COMMAND A
*K*ING'S SHIP

Selected Historical Fiction Published by McBooks Press

BY ALEXANDER KENT
*The Complete
  Midshipman Bolitho
Stand Into Danger
In Gallant Company
Sloop of War
To Glory We Steer
Command a King's Ship
Passage to Mutiny
With All Despatch
Form Line of Battle!
Enemy in Sight!
The Flag Captain
Signal–Close Action!
The Inshore Squadron
A Tradition of Victory
Success to the Brave
Colours Aloft!
Honour This Day
The Only Victor
Beyond the Reef
The Darkening Sea
For My Country's Freedom
Cross of St George
Sword of Honour
Second to None
Relentless Pursuit
Man of War*

BY PHILIP MCCUTCHAN
*Halfhyde at the Bight
  of Benin
Halfhyde's Island
Halfhyde and the
  Guns of Arrest
Halfhyde to the Narrows
Halfhyde for the Queen
Halfhyde Ordered South
Halfhyde on Zanatu*

BY R.F. DELDERFIELD
*Too Few for Drums
Seven Men of Gascony*

BY JAMES L. NELSON
*The Only Life That
  Mattered*

BY DEWEY LAMBDIN
*The French Admiral
The Gun Ketch
Jester's Fortune*

What Lies Buried

BY JULIAN STOCKWIN
*Mutiny
Quarterdeck
Tenacious*

BY JAN NEEDLE
*A Fine Boy for Killing
The Wicked Trade
The Spithead Nymph*

BY DUDLEY POPE
*Ramage
Ramage & The Drumbeat
Ramage & The Freebooters
Governor Ramage R.N.
Ramage's Prize
Ramage & The Guillotine
Ramage's Diamond
Ramage's Mutiny
Ramage & The Rebels
The Ramage Touch
Ramage's Signal
Ramage & The Renegades
Ramage's Devil
Ramage's Trial
Ramage's Challenge
Ramage at Trafalgar
Ramage & The Saracens
Ramage & The Dido*

BY FREDERICK MARRYAT
Frank Mildmay OR
  *The Naval Officer
Mr Midshipman Easy
Newton Forster* OR
  *The Merchant Service
Snarleyyow* OR
  *The Dog Fiend
The Privateersman*

BY V.A. STUART
*Victors and Lords
The Sepoy Mutiny
Massacre at Cawnpore
The Cannons of Lucknow
The Heroic Garrison*

*The Valiant Sailors
The Brave Captains
Hazard's Command
Hazard of Huntress
Hazard in Circassia
Victory at Sebastopol
Guns to the Far East
Escape from Hell*

BY JAMES DUFFY
Sand of the Arena

BY JOHN BIGGINS
*A Sailor of Austria
The Emperor's Coloured Coat
The Two-Headed Eagle*

BY ALEXANDER FULLERTON
*Storm Force to Narvik
Last Lift from Crete
All the Drowning Seas
A Share of Honour
The Torch Bearers
The Gatecrashers*

BY C.N. PARKINSON
*The Guernseyman
Devil to Pay
The Fireship
Touch and Go
So Near So Far
Dead Reckoning*

*The Life and Times of
  Horatio Hornblower*

BY NICHOLAS NICASTRO
*The Eighteenth Captain
Between Two Fires*

BY DOUGLAS REEMAN
*Badge of Glory
First to Land
The Horizon
Dust on the Sea
Knife Edge*

*Twelve Seconds to Live
Battlecruiser
The White Guns
A Prayer for the Ship
For Valour*

BY DAVID DONACHIE
*The Devil's Own Luck
The Dying Trade
A Hanging Matter
An Element of Chance
The Scent of Betrayal
A Game of Bones*

*On a Making Tide
Tested by Fate
Breaking the Line*

BY BROOS CAMPBELL
No Quarter

Alexander Kent

COMMAND A KING'S SHIP

the Bolitho novels: 6

McBooks Press, Inc.
www.mcbooks.com

ITHACA, NY

First published by McBooks Press 1998

Copyright © 1973 by Alexander Kent
First published in the United Kingdom by Hutchinson 1973

Cover painting by Geoffrey Huband

Library of Congress Cataloging-in-Publication Data

Kent, Alexander.
  Command a king's ship / by Alexander Kent.
    p. cm. — (Richard Bolitho novels ; no. 6)
  ISBN 0-935526-50-1 (trade paper)
    1. Great Britain—History, Naval—18th century—Fiction.
  I. Title. II. Series: Kent, Alexander. Richard Bolitho novels ;
  no. 3.
  PR6061.E63 C64 1998
  823'.914—dc21   98-040950

Additional copies of this book may be ordered from any bookstore or directly
from McBooks Press, Inc., ID Booth Building, 520 North Meadow St.,
Ithaca, NY 14850. Please include $5.00 postage and handling with mail orders.
New York State residents must add sales tax to total remittance (books &
shipping). All McBooks Press publications can also be ordered by calling
toll-free 1-888-BOOKS11 (1-888-266-5711).
Please call to request a free catalog.

Visit the McBooks Press website at www.mcbooks.com.

Printed in the United States of America

9 8

COMMAND A
*K*ING'S SHIP

"Danger and Death dance to the wild music of the gale, and when it is night they dance with fiercer abandon, as if to allay the fears that beset the sailormen who feel their touch but see them not."

GEORGE H. GRANT

I

THE $\mathcal{A}$DMIRAL'S CHOICE

AN ADMIRALTY messenger opened the door of a small anteroom and said politely, "If you would be so good as to wait, sir." He stood aside to allow Captain Richard Bolitho to pass and added, "Sir John knows you are here."

Bolitho waited until the door had closed and then walked to a bright fire which was crackling below a tall mantel. He was thankful that the messenger had brought him to this small room and not to one of the larger ones. As he had hurried into the Admiralty from the bitter March wind which was sweeping down Whitehall he had been dreading a confrontation in one of those crowded waiting-rooms, crammed with unemployed officers who watched the comings and goings of more fortunate visitors with something like hatred.

Bolitho had known the feeling, too, even though he had told himself often enough that he was better off than most. For he had come back to England a year ago, to find the country at peace, and the towns and villages already filling with unwanted soldiers and seamen. With his home in Falmouth, an established estate, and all the hard-earned prize money he had brought with him, he knew he should have been grateful.

He moved away from the fire and stared down at the broad roadway below the window. It had been raining for most of the morning, but now the sky had completely cleared, so that the many puddles and ruts glittered in the harsh light like patches of pale blue silk. Only the steaming nostrils of countless horses which passed this way and that, the hurrying figures bowed into the wind, made a lie of the momentary colour.

He sighed. It was March, 1784, only just over a year since his return home from the West Indies, yet it seemed like a century.

Whenever possible he had quit Falmouth to make the long journey to London, to this seat of Admiralty, to try and discover why his letters had gone unanswered, why his pleas for a ship, *any* ship, had been ignored. And always the waiting-rooms had seemed to get more and more crowded. The familiar voices and tales of ships and campaigns had become forced, less confident, as day by day they were turned away. Ships were laid up by the score, and every seaport had its full quota of a war's flotsam. Cripples, and men made deaf and blind by cannon fire, others half mad from what they had seen and endured. With the signing of peace the previous year such sights had become too common to mention, too despairing even for hope.

He stiffened as two figures turned a corner below the window. Even without the facings on their tattered red coats he knew they had been soldiers. A carriage was standing by the roadside, the horses nodding their heads together as they explored the contents of their feeding bags. The coachman was chatting to a smartly dressed servant from a nearby house, and neither took a scrap of notice of the two tattered veterans.

One of them pushed his companion against a stone balustrade and then walked towards the coach. Bolitho realised that the man left clinging to the stonework was blind, his head turned towards the roadway as if trying to hear where his friend had gone. It needed no words.

The soldier faced the coachman and his companion and held out his hand. It was neither arrogant nor servile, and strangely moving. The coachman hesitated and then fumbled inside his heavy coat.

At that moment another figure ran lightly down some steps

and wrenched open the coach door. He was well attired against the cold, and the buckles on his shoes held the watery sunlight like diamonds. He stared at the soldier and then snapped angrily at his coachman. The servant ran to the horses' heads, and within seconds the coach was clattering away into the busy press of carriages and carts. The soldier stood staring after it and then gave a weary shrug. He returned to his companion, and with linked arms they moved slowly around the next corner.

Bolitho struggled with the window catch, but it was stuck fast, his mind reeling with anger and shame at what he had just seen.

A voice asked, "May I help, sir?" It was the messenger again.

Bolitho replied, "I was going to throw some coins to two crippled soldiers!" He broke off, seeing the mild astonishment in the messenger's eyes.

The man said, "Bless you, sir, you'd get used to such sights in London."

"Not me."

"I was going to tell you, sir, that Sir John will see you now!"

Bolitho followed him into the passageway again, conscious of the sudden dryness in his throat. He remembered so clearly his last visit here, a month ago almost to the day. And that time he had been summoned by letter, and not left fretting and fuming in a waiting-room. It had seemed like a dream, an incredible stroke of good fortune. It still did, despite all the difficulties which had been crammed into so short a time.

He was to assume command immediately of His Britannic Majesty's Ship *Undine,* of thirty-two guns, then lying in the dockyard at Portsmouth completing a refit.

As he had hurried from the Admiralty on that occasion he had felt the excitement on his face like guilt, aware of the other watching eyes, the envy and resentment.

The task of taking command, of gathering the dockyard's resources to his aid to prepare *Undine* for sea, had cost him dearly. With the Navy being cut down to a quarter of its wartime strength he had been surprised to discover that it was harder to obtain spare cordage and spars rather than the reverse. A weary shipwright had confided in him that dockyard officials were more intent on making a profit with private dealers than they were on aiding one small frigate.

He had bribed, threatened and driven almost every man in the yard until he had obtained more or less what he needed. It seemed they saw his departure as the only way of returning to their own affairs.

He had walked around his new command in her dock with mixed feelings. Above all, the excitement and the challenge she represented. Gone were the pangs he had felt in Falmouth whenever he had seen a man-of-war weathering the headland below the castle. But also he had discovered something more. His last command had been *Phalarope,* a frigate very similar to *Undine,* if slightly longer by a few feet. To Bolitho she had been everything, perhaps because they had come through so much together. In the West Indies, at the battle of the Saintes he had felt his precious *Phalarope* battered almost to a hulk beneath him. There would never, *could* never, be another like her. But as he had walked up and down the stone wall of the dock he had sensed a new elation.

Halfway through the hurried overhaul he had received an unheralded visit from Rear Admiral Sir John Winslade, the man who had greeted him at the Admiralty. He had given little away, but after a cursory inspection of the ship and Bolitho's preparations he had said, "I can tell you now. I'm sending you to India. That's all I can reveal for the moment." He had run his eye over the few riggers working on yards and shrouds and had added dryly, "I only hope for your sake you'll be ready on time."

There was a lot in what Winslade had hinted. Officers on half-pay were easy to obtain. To crew a King's ship without the urgency of a war or the pressgang was something else entirely. Had *Undine* been sailing in better-known waters things might have been different. And had Bolitho been a man other than himself he might have been tempted to keep her destination a secret until he had signed on sufficient hands and it was too late for them to escape.

He had had the usual flowery-worded handbills distributed around the port and nearby villages. He had sent recruiting parties as far inland as Guildford on the Portsmouth Road, but with small success. And now, as he followed the messenger towards some high gilded doors he knew *Undine* was still fifty short of her complement.

In one thing Bolitho had been more fortunate. *Undine*'s previous captain had kept a shrewd eye on his ship's professional men. Bolitho had taken charge to discover that *Undine* still carried the hard core of senior men, the warrant officers, a first class sailmaker, and one of the most economical carpenters he had ever watched at work. His predecessor had quit the Navy for good to seek a career in Parliament. Or as he had put it, "I've had a bellyful of fighting with iron. From now on, my young friend, I'll do it with slander!"

Rear Admiral Sir John Winslade was standing with his back to a fire, his coat-tails parted to allow the maximum warmth to reach him. Few people knew much about him. He had distinguished himself vaguely in some single-ship action off Brest, and had then been neatly placed inside the Admiralty. There was nothing about his pale, austere features to distinguish him in any way. In fact, he was so ordinary that his gold-laced coat seemed to be wearing him rather than the other way round.

Bolitho was twenty-seven and a half years old, but had already held two commands, and knew enough about senior officers not to take them at face value.

Winslade let his coat-tails drop and waited for Bolitho to reach him. He held out his hand and said, "You are punctual. It is just as well. We have much to discuss." He moved to a small lacquered table. "Some claret, I think." He smiled for the first time. It was like the sunlight in Whitehall. Frail, and easily removed.

He pulled up a chair for Bolitho. "Your health, Captain." He added, "I suppose you know why I asked for you to be given this command?"

Bolitho cleared his throat. "I assumed, sir, that as Captain Stewart was entering politics that you required another for . . ."

Winslade gave a wry smile. "*Please,* Bolitho. Modesty at the expense of sincerity is just so much top-hamper. I trust you will bear that in mind?"

He sipped at his claret and continued in the same dry voice, "For this particular commission I have to be sure of *Undine's* captain. You will be on the other side of the globe. I have to know what you are thinking so that I can act on such despatches as I might receive in due course."

Bolitho tried to relax. "Thank you." He smiled awkwardly. "I mean, for your trust, sir."

"Quite so." Winslade reached for the decanter. "I know your background, your record, especially in the recent war with France and her Allies. Your behaviour when you were on the American station reads favourably. A full scale war and a bloody rebellion in America must have been a good schoolroom for so young a commander. But that war is done with. It is up to us," he smiled slightly, "*some* of us, to ensure that we are never forced into such a helpless stalemate again."

Bolitho exclaimed, "We did not lose the war, sir."

"We did not win it either. That is more to the point."

Bolitho thought suddenly of the last battle. The screams and yells on every side, the crash of gunfire and falling spars. So many had died that day. So many familiar faces just swept away. Others had been left, like the two ragged soldiers, to fend as best they could.

He said quietly, "We did our best, sir."

The admiral was watching him thoughtfully. "I agree. You may not have won a war, but you did win a respite of sorts. A time to draw breath and face facts."

"You think the peace will not last, sir?"

"An enemy is always an enemy, Bolitho. Only the vanquished know peace of mind. Oh yes, we will fight again, be sure of it."

He put down his glass and added sharply, "Now, about your ship. Are you prepared?"

Bolitho met his gaze. "I am still short of hands, but the ship is as ready as she will ever be, sir. I had her warped out of the dock-yard two days ago, and she is now anchored at Spithead awaiting final provisioning."

"How short?"

Two words, but they left no room for manoeuvre.

"Fifty, sir. But my lieutenants are still trying to gather more."

The admiral did not blink. "I see. Well, it's up to you. In the meantime I will obtain a warrant for you to take some 'volunteers' from the prison hulks in Portsmouth harbour."

Bolitho said, "It's a sad thing that we must rely on convicts."

"They are men. That is all you require at the moment. As it is, you will probably be doing some of the wretches a favour. Most of 'em were to be transported to the penal colonies in America. Now, with America gone, we will have to look elsewhere for new settle-ments. There is some talk of Botany Bay, in New Holland, but it may be rumour, of course."

He stood up and walked to a window. "I knew your father. I was saddened to hear of his death. While you were in the West Indies, I believe?" He did not wait for a reply. "This mission would have been well cut for him. Something to get his teeth into. Self-dependence, decisions to be made on the spot which could make or break the man in command. Everything a young frigate captain dreams of, right?"

"Yes, sir."

He pictured his father as he had last seen him. The very day he had sailed for the Indies in *Phalarope*. A tired, broken man. Made bitter by his other son's betrayal. Hugh Bolitho had been the apple of his eye. Four years older than Richard, he had been a born gambler, and had ended in killing a brother officer in a duel. Worse, he had fled to America, to join the Revolutionary forces and later to command a privateer against the British. It had been that knowledge which had really killed Bolitho's father, no matter what the doctor had said.

He tightened his grip on his glass. Much of his prize money had gone into buying back land which his father had sold to pay Hugh's debts. But nothing could buy back his honour. It was fortunate that Hugh had died. If they had ever met again Bolitho imagined he might kill him for what he had done.

"More claret?" Winslade seemed absorbed with his own thoughts. "I'm sending you to Madras. There you will report to . . . well, it will be in your final orders. No sense in idle gossip." He added, "Just in case you cannot get your ship manned, eh?"

"I'll get them, sir. If I have to go to Cornwall."

"I hope that will not be necessary."

Winslade changed tack again. "During the American campaign you probably noticed that there was little co-operation between military and civilian government. The forces on the ground fought the battles and confided in neither. That must not happen again. The task I am giving you would be better handled by a squadron, with an admiral's flag for good measure. But it would invite attention, and *that* Parliament will not tolerate in this uneasy peace."

He asked suddenly, "Where are you staying in London?"

"The George at Southwark."

"I will give you an address. A friend's residence in St. James's Square." He smiled at Bolitho's grave features. "Come, don't look so gloomy. It is time you made your way in affairs and put the line of battle behind you. Your mission may bring you to eyes other than those of jaded flag officers. Get to know people. It can do nothing but good. I will send a courier with instructions for your first lieutenant." He darted him a quick glance. "Herrick, I gather. From your last ship."

"Yes, sir." It sounded like "of course." There had never been any doubt whom he would ask for if he got another ship.

"Well then, Mr. Herrick it is. He can take charge of local

matters. I'll need you in London for four days." He hardened his tone as Bolitho looked about to protest. *"At least!"*

The admiral regarded Bolitho for several seconds. Craving to get back to his ship, uncertain of himself in these overwhelming surroundings. It was all there and more besides. As Bolitho had entered the room it had been like seeing his father all those long years ago. Tall, slim, with that black hair tied at the nape of his neck. The loose lock which hung above his right eye told another story. Once as he had raised his glass it had fallen aside to display a livid scar which ran high into the hairline. Winslade was glad about his choice. There was intelligence on Bolitho's grave features, and compassion too, which even his service in seven years of war had not displaced. He could have picked from a hundred captains, but he had wanted one who needed a ship and the sea and not merely the security such things represented. He also required a man who could think and act accordingly. Not one who would rest content on the weight of his broadsides. Bolitho's record had shown plainly enough that he was rarely content to use written orders as a substitute for initiative. Several admirals had growled as much when Winslade had put his name forward for command. But he had got his way, for Winslade had the weight of Parliament behind him, which was another rarity.

He sighed and picked up a small bell from the table.

"You go and arrange to move to the address I will give you. I have much to do, so you may as well enjoy yourself while you can."

He shook the bell and a servant entered with Bolitho's cocked hat and sword. Winslade watched as the man buckled the sword deftly around his waist.

"Same old blade, eh?" He touched it with his fingers. It was very smooth and worn, and a good deal lighter than more modern swords.

Bolitho smiled. "Aye, sir. My father gave it to me after . . ."

"I know. Forget about your brother, Bolitho." He touched the hilt again. "Your family have brought too much honour for many generations to be brought down by one man."

He thrust out his hand. "Take care. I daresay there are quite a few tongues wagging about your visit here today."

Bolitho followed the servant into the corridor, his mind moving restlessly from one aspect of his visit to another. Madras, another continent, and that sounded like a mere beginning to whatever it was he was supposed to do.

Every mile sailed would have its separate challenge. He smiled quietly. And reward. He paused in the doorway and stared at the bustling people and carriages. Open sea instead of noise and dirt. A ship, a living, vital being instead of dull, pretentious buildings.

A hand touched his arm, and he turned to see a young man in a shabby blue coat studying him anxiously.

"What is it?"

The man said quickly, "I'm Chatterton, Captain. I was once second lieutenant in the *Warrior*, seventy-four." He hesitated, watching Bolitho's grave face. "I heard you were commissioning, sir, I was wondering . . ."

"I'm sorry, Mr. Chatterton. I have a full wardroom."

"Yes, sir, I had guessed as much." He swallowed. "I could sign as master's mate perhaps?"

Bolitho shook his head. "It is only seamen I lack, I'm afraid."

He saw the disappointment clouding the man's face. The old *Warrior* had been in the thick of it. She was rarely absent from any battle, and men had spoken her name with pride. Now her second lieutenant was waiting like a beggar.

He said quietly, "If I can help." He thrust his hand into his pocket. "Tide you over awhile."

"Thank you, no, sir." He forced a grin. "Not yet anyway." He pulled up his coat collar. As he walked away he called, "Good luck, Captain!"

Bolitho watched him until he was out of sight. It might have been Herrick, he thought. Any of us.

His Majesty's frigate *Undine* tugged resentfully at her cable as a stiffening south-easterly wind ripped the Solent into a mass of vicious whitecaps.

Lieutenant Thomas Herrick turned up the collar of his heavy watchcoat and took another stroll across the quarterdeck, his eyes slitted against a mixture of rain and spray which made the rigging shine in the poor light like black glass.

Despite the weather there was still plenty of activity on deck and alongside in the pitching store boats and water lighters. Here and there on the gangways and right forward in the eyes of the ship the red coats of watchful marines made a pleasant change from the mixtures of dull grey elsewhere. The marines were supposed to ensure that the traffic in provisions and last moment equipment was one way, and none was escaping through an open port as barter for cheap drink or other favours with friends ashore.

Herrick grinned and stamped his feet on the wet planking. They had done a lot of work in the month since he had joined the ship. Others might curse the weather, the uncertainties offered by a long voyage, the prospect of hardship from sea and wind, but not he. The past year had been far more of a burden for him, and he was glad, no thankful, to be back aboard a King's ship. He had entered the Navy when he was still a few weeks short of twelve years old, and these last long months following the signing of peace with France and the recognition of American independence had been his first experience of being away from the one life he understood and trusted.

Unlike many of his contemporaries, Herrick had nothing but his own resources to sustain him. He came of a poor family, his father being a clerk in their home town of Rochester in Kent. When he had gone there after paying off the *Phalarope* and saying his farewell to Bolitho, he had discovered things to be even worse than he had expected. His father's health had deteriorated, and he seemed to be coughing his life away, day in, day out. Herrick's only sister was a cripple and incapable of doing much but help her mother about the house, so his homecoming was seen in rather different ways from his own sense of rejection. A friend of his father's employer had gained him an appointment as mate in a small brig which earned a living carrying general cargo up and down the east coast and occasionally across the channel to Holland. The owner was a miserly man who kept the brig so shorthanded that there were barely enough men to work ship, let along handle cargo, load lighters and keep the vessel in good repair.

When he had received Bolitho's letter, accompanied by his commission from the Admiralty charging him to report on board *Undine*, he had been almost too stunned to realise his good fortune. He had not seen Bolitho since that one last visit to his home in Falmouth, and perhaps deep inside he had believed that their friendship, which had strengthened in storm and under bloody broadsides, would be no match for peace.

Their worlds were, after all, too far apart. Bolitho's great stone house had seemed like a palace to Herrick. His background, his ancestry of seafaring officers, put him in a different sphere entirely. Herrick was the first in his family to go to sea, and that was the least of their differences.

But Bolitho had not changed. When they had met on this same quarterdeck a month ago he had known it with that first glance. It was still there, the quiet sadness, which could give way to something like boyish excitement in the twinkling of an eye.

Above all, Bolitho too was pleased to be back, keen to test himself and his new ship whenever a chance offered itself.

A midshipman scuttled over the deck and touched his hat.

"Cutter's returning, sir."

He was small, pinched with cold. He had been aboard just three weeks.

"Thank you, Mr. Penn. That'll be some new hands, I hope." He eyed the boy unsympathetically. "Now smarten yourself, the captain may be returning today."

He continued his pacing.

Bolitho had been in London for five days. It would be good to hear his news, to get the order to sail from this bitter Solent.

He watched the cutter lifting and plunging across the white-caps, the oars moving sluggishly despite the efforts of the boat's coxswain. He saw the cocked hat of John Soames, the third lieutenant, in the sternsheets, and wondered if he had had any luck with recruits.

In the *Phalarope* Herrick had begun his commission as third lieutenant, rising to Bolitho's second-in-command as those above him died in combat. He wondered briefly if Soames was already thinking of his own prospects in the months ahead. He was a giant of a man and in his thirtieth year, three years older than Herrick. He had got his commission as lieutenant very late in life, and by a roundabout route, mostly, as far as Herrick could gather, in the merchant service and later as master's mate in a King's ship. Tough, self-taught, he was hard to know. A suspicious man.

Quite different from Villiers Davy, the second lieutenant. As his name suggested, he was of good family, with the money and proud looks to back up his quicksilver wit. Herrick was not sure of him either, but told himself that any dislike he might harbour was because Davy reminded him of an arrogant midshipman they had carried in *Phalarope*.

Feet thumped on deck and he turned to see Triphook, the purser, crouching through the drizzle, a bulky ledger under his coat.

The purser grimaced. "Evil day, Mr. Herrick." He gestured to the boats alongside. "God damn those thieves. They'd rob a blind man, so they would."

Herrick chuckled. "Not like you pursers, eh?"

Triphook eyed him severely. He was stooped and very thin, with large yellow teeth like a mournful horse.

"I hope that was not seriously meant, *sir?*"

Herrick craned over the dripping nettings to watch the cutter hooking on to the chains. God, their oarsmanship was bad. Bolitho would expect far better, and before too long.

He snapped, "Easy, Mr. Triphook. But I was merely *reminding* you. I recall we had a purser in my last ship. A man called Evans. He lined his pockets at the people's expense. Gave them foul food when they had much to trouble them in other directions."

Triphook watched him doubtfully.

"What happened?"

"Captain Bolitho made him pay for fresh meat from his own purse. Cask for cask with each that was rotten." He grinned. "So be warned, my friend!"

"He'll have no cause to fault *me*, Mr. Herrick." He walked away, his voice lacking conviction as he added, "You can be certain of that."

Lieutenant Soames came aft, touching his hat and scowling at the deck as he reported, "Five hands, sir. I've been on the road all day, I'm fair hoarse from calling the tune of those handbills."

Herrick nodded. He could sympathise. He had done it often enough himself. Five hands. They still needed thirty. Even then it would not allow for death and injury to be expected on any long voyage.

Soames asked thickly, "Any more news?"

"None. Just that we are to sail for Madras. But I think it will be soon now."

Soames said, "Good riddance to the land, I say. Streets full of drunken men, prime hands we could well do with." He hesitated. "With your permission I might take a boat away tonight and catch a few as they reel from their damn ale houses, eh?"

They turned as a shriek of laughter echoed up from the gun deck, and a woman, her breasts bare to the rain, ran from beneath the larboard gangway. She was pursued by two seamen, both obviously the worse for drink, who left little to the imagination as to their intentions.

Herrick barked, "Tell that slut to get below! Or I'll have her thrown over the side!" He saw the astonished midshipman watching the spectacle with wide-eyed wonder and added harshly, "Mr. Penn! *Jump to it,* I say!"

Soames showed a rare grin. "Offend your feelings, Mr. Herrick?"

Herrick shrugged. "I know it is supposed to be the proper thing to allow our people women and drink in harbour." He thought of his sister. Anchored in that damned chair. What he would give to see her running free like that Portsmouth trollop. "But it never fails to sicken me."

Soames sighed. "Half the bastards would desert otherwise, signed on or not. The romance of Madras soon wears off when the rum goes short."

Herrick said, "What you asked earlier. I cannot agree. It would be a bad beginning. Men taken in such a way would harbour plenty of grievances. One rotten apple can sour a full barrel."

Soames eyes him calmly. "It seems to me that this ship is almost *full* of bad apples. The volunteers are probably on the run from debt, or the hangman himself. Some are aboard just to see what they can lay their fingers on when we are many miles from proper authority."

Herrick replied, "Captain Bolitho will have sufficient authority, Mr. Soames."

"I forgot. You were in the same ship. There was a mutiny."

It sounded like an accusation.

"Not of his making." He turned on him angrily. "Be so good as to have the new men fed and issued with slop clothing."

He waited, watching the resentment in the big man's eyes.

He added, "Another of our captain's requirements. I suggest you acquaint yourself with his demands. Life will be easier for you."

Soames strode away and Herrick relaxed. He must not let him get into his skin so easily. But any criticism, or even hint of it, always affected him. To Herrick, Bolitho represented all the things he would like to be. The fact he also knew some of his secret faults as well made him doubly sure of his loyalty. He shook his head. It was stronger even than that.

He peered over the nettings towards the shore, seeing the walls of the harbour battery glinting like lead in the rain. Beyond Portsmouth Point the land was almost hidden in murk. It would be good to get away. His pay would mount up and go towards helping out at home. With his share of prize money, which he gained under Bolitho in the West Indies he had been able to buy several small luxuries to make their lot easier until his next return. And when might that be? Two years? It was better never to contemplate such matters.

He saw a ship's boy duck into the rain to turn the hour-glass beside the deserted wheel, and waited for him to chime the hour on the bell. Time to send the working part of the watch below. He grimaced. The wardroom might be little better. Soames under a cloud of inner thought. Davy probing his guard with some new, smart jest or other. Giles Bellairs, the captain of marines, well on the way to intoxication by this time, knowing his hefty sergeant could deal with the affairs of his small detachment. Triphook probably brooding over the issue of clothing to the new men. Typical of the purser. He could face the prospect of a great sea voyage, with each league measured in salt pork and beef, iron-hard biscuit, juice to prevent scurvy, beer and spirits to supplement fresh water which would soon be alive in its casks, and all the thousand other items under his control, with equanimity. But one small issue of clothing, while they still wore what they had come aboard in, was too much for his sense of values. He would learn. He grinned into the cold wind. They all would, once Bolitho brought the ship alive.

More shouts from alongside, and Penn, the midshipman, called anxiously, "Beg pardon, sir, but I fear the surgeon is in difficulties."

Herrick frowned. The surgeon's name was Charles Whitmarsh. A man of culture, but one with something troubling him.

Most ship's surgeons, in Herrick's experience, had been butchers. Nobody else would go to sea and face the horrors of mangled men screaming and dying after a savage battle with the enemy. In peacetime he had expected it might be different.

Whitmarsh was a drunkard. As Herrick peered down at the jolly boat as it bobbed and curtsied at the chains, he saw a boatswain's mate and two seamen struggling to fit the surgeon into a bowline to assist his passage up the side. He was a big man, almost as large as Soames, and in the grey light his features shone with all the brightness of a marine's coat.

Herrick snapped, "Have a cargo net lowered, Mr. Penn. It is not dignified, but neither is this, by God!"

Whitmarsh landed eventually on the gun deck, his hair awry, his face set in a great beaming smile. One of his assistants and two marines lifted him bodily and took him aft below the quarterdeck. He would sleep in his small sickbay for a few hours, and then begin again.

Penn asked nervously, "Is he unwell, sir?"

Herrick looked at the youth gravely. "A thought tipsy, lad, but well enough to remove a limb or two, I daresay." He relented and touched his shoulder. "Go below. Your relief will be up soon."

He watched him hurry away and grinned. It was hard to recall that he had been like Penn. Unsure, frightened, with each hour presenting some new sight and sound to break his boy's illusions.

A marine yelled, "Guardboat shovin' off from the sallyport, sir!"

Herrick nodded. "Very well."

That would mean orders for the *Undine*. He let his gaze move forward between the tall, spiralling masts with their taut maze of shrouds and rigging, the neatly furled canvas and to the bowsprit, below which *Undine*'s beautiful, full-breasted figurehead of a water-nymph stared impassively to every horizon. It also meant that Bolitho would be returning. *Today*.

And for Thomas Herrick that was more than enough.

2

FREE OF THE *L*AND

CAPTAIN Richard Bolitho stood in the shelter of the stone wall beside the sallyport and peered through the chilling drizzle. It was afternoon, but with the sky so overcast by low cloud it could have been much later.

He was tired and stiff from the long coach ride, and the journey had been made especially irritating by his two jovial companions. Businessmen from the City of London, they had become more loud-voiced after each stop for change of horses and refreshment at the many inns down the Portsmouth road. They were off to France in a packet ship, to contact new agencies there, and so, with luck, expand their trade. To Bolitho if was still hard to accept, just a year back the Channel had been the only barrier between this country and their common enemy. The moat. The last ditch, as some news-sheet had described it. Now it seemed as if it was all forgotten by such men as his travelling companions. It had become merely an irritating delay which made their journey just so much longer.

He shrugged his shoulders deeper inside his boat-cloak, suddenly impatient for the last moments to pass, so that he could get back to the ship. The cloak was new, from a good London tailor. Rear Admiral Winslade's friend had taken him there, and managed to do so without making Bolitho feel the complete ignoramus. He smiled to himself despite his other uncertainties. He would never get used to London. Too large, too busy, where nobody had time to draw breath. And noisy. No wonder the rich houses around St. James's Square had sent servants out every few hours to spread fresh straw on the roadway. The grinding roar of carriage wheels was enough to wake the dead. It had been a beautiful house, his hosts charming, if slightly amused by his questions. Even now, he was still unsure of their strange ways. It was not just enough to live in that fine, fashionable residence, with its splendid spiral staircase and huge chandeliers. To be *right*, you had to live on the best side of the square, the east side. Winslade's friends lived there. Bolitho smiled again. They would.

Bolitho had met several very influential people, and his hosts had given two dinner parties with that in mind. He knew well enough from past experience that without their help it would have been impossible. Aboard ship a captain was next only to God. In London society he hardly registered at all.

But that was behind him now. He was back. His orders would be waiting, and only the actual time of weighing anchor was left to conjecture.

He peered round the wall once more, feeling the wind on his face like a whip. The signal tower had informed *Undine* of his arrival, and very soon now a boat would arrive at the wooden pier below the wall. He wondered how his coxswain, Allday, was managing. His first ship as captain's coxswain, but Bolitho understood him well enough to know there was little to fear on his behalf. It would be good to see him, too. Something familiar. A face to hold on to.

He glanced up the narrow street to where some servants from the George Inn, where the coach had finally come to rest, were guarding his pile of luggage. He thought of the personal purchases he had made. Maybe London had got some hold on him after all.

When Bolitho had got his first command of the sloop *Sparrow* during the American Revolution, he had had little time to acquaint himself with luxuries. But in London, with the remains of his prize money, he had made up for it. New shirts, and some comfortable shoes. This great boat-cloak, which the tailor had assured him would keep out even the heaviest downpour. It had been partly Winslade's doing, he was certain of that. His host had casually mentioned that Bolitho's mission in *Undine* required not merely a competent captain, but one who would look the part, no matter what sort of government official he might meet. There was, he had added gently, a matter of wine.

Together they had gone to a low-beamed shop in St. James's Street. It was not a bit what Bolitho might have imagined. It had the sign of a coffee mill outside its door, and the owners' names, Pickering and Clarke, painted in gold leaf above. It was a friendly place, even intimate. It could almost have been Falmouth.

It was to be hoped the wine had already arrived aboard *Undine.* Otherwise, it was likely he would have to sail without it, and leave a large hole in his purse as well.

It would be a strange and exciting sensation to sit in his cabin, hundreds of miles from England, and sample some of that beautiful madeira. It would bring back all those pictures of London again. The buildings, the clever talk, the way women looked at you. Once or twice he had felt uneasy about that. It had reminded him bitterly of New York during the war. The boldness in their faces. The confident arrogance which had seemed like second nature to them.

An idler called, "Yer boat's a-comin', Cap'n!" He touched his hat. "I'll give 'ee a 'and!" He hurried away to call the inn servants, his mind dwelling on what he might expect from a frigate's captain.

Bolitho stepped out into the wind, his hat jammed well down over his forehead. It was the *Undine*'s launch, her largest boat, the oars rising and falling like gulls' wings as she headed straight for the pier. It must be a hard pull, he thought. Otherwise Allday would have brought the gig.

He found he was trembling, and it was all he could do to prevent a grin from splitting his face in two. The dark green launch, the oarsmen in their checked shirts and white trousers, it was all there. Like a homecoming.

The oars rose in the air and stood like twin lines of swaying white bones, while the bowman made fast to the jetty and aided a smart midshipman to step ashore.

The latter removed his hat with a flourish and said, "At your service, sir."

It was Midshipman Valentine Keen, a very elegant young man who was being appointed to the *Undine* more to get him away from England than to further his naval advancement, Bolitho suspected. He was the senior midshipman, and if he survived the round voyage would probably return as a lieutenant. At any rate, as a man.

"My boxes are yonder, Mr. Keen."

He saw Allday standing motionless in the sternsheets, his blue coat and white trousers flapping in the wind, his tanned features barely able to remain impassive.

Theirs was a strange relationship. Allday had come aboard Bolitho's last ship as a pressed man. Yet when the ship had paid off at the end of the war Allday had stayed with him at Falmouth. Servant; guardian. Trusted friend. Now as his coxswain he would be ever nearby. Sometimes an only contact with that other, remote world beyond the cabin bulkhead.

Allday had been a seaman all his life, but for a period when he had been a shepherd in Cornwall, where Bolitho's pressgang had found him. An odd beginning. Bolitho thought of his previous coxswain, Mark Stockdale. A battered ex-prizefighter who could hardly speak because of his maimed vocal cords. He had died protecting Bolitho's back at the Saintes. Poor Stockdale. Bolitho had not even seen him fall.

Allday clambered ashore.

"Everything's ready, Captain. A good meal in the cabin." He snarled at one of the seamen, "Grab that chest, you oaf, or I'll have your liver!"

The seaman nodded and grinned.

Bolitho was satisfied. Allday's strange charm seemed to be working already. He could curse and fight like a madman if required. But Bolitho had seen him caring for wounded men and knew his other side. It was no wonder that the girls in farms and villages around Falmouth would miss him. Better though for Allday, Bolitho decided. There had been rumours enough lately about his conquests.

Then at last it was all done. The boat loaded, the idler and servants paid. The oars sending the long launch purposefully through the tossing water.

Bolitho sat in silence, huddled in his cloak, his eyes on the distant frigate. She was beautiful. In some ways more so than *Phalarope*, if that were possible. Only four years old, she had been built in a yard at Frindsbury on the River Medway. Not far from Herrick's home. One hundred and thirty feet long on her gun deck, and built of good English oak, she was the picture of a shipbuilder's art. No wonder the Admiralty had been loath to lay her up in ordinary like so many of her consorts at the end of the war. She had cost nearly fourteen thousand pounds, as Bolitho had been told more than once. Not that he needed to be reminded. He was lucky to get her.

There was a brief break in the scudding clouds, and the watery light played down along *Undine*'s gun ports to her clean sheathing as she rolled uneasily in the swell. Best Anglesey copper. Stout enough for anything. Bolitho recalled what her previous captain, Stewart, had confided. In a fierce skirmish off Ushant he had been raked by heavy guns from a French seventy-four. *Undine* had taken four balls right on her waterline. She had been fortunate to reach England afloat. Frigates were meant for speed and hit-and-run fighting, not for matching metal with a line-of-battle ship. Bolitho knew from his own grim experience what that could do to so graceful a hull.

Stewart had added that despite careful supervision he was still unsure as to the perfection of the repairs. With the copper replaced, it took more than internal inspection to discover the true value of a dockyard's overhaul. Copper protected the hull from many sorts of weed and clinging growth which could slow a ship to a painful crawl. But behind it could lurk every captain's real enemy, rot. Rot which could change a perfect hull into a ripe, treacherous trap for the unwary. Admiral Kempenfelt's own flagship, the *Royal George*, had heeled over and sunk right here in Portsmouth just two years ago, with the loss of hundreds of lives. It was said that her bottom had fallen clean away with rot. If it could happen to a lofty first-rate at anchor, it would do worse to a frigate.

Bolitho came out of his thoughts as he heard the shrill of boatswain's calls above the wind, the stamp of feet as the marines prepared to receive him. He stared up at the towering masts, the movement of figures around the entry port and above in the shrouds. They had had a month to get used to seeing him about the ship, except for the unknown quantity, the newly recruited part of the company. They might be wondering about him now. What he was like. Too harsh, or too easy-going. To them, once the anchor was catted, he was everything, good or bad, skilful or incompetent. There was no other ear to listen to their complaints, no other voice to reward or punish.

"Easy all!" Allday stood half poised, the tiller bar in his fist. "Toss your oars!"

The boat thrust forward and the bowman hooked on to the main chains at the first attempt. Bolitho guessed that Allday had been busy during his stay in London.

He stood up and waited for the right moment, knowing Allday was watching like a cat in case he should slip between launch and ship, or worse, tumble backwards in a welter of flailing arms and legs. Bolitho had seen it happen, and recalled his own cruel amusement at the spectacle of his new captain arriving aboard in a dripping heap.

Then, with the spray barely finding time to catch his legs, he was up and on board, his ears ringing to the shrill of calls and to the slap of marines' muskets while they presented arms. He doffed his hat to the quarterdeck, and nodded to Herrick and the others.

"Good to be back, Mr. Herrick." His tone was curt.

"Welcome aboard, sir." Herrick was equally so. But their eyes shone with something more than routine formality. Something which none of the others saw, or shared.

Bolitho removed his cloak and handed it to Midshipman Penn. He turned to allow the fading light to play across the broad white lapels of his dress coat. They would all know he was here. He saw the few hands working aloft on last minute splicing, others crowded on gangways and down on the main deck between the twin lines of black twelve-pounder guns.

He smiled, amused at his own gesture. "I will go below now."

"I have placed the orders in your cabin, sir."

Herrick was bursting with questions. It was obvious from his flat, formal voice. But his eyes, those eyes which were so blue, and which could look so hurt, made a lie of his rigidity.

"Very well, I will call you directly."

He made to walk aft to the cabin hatchway when he saw some figures gathered just below the quarterdeck rail. In mixed garments, they were in the process of being checked against a list by Lieutenant Davy.

He called, "New hands, Mr. Davy?"

Herrick said quietly, "We are still thirty under strength, sir."

"Aye, sir." Davy squinted up through the light drizzle, his handsome face set in a confident smile. "I am about to get them to make their marks."

Bolitho crossed to the ladder and ran down to the gun deck. God, how wretched they all looked. Half-starved, ragged, beaten. Even the demanding life aboard ship could surely be no worse than what had made them thus.

He watched Davy's neat, elegant hands as he arranged the book on top of a twelve-pounder's breech.

"Come along now, make your marks."

They shuffled forward, self-conscious, awkward, and very aware that their new captain was nearby.

Bolitho's eye stopped on the one at the end of the line. A sturdy man, well-muscled, and with a pigtail protruding from beneath his battered hat. One prime seaman at least.

He realised Bolitho was watching him and hurried forward to the gun.

Davy snapped, "Here now, hold your damn eagerness!"

Bolitho asked, "Your name?"

He hesitated. "Turpin, sir."

Davy was getting angry. "Stand still and remove your hat to the captain, damn your eyes! If you know anything, you should know respect!"

But the man stood stockstill, his face a mixture of despair and shame.

Bolitho reached out and removed an old coat which Turpin had been carrying across his right forearm.

He asked gently, "Where did you lose your right hand, Turpin?"

The man lowered his eyes. "I was in the *Barfleur*, sir. I lost it at the Chesapeake in '81." He looked up, his eyes showing pride, but only briefly. "Gun captain, I was, sir."

Davy interjected, "I am *most* sorry, sir. I did not realise the fellow was crippled. I will have him sent ashore."

Bolitho said, "You intended to sign the articles with your left hand. Is it *that* important?"

Turpin nodded. "I'm a seaman, sir." He looked round angrily as one of the recruited men nudged his companion. "Not like *some!*" He turned back to Bolitho, his voice falling away. "I can do anything, sir."

Bolitho hardly heard him. He was thinking back to the Chesapeake. The smoke and din. The columns of wheeling ships, like armoured knights at Agincourt. You never got away from it. This man Turpin had been nearby, like hundreds of others. Cheering and dying, cursing and working their guns like souls possessed. He thought of the two fat merchants on the coach. So men like that could grow richer.

He said harshly, "Sign him on, Mr. Davy. One hand from the old *Barfleur* will be more use to me than many others."

He strode aft beneath the quarterdeck, angry with himself, and with Davy for not having the compassion to understand. It was a stupid thing to do. Pointless.

Allday was carrying one of the chests aft to the cabin, where a marine stood like a toy soldier beneath the spiralling deckhead lantern.

He said cheerfully, "That was a good thing you just did, Captain."

"Don't talk like a fool, Allday!" He strode past him and winced as his head grazed an overhead beam. When he glared back at Allday his coxswain's homely features were quite expressionless. "He could probably do *your* work."

Allday nodded gravely. "Aye, sir, it is true that I am overtaxed!"

"Damn your impertinence!" It was useless with Allday. "I don't know why I tolerate you!"

Allday took his sword and walked with it to the cabin bulkhead.

"I once knew a man in Bodmin, Captain." He stood back and studied the sword critically. "Used to hammer a block of wood with a blunt axe, he did. I asked him why he didn't use a sharper blade and finish the job properly." Allday turned and smiled calmly. "He said that when the wood was broken he'd have nothing to work his temper on."

Bolitho sat down at the table. "Thank you. I must remember to get a better axe."

Allday grinned. "My pleasure, Captain." He strode out to fetch another chest.

Bolitho pulled the heavy sealed envelope towards him. With some education behind him Allday might have become almost anything. He slit open the envelope and smiled to himself. Without it he was quite bad enough.

Herrick stepped into the cabin, his hat tacked under one arm. "You sent for me, sir?"

Bolitho was standing by the great stern windows, his body

moving easily with the ship's motion. *Undine* had swung her stern to the change of tide, and through the thick glass Herrick could see the distant lights of Portsmouth Point, glimmering and changing shape through the droplets of rain and spray. In the pitching deckhead lanterns the cabin looked snug and inviting. The bench seat around the stern was covered with fine green leather, and Bolitho's desk and chairs stood out against the deck covering of black and white checked canvas like ripe chestnut.

"Sit down, Thomas."

Bolitho turned slowly and looked at him. He had been back aboard for over an hour, reading and re-reading his orders to ensure he would miss nothing.

He added, "We will weigh tomorrow afternoon. I have a warrant in my orders which entitles me to accept 'volunteers' from the convict hulks in Portsmouth. I would be obliged if you would attend to that as soon after first light as is convenient."

Herrick nodded, watching Bolitho's grave features, noting the restless movements of his hands, the fact that his carefully prepared meal lay untouched in the adjoining dining space. He was troubled. Uncertain about something.

Bolitho said, "We are to sail for Teneriffe." He saw Herrick stiffen and added quietly, "I know, Thomas. You are like me. It comes hard to tack freely into a port where months back we could have expected a somewhat different welcome."

Herrick grinned. "Heated shot, no doubt."

"There we will embark two, maybe three passengers. After replenishing whatever stores we lack, we will proceed without further delay to our destination, Madras." He seemed to be musing aloud. "Over twelve thousand miles. Long enough to get to know one another. And our ship. The orders state that we will proceed with all haste. For that reason we must ensure our people learn their work well. I want no delays because of carelessness or unnecessary damage to canvas and rigging."

Herrick rubbed his chin. "A long haul."

"Aye, Thomas. A hundred days. That is what I intend." He smiled, the gravity fading instantly. "With your help, of course!

Herrick nodded, "May I ask what we are expected to accomplish?"

Bolitho looked down at the folded sheets of his orders. "I still know very little. But I have read quite a lot between the lines."

He began to pace from side to side, his shadow moving unevenly with the roll of the hull.

"When the war ended, Thomas, it was necessary to make concessions. To restore a balance. We had captured Trincomalee in Ceylon from the Dutch. The finest naval harbour and the best place in the Indian Ocean. The French admiral, Suffren, captured it from us, and when war ended gave it back to Holland. We have returned many West Indian islands to France, as well as her Indian stations. And Spain, well, she has been given back Minorca." He shrugged. "Many men on both sides died for nothing, it seems."

Herrick sounded confused. "But what of us, sir? Did we get nothing out of all this?"

Bolitho smiled. "I believe we are about to do so. Hence the extreme secrecy and our vague orders concerning Teneriffe."

He paused and looked down at the stocky lieutenant.

"Without Trincomalee we are in the same position as before the war. We still need a good harbour for our ships. A base to control a wide area. A stepping-stone to expand the East Indies trade."

Herrick grunted. "I'd have thought the East India Company had got all it wanted."

Bolitho's mind returned to the men on the coach. Others he had met in London.

"There are those in authority who see power as the essential foundation of national superiority. Commercial wealth as a means to such power." He glanced at a twelve-pounder gun at the forward end of his cabin, its squat outline masked by a chintz cover. "And war as the means to all three."

Herrick bit his lip. "And we are to be the 'probe,' so to speak?"

"I may be quite wrong, Thomas. But you must know my thinking. Just in case things go against us."

He remembered Winslade's words at the Admiralty. *The task I am giving you would be better handled by a squadron.* He wanted someone he could trust. Or did he merely need a scapegoat should things go wrong? Bolitho had always complained bitterly about being tied to too strict orders. His new ones were so vague that he felt even more restricted. Only one thing was clear. He would take on board a Mr. James Raymond at Teneriffe, and place the ship at his disposal. Raymond was a trusted government courier, and would be carrying the latest despatches to Madras.

Herrick remarked, "It will take some getting used to. But being at sea again in a ship such as *Undine* will make a world of difference."

Bolitho nodded. "We must ensure that our people are prepared for anything, peace or no peace. Where we are going they may be less inclined to accept our views without argument."

He sat down on the bench and stared through the spattered glass.

"I will speak with the other officers at eight bells tomorrow while you are in the hulks." He smiled at Herrick's reflection. "I am sending *you* because you will understand. You'll not frighten them all to death!"

He stood up quickly.

"Now, Thomas, we will take a glass of claret."

Herrick leaned forward. "That was a goodly selection you had sent from London, sir."

Bolitho shook his head. "We will save *that* for more trying times." He lifted a decanter from its rack. "This is more usual to our tastes!"

They drank their claret in comfortable silence. Bolitho was thinking how strange it was to be sitting quietly when the voyage which lay ahead demanded so much of all of them. But it was useless to prowl about the decks or poke into stores and spirit rooms. *Undine* was ready for sea. As ready as she could ever be. He thought of his officers, the extensions of his ideas and authority. He knew little of any of them. Soames was a competent seaman, but was inclined to harshness when things did not go right immediately. His superior, Davy, was harder to know. Outwardly cool and unruffled, he had a ruthless streak like many of his kind. The sailing master was called Ezekiel Mudge, a broad lump of a man who looked old enough to be his grandfather. In fact he was sixty, and certainly the oldest master Bolitho had met. Old Mudge would prove to be one of the most important when they reached the Indian Ocean. He had originally served in the East India Company, and had endured more storms, shipwrecks, pirates and a dozen other hazards than any man alive, if his record was to be believed. He had a huge beaked nose, with the eyes perched on either side of it like tiny, bright stones. A formidable person, and one who would be watching his captain's seamanship for flaws, Bolitho was certain of that.

The three midshipmen seemed fairly average. Penn was the youngest, and had come aboard three days after his twelfth birthday. Keen and Armitage were both seventeen, but whereas the former showed the same elegant carelessness as Lieutenant Davy, Armitage appeared to be forever looking over his shoulder. A mother's boy. Four days after he had reported aboard with his gleaming new uniform and polished dirk his mother had in fact come to Portsmouth to visit him. Her husband was a man of some influence, and she had swept into the dockyard in a beautiful carriage like some visiting duchess.

Bolitho had greeted her briefly and allowed her to meet Armitage in the seclusion of the wardroom. If she had seen the actual quarters where her child was to serve his months at sea she would probably have collapsed.

He had had to send Herrick in the end to interrupt the embraces and the mother's plaintive sobs with a feeble excuse about Armitage being required for duty. Duty; he could hardly move about the ship without falling headlong over a block or a ringbolt.

Giles Bellairs, the debonair captain of marines, was more like a caricature than a real person. Incredibly smart, shoulders always rigidly squared, he looked as if he had had his uniforms moulded around his limbs like wax. He spoke in short, clipped sentences, and barely extended much beyond matters of hunting, wildfowling and, of course, drill. His marines were his whole life, although he hardly ever seemed to utter much in the way of orders. His massive sergeant, Coaker, took care of the close contact with the marines, and Bellairs contented himself with an occasional "Carry on, Sar'nt Coaker!" or "I say, Sar'nt, that fellah's like a bundle of old rags, what?" He was one of the few people in Bolitho's experience who could get completely drunk without any outward change of expression.

Triphook, the purser, appeared very competent, if grudging with his rations. He had taken a lot of care to ensure that the victualling yard had not filled the lower hold with rotten casks, to be discovered too late to take action. That in itself was rare. Bolitho's thoughts came back to the surgeon. He had been aboard for two weeks. Had he been able to get a replacement he would have done so. Whitmarsh was a drunkard in the worst sense. Sober he had a quiet, even gentle manner. Drunk, which was often, he seemed to come apart like an old sail in a sudden squall.

He tightened his jaw. Whitmarsh would mend his ways. Or else . . .

Feet scraped across the planks overhead and Herrick said, "There's a few below decks tonight who'll be wondering if they've done a'right by signing on." He chuckled. "Too late now."

Bolitho stared astern at the black, swirling water, hearing the urgent tide banging and squeaking around the rudder.

"Aye. It's a long step from land to sea. Far more so than most people realise!" He returned his glass to the rack. "I think I shall turn in now. It will be a long day tomorrow."

Herrick stood up and nodded. "I'll bid you goodnight, sir."

He knew full well that Bolitho would stay awake for hours yet. Pacing and planning, searching for last-minute faults, possible mistakes in the arrangement of watch-bills and delegation of duties. Bolitho would know he was aware of this fact, too.

The door closed and Bolitho walked right aft to lean his hands on the centre sill. He could feel the woodwork vibrating under his palms, the hull trembling all around him in time to the squeak of stays, the clatter and slap of halliards and blocks.

Who would watch them go? Would anyone care? One more ship slipping down channel like hundreds before her.

There was a nervous tap at the door, and Noddall, the cabin servant, pattered into the lantern light. A small man, with the pointed face of an anxious rodent. He even held his hands in front of him like two nervous paws.

"Yer supper, sir. You've not touched it." He started to gather up the plates. "Won't do, sir. It won't *do*."

Bolitho smiled as Noddall scampered away to his pantry. He was so absorbed in his own little world it seemed as if he had not even noticed there was a change of command.

He threw his new cloak across his shoulders and left the cabin. On the pitch-dark quarterdeck he groped his way aft to the taffrail and stared towards the land. Countless lights and hidden houses. He turned and looked along his ship, the wind blowing his hair across his face, the chill making him hold his breath. The riding light reflected on the taut shrouds like pale gold, and right forward he saw a smaller lantern, where the lonely anchor watch kept a wary eye on the cable.

It *felt* different, he decided. No sentries on each gangway to watch for a sneak attack or a mass attempt at desertion. No nets to delay a sudden rush of enemy boarders. He touched a quarterdeck six-pounder with one hand. It felt like wet ice. But for how long, he wondered?

The master's mate of the watch prowled past, and then sheered away as he saw his captain by the rail.

"All's well, zur!" he called.

"Thank you."

Bolitho did not know the man's name. Not yet. In the next hundred days he would know more than their names, he thought. As they would about him.

With a sigh he returned to his cabin, his hair plastered to his head, his cheeks tingling from the cold. There was no sign of Noddall, but the cot was ready for him, and there was something hot in a mug nearby.

A minute after his head was on the pillow he was fast asleep.

The next day dawned as grey as the one before, but overnight the rain had stopped, and the wind held firm from the southeast.

All forenoon the work went on without relaxation, the petty officers checking and re-checking their lists of names, putting them to faces, making sure seasoned hands were spaced among the untried and untrained.

Bolitho dictated a final report to his clerk, a dried-up man named Pope, and then signed it in readiness for the last boat. He found time to speak with his officers, and seek out Mr. Tapril, the gunner, in his magazine to discuss moving some of the spare gun parts and tackle further aft and help adjust the vessel's trim until she had consumed some of her own stores to compensate for it.

He was changing into his seagoing coat, with its faded lace and dull buttons, when Herrick entered the cabin and reported he had brought fifteen new men from the hulks.

"What was it like?"

Herrick sighed. "It was a sort of hell, sir. I could have got treble the number, a whole company of 'em if I'd been able to bring their women and wives, too."

Bolitho paused as he tied his neckcloth. "*Women?* In the hulks?"

"Aye, sir." Herrick shuddered. "I hope I never see the like again."

"Very well. Sign them on, but don't give them anything to do just yet. I doubt they've the strength to lift a marlin spike after being penned up like that."

A midshipman appeared in the open door.

"Mr. Davy's respect, sir." His eyes darted around the cabin, missing nothing. "And the anchor's hove short."

"Thank you." Bolitho smiled. "Next time stay awhile, Mr. Penn, and have a better look."

The boy vanished, and Bolitho looked steadily at Herrick.

"Well, Thomas?"

Herrick nodded firmly. "Aye, sir. I'm ready. It's been a long wait."

They climbed up to the quarterdeck together, and while Herrick moved to the forward rail with his speaking trumpet, Bolitho stood aft, a little apart from the others who were gathered restlessly at their stations.

Clink, clink, clink, the capstan was turning more slowly now, the men's backs bent almost double as the hull pulled heavily on the anchor.

Bolitho looked at the master's untidy shape beside the double wheel. He had four helmsmen. He was taking no chances, it seemed. With the helm, or his new captain's skill.

"Get the ship under way, if you please." He saw Herrick's trumpet moving. "Once clear of this local shipping we will lay her on the larboard tack and steer sou'-west by west."

Old Mudge nodded heavily, one eye hidden beyond the headland of a nose.

"Aye, aye, sir."

Herrick yelled, "Stand by on the capstan!" He shaded his eyes to peer up at the masthead pendant. "Loose heads'ls!"

The answering flip and clatter of released canvas made several new men peer round, confused and startled. A petty officer thrust a line into a man's hand and bellowed, "'Old it, you bugger! Don't stand there like a bloody woman!"

Bolitho saw a bosun's mate right forward astride the bowsprit, one arm circling above his head as the cable grew stiffer and more vertical beneath the gilded water-nymph.

"Hands aloft! Loose tops'ls!"

Bolitho relaxed slightly as the nimble-footed topmen swarmed up the ratlines on either beam. No sense in rushing it this first time. The watching eyes ashore could think what they liked. He'd get no thanks for letting her drive ashore.

"Man the braces!"

Herrick was hanging over the rail, his trumpet moving from side to side like a coachman's blunderbuss.

"Lively there! Mr. Shellabeer, get those damned idlers aft on the double, I say!"

Shellabeer was the boatswain, a swarthy, taciturn man who looked more like a Spaniard than a Devonian.

Bolitho leaned back, his hands on his hips, watching the swift figures dashing out on the vibrating yards like monkeys. It made him feel sick to watch their indifference to such heights.

First one, then the next great topsail billowed and banged loosely in confusion, while the seamen on the yards clung on, calling to each other, or jeering at their opposite numbers on the other masts.

"Anchor's aweigh, sir!"

Like a thing released from chains the frigate swung dizzily across the steep troughs, men falling and slithering at the braces as they fought to haul the great yards round, to cup the wind and master it.

"Lee braces there! Heave away!" Herrick was hoarse.

Bolitho gritted his teeth and forced himself to remain quite still as she plunged further astride the wind. Here and there a bosun's mate struck out with his rope starter or pushed a man bodily to brace or halliard.

Then with a booming roar like thunder the sails filled and hardened to the wind's steady thrust, the deck canting over and holding steady as the helmsmen threw themselves on their spokes.

He made himself take a glass from Midshipman Keen and trained it across the starboard quarter, keeping his face impassive, even though he was almost shaking with excitement and relief.

The sail drill was very bad, the placing of trained men too sketchy for comfort, but they were away! Free of the land.

He saw a few people on the Point watching them heel over on the larboard tack, the top of a shining carriage just below the wall. Perhaps it was Armitage's mother, weeping as she watched her offspring being taken from her.

The master shouted gruffly, "Sou'-west by west, sir! Full an' bye!"

When Bolitho turned to answer him he saw that the master was nodding with something like approval.

"Thank you, Mr. Mudge. We will get the courses on her directly."

He walked forward to join Herrick at the rail, his body angled steeply to the deck. Some of the confusion was being cleared, with men picking their way amidst loose coils of rope like survivors from a battle.

Herrick looked at him sadly. "It was terrible, sir."

"I agree, Mr. Herrick." He could not restrain a smile. "But it will improve, eh?"

By late afternoon *Undine* had beaten clear of the Isle of Wight and was standing well out in the Channel.

By evening only her reefed topsails were visible, and soon even they had disappeared.

3

A *M*IXED GATHERING

ON THE morning of the fourteenth day after weighing anchor at Spithead Bolitho was in his cabin sipping a mug of coffee and pondering for the countless time on what he had achieved.

The previous evening they had sighted the dull hump of Teneriffe sprawled like a cloud across the horizon, and he had decided to heave-to and avoid the hazards of a night approach. *Fourteen days.* It felt an eternity. They had been plagued by foul weather for much of that time. Flicking over the pages of his personal log he could see the countless, frustrating entries. Headwinds, occasional but fierce gales, and the constant need to shorten sail, to reef down and ride it out as best they could. The dreaded Bay of Biscay had been kind to them, that at least was a mercy. Otherwise, with almost half the ship's company too seasick to venture aloft, or too terrified to scramble out along the dizzily pitching yards without physical violence being used on them, it was likely *Undine* might have reached no further.

Bolitho appreciated what it must be like for many of his men. Shrieking winds, overcrowded conditions in a creaking, rolling hull where their food, if they could face it, often ended up in a mess of bilge water and vomit. It produced a kind of numbness, like that given to a man left abandoned in the sea. For a while he strikes out bravely, swimming he knows not where, until he is too exhausted, too dazed to care. He is without authority or any sort of guidance. It is his turning point.

Bolitho recognised all the signs well enough, and knew it was the same sort of challenge for him. Give in to his own understanding and sympathy, listen too much to excuses from his hard-worked lieutenants and warrant officers, and he would never regain control, or be able to rally his company when the real pressure came.

He knew that many cursed him behind his back, prayed for him to fall dead or vanish overboard in the night. He saw their glances, sensed their resentment as he pushed them through each day, each hour of every one of those days. Sail drill, and more drill against Herrick's watch, while he himself made sure all engaged knew he was following their efforts. He made the men on *Undine's* three masts race each other in their struggle to shorten or make more sail, until finally he drove them even harder to work not in competition but as a gasping, silently cursing team.

Now, as he sat with the mug in his hands he found some grudging satisfaction in what they had done. What they had achieved together, willingly or otherwise. When *Undine* dropped her anchor in the roads of Santa Cruz today, the watching Spaniards would see a semblance of order and discipline, of efficiency which they had come to know and fear in times of war.

But if he had driven his company to the limit he had not spared himself either. And he was feeling it, despite the inviting rays of early sunshine which made reflections dance across the low deckhead. Barely a watch had passed without his going on deck to lend his presence. Lieutenant Davy had little experience of handling a ship in foul weather, but would learn, given time. Soames was too prone to lose patience when faced with a disaster on deck. He would knock some luckless seaman aside and leap into his place yelling, "You're useless! I'd rather do it myself!" Only Herrick rode out the storm of Bolitho's persistent demands, and Bolitho felt sorry that his friend had been made to carry the brunt of the work. It was too easy to punish men, when in fact it was an officer's fault for losing his own head, or not being able to find the right words in the teeth of a raging gale. Herrick stood firmly between wardroom and lower deck, and twixt captain and company.

There had even been two floggings, something which he had hoped to avoid. Each case had been within the private world of the lower deck. The first a simple one of stealing from another sailor's small hoard of money. The second, far more serious, had been a savage knife-fight which had ended in a man having his face opened from ear to jaw. It was still not certain if he would live.

A real grudge fight, a momentary spark of anger caused by fatigue and constant work, he did not really know. In a well-trained ship of war it was likely he would never have heard about either case. The justice of the lower deck was far more drastic and instant when their own world was threatened by a thief or one too fond of his knife.

Bolitho despised captains who used authority without consideration for the misery it might entail, who meted out savage punishment without getting to the root of the trouble and thereby avoiding it. Herrick knew how he felt. When Bolitho had first met him he had been the junior lieutenant in his ship. A ship where the previous captain had been so severe, so unthinkingly brutal with his punishments that the seeds of mutiny had been well and truly laid.

Herrick knew better than most about such things, and yet he had intervened personally to persuade Bolitho to avoid the floggings. It was their first real disagreement, and Bolitho had hated to see the sudden hurt in Herrick's eyes.

Bolitho had said, "This is a new company. It takes time to weld people together so that each can rely on his companion under all circumstances. Many are entirely ignorant of the Navy's ways and its demands. They hate to see 'others' getting away with crimes they themselves avoid. At this stage we cannot allow them to split into separate groups. Old hands and the new recruits, professional criminals and the weak ones who have no protection but to ally themselves with some other faction."

Herrick had persisted, "But in *peacetime*, sir, maybe it takes all the longer."

"We can't afford the luxury of finding out." He had hardened voice. "You know how I feel. It is not easy."

The thief had taken his punishment without a whimper, a dozen lashes at the gratings while *Undine* had cruised along beneath a clearing sky, some gulls throwing their shadows round and round across the tense drama below.

As he had read from the Articles of War, Bolitho had looked along his command at the watching men in shrouds and rigging, the sharp red lines of Bellairs's marines, Herrick and all the rest. The second culprit had been a brute of a man called Sullivan. He had volunteered to a recruiting party outside Portsmouth, and had all the looks of a hardened criminal. But he had served in a King's ship before and should have been an asset.

Three dozen lashes. Little enough in the Navy's view for half killing a fellow seaman. Had he laid a hand on an officer he would have faced death rather than a flogging.

The actual punishment was terrible. Sullivan had broken down completely at the first blow across his naked back, as the boatswain's mates took turns to lay the lash over shoulders and spine he had wriggled and screamed like a madman, his mouth frothing with foam, his eyes like marbles in his distorted face.

Mr. Midshipman Armitage had almost fainted, and some of those who had just recovered from their own sickness had vomited in unison, despite the harsh shouts from their petty officers.

Then it had ended, the watching men giving a kind of sigh as they were dismissed below.

Sullivan had been cut down and carried to Whitmarsh's sickbay, where no doubt he had been restored by a plentiful ration of rum.

Each day following the punishment, as he had paced the quarterdeck or supervised a change of tack, Bolitho had the eyes watching him. Seeing him perhaps as enemy rather than commander. He had told himself often enough that when you accepted the honour of command you carried all of it. Not just the authority and the pride of controlling a living, vital ship, but the knocks and kicks as well.

There was a tap on the door and Herrick stepped into the cabin.

"About another hour, sir. With your permission I will give the order to clew up all canvas except tops'ls and jib. It will make our entrance more easy to manage."

"Have some coffee, Thomas." He relaxed as Herrick seated himself across the table. "I am burning to know what we are about."

Herrick took a mug and tested the coffee with his tongue.

"Me, too." He smiled over the rim. "Once or twice back there I thought we might never reach land!"

"Yes. I can feel for many of our people. Some will never have seen the sea, let alone driven so far from England. Now, they know that Africa lies somewhere over the larboard bulwark. That we are going to the other side of the earth. Some are even beginning to feel like seamen, when just weeks back they had thumbs where their fingers should be."

Herrick's smile widened. "Due to you, sir. I am sometimes very thankful that I hold no command. Or chance of one either."

Bolitho watched him thoughtfully. The rift was healed.

"I am afraid the choice may not be yours, Thomas." He stood up. "In fact, I shall see that you get command whenever the opportunity offers itself, if only to drive some of your wild idealism into the bilges!"

They grinned at each other like conspirators.

"Now be off with you while I change into a better coat." He grimaced. "To show our Spanish friends some respect, eh?"

A little over an hour later, gliding above her own reflection, *Undine* moved slowly towards the anchorage in the roads. In the bright sunlight the island of Teneriffe seemed to abound with colour, and Bolitho heard several of the watching seamen gasping with awe. The hills were no longer hidden in shadow, but danced on the glare with every shade and hue. And everything was brighter and larger, at least it appeared so to the new hands. Shimmering white buildings, brilliant blue sea, with beaches and surf to make a man catch his breath and stare.

Allday stood aft by the cabin hatch and remarked, "I'll bet some Don'd like to rake us as we come by!"

Bolitho ran his eye quickly along his ship, trying to see her as those ashore would. She looked very smart, and gave little hint of the sweat and effort which had gone to make her so. The best ensign fluttered from the gaff, the scarlet matching that of the marines' swaying lines athwart the quarterdeck. On the larboard gangway Tapril, the gunner, was having a last hurried discussion with his mates in readiness to begin a salute to the Spanish flag which flew so proudly above the headland battery.

Old Mudge was beside the wheel, hands hidden in the folds of his watchcoat. He seemed to retain the same clothing no matter what the weather might do, hot or cold, rain or fine. He kept a variety of instruments and personal items in his capacious pockets, and Bolitho guessed that sometime, long past, he had been made to rush on deck and stay there with half of his things still scattered around his cabin.

He growled to the helmsmen and they edged the wheel over a few spokes, the main topsail filling and then drooping again as the ship idled beneath the land's protection.

Herrick trained his glass on the land and then said, "Passing the point now, sir!"

"Very well." Bolitho waved his hand to Tapril. "Begin salute."

And as the English frigate continued slowly towards her anchorage the frail morning air shook and trembled to the regular crash of cannon fire. Gun for gun the Spanish replied, the smoke hanging almost motionless above the shallowing water.

Bolitho gripped his hands together behind him, feeling the sweat exploring his spine under his heavy dress coat and making one of his new shirts cling like a wet towel.

It was strange to stand so impassively as the slow barrage went on around him. Like some trick or dream. At any moment, he half-expected to see the bulwark blast apart, or a ball to come screaming amongst the rigid marines and cut them to a bloody gruel.

The last shot hammered his ears, and as the drifting smoke moved away from the decks he saw another frigate anchored at the head of the roads. Spanish, larger than *Undine,* her colours and pendants very bright against the green shore beyond. Her captain, too, had probably been remembering, he thought.

He glanced up at the masthead pendant as it whipped half-heartedly in the breeze. Soon now. More orders. A new piece to fit into the puzzle.

Mudge blew his great nose loudly, a thing he always did before carrying out some part of his duties.

"Ready, sir."

"Very well. Man the braces. Hands wear ship, if you please."

Bare feet padded across the newly-scrubbed decks in a steady rush to obey his repeated order, and Bolitho slowly breathed out as each man reached his station without mishap.

"Tops'l sheets!"

The flag above the battery dipped in the glare and then returned to its proper place. Some small boats were shoving off from the land, and Bolitho saw that many were loaded with fruit and other items for barter. With all their bread ruined in the first storm, and few fresh fruits to rival those in the boats, Triphook, the purser, would be busy indeed.

"Tops'l clew lines!"

A boatswain's mate shook his fist at some anonymous figure on the fore topsail yard. "Yew clumsy bugger! You 'old on with one 'and or yew'll never see yer doxy again!"

Bolitho watched the narrowing strip of water, his eyes half-closed against the searing glare.

"Helm a'lee!"

He waited, as with dignity *Undine* turned quietly into the wind, her remaining canvas shivering violently.

"*Let go!*"

There was a yell from forward, followed by a splash as the anchor plunged down beneath the golden figurehead.

Herrick waited until the last of the canvas had vanished as if by magic along the yards and said, "They did quite well, I thought, sir?"

Bolitho watched him, holding back the smile. Then, relenting, he replied, "*Quite* well, Mr. Herrick."

Herrick grinned. "You'll not need the gig today, sir. A boat's heading out to us in fine style."

Allday strode forward and presented Bolitho's sword. He frowned and muttered, "Not the gig, Captain?" He sounded aggrieved.

Bolitho held out his arms to allow the coxswain to buckle the belt around his waist.

"Not this time, Allday."

It was terrible how both Herrick and Allday watched over his every move.

The marines were stamping and shuffling into a new formation by the entry port, Sergeant Coaker's face shining beneath his black shako like a great sweating fruit.

Bolitho turned to watch the approaching launch, a grand affair with a gilded and canopied cockpit. Beside it, Allday's poor gig would look like a Falmouth harbour boat. A resplendent officer stood watching the anchored frigate, a scroll under one arm. The usual welcoming words. The first link to whatever lay ahead.

He said quietly, "You will remain aboard, Mr. Herrick. Mr. Davy will accompany me ashore." He ignored the obvious disappointment. "Take good care of matters here, and make certain our people are ready for anything!"

Herrick touched his hat. "Aye, aye, sir." He hurried away to tell Davy of his good fortune.

Bolitho smiled gravely. With shore boats and other temptations it would need all of Herrick's skill to keep the ship from being swamped by traders and less respectable visitors.

He heard Herrick say, "So *you* are to accompany the captain, Mr. Davy."

Davy hesitated, gauging the moment and Herrick's mood. Then he said calmly, "A wise choice, if I may say so, Mr. Herrick."

Bolitho turned away, hiding his smile, as Herrick snapped, "Well, you are damn little use here, are you?"

Then as the four minute drummer boys struck up with their flutes and drums "Heart of Oak" and Bellairs's sweating guard presented muskets, Bolitho stepped forward to greet his visitor.

The Governor's Residence was well situated on a gently sloping road above the main anchorage. On his way from the ship by barge and carriage Bolitho was relieved to discover that his official escort, a major of artillery, spoke very little English, and contented himself with occasional exclamations of pleasure whenever they passed anything unusual.

It was obvious that everything was well planned, and that from the moment *Undine*'s topgallants had been sighted the previous evening things had begun to move.

Bolitho barely remembered meeting the Governor. A bearded, courteous man who shook his hand, received Bolitho's formal greetings on behalf of King George, and who then withdrew to allow an aide to conduct the two British officers to another room.

Davy, who was not easily impressed, whispered, "By God, sir, the Dons live well. No wonder the treasure ships stop here en route for Spain. A ready market for 'em, I would think."

The room into which they were ushered was spacious indeed. Long and cool, with a tiled floor and a plentiful selection of well-carved furniture and handsome rugs. There was one huge table in the centre, made entirely of marble. It would take seven gun crews to move it, Bolitho decided.

There were about a dozen people standing around the table, *arranged*, he thought, so that without wasting time he could distinguish those who counted from those who did not.

The man he guessed to be James Raymond stepped forward and said quickly, "I am Raymond, Captain. Welcome. We had expected you earlier perhaps." He spoke very abruptly. Afraid of wasting time? Unsure of himself? It was hard to tell.

He was in his early thirties, well dressed, and had features which could pass as handsome but for his petulant frown.

He said, "And this is Don Luis Puigserver, His Most Catholic Majesty's personal emissary."

Puigserver was a sturdy man, with biscuit-coloured features and a pair of black eyebrows which dominated the rest of his face. He had hard eyes, but there was charm, too, as he stepped forward and took Bolitho's hand.

"A pleasure, *Capitan*. You have a fine ship." He gestured to a tall figure by the window. "Capitan Alfonso Triarte of the *Nervion* had much praise for the way she behaved."

Bolitho looked at the other man. Very senior. He would be, to command the big frigate in the roads. He returned Bolitho's examination without much show of pleasure. Like two dogs who have fought once too often, perhaps.

He forgot all about Triarte as the emissary said smoothly, "I will be brief. You will wish to return to your ship, to make last arrangements for sailing to our destination."

Bolitho watched him curiously. There was something very compelling about the man. His stocky figure, his legs which looked so muscled, despite the fine silk stockings, even the rough handshake could not disguise his confident assurance.

No wonder the Governor had been quick to pass Bolitho on to him; Puigserver obviously commanded respect.

He snapped his spatulate fingers and a nervous aide hurried forward to take Bolitho's hat and sword. Another beckoned to some servants, and in minutes everyone was seated around the altar-like table, a beautifully cut goblet at his elbow.

Only Puigserver remained standing. He watched the servants filling the goblets with sparkling wine, his face completely unruffled. But when Bolitho glanced down he saw one of his feet tapping very insistently on the tiled floor.

He raised his glass. "Gentlemen. To our friendship."

They stood up and swallowed the wine. It was excellent, and Bolitho had a mental picture of his own doubts and fumblings in the shop at St. James's Street.

Puigserver continued, "Little came out of the war but a need to avoid further bloodshed. I will not waste our time by making empty promises which I cannot keep, but I can only hope that we may further our separate causes in peace."

Bolitho glanced quickly at the others. Raymond leaning back in his chair, trying to appear relaxed, but as taut as a spring. The Spanish captain looking at his wine, eyes distant. Most of the others had the empty expressions of those who pretend to understand when in fact they do not. It seemed likely to Bolitho that they only understood one word in ten.

Davy sat stiffly on the opposite side of the table, his clean features glowing with heat, his face set in a mask of formality.

It all boiled down to the three of them. Don Luis Puigserver, Raymond and himself.

The former said, "Thankfully, Spain has received back Minorca and certain other islands as concessions following the *unfortunate* war." His eyes rested on Bolitho very briefly. Dark, almost black. They were like Spanish olives. "In return, His Most Catholic Majesty has seen fit to bless this new venture between us." He looked at Raymond. "Perhaps you would be good enough to expand the details, yes?"

Raymond made to stand up and changed his mind.

"As you will know, Captain Bolitho, the French Admiral Suffren was responsible for many attacks on our ships and possessions in the East Indies and India itself. Holland and Spain"—he hesitated as Capitan Triarte coughed gently—"were France's allies but they had not the available squadrons and men to protect their possessions in that area. Suffren did it for them. He captured

Trincomalee from us and restored it to the Dutch after the war. There were several other instances, but you will know of most of them, Captain. Now, in exchange for certain other considerations which need not concern you, Spain has agreed in principle to hand over to Britain one of her remaining possessions in, er, Borneo." He eyed Bolitho flatly. "Which is where you will eventually be going, of course."

Of course. It sounded so simple. Another two or three thousand miles added to their present voyage. The way Raymond spoke it could have been Plymouth.

Bolitho said quietly, "I am not certain I understand the purpose of all this."

Puigserver interjected, "Of that I am sure, *Capitan.*" He glanced coldly at Raymond. "Let us be frank. To avoid further trouble in this uneasy truce, for that is what it is, we must move with caution. The French gained next to nothing in the Indies despite all their efforts, and they are, how you say? *Touchy* about any swift expansions around their dwindling influence there. Your final destination will be Teluk Pendang. A fine anchorage, a commanding position for any country with the will to expand elsewhere in that area. A bridge to empire, as some Greek once remarked."

Bolitho nodded. "I see, *Señor.*"

He did not, nor had he even heard of the place mentioned.

Raymond said sharply, "When peace was signed last year, our Government despatched the frigate *Fortunate* to Madras with the bones of this present agreement in her care. On her way around the Cape of Good Hope she met with two of Suffren's frigates which were returning to France. Naturally enough, they knew nothing of the peace, and *Fortunate's* captain was given no time to explain the point. They fought, and *Fortunate* so battered one of the enemy that she took fire and sank. Unfortunately, she, too, was set ablaze and was lost with most of her company."

Bolitho could picture the scene. Three ships on an open sea.

Countries at peace at last, but their captains eager to fight, as they had been conditioned to do.

"However, one of the French captains, the surviving one, was a veteran called Le Chaumareys. One of France's best."

Bolitho smiled. "I have heard of him."

Raymond seemed flustered. "Yes. I am sure, of it. Well, it is believed in some quarters that France, through Le Chaumareys, now knows about this arrangement we are making with Spain. If that is so, then France will be troubled at the prospect of our gaining another possession, one which *she* fought for on Spain's behalf."

Bolitho did understand now. All the veiled remarks at the Admiralty. The secrecy. No wonder. One hint that England was about to push her way further into the East Indies, no matter for what outward reason, and a war might burst out again like an exploding magazine.

He asked, "What are we to do?"

Raymond replied, "You will sail in company with the *Nervion*." He swallowed hard. "*She* will be the senior ship, and you will act accordingly. Upon arrival at Madras you will embark the new British Governor and convey him, with whatever forces he may have, to his new destination. Teluk Pendang. I will accompany you with despatches for him, and to advise in any way I can."

Puigserver beamed at them, his black eyebrows arched like great bows. "And *I* will be there to ensure that there is no nonsense from our people, eh?"

Raymond added wearily, "The French have a forty-four-gun frigate in that area, the *Argus*. It is said that Le Chaumareys is with her. He knows the Sunda Isles and Borneo as well as any European can."

Bolitho breathed out slowly. It was a good plan as far as it went. A British squadron would invite an open battle sooner or later, but two frigates, one from each nation, would be more than a match for the heavily-armed *Argus* both verbally and in artillery.

Puigserver walked slowly to the broad window and stared down at the anchored ships.

"A long voyage, gentlemen, but I hope a rewarding one for us all." He turned towards Bolitho, his square face in shadow.

"Are you ready to sail again?"

"Aye, *Señor*. My people are preparing to take in more water and fresh fruit, if that is possible."

"It is being attended to, *Capitan*." He showed his teeth. "I am sorry I cannot entertain you now, but in any case, this island is a dismal place. If you come to Bilbao." He kissed his fingertips. "*Then* I will show you how to live, eh?" He laughed at Raymond's grim features. "And I suspect we will all know ourselves *much* better after this voyage is done!"

The Spanish aides bowed politely as Puigserver walked to the door, and he called, "We will meet before we sail." He turned away. "But tomorrow we raise our anchors, come what may."

Raymond walked round the table as the babble of conversation broke out again. He whispered fiercely, "That damned fellow! One more day with him and I would have told him a thing or two!"

Bolitho asked, "In which vessel will you be sailing? Mine's a fine ship, but smaller by far than the Spaniard."

Raymond twisted round to watch the Spanish captain who was discussing something with his companions in a low voice.

"Sail in the *Nervion?* If your ship were a damned collier brig I'd take her in preference!"

Davy whispered, "I think they expect us to leave, sir."

Raymond scowled. "I will come to your ship and arrange things there. Where no ears listen even to one's breathing!"

Bolitho saw his escort waiting outside the door and smiled to himself. Raymond seemed to have a very vital role in things. Tact, however, was beyond him.

They returned to the jetty with hardly a word, but Bolitho was very conscious of the tension within the man Raymond. On a knife edge. Tortured by something. His work was over-reaching him perhaps.

As the scarlet-coated oarsmen propelled the Governor's barge towards *Undine* Bolitho felt a sense of relief. A ship he could understand. Raymond's life was as alien as the moon.

Raymond clambered up from the barge and stared vaguely at the assembled side-party, at the comings and goings of *Undine's* seamen as they worked the tackles on the opposite side. Casks and nets of fruit, and straw hats to protect the unwary from sunburn.

Bolitho nodded to Herrick. "All well?" He touched Raymond's arm. "Mr. Raymond will be a passenger with us." He turned sharply as he heard a shrill of laughter from the cabin hatch. "Who let that woman on board? In God's name, Mr. Herrick, this is not the Nore or Portsmouth Point!"

Then he saw the girl. Small and dark, in a bright red dress, she was talking to Allday, who was obviously enjoying himself.

Raymond said heavily, "I had hoped to explain earlier, Captain. That girl is a maid-servant. My *wife's* maid." He looked as if he was going to be sick.

Herrick tried to dispel Bolitho's sudden anger. "She came out with her lady just an hour back, sir. She had authority." He looked worried. "I had little choice in the matter."

"I see."

Bolitho strode aft. All those thousands of miles in a small crowded ship-of-war. Raymond was bad enough, but his wife and a maid were too much. He saw some seamen nudging each other. They had probably been waiting just to see his reactions.

Very calmly he said, "Perhaps you would, er, introduce me, Mr. Raymond?"

They went aft together, and Davy whispered, "God's teeth, Mr. Herrick, what a mixed gathering we are fast becoming!"

Herrick glared at him. "And I suppose you have been out there damn well enjoying yourself!"

"A little wine. Some fair company." He chuckled. "But I thought, too, of you, *sir*."

Herrick grinned. "To hell with you! Get into your working clothes and help with this loading. You need a million eyes today!"

In the meantime Bolitho had reached his cabin, and stared at it in dismay. There were boxes everywhere, and clothing spilled across furniture and guns, as if there had been a violent robbery aboard.

Mrs. Raymond was tall, unsmiling, and almost beside herself with anger.

Her husband exclaimed, "You should have *waited*, Viola. This is our captain."

Bolitho bowed slightly. "Richard Bolitho, ma'am. I had just mentioned that a thirty-two-gun frigate has barely the room for luxury. However, since you have chosen to sail with us, I will do all that I can to—" He got no further.

"Chosen?" Her voice was husky with scorn. "Please do not delude yourself, Captain. *He* does not wish me to travel in the *Nervion*." Her mouth twisted in contempt. "He fears for my safety when I am with Spanish *gentlemen!*"

Bolitho noticed Noddall hovering anxiously by the dining compartment and snapped, "Help Mrs. Raymond's maid to stow all this"—he looked round helplessly—"gear." He saw Raymond slump down on the bench seat like a dying man. No wonder he looked troubled. "And pass the word for the first lieutenant." He glanced around the cabin, speaking his thoughts aloud. "We will have these twelve-pounders removed temporarily and put quakers in their place. That will allow a little more room."

Raymond looked up dully. "Quakers?"

"Wooden muzzles. They give an appearance that we are still fully armed." He forced a smile. "Quakers having an opposition to war."

Herrick appeared by the door. "Sir?"

"We will rig extra screens here, Mr. Herrick. A larger sleeping compartment for our passengers. To larboard, I think."

Mrs. Raymond said calmly, "For me and my maid, if you please." She looked at her husband. "He will bed elsewhere on *this* ship."

Herrick studied her curiously but said, "Mr. Raymond to starboard then. And what about you, sir?"

Bolitho sighed. "Chart space." He looked at the others. "We will dine together here, if you agree."

Nobody answered.

Midshipman Keen hovered by the door, his eyes on the woman.

"Mr. Soames's respects, sir, and the captain of *Nervion* is about to board us."

Bolitho swung round and then gasped as his shin cracked against a heavy chest.

He said between his teeth, "I will endeavour to be hospitable, Mr. Herrick!"

Herrick kept his face blank. "I am certain of it, sir."

It was early morning by the time Bolitho had pulled himself wearily into his cot, his mind still reeling from entertaining Capitan Triarte and some of his officers. He had been made to go across to the *Nervion* where the captain had again made a point of comparing the spacious comfort with *Undine*'s over-crowded quarters. It had not helped at all. Now the ship lay quiet again, and he tried to picture Mrs. Raymond who was sleeping beyond the newly-rigged screen. He had seen her in the cabin when the Spanish officers had come aboard. Aloof yet tempting, with little to reveal her true feelings for her husband. A dangerous woman to cross, he thought.

How still the ship felt. Perhaps, like himself, everyone was too weary to move. Guns had been trundled away and lowered with difficulty into the holds. More stores and heavy gear had had to be swayed aft to readjust the trim once again. It was surprising how much larger the cabin looked without the guns there.

He groaned as his head found some new ache to offer him. He

would not see much of it though. He turned his face to the pillow, the sweat running across his chest with the effort. One thing was certain. He had rarely had better incentive for a fast passage.

He was up and about at first light, eager to get his work done before the heat of the day made thinking more difficult. In the afternoon, to the distant strains of a military band and the cheers of a crowd along the waterfront, *Undine* weighed anchor, and with *Nervion* in the lead, her great foresail displaying a resplendent cross of scarlet and gold, worked clear of the roads before setting more canvas to the wind.

Some small craft followed them across the glittering water, but were soon outpaced by the graceful frigates. By dusk they had the sea to themselves, with only the stars for company.

4

DEATH OF A *S*HIP

EZEKIEL MUDGE, *Undine*'s sailing master, sat comfortably in one of Bolitho's chairs and peered at the chart which was laid across the desk. Without his hat he looked even older, but there was assurance in his voice as he said, "This wind'll freshen in the next day or so, sir. You mark my words." He tapped the chart with his own brass dividers which he had just fished from one of his pockets. "For now, the nor'-east trades will suit us, and we'll be up to the Cape Verde Islands in a week, with any luck." He sat back and studied Bolitho's reactions.

"Much as I thought."

Bolitho walked to the stern windows and leaned his hands on the sill. It was hot, like wood from a fire, and beyond the frigate's small, frothing wake the sea was blinding in the glare. His shirt was open to the waist, and he could feel the sweat running down his shoulders, a dryness in his throat like dust.

It was almost noon, and Herrick would be waiting for the midshipmen to report to him on the quarterdeck to shoot the sun for their present position. A full week, but for a few hours, since they had sailed from Santa Cruz, and daily the sun had pinned them down, had defied the light airs which had tried to give them comfort. Today the wind had strengthened slightly, and *Undine* was ghosting along on the starboard tack with all sails drawing well.

There was little satisfaction in Bolitho's thoughts. For *Undine* had suffered her first casualty, a young seaman who had fallen overboard just as darkness had been closing in the previous day. Signalling his intention to the Spanish captain, Bolitho had gone about to begin a search for the luckless man. He had been working aloft on the main topsail yard, framed against the dying sunlight like a bronze statue. Had he been a raw recruit, or some heavy-handed landsman, it was likely he would still be alive. But he had been too confident, too careless perhaps for those last vital seconds as he had changed his position. One cry as he had fallen, and then his head had broken surface almost level with the mizzen, his arms beating at the sea as he tried to keep pace with the ship.

Davy had told him that the seaman was a good swimmer, and that fact had given some hope they might pick him up. They had lowered two boats, and for most of the night had searched in vain. Dawn had found them on course again, but to Bolitho's anger he had discovered that the *Nervion* had made no attempt to shorten sail or stay in company, and only in the last half-hour had the masthead reported sighting her topgallant sails once again.

The seaman's death had been an additional thorn to prod at his determination to weld the ship together. He had seen the Spanish officers watching their first attempts at gun drill through their telescopes, slapping their thighs with amusement whenever something went wrong, which was often. They themselves never drilled

at anything. They seemed to treat the voyage as a form of enter-
tainment.

Even Raymond had remarked, "Why bother with gun drill,
Captain? I do not know much about such matters, but surely your
men find it irksome in this damned heat?"

He had replied, "It is my responsibility, Mr. Raymond. I
daresay it may be unnecessary for this mission, but I'll take no
chances."

Raymond's wife had kept aloof from all of them, and during
the day spent much of her time under a small awning which
Herrick's men had rigged for her and the maid right aft by the
taffrail. Whenever they met, usually at meal times, she spoke only
briefly, and then touched on personal matters which Bolitho barely
understood. She appeared to enjoy hinting to her husband that he
was too backward, that he lacked assurance when it was most
needed. Once he had heard her say hotly, "They ride right over
you, James! How can I hold up my head in London when you
suffer so many insults! Why, Margaret's husband was knighted for
his services, and he is five years your junior!" And so on.

Now, as he turned to look at Mudge, he wondered what he and
the others were thinking of their captain. Driving them all too
hard, and for no purpose. Making them turn to and work at those
stubborn guns while aboard the Spaniard the offwatch hands
sprawled about sleeping or drinking wine like passengers.

As if reading his thoughts, Mudge said, "Don't mind what
some o' the buggers are sayin', sir. You're young, but you've a mind
for the right thing, if you'll pardon the liberty." He plucked at his
great nose. "I've seen many a cap'n taken all aback 'cause he worn't
ready when the time came." He chuckled, his small eyes vanishing
into his wrinkles. "An' as you well knows, sir, when things *do* go
wrong it's no blamed use slappin' yer hip an' blastin' yer eye, an'
blamin' all else." He tugged a watch the size of a turnip from an
inner pocket. "I must away on deck, if you can spare me, sir. Mr.
'Errick likes me to be there when we compares our reckonin'." It

seemed to amuse him. "As I said, sir, you stand firm. You don't 'ave to *like* a cap'n, but by God you've got to trust 'un!" He lumbered from the cabin, his shoes making the deck creak as he passed.

Bolitho sat down and tugged at his open shirt. It was a beginning.

Allday peered into the cabin. "Can I send your servant in now, Captain?" He darted a glance at the table. "He'll be wanting to get your meal laid."

Bolitho smiled. "Very well."

It was stupid to let small things prey on his mind. But with Mudge it was different. Important. He had probably sailed with more captains than Bolitho had met in his whole life.

They both looked round as Midshipman Keen stood in the doorway. Already he was well tanned, and looked as healthy and fresh as a veteran sailor.

"Mr. Herrick's respects, sir. Masthead has just reported sighting another vessel ahead of the Spaniard. On a converging tack. Small. Maybe a brig."

"I will come up." Bolitho smiled. "The voyage appears to agree with you, Mr. Keen."

The youth grinned. "Aye, sir. Though I fear my father sent me away for other reasons but my health."

As he hurried away Allday murmured, "Young devil, that one! Got some poor girl into trouble, I'll wager!"

Bolitho kept his face impassive. "Not like you, of course, Allday."

He strode out past the sentry and climbed quickly to the quarterdeck. Even though he was expecting it, the heat came down on him like the mouth of an open furnace. He felt the deck seams sticking to his shoes, the searing touch on his face and neck as he crossed to the weather side and looked along his command.

With her pale, lightweight canvas bent on, and her deck tilting to the wind, *Undine* was moving well. Spray leapt up and round the jib boom at irregular intervals, and far above his head he saw the pendant streaming abeam like a thin whip.

Mudge and Herrick were muttering together, their sextants gleaming in the sunlight like gold, while two midshipmen, Armitage and Penn, compared notes, their faces screwed in worried concentration.

Soames was by the quarterdeck rail and turned as Bolitho asked, "About this newcomer. What is she, do you reckon?"

Soames looked crushed with the heat, his hair matted to his forehead, as if he had been swimming.

"Some trader, I expect, sir." He did not sound as if he cared. "Maybe she intends to ask the Spaniard for her position." He scowled. "Not that they'll know much!"

Bolitho took a glass from the rack and climbed into the mizzen shrouds. Moving it gradually he soon found the *Nervion*, far ahead on the larboard bow, a picture of beauty under her great spread of canvas, her hull gleaming in the sun like metal. He trained the glass further to starboard and then held it steady on the other vessel. Almost hidden in heat haze, but he could see the tan-coloured sails well enough, the uneven outline of her rig. Square on the fore, fore-and-aft on the mainmast. He felt vaguely angry.

"A brigantine, Mr. Soames."

"Aye, sir."

Bolitho looked at him and then climbed back to the deck.

"In future, I want a full report of each sighting, no matter how trivial it might appear at the time."

Soames tightened his jaw. "Sir."

Herrick called, "It was my fault, sir. I should have told Mr. Keen to pass a full description to you."

Bolitho walked aft. "Mr. Soames has the watch, I believe."

Herrick followed him. "Well, yes, sir."

Bolitho saw the two helmsmen stiffen as he moved to the compass. The card was steady enough. South by west, and with plenty of sea room. The African coast lay somewhere across the larboard beam, over thirty leagues distant. There was nothing on their ocean but the three ships. Coincidence? A need to make contact perhaps?

Soames's indifference pricked at his mind like a burr and he snapped, "Make certain our watchkeepers know what they are about, Mr. Herrick." He saw Keen leaning against the nettings. "Send *him* aloft with a glass. An untried eye might tell us more."

Mudge ambled towards him and said gruffly, "Near as makes no difference, sir. Cape Blanco should be abeam now." He rubbed his chin. "The most westerly point o' that savage continent. An' quite close enough, if you ask me!"

His chest went up and down to a small wheezing accompaniment. It was as near as he ever got to laughing.

Keen's voice came down from the masthead. "Deck there! Brigantine is still closing the *Nervion!*"

Herrick cupped his hands. "Does she show any colours?"

"None, sir!"

Herrick clambered into the shrouds with his own telescope. After a while he called, "The Dons don't seem worried, sir."

Mudge growled. "'Ardly likely to be bothered about that little pot o' paint, is they?"

Bolitho said, "Bring her up a point, Mr. Mudge. It would be best if we regain company with our companion."

He turned as a voice asked, "Are you *troubled*, Captain?"

Mrs. Raymond was standing by the trunk of the mizzen mast, her face shadowed by a great straw hat which she had brought from Teneriffe.

He shook his head. "Merely curious, ma'am." In his crumpled shirt and breeches he felt suddenly clumsy. "I'm sorry there is not more to amuse you during the day."

She smiled. "Things may yet improve."

"Deck there!" Keen's voice made them all look up. "The other vessel is going about, sir!"

Herrick called, "He's right. The brigantine's going to cross clean over the Don's bows!" He turned, grinning broadly. "That'll make 'em hop about!"

The grin vanished as a dull bang echoed and re-echoed over the water.

Keen yelled, "She's fired on the *Nervion!*" A second bang reached the quarterdeck and he cried again, "And another!" He was almost screaming with excitement. "He's put a ball through her forecourse!"

Bolitho ran to the shrouds and joined Herrick.

"Let me see."

He took the big glass and trained it on the two ships. The brigantine's shape had shortened, and she was presenting her stern to him even as she idled across the frigate's broader outline. Even at such a distance it was possible to see the confusion aboard the Spanish frigate, the glint of sunlight on weapons as her company ran to quarters.

Herrick said hoarsely, "That brigantine's master must be mad. No one but a crazy man would cross swords with a frigate!"

Bolitho did not reply. He was straining his eye to watch the little drama framed in his lens. The brigantine had fired two shots, one of which, if not both, had scored a mark. Now she was tacking jauntily away, and it was evident, as the *Nervion* began to spread more sail, that Capitan Triarte intended to give chase.

He said, "*Nervion*'ll be up to her within the hour. They're both changing tack now."

"Perhaps that fool imagined *Nervion* was a fat merchantman, eh?" Davy had arrived on deck. "But no, it is not possible."

Herrick followed Bolitho down from the shrouds and watched him dubiously.

"Shall we join in the chase, sir?"

Mudge almost pushed him aside as he barked, "Chase be damned, I say!"

They looked at him.

"We must stop that mad Don, sir!" He waved his big hand across the nettings. "Off Cape Blanco, sir, there's a powerful great reef, an' it runs near on a 'undred miles to seaward. *Nervion's* in risk now, but if 'er master brings 'er up another point he'll be across that damned reef afore 'e knows it!"

Bolitho stared at him. "Get the royals on her, Mr. Herrick! Lively now!" He walked quickly to the helm. "We must make more speed."

Soames called, "The Don's come up another point by the look of her, sir!"

Mudge was already squinting at the compass bowl. "Jesus! 'E's steerin' sou'sou'-east!" He looked at Bolitho imploringly. "We'll never catch 'im in time!"

Bolitho paced to the quarterdeck rail and back again. Weariness, the scorching heat, all was forgotten but that distant pyramid of white sails, with the smaller, will-o'-the-wisp brigantine dancing ahead. Mad? A confused pirate? It made no difference now.

He snapped, "Clear away a bow chaser, Mr. Herrick. We will endeavour to distract the *Nervion*."

Herrick was peering aloft, shading his eyes with his speaking trumpet as the topmen set the additional sails.

"Aye, aye, sir!" He yelled, "Fetch Mr. Tapril!"

But the gunner was already forward, supervising the crew of a long nine-pounder.

Bolitho said sharply, "*Nervion's* pulled over still further, Mr. Mudge." He could not hide the anguish in his voice.

How could it be happening? The sea so huge, so empty. And yet, the reef was there. He had heard of it before from men who had passed this way. Many good ships had foundered on its hard spine.

"Larboard gun ready, sir!"

"*Fire!*"

It crashed out, the brown smoke drifting downwind and dispersing long before the telltale waterspout lifted like a feather far astern of the other frigate.

"Another. Keep firing." He looked at Mudge. "Bring her up a point."

Mudge protested, "I'll not be responsible, sir."

"No. *I will.*"

He strode forward to the rail again, his shirt flapping open across his chest, yet feeling no benefit from the wind. When he looked up he saw the sails drawing firmly, as would the Spaniard's. With such power to drive her, she would disembowel herself on the reef, unless Triarte acted, and at once.

The deck shook as another ball, whined and ricocheted across the blue water.

Bolitho yelled, "Masthead! What are they doing?"

The lookout replied, his rougher voice leaving no doubt in Bolitho's mind, "Th' Dons is gainin', sir! They're runnin' out their guns right this moment!"

Maybe the Spaniards had heard the bow chaser, even observed a fall of shot, but imagined the stupid British were still exercising gunnery. Or perhaps they believed *Undine* was so furious at missing the chase that Bolitho was firing at this impossible range merely to take the edge off his temper.

He heard himself ask, "How long, Mr. Mudge?"

Mudge replied thickly, "She should 'ave struck, sir. That damned brigantine must 'ave crossed the reef in safety. She'll draw little enough, I'm thinkin'."

Bolitho stared at him. "But if *she* got through, then perhaps . . ."

The master shook his head. "No chance, sir."

A great yell came from the watching seamen in the bows. When Bolitho swung round he stared with horror as the Spanish frigate lifted, drove forward again and then slewed round on the hidden reef. Over and around her all her masts and yards, the flailing sails and rigging splashed and cascaded in a chaos which was terrible to see. So great was the impact that she had presented her larboard side to the reef, and through the open gunports the water must now be surging in a triumphant flood, while men trapped in the tangled rigging and broken spars floundered in terror, or were being crushed by the cannon as they tore from their lashings.

The brigantine had changed tack. She was not even pausing to watch the full extent of her work.

Bolitho said harshly, "Shorten sail, Mr. Herrick. We will heave-to presently and get every boat in the water. We must do all we can to save them."

He saw some of the men by the bow chasers pointing and chattering as *Nervion* yawed still further on her side, spilling more broken timber and shattered planking into the swell above the reef.

"And get those hands to *work*, Mr. Herrick!" He swung away. "I'll not have them watch others drown, as if it was a day's amusement!"

He made himself cross the deck once more, and when he looked towards the reef he almost expected to see *Nervion*'s proud silhouette standing before the wind. That this was a bad dream. A nightmare.

But why? *Why?* The question seemed to mock him. To hammer at his brain. How could it have happened?

"I'd not venture any closer, sir." Mudge was watching him grimly. "If we gets a shift of wind we could still run foul of the reef."

Bolitho nodded heavily. "I agree." He looked away. "And thank you."

Mudge said quietly, "It worn't your fault. You done all you could."

"Heave to, Mr. Herrick." He could barely keep his voice level. "Have the boats swayed out."

Soames remarked, "A long pull, sir. Near on three miles."

Bolitho did not even hear him. He was seeing the little brigantine. It was no coincidence. No rash act of the moment.

Mudge said, "There'll not be many, sir." He fumbled in his pockets. "There's sharks a'plenty in these waters."

As *Undine* came up into the wind, her remaining sails thundering and flapping noisily in protest, the boats were lowered with surprisingly little delay. It was as if something had reached out across the three miles of smiling water to touch each and every one of them. A plea for help, a cry of warning, it was difficult to define. But as the first boat shoved off from the side, and the seamen at the oars picked up the stroke, Bolitho saw that their faces were grim and suddenly determined. As he had not seen them before.

Allday said, "I'll take the gig, if I may, Captain."

"Yes." Their eyes met. "Do what you can."

"I will."

Then he was gone, yelling for his men.

"Warn the surgeon to be prepared, Mr. Herrick." He saw the quick exchange of glances and added coldly, "And if he is the worse for drink I will have him flogged."

All the boats were away now, while far beyond their busy oars he could see the remains of the other ship writhing on the invisible reef, the great foresail with its red and gold crucifix still floating around the wreckage like a beautiful shroud.

Bolitho began to pace up and down below the nettings, his hands behind him, his body swaying to the untidy motion as the ship rolled in each undulating trough.

He heard Raymond say, "Captain Triarte was wrong. He made a stupid error of judgement."

He paused and looked at him. "He has paid for it, Mr. Raymond!"

Raymond saw the contempt in Bolitho's grey eyes and walked away. "I was only saying . . ." But nobody looked at him.

Herrick watched Bolitho pacing back and forth and wished he could say something to ease his despair. But better than most, he knew that at such moments Bolitho was the only one who could help himself.

Hours later, as the boats pulled wearily back towards their ship, Bolitho was still on deck, his shirt dark with sweat, his mind aching from his deliberations.

Herrick reported, "No more than forty survivors, sir. Some are in a bad way, I fear." He saw the question in Bolitho's eyes and nodded. "The surgeon's ready, sir. I saw to that."

Bolitho walked slowly to the nettings and craned over to watch the first boat, the gig, as it hooked on to the chains. One man, cradled against Allday's legs, and held firmly by two seamen, was shrieking like a tortured woman. A shark had taken a piece from his shoulder big enough to thrust a round-shot through. He turned away, sickened.

"In God's name, Thomas, send more hands to help those poor devils."

Herrick said, "It is being done, sir."

Bolitho looked up at the flapping ensign at the gaff. "By heaven, if this is how we behave in peace, then I would we were at war."

He watched some of the oarsmen clambering aboard. Hands blistered, backs and faces raw from the sun, they said very little as they went below.

Perhaps what they had seen at the reef had taught them more than drill, and would act as a warning to all of them.

He began to pace again. *And to me.*

Bolitho strode into the cabin and paused below the skylight. It was almost sunset, and the open stern windows shone in the dying glare like burnished copper. Within the cabin the shadows bobbed this way and that to the frigate's steady motion and the swinging deckhead lanterns, and he watched the little group by the windows with something like disbelief.

Don Luis Puigserver sat awkwardly on the bench seat one arm in a sling, his chest and ribs encased in bandages. When he had been dragged aboard with the other survivors a few hours earlier he had passed unrecognised until a gasping Spanish lieutenant, the only one of *Nervion's* officers to be rescued, had managed to explain the truth. Then, Bolitho had thought it was too late. The thickset Spaniard had been unconscious and covered with angry scars and bruises. The fact he had survived that long had been hard to accept when Bolitho had recalled the *Nervion*'s final destruction. Of the forty or so to reach *Undine*'s protection, ten had already died, and several of the remainder were in a bad state. Crushed under falling spars, half drowned by the inrush of water, the *Nervion*'s original complement of two hundred and seventy men had been totally unprepared for the horror which had awaited them on the reef. While their vessel had foundered and smashed herself to pieces, the surging waters had suddenly erupted in a maelstrom of dashing shapes as the sharks had hurried to the attack. Terrified men had seen their companions torn to bloody remnants, when moments before they had been setting more sail and manning their guns to run down the impudent brigantine.

When *Undine*'s boats had arrived it had been nearly over. A few men had swum desperately back to the capsized frigate, only to be dragged down as she had slid from the reef for her last plunge. Others had clung to floating spars and upturned boats and had watched in terror as one by one their grey attackers had plucked them screaming into the churned, scarlet water.

And now, Puigserver was sitting here in the cabin, his face almost composed as he sipped steadily from a goblet of wine. He was naked to the waist, and Bolitho could see some extent of the bruising on his body, evidence of his will to survive.

He said quietly, "I am grateful that you are in better spirits, *Señor*."

The Spaniard made to grin, but winced at the effort. He waved the surgeon and one of his assistants aside and asked, "My men? How many?"

Bolitho looked past him towards the horizon. A thread of copper, fading even as he watched.

"Thirty." He shrugged. "Many were badly mauled."

Puigserver took another swallow. "It was terrible to behold." His dark eyes hardened. "Capitan Triarte was so enraged by that other ship's attack that he went after her like a man possessed. He was too hot-blooded. Not like you."

Bolitho smiled gravely. *Not like you.* But suppose he had not had a sailing master like Mudge? One so experienced, so travelled as to *feel* the reef's danger like another of his stored memories. It was likely *Undine* might have shared the Spaniard's fate. It made him chill, despite the lifeless air in the cabin.

Somewhere beyond the bulkhead a man screamed. A thin, long-drawn sound which stopped abruptly as if a door had been slammed on it.

Whitmarsh wiped his hands on his apron and straightened his back, his head bowed beneath the beams.

He said, "Don Puigserver will be comfortable for a while, sir. I would like to return to my other charges." He was sweating very badly, and a muscle at one corner of his face twitched uncontrollably.

Bolitho nodded. "Thank you. Please inform me of any help you might require."

The surgeon touched the Spaniard's bandages vaguely. "God's help perhaps." He gave a wry smile. "Out here, we have little else."

As he left with his assistant Puigserver murmured, "A man with an inner torment, *Capitan.*" He grimaced. "But a gentle one for his trade."

Allday was folding up a towel and some unused dressings and said, "Mr. Raymond was asking to see you, Captain." He frowned. "I told him you had given orders that the cabin was to be kept for the surgeon until his work was done with Don Puig—" he coughed, ". . . the Spanish gentleman."

"What did he want?"

Bolitho was so weary he hardly cared. He had seen little of Raymond since the survivors had been brought aboard, and had heard he had been in the wardroom.

Allday replied, "He was wishing to make a complaint, Captain.

His wife took a displeasure at you asking her to help tend the injured." He frowned again. "I told him you had more important work to do." He picked up his things and walked to the door.

Puigserver leaned back and closed his eyes. Without the others present he seemed willing to reveal the pain he was really enduring.

He said, "Your Allday is a remarkable fellow, eh? With a few hundred of his kind I might think again about a campaign in the South Americas."

Bolitho sighed. "He worries too much."

Puigserver opened his eyes and smiled. "He seems to think you are worth worrying about, *Capitan.*"

He leaned forward, his face suddenly intense. "But before Raymond and the others come amongst us, I must speak. I want your opinion about the wreck. I *need* it."

Bolitho walked to the bulkhead and touched the sword with his fingers.

He said, "I have thought of little else, *Señor.* At first I believed the brigantine to be a pirate, her captain so confused or so in dread of his crew as to need a battle to keep them together. But I cannot believe it in my heart. Someone knew of our intentions."

The Spaniard watched him intently. "The French perhaps?"

"Maybe. If their government is so concerned at our movements it must mean that when they sank the *Fortunate* they did indeed capture her despatches intact. It would have to be something really vital to play such a dangerous game."

Puigserver reached for the wine bottle. "A game which *did* work."

"Then you, too, are of the same mind, *Señor!*" He watched the man's outline, paler now against the darkened windows.

He did not reply directly. "If, and I am only saying *if,* this someone intended such a course of action, he will have known we were two ships in company." He paused and then said sharply, "A reaction, *Capitan!* Quickly!"

Bolitho said, "It would make no difference. He would realise that this is a combined mission. One ship without the other makes further progress impossible, and . . ."

Puigserver was banging his hip with the goblet, wine slopping over his leg like blood.

He shouted excitedly, "*And?* Go on, *Capitan! And what?*"

Bolitho looked away and replied firmly, "I must return either to England or to Teneriffe and await further orders."

When he looked again at the Spaniard he saw he was slumped back on the seat, his square features strained, his chest heaving as if from a fight.

Puigserver said thickly, "When you came to Santa Cruz, I knew you were a man of thoughts and not merely of words." He shook his head. "Let me finish. This man, these creatures, whoever they are, who would let my people die so horribly, *want you to turn back!*"

Bolitho watched him, fascinated, awed by his strength.

"Without you being here, *Señor,*" he looked away, "I would have had no option."

"Exactly, *Capitan.*"

He peered at Bolitho over the rim of the goblet, his eyes shining in the lantern light like tawny stones.

Bolitho added, "By the time I returned to England, and new plans were made and agreed upon, something might have happened in the East Indies or elsewhere which we could not control."

"Give me your hand, *Capitan.*" He groped forward, his breathing sharper. "In a moment I will sleep. It has been a wretched day, but far worse for many others."

Bolitho took his hand, suddenly moved by Puigserver's obvious sincerity.

The latter asked slowly, "How many have you in this little ship?"

Bolitho pictured the riffraff brought aboard at Spithead. The ragged men from the prison hulks, the smartly-dressed ones fleeing from some crime or other in London. The gun captain with only one hand. All of them.

He said, "They have the makings, *Señor.* Two hundred, all told, including my marines." He smiled, if only to break the tension. "And I will sign on those of your men who have survived, if I may?"

Puigserver did not seem to hear. But his grip was like iron as he said, "Two hundred, eh?"

He nodded grimly. "It will be sufficient."

Bolitho watched him. "We go on, *Señor?*"

"You are *my capitan* now. What do *you* say?"

Bolitho smiled. "But you know already, *Señor.*"

Puigserver gave a great sigh. "If you will send that fool Raymond in to me, and your clerk, I will put my seal on this new undertaking." His voice hardened. "Today I saw and heard many men die in fear and horror. Whatever made that foul deed necessary, I intend to set the record right. And when I do, *Capitan,* I will make it a reckoning which our enemies will long remember."

There was a tap at the door and Midshipman Armitage stood outlined by the swinging lantern in the passageway.

"Mr. Herrick's respects, sir. The wind's freshening from the nor'-east." He faltered, like a child repeating a lesson to his tutor.

"I will come up directly."

Bolitho thought suddenly of Mudge, how he had prophesied a better wind. He would be up there with Herrick, waiting for the orders. Armitage's message told him all that and more. Whatever was decided now might settle the fate of the ship and every man aboard.

He looked at Puigserver. "It is settled then, *Señor?*"

"Yes, *Capitan.*" He was getting more drowsy. "You can leave me now. And send Raymond before I sleep like some drunken goatherd."

Bolitho followed the midshipman from his cabin, noting how stiffly the sentry at the door was holding his musket. He had probably been listening, and by tonight it would be all over the ship.

Not merely a voyage to display the Navy's reach in foreign parts, but one with a real prospect of danger. He smiled grimly as he reached the quarterdeck ladder. It might make gun drill less irksome for them in future.

He found Herrick and Mudge near the helm, the master with a shaded lantern held over his slate, upon which he made his surprisingly neat calculations.

Bolitho walked up the weather side, looking aloft at the bulging canvas, hearing the sea creaming along the hull like water in a mill sluice.

Then he returned to where they were waiting and said, "You may shorten sail for the night, Mr. Herrick. Tomorrow you can sign on any of the *Nervion*'s people you find suitable." He paused as another frantic cry floated up from the orlop deck. "Though I fear it may not be many."

Herrick asked, "We are not going about then, sir?"

Mudge exclaimed, "An' a good thing, too, if I may say so, sir." He rubbed his bulging rump with one hand. "Me rheumatism will sheer off when we gets to a 'otter climate."

Bolitho looked at Herrick. "We go forward, Thomas. To finish what was begun back there on the reef."

Herrick seemed satisfied. "I'm for that."

He made to walk to the rail where a bosun's mate awaited his orders, but Bolitho stopped him, saying, "From this night on, Thomas, we must keep our wits about us. No unnecessary pauses for fresh water if prying eyes are nearby. We will ration every drop if necessary, and stand or fall by our own resources. But we must stay clear of the land where an enemy might betray our course or intentions. If, as I now believe, someone is working against us, we must use his methods against him. Gain ourselves time by every ruse we can invent."

Herrick nodded. "That makes good sense, sir."

"Then I hope it may seem so to our people." He walked to the weather side. "You may carry on now."

Herrick turned away. "Call the hands. We will shorten sail."

As the shouts echoed between decks and the seamen came dashing on to the gangways, Herrick said, "I almost forgot, sir. Mrs. Raymond is worried about her accommodation."

"It is arranged." He paused and watched the hands scampering to the shrouds. "Don Puigserver will sleep in the main cabin. Mrs. Raymond can retain her own cot with the maid."

Herrick sounded cautious. "I doubt she will like that, sir."

Bolitho continued his pacing. "Then she may say so, Mr. Herrick. And when she does I will explain what I think of a woman so pampered she will not lift a finger to help a dying man!"

A master's mate strode along the gangway. "All mustered, sir!"

Herrick was still watching the pacing figure, the open white shirt clearly etched against the nettings and the sea beyond. In the next few weeks *Undine* would get much smaller, he thought.

"Very well, Mr. Fowlar. Get the to'gan's'ls off her. If the weather freshens up we may have to reef tops'ls before the night's done."

Old Mudge rubbed his aching back. "The weather is a fool!" But nobody heeded him.

Bolitho saw the topmen sliding down to the deck, with barely a word to each other as they were checked again by their petty officers. Around the vibrating bowsprit the spindrift rode in the wind like pale arrows, and high above the deck he saw the topsails hardening and puffing out their bellies to a combined chorus of creaking rigging and blocks.

"Dismiss the watch below." Herrick's voice was as usual. He took Bolitho's word as he would a rope to save himself from drowning.

In the darkness Bolitho smiled. Perhaps it was better to be so.

In the cabin Don Puigserver sat at the desk and watched the clerk's quill scraping across his written orders. Raymond was leaning against the quarter windows, his face expressionless as he peered into the darkness

Then across his shoulder he said, "It is a great responsibility,

Don Puigserver. I am not sure I can advise in its favour."

The Spaniard leaned painfully against the chair-back and listened to the regular footsteps across the deck overhead. Up and down.

"It is not mine alone, Señor Raymond. I am in good company, believe me."

Above and around them the *Undine* moved and murmured in time with sea and wind. Right forward below the bowsprit the golden nymph stared unwinkingly at the darkened horizon. Decision and destiny, triumph and disappointment meant nothing to her. She had the ocean, and that was life itself.

5

THE *W*ORK OF A DEMON

BOLITHO stood loosely by the quarterdeck rail, his body partly shaded from the harsh glare by the thick mainmast trunk, and watched the routine work around him. Eight bells chimed from the forecastle, and he could hear Herrick and Mudge comparing notes from their noon sights, while Soames, who was officer of the watch, prowled restlessly by the cabin hatch as he awaited his relief.

Just to watch the slow, lethargic movements of the men on the gangways and gun deck was enough. Thirty-four days since they had seen *Nervion*'s destruction on the reef, and nearly two months since weighing anchor at Spithead. It had been hard work all the way, and from the moment the Spanish ship had foundered the atmosphere aboard had been compressed and strained to the limit.

The last few days had been the worst part, he thought. For a while his company had gained some excitement at crossing the Equator, with all its mysteries and myths. He had issued an extra ration of rum, and for a time he had observed some benefit from the change. The new hands had seen the line-crossing as a kind of test which they had somehow managed to pass. The old seamen had grown in stature as they had recounted or lied about the number of occasions they had sailed these waters in other ships. A fiddler had emerged, and after a self-conscious overture had brought some music and scratchy gaiety to their daily lives.

And then, the last of the badly injured Spaniards had begun to die. It had been like the final pressure on them all. Whitmarsh had done all he could. He had carried out several amputations, and as the pitiful cries had floated up from his sickbay Bolitho had felt the brief satisfaction of drawing his company together fading once again. The dying Spaniard had dragged it out for many days. Nearly a month he had ebbed and rallied, sobbing and groaning, or sleeping peacefully while Whitmarsh had stayed with him hour by hour. It had seemed as if the surgeon was testing his own resources, searching for some new cracking point. The last of his patients to die had been the ones mauled by sharks, those which because of their wounds could not be saved or despatched by amputations. Gangrene had set into their flesh, and the whole ship had been pervaded by a stench so revolting that even the most charitable had prayed for the sufferers to die.

He saw the afternoon watch mustering below the quarter-deck, while Lieutenant Davy strode aft and waited for Soames to sign his report in the log. Even Davy looked weary and bedraggled, his handsome face so tanned by hours on duty he could have been a Spaniard.

They all avoided Bolitho's eye. As if they were afraid of him, or that they needed all their energies merely to get through another day.

Davy reported, "The watch is aft."

Soames glared at him. "A moment *late*, Mr. Davy."

Davy regarded him disdainfully and then turned to his master's mate. "Relieve the wheel."

Soames stamped to the hatch and disappeared below.

Bolitho clenched his hands behind him and took a few steps away from the mast. The only satisfaction was the wind. The previous day, as they had changed tack towards the east and the masthead had reported sighting land far abeam, the westerlies had made themselves felt. As he shaded his eyes to peer aloft he could see the impatient thrust of power in every sail, the mainyard bending and trembling like one giant bow. That blur of land had been Cape Agulhas, the southernmost tip of the African continent. Now, stretching before the crisscross of rigging and shrouds lay the blue emptiness of the Indian Ocean, and like many of his new seamen who had contemplated their crossing the Equator, he was able to consider what together they had achieved to reach this far. The Cape of Good Hope was to all intents the halfway of their voyage, and to this day he had kept his word. Mile upon mile, day after scorching day, driving wildly in blustery squalls, or lying becalmed, with every sail hanging lifeless, he had used everything he knew to keep up their spirits. When that had faltered he had speeded up the daily routine. Gun and sail drill, and competitions between messes for the offwatch hands.

He saw the purser and his assistant waiting beside a puncheon of pork which had just been swayed up from the forward hold. Midshipman Keen stood nearby, trying to appear knowledgeable as Triphook had the new cask opened and proceeded to check through each four-pound piece of salt pork before he allowed it to be carried to the galley. Keen, whose junior authority as midshipman of the watch made him the captain's representative on such occasions, probably imagined it to be a waste of time. Bolitho knew otherwise from past experience. It was well known for dishonest victualling yards to give short measure, or to make up the contents of a cask with hunks of rotten meat, even pieces of old canvas, knowing as they did that by the time a ship's purser discovered the fault he would be well clear of the land and unable to complain. Pursers, too, were known to line their own pockets by sharp practice with their opposite numbers ashore.

Bolitho saw the gaunt purser nod mournfully and mark his ledger, apparently satisfied. Then he followed the little procession forward to the galley, his shoes squeaking as they clung to the sun-heated pitch between the deck seams.

The heat, the relentless, unbroken days were testing enough. But Bolitho knew it only needed a hint of corruption, some suggestion that the ship's company were being cheated by their officers, and the whole voyage might explode. He had asked himself over and over again if he was allowing his last experience to pray on his mind. Even the word itself, *mutiny,* had struck fear into the heart of many a captain, especially one far from friendly company and higher authority.

He took a few paces along the side and winced as his wrist brushed against the bulwark. The timbers were bone-dry, the paint cracking, despite regular attention.

He paused and shaded his eyes to watch some large fish jumping far abeam. *Water.* It was usually uppermost in his mind. With the new hands, and the need to use much of their precious water supply to help the sick and injured, even rationing might not be enough.

He saw two Negro seamen lounging by the larboard gangway. It was a mixed company indeed. When they had sailed from Spithead it had been varied enough. Now, with the small list of Spanish survivors, they were even more colourful. Apart from the sole Spanish officer, a sad-eyed lieutenant named Rojart, there were ten seamen, two boys who were little more than children, and five soldiers. The latter, at first grateful to have survived, were now openly resentful of their new status. Carried aboard *Nervion* as part of Puigserver's personal guard, they were now neither fish nor fowl, and while they tried to act as seamen, they were usually found watching *Undine*'s sweating marines with both envy and contempt.

Herrick stepped into his thoughts and reported, "The master and I agree." He held out the slate. "If you would care to examine this, sir." He sounded unusually guarded.

Mudge ambled into the shadow of the hammock nettings and said, "If you are about to alter course, sir." He dragged out his handkerchief. "It is as good a time as any." He blew his nose violently.

Herrick said quickly, "I would like to make a suggestion, sir."

Mudge moved away and stood patiently near the helmsman.

It was hard to tell if Herrick had just thought of his suggestion, or if he had discussed it with the others.

"Some were a mite surprised when you stood clear of Cape Town, sir." His eyes were very blue in the glare. "We could have landed our remaining sick people and taken in fresh water. I doubt that the Dutch governor there would pay much heed to our movements."

"Do you, Mr. Herrick?"

He saw a puff of dull smoke from the galley. Soon now the offwatch men would be having a meal in the sweltering heat of their messes. The remains of yesterday's salt beef. Skillygolee, as they named it. A mixture of oatmeal gruel, crushed biscuits and lumps of boiled meat. And all that washed down with a full ration of beer. It was likely the latter was stale and without life. But anything was better than the meagre ration of water.

He jerked himself back to Herrick, suddenly irritated. "And who put you up to this remarkable assessment?" He saw Herrick's face cloud over but added, "It has an unfamiliar ring to it."

Herrick said, "It's just that I do not wish to see you driving yourself, sir. I felt as you did about *Nervion*'s loss, but it is done, and there's an end to it. You did all you could for her people . . ."

Bolitho said, "Thank you for your concern, but I am not driving myself or our people to no purpose. I believe we may be needed, even at this moment."

"Perhaps, sir."

Bolitho regarded him searchingly. "Perhaps indeed, but then that is my responsibility. If I have acted wrongly, then you may receive promotion more quickly than you thought." He turned away. "When the hands have eaten we will lay her on the new course. Nor'-east by east." He looked at the masthead pendant. "See how it blows. We'll get the royals on her directly and run with the wind under our coat-tails while it lasts."

Herrick bit his lip. "I still believe we should touch land, sir, if only to collect water."

"As I do, Mr. Herrick." He faced him coldly. "And that I will do whenever I can without arousing interest elsewhere. I have my orders. I intend to carry them out as best I can, do you understand?"

They watched each other, their eyes angry, troubled, and concerned by the sudden flare-up between them.

"Very good, sir." Herrick stood back, his eyes squinting in the sun. "You can rely on me."

"I was beginning to wonder, Mr. Herrick." Bolitho half stepped forward, one hand outstretched as Herrick swung away, his face taut with dismay.

He had not meant the words to form in that way. If he had ever doubted anything in his life, Herrick's loyalty was not one of them. He felt ashamed and angry. Perhaps the strain of this empty monotony, of carrying men who wanted to do nothing but crawl away from work and the sun, of torturing his mind with plans and doubts, had taken a far greater toll than he had imagined.

He turned on his heel and saw Davy watching him curiously.

"Mr. Davy, you have only just taken over your watch, and I would not wish to disrupt your thoughts. But examine the forecourse, if you please, and set some of your hands to put it to rights." He saw the lieutenant fall back from his anger and, added "It looks as slack as the watch on deck!"

As he strode to the cabin hatch he saw the lieutenant hurrying to the rail. The fact that the forecourse was not drawing as it should was no excuse for taking out his temper on Davy.

He strode past the sentry and slammed the cabin door behind him. But there was no escape here. Noddall was laying plates on the table, his face stiffly resentful as Mrs. Raymond's maid followed him around the cabin like an amused child.

Raymond was slumped in a chair by the stern windows, apparently dozing, and his wife sat on the bench seat, fanning herself, and watching Noddall's preparations, a look of complete boredom on her face.

Bolitho made to go but she called, "Come *along*, Captain. We barely see you from day to day." She patted the bench seat with the fan. "Sit awhile. Your precious ship will survive, I think."

Bolitho sat down and leaned one elbow on the sill. It was good to feel life in the wind again, to watch the lift and swirl of foam as it surged freely from the counter, or came up gurgling around the rudder.

Then he turned slightly and looked at her. She had been aboard all this time and yet he knew little of her. She was watching him now, her eyes partly amused, partly questioning. Probably two or three years older than himself, he thought. Not beautiful, but with the aristocratic presence which commanded instant attention. She had fine, even teeth, and her hair, which she had allowed to flow loosely across her shoulders, was the colour of autumn. While he and the rest of his officers had found difficulty in keeping cool, or finding a clean shirt after the sun's tyranny or some fierce squall in the South Atlantic, she had always managed to remain perfect. As she was now. Her gown was not merely worn, it was *arranged*, so that he and not she looked out of place against the stern windows. Her earrings were heavy, and he guessed their value would pay most of his marines for a year or more.

She smiled. "Do you enjoy what you see, Captain?"

Bolitho started. "I am sorry, ma'am. I am tired."

She exclaimed, "How gallant! I am sorry it is only weariness which makes you look at me." She held up the fan and added, "I am mocking you, Captain. Do not look so depressed."

Bolitho smiled. "Thank you."

He thought suddenly of that other time. In New York, three

years ago. Another ship, his first command, and the world opening up just for him. A woman had shown him that life was not so kind, nor was it easy.

He admitted, "I have had a lot on my mind. I have been used to action and sharp decisions for most of my life. Merely to make sail and face an empty sea day by day is something alien to me. Sometimes I feel more like a grocery-captain than that of a man-o'-war."

She watched him thoughtfully. "I can believe it. I should have realised earlier." She gave a slow smile, her lashes hiding her eyes. "Then maybe I would not have offended you."

Bolitho shook his head. "Much of it was my fault. I have been so long in ships of war that I have become used to expecting others to share my dedication. If there is a fire I expect all close by to quench it. If a man tries to overrun authority by mutiny or in an enemy's name I would call for others to strike him down, or do so myself." He faced her gravely. "That is why I expected you to aid the men injured in the wreck." He shrugged. "Again, I *expected* it. I did not ask."

She nodded. "That admission must have surprised you, as much as it did me, Captain." She showed her teeth. "It has cleared the air a little?"

"Yes."

He touched his forehead unconsciously, plucking at the rebellious lock of black hair which clung to the skin with sweat.

He saw her eyes widen as she caught sight of the livid scar beneath and said quickly, "Forgive me, ma'am. I must go and examine my charts before we dine."

She watched him as he stood up and said, "You wear your authority well, Captain." She glanced at her sleeping husband. "Unlike some."

Bolitho did not know how to reply. "I am afraid that is hardly for me to discuss, ma'am."

He looked up as feet thudded across the deck and shadows flitted above the open skylight.

She asked, "What is it?"

He did not see the annoyance in her eyes.

"I am not sure. A ship perhaps. I gave orders I was to be informed so that I can take avoiding action."

Noddall paused, two forks in his hand. "I 'eard no 'ail from th' mast'ead, sir."

There was a rap at the door and Herrick stood in the entrance, his chest heaving from exertion.

"I am sorry to burst in." He looked past Bolitho towards the woman. "It would be better if you came with me, sir."

Bolitho stepped from the cabin and pulled the door behind him. In the doorway which opened on to the ship's wardroom he saw a small group waiting for him. They looked confused. Stricken. Like strangers. There was Bellairs, accompanied by his towering sergeant. Triphook, his horse teeth bared as if to snap at an unseen attacker, and cowering just behind him was the ship's cooper, a small hunched petty officer named Joseph Duff. He was the second oldest man aboard, and wore steel-rimmed spectacles at his work, although he usually managed to hide them from his messmates for much of the time.

Herrick said quietly, "Duff has reported that most of the fresh water is undrinkable, sir." He swallowed under Bolitho's stare. "He was doing his usual inspection and has just reported to the ship's corporal."

Triphook was murmuring fervently, "In all my days. Never, *never* have I seen the like!"

Bolitho beckoned to the cooper. "Well, Duff, I am waiting. What is this find which you have discovered?"

Duff blinked at him through the oval glasses. He looked like a grey-haired mole.

"Me usual inspection, sir."

He grew smaller as they crowded round him. Soames had come from his own cabin, and loomed over Bellairs's shoulder like a cliff.

Duff continued shakily, "The casks was all good 'uns, I saw to that, sir. First thing I always looks for. I learned me work under a fine old cooper in the *Gladiator* when I first took on, sir, an'—"

"For God's sake, Duff!" Herrick sounded desperate. *"Tell the captain!"*

Duff lowered his head. "Most of the casks is foul, sir. They *'as* to be."

Sergeant Coaker stepped forward, his boots creaking as the ship tilted in a sudden trough. He was holding a small bundle, but keeping it away from his tunic as if it were alive.

"Open it."

The sergeant unfolded the parcel very carefully, his face set like stone.

Bolitho felt the deck soaring violently, tasted the vomit clawing at his throat. Screwed up, as if at the instant shock of imputation, it was a human hand.

Soames choked, "In the name of Christ!"

Duff said in a small voice, "In all of 'em, sir. 'Cept the last two casks by the bulk'ead."

Triphook said heavily, "He's right, sir. Bits of flesh." He trembled violently, his face breaking out in sweat. "The work of a demon!"

There was a sharp cry of horror, and Bolitho stepped in front of the cooper as Mrs. Raymond gasped, "I'm going to be sick." He saw her leaning against the marine sentry, her face like chalk as she stared fixedly at the group by the wardroom.

Bolitho snapped, "Get rid of that object!" To Noddall's hovering shadow he added, "Call that damned maid and attend to the lady!" His mind was reeling from Duff's gruesome discovery. What it meant, and what he now had to do. "Fetch the surgeon."

Bellairs dabbed his lips with a handkerchief. "Carry on Sar'nt Coaker. Pass the word for Mr. Whitmarsh." He glanced at the others. "Though I doubt he will be able to assist, what?"

Herrick asked, "Would you care to come in here, sir?" He stood aside to allow Bolitho to enter the wardroom.

It was small and compact, the table laid for a meal, and at odds with the twelve-pounders which were lashed at each open port. Bolitho sat down heavily on a sea chest and stared through the nearest gun port. The fair wind and dancing water held no more attraction. Danger was within the ship. His ship.

Herrick prompted, "Some wine, sir."

When he turned Bolitho saw the others watching him. Soames at the top of the table. Bellairs and Triphook seated on the opposite side. In those fleeting seconds he recalled his own life as a junior lieutenant in a frigate. The wardroom was the place you shared not merely your food and your life, you shared your doubts, and drew on your companions for help whenever it was needed. Aft, behind his bulkhead, the captain had been a remote, godly character beyond reach. At no time that he could recall had he imagined a captain required anything but obedience.

It even *felt* different here. Pistols in a rack. Some shirts hanging to air which the wardroom servant had just washed. The smell of something simmering in a pot.

He replied, "Thank you. I would relish a glass just now."

They relaxed slightly and Soames said, "It will mean turning back, sir." He thought about it. "Or making for the African coast mebbee."

Feet creaked outside the door and then Mudge pushed his way into the wardroom, his grey hair sprouting as he threw his hat into a corner.

"God blast me eyes, but what's this bloody deed I've bin told?" He saw Bolitho and muttered, "Beggin' yer pardon, sir. I was not expectin' to discover you in 'ere."

Herrick held out a glass. "Some Rhenish, sir." He did not smile, but his eyes were calm. Almost pleading. "Still fairly fresh, I think."

Bolitho sipped it gratefully. "Thank you." He tasted the sourness in his throat. "After what I have just witnessed . . ." He swung round as the surgeon lurched through the door, his shirt unbuttoned, his gaze bleary.

"You have been told the news, Mr. Whitmarsh?"

He watched the effort he was making to focus his eyes, the growth of stubble on his chin. Whitmarsh had been quietly making up for all the time he had stayed with his patients.

"Well?"

Whitmarsh groped his way to a gun and leaned on it with both hands, sucking air through the open port like a drowning man.

"I heard, sir." He retched. "I heard."

Bolitho watched him impassively. "As the water casks were fresh when stowed aboard at Spithead, it would seem likely that these human fragments came from your surgery." He waited, feeling pity for the man, but knowing the need for haste. "Would you agree?"

"I expect so."

Whitmarsh lurched to the table and poured a large measure of wine.

Bolitho said sharply, "If you drink that, Mr. Whitmarsh, I will see to it that you do not get another drop while you are under my command." He stood up. "Now, think, man! Who could have done this?"

Whitmarsh stared at the glass in his hand, his body swaying badly, despite the easy motion.

"I was kept busy. They were in a poor way, sir. I had my loblolly boys and my mate to assist me." He screwed up his red face in an effort to remember, the sweat dripping off his chin like rain. "It was Sullivan. I gave him the job of clearing amputated limbs and the like from my sickbay. He was very helpful." He nodded vaguely. "It's all coming to me now. Sullivan." He turned and stared fixedly at Bolitho. "The man *you* had flogged, sir."

Herrick said harshly, "Don't be so bloody impertinent to the captain!"

Bolitho found he was suddenly very calm. "In your opinion, Mr. Whitmarsh, will the casks be any further use after this?"

"None." The surgeon was still glaring at him. "They must be scoured at once. The contents thrown overboard. A mouthful of that water, after gangrenous flesh has been in it, and you'll have a raging fever aboard! I've known it happen. There's no cure."

Bolitho placed his glass on the table very slowly. Giving his mind time to steady.

"It seems that you are not the only one who wishes to turn back, Mr. Herrick. Now take hold of Sullivan and guard him before he does some other mischief." He turned to Whitmarsh. "I have not finished with you yet!"

Feet clattered on the quarterdeck ladder and Herrick reappeared in the doorway.

"Sir! That fool Sullivan is aloft on the cro'jack yard! He's raving mad! Nobody can get near him!"

Bolitho heard men shouting, more feet pounding overhead.

He said, "I will go up."

He found the gangways crowded with seamen and marines, while Don Puigserver and his Spanish lieutenant had joined Davy by the quarterdeck rail to watch a bosun's clinging to the mizzen shrouds and trying to reach Sullivan.

The seaman was perched on the yard, totally indifferent to the great billowing sail at his back and the hard sunlight which lanced across his body. He was completely naked, but for his belt, where he carried the broad-bladed dirk which had brought about his flogging in the first place.

Davy said anxiously, "I did not know what to do, sir. The man is obviously moonstruck or worse."

The bosun's mate bellowed, "Now yew get down on deck, or by the livin' Jesus I'll pitch you there meself!"

Sullivan threw back his head and laughed. It was a shrill, unnerving sound.

"Now, now, Mr. Roskilly! What would you do then? Lay your little rope's end on me?" He laughed again and then pulled out the knife. "Come along then, matey! I'm awaitin' you, you goddamned lickspittle!"

Bolitho called, "Come down, Roskilly! You'll do no good by getting killed!"

Sullivan craned under the vibrating yard. "Well, blow me down, mates, an' who 'ave we 'ere? Our gallant captain, no less!" He rocked with laughter. "An' 'e's all aback 'cause poor old Tom Sullivan's spoiled the water for him!"

Some of the watching seamen had been grinning at the spectacle on the quarterdeck. The mention of water soon altered that.

Bolitho looked at the upturned faces, feeling the spreading alarm like the edge of a fire.

He walked aft, his shoes loud in the sudden hush around him. Below the yard he stopped and looked up.

"Come along, Sullivan." He was in the sunlight and with no shade from the bellying sail above. He felt the sweat pouring down his chest and thighs, just as he could sense the other man's hatred. "You have done enough today!"

Sullivan cackled. "Did you hear that, lads? Done enough!"

He twisted on the yard, the glare playing across the scars on his back, pale against the tanned skin. "You've done enough to me, Cap'n bloody Bolitho!"

Herrick snapped, "Sergeant Coaker! Have one of your marksmen brought aft! That man is a damned danger up there!"

"Belay that!" Bolitho kept his eyes on the crossjack yard. "He is past reason. I'll not have him shot down like some mad dog."

He sensed Puigserver was watching him and not the man on the yard, and that Allday was close by, a cutlass in his hand. But they were all excluded. It was between him and Sullivan.

He called, "I am *asking* you, Sullivan!" He recalled the woman's face in the cabin. *I did not ask.*

"You go to hell, Captain!" Sullivan was screaming now, his naked body twisting on the yard as if in torment. "An' I'll take you there now!"

Bolitho hardly saw his hand move, just the brief flash of sunlight on the blade, and then gasped as the knife cut through his sleeve before embedding itself in the deck by his right shoe. So great was the force that nearly an inch of blade was driven into the planking.

Sullivan was transfixed, a long streamer of spittle trailing to the wind as he stared down at Bolitho at the foot of the mast.

Bolitho remained motionless, feeling the blood running down his elbow and forearm and on to the deck. He did not take his eyes off Sullivan, and the concentration helped to overcome the searing pain left by the blade.

Sullivan stood up wildly and began to scramble outboard along the yard. Everybody began to yell at once, and Bolitho felt Herrick gripping his arm, another wrapping a cloth around it, deadening the pain.

Whitmarsh had appeared below the nettings, and he, too, was shouting at the man framed against the clear sky.

Sullivan turned and spoke in a level voice for the first time. "And you, too, *Doctor!* God damn you to *hell!*" Then he jumped out and down, his body hitting the water with a violent splash.

For a moment he floated past the quarter, and as the spanker's great shadow passed over him he clasped his hands above his head and vanished.

Herrick said, "We could never pick him up. If we tried to heave-to under this canvas, we'd tear the sticks out of her."

Bolitho did not know to whom he was speaking. Perhaps to himself.

He walked to the hatch, holding his torn and bloodied sleeve with one hand. He saw the bosun's mate, Roskilly, pulling the knife out of the deck. He was a strong man, but it took him two attempts to tug it clear.

Puigserver followed him below, then stepped in front of him. "That was a brave thing you did, *Capitan.*" He sighed. "But he could have killed you."

Bolitho nodded. The pain was getting worse. "We have some hard times ahead, *Señor.* We must find water, and soon." He tightened his jaw. "But I am not turning back."

Puigserver eyed him sadly. "You made a gesture. One which might have ended your life. And all for a madman."

Bolitho walked to the cabin. "Maybe we were both mad."

Herrick hurried after him, and as they entered the cabin Bolitho saw there was a chair directly under the skylight. Raymond must have been standing on it to watch the drama overhead.

Mrs. Raymond was aft by the windows. She looked very pale, but came towards him saying, "Your arm, Captain." She shouted to her maid, "Bandages!"

Bolitho realised that Herrick was in the cabin. "Well?"

Herrick watched him worriedly. "What you did—"

"It could have killed me. I know." Bolitho forced a smile. "I have already been told."

Herrick breathed out slowly. "And I believed I knew you, sir."

"And now?" He looked at him steadily. "Thomas?"

Herrick grinned. "I only know that you never cease to surprise me. *And* others." He gestured to the deckhead. "A seaman who has been cursing and complaining for near on a month was just heard to damn Sullivan's soul for threatening the life of *his* captain." His grin faded. "But I'd rather you rallied our people in some other way, sir."

Bolitho held out his arm as the maid carried a basin to the desk.

"If you *know* of any way to keep up their spirits, Thomas, I'd be obliged to hear it. In the meantime, call the hands and get the royals on her. I want every stitch she can carry." He checked him as he made for the door. "And pass the word. One pint of water per day." He glanced around the cabin, "Officers and passengers included."

Herrick hesitated. "And the surgeon, sir?"

Bolitho looked down at the maid as she cleaned the deep cut on his arm. She returned his glance boldly.

He said, "I am in good hands, it seems. I will think about Mr. Whitmarsh when I have more time." He added grimly, "And at this moment, time is of the greatest value in the world."

Bolitho waited by the open stern windows and watched the moon making a fine path across the water. The sea looked unusually choppy, but he knew it was from a steep undertow which explored the depths many miles from the African coast. At his back he heard the others moving into the cabin and finding somewhere to sit, the sounds of goblets and wine as Noddall went about his business. Despite the cool air after the day's blazing sunlight his body felt drained and stiff, and about him the ship creaked and groaned, her timbers so dried-out that it was a wonder she was not leaking like on old bucket.

A week since Sullivan had jumped to his death, seven long days while he had taken his ship inshore time and time again, only to stand off at the report of some sail, or an unexplained sighting of a native craft.

Now, he could delay no longer. He had been visited by Whitmarsh that afternoon, a man so tormented by his own worries that it had been a difficult interview. Whitmarsh had made it quite definite that he could no longer be held responsible if Bolitho persisted in staying clear of land. The two remaining casks of water were almost empty, and what remained was little better than scum. More men were lying ill on the orlop deck, and those fit enough to work ship had to be watched by the minute. Tempers flared, and petty officers went about their duties with an eye on their backs for a knifethrust in a momentary display of madness.

Herrick reported, "All ready, sir." Like the others. Tense. Watchful.

Bolitho turned and looked around his officers. All but Soames, who was on duty, were present. Even the three midshipmen. He watched them gravely. It might teach them something, he thought.

"I intend to close the land again tomorrow."

He saw Don Puigserver by the bulkhead with his lieutenant. Raymond a few feet away from him, rubbing his face in sharp, agitated movements.

Davy said, "Makes fine sense, sir." He swallowed some wine. "If we give our people more rum to drink as we cut down the water, we'll be too tipsy to do anything!" He forced a smile. "A fine situation it would be!"

Bolitho turned to Mudge. He was in the largest chair, still wearing his thick coat, and staring up at the open skylight as a moth darted into the lantern's beam. He saw Bolitho's expression and sighed.

"I called at this place just the once, sir. When I was master's mate in the *Windsor,* Indiaman. We was in much the same trouble ourselves then. No water, becalmed for weeks on end, an' with 'alf the people goin' wild with thirst."

Bolitho asked, "But there *is* water available?"

Mudge moved his chair towards the desk in short, squeaky jerks. Then he jabbed the open chart with his thumb.

"We'm now in th' Mozambique Channel, as we all knows." He glared at Midshipman Armitage. "Cept for some too hignorant to *learn* aright!" He continued in a more unruffled tone, "Th' African coast is fair wild 'ereabouts, an' not a lot be known about it. Ships put in, of course." His eyes gleamed as he looked up at Bolitho. "For water. To trade mebbee. An' to find theirselves some black ivory from time to time."

Midshipman Keen was leaning over his shoulder, his face the only one present which showed little sign of strain.

"Black ivory, sir?"

Herrick said sharply, "Slaves."

Mudge leaned back comfortably. "It follows that we must be careful. Land in force, get the water, if I can recall exactly where it is, and stand out to sea agin."

Bellairs said, "My marines will give a good account, thank you!"

Mudge regarded him scornfully. "Just so, Cap'n Bellairs, sir. In their pretty coats, with their drums and fifes, I can picture it a fair treat!" He added harshly, "They'd 'ave 'em for breakfast afore they could polish their bloody boots!"

"Well, *really!*" Bellairs was shocked.

Bolitho nodded. "Very well then. The wind is staying with us, so we should be able to anchor by noon tomorrow."

Mudge agreed. "Aye. But not close inshore, sir. There's a fair bit o' reef just around the point. It'll mean every boat in th' water, an' a 'ard pull for all 'ands."

"Yes." Bolitho looked at Davy. "You can arrange the arming of each boat with the gunner. Swivels for launch and cutter. Musketoons for the rest." He glanced round at their intent faces. "I'll want an officer with each party. Some of our people will need watching, if only for their own sakes." He let his words sink in. "Remember it well. Many of them are quite raw to this sort of work, although because we have been together for over two months, you may see them as veterans. They are not, so treat them accordingly. *Lead* them, do not be content to leave your work to others less qualified."

He saw the midshipmen exchanging glances like boys about to take part in some private escapade. Keen, his eyes sparkling with excitement. Little Penn, openly impressed by being included. Poor Armitage, his forehead raw red from being on watch for a few moments without a hat. They were even less experienced than most of the men.

He looked at the chart. But for Sullivan they might have made the whole voyage to Madras without a pause, despite their shortages. Herrick had tried to help by saying it was bad luck. Puigserver had stated that he was behind him, whatever he decided was best for the ship. But it was still his decision, and nobody else could change that.

Some of those present in the cabin had stopped speaking with the surgeon altogether, and perhaps for that reason alone Bolitho had made no further comment about his choice of Sullivan as a helper, giving him the opportunity, crazy or not, of fouling the water supply. He saw him only on matters of sick reports, and each time was shocked by his appearance. The man was boiling inside, bitter, and yet unable to share his problems. He did not even want to.

He heard a woman's voice, saw the others look up at the skylight as feet passed overhead. Mrs. Raymond and her maid taking their usual stroll under the stars. He hoped Soames would ensure they did not stray from the quarterdeck. He would not answer for their safety at the hands of some of the seamen. He could understand how many of them felt.

To the volunteers it must seem a far cry from the recruiting posters, and to the men from the prison hulks it might now appear to be a bad exchange of circumstances. Even those hiding from crimes committed ashore would find room for doubt and resentment. The crimes would have faded with the fear of arrest and trial. But the heat and thirst, and the daily grind of disciplined duty were only too real.

He saw Raymond biting his lip, his eyes following the footsteps as if he was seeing through the deckhead itself. If anything, he and his wife were moving further apart by being confined in the ship. It was a strange relationship.

He thought back over the past days and one particular incident. He had been in his small makeshift cabin in the chart space, and Allday had been changing the bandage on his arm for him. She had entered the cabin without knocking, in fact, neither of them had heard her approach. She had stood by the open port, quite relaxed, and had watched him without saying a word. Bolitho had been stripped to the waist, and as he reached for a fresh shirt she had said softly, "I see you bear yet another scar, Captain."

Bolitho's hand had gone to his side, suddenly conscious of the ragged mark where a pistol ball had missed his ribs by a thread. He had seen it exactly, as he was seeing it now. The privateer's tilting deck, the American lieutenant running towards him, taking aim. The crash of a shot. The sharp stabbing agony. Oblivion.

Allday had said rudely, "The captain's dressing! Ships' ways are different from those ashore, it seems!"

But she had stood firm, her lips slightly parted, while she watched him. But how could she have understood what he was thinking? That the ball had been fired by one of his own brother's officers. A traitor. A wanted renegade, now dead and forgotten by most.

But not by me.

He shook himself out of his brooding thoughts. Nothing mattered now but the work in hand. Water. All that he needed to take them to Madras. Beyond that was another challenge. It could wait.

He said, "That is all, gentlemen." He realised he had spoken more abruptly than intended and added, "We have a fine ship. One of the most efficient and modern devices created by man. We can give a good account of ourselves to any vessel but a ship of the line." He paused as Herrick smiled at him, bridging the gap between them as he, too, remembered. "Except for rare, and not to be encouraged, occasions! But without water to drink we are like stumbling old men, with neither the means nor the will to face another day. Remember what I have said. Be vigilant. For the moment that is all I ask of you."

They filed out of the cabin, leaving him with Puigserver and Raymond. Raymond looked hopefully at the Spaniard, but when he made no attempt to take his usual walk on deck he, too, left the cabin.

Bolitho sat down and watched the moonlight as it played across the *Undine*'s bubbling wake.

"What is the matter with him, *Señor?*" It was strange how easy it was to talk to him.

Just over a year back he had been an enemy. One Bolitho would have killed in battle had he not called for quarter. He smiled to himself. Or the other way round. He was a powerful man, that was certain, and much of his counsel he kept to himself. But Bolitho trusted him. The ship's company, for the most part, had also accepted him as their own. Like Allday, who had long given up trying to pronounce his name, they called him *Mister Pigsliver.* But they said it with something near to affection.

Puigserver regarded him with quiet amusement.

"My dear *Capitan,* he is like a watchdog. He fears for his wife, what *she* will do, rather than what others will do to her!" He chuckled, the sound rising from his belly. "She, I think, is beginning to enjoy the game, knowing that every man aboard sees her in a different eye. She stands proudly, a tigress in our midst."

"You seem to know a great deal about her, *Señor.*"

The smile broadened. "You know your ships, *Capitan.* Unlike me, I fear you still have much to learn about women, eh?"

Bolitho made to protest and then changed his mind. The memory was still too painful to leave room for a denial.

6

*A*TTACK OVERLAND

"WELL, THOMAS, what d'you make of it at close quarters?" Bolitho's voice was hushed, as with the others around him he stared towards the shore.

They had made a careful approach since dawn, seeing the land gaining shape and substance, and then as the sun had found them again, they had watched the colour, the endless panorama of green.

With two experienced leadsmen in the chains, and under minimum canvas, *Undine* had felt her way towards the land. It had looked like an untouched world with jungle so thick it seemed impossible for anything to move freely away from the sea.

Herrick replied quietly, "The master seems satisfied, sir." He trained his telescope over the hammock nettings. "As he described it. A round headland to the north. And that strange-looking hill about a mile inland."

Bolitho stepped on to a bollard and peered down over the nettings. *Undine* had finally dropped anchor some four cables off-shore to give her sea-room and a safe depth at all times. Nevertheless, it looked very shallow, and he could even see the great shadow of *Undine*'s coppered hull on the bottom. Pale sand. Like that on the various small, crescent-shaped beaches they had seen on their cautious approach.

Long trailers of strange weed, writhing to the current far below the ship as if in a tired sort of dance. But to larboard, as the ship swung to her cable he saw other shapes, browns and greens, like stains in the water. Reefs. Mudge was right to be so careful. Not that anyone would need reminding after *Nervion*'s fate.

Alongside, the first boats had already been swayed out, and Shellabeer, the boatswain, was gesticulating with his fists at some Spanish seamen who were baling one of them. It would do the frail hulls good to be afloat again, Bolitho thought.

He said absently, "I shall go with the boats, and you will keep a good watch in case of trouble."

He could almost feel Herrick's unspoken protest, but added, "If anything goes wrong ashore it might help some of our people if they see I'm sharing it with them." He turned and clapped Herrick's shoulder. "Besides which, I feel like stretching my legs. It is my prerogative."

On the gun deck Davy was striding back and forth inspecting

the men mustered for the boats, checking weapons and the tackle for hoisting and lowering water casks when the work was begun.

Overhead the sky was very pale, as if the sun had boiled the colour from it and had spread it instead across the glittering stretch of sea between ship and shore.

Bolitho marvelled at the stillness. Just an occasional necklace of white surf along the nearest beach and at the foot of the headland. It was as if it was holding its breath, and he could imagine a thousand eyes watching the anchored frigate from amongst the trees.

There were loud thumps as the swivel guns were lowered into the bows of launch and cutter, and more shouted orders while the bell-mouthed musketoons found their proper mountings in gig and pinnace. The jolly boat was to remain with the ship. It was too small for the great casks, and might be needed in an emergency.

He rubbed his chin and stared at the land. Emergency. It appeared safe enough. All the way along the coast, as they had slipped past one bay or inlet after another, and all of which had seemed identical to everyone but Mudge, he had waited for some sign, a hint of danger. But not a boat drawn up on the sand, not a wisp of smoke from a fire, not even a bird had broken the stillness.

"Boats ready, sir!" Shellabeer tilted his swarthy face in the glare.

Bolitho walked to the rail and looked down at the gun deck. The seamen seemed altered yet again. Perhaps because of their cutlasses, the way they glanced at each other, their torment of thirst momentarily put aside. Most of them were very different, from the men who had first joined the ship. Their bared backs were well browned, with only an occasional scar of sunburn to mark the foolish or the unwary.

He called, "Over yonder is Africa, lads." He felt the rustle of excitement expanding like a wind over corn. "You'll be seeing many more places before we are homeward bound again. Do as you are bid, stay with your parties, and no harm should come to you." He hardened his tone. "But it is a dangerous country, and the natives hereabouts have had little cause to like or trust the foreign sailorman. So keep a good watch, and work well with the casks." He nodded. "Man your boats."

Mudge joined him at the gangway as the first men swung their way down the side.

"I should be a'goin' with you, sir. I've told me best master's mate, Fowlar, what to look for, an' 'e's a good man, that 'e be."

Bolitho lifted his arms as Allday buckled on his sword.

"Then what troubles you, Mr. Mudge?"

Mudge scowled. "Time was when I could swim 'alf a mile an' then march another with a full load on me back!"

Herrick, grinned. "And still have the wind to bed a fine wench, I'll be bound!"

Mudge glared at him. "Your time'll come, Mr. 'Errick. It ain't no pleasure, gettin' old!"

Bolitho smiled. "Your value is here."

To Herrick he said, "Rig boarding nets during our stay. With only an anchor watch and the marines at your back, you might be in bother if someone tries to surprise you." He touched his arm. "I know. I am over-cautious. I can read your face like a chart. But better so than dead." He glanced at the shore. "Especially here."

He walked to the entry port. "The boats will return two by two. Send the rest of the men as soon as you can. They'll tire easily enough in this heat."

He saw Puigserver wave to him from the gangway, and Raymond watching from right aft by his wife's little canopy. He touched his hat to the side party and climbed quickly down into the gig where Allday waited by the tiller.

"Shove off!"

One by one the boats idled clear of the frigate's shadow, and then with oars moving in unison turned towards the land. Bolitho remained standing to examine his little flotilla.

Lieutenant Soames with the launch, *Undine*'s largest boat, every inch of space filled with men and casks, while in the bows a gun captain crouched over the loaded swivel like some kind of figurehead. Then the cutter, also deeply laden, with Davy in control, his figure very slim against that of Mr. Pryke, *Undine*'s portly carpenter. As was proper, Pryke was going ashore in the hopes of finding timber suitable for small repairs about the ship.

Midshipman Keen, accompanied by little Penn, had the pinnace, and Bolitho could see them bobbing about with obvious excitement as they pulled steadily across the water.

Bolitho glanced astern at his ship, seeing the figures on her deck already small and impersonal. Someone was in the cabin, and he guessed it was Mrs. Raymond, watching the boats, avoiding her husband, probably neither.

Then he looked down at the men in the gig, at the weapons between their straddled legs, at the way they avoided his scrutiny. Right forward he saw a man moving the musketoon from side to side to free the mount from caked salt, and realised it was Turpin, the one who had tried so desperately to deceive Davy at Spithead. He saw Bolitho watching him and held up his arm. In place of his hand he had a hook of bright steel. He called, "The gunner had it fixed up for me, sir!" He was grinning. "Better'n the real thing!"

Bolitho smiled at him. He at least seemed in good spirits.

He watched the slow moving hulls. About eighty officers and men with more to follow when he could spare the boats. He sat down and shaded his eyes with his hat. As he did so he touched the scar above his eye, remembering that other watering party he had been with so long ago. The sudden charge, screams all about him, that great towering savage brandishing a cutlass he had just seized from a dying sailor. He had seen it only for a second, and then fallen senseless, his face a mask of blood. It had been a close-run thing. But for his coxswain, it would have been the end.

Herrick probably resented his landing with this watering party. It was work normally given to a lieutenant. But that memory, like the scar, was a constant reminder of what could go wrong without any sort of warning.

"Cable to go, Captain!" Allday eased the tiller bar slightly.

Bolitho started. He must have been dreaming. *Undine* looked far away now. A graceful toy. While right across the bows and reaching out on either hand like huge green arms, was the land.

Once again Mudge's memory proved to be sure and reliable. Within two hours of beaching the boats and sorting the hands into working parties, the master's mate, Fowlar, reported finding a little stream, and that the water was the freshest thing he had tasted for years.

The work was begun immediately. Armed pickets were placed at carefully chosen vantage points, and lookouts sent to the top of the small hill, below which Mudge's stream gurgled away into the dense jungle. After the first uncertainty of stepping on to dry land, with all the usual unsteadiness to their sea-legs, the sailors soon settled down to the task. Pryke, the carpenter, and his mates quickly assembled some heavy sledges upon which the filled casks would be hauled down to the boats, and while the cooper stood watchfully at the stream the other men were busy with axes, clearing a path through the trees under Fowlar's personal supervision.

With Midshipman Penn trotting at his heels to act as messenger, Bolitho retained contact between beach and stream, making several journeys to ensure the operation was working smoothly. Lieutenant Soames was in charge of the beach, and of allocating more men to the work as they were ferried ashore. Davy had the inland part, while Keen was usually to be seen with some armed men at his back trudging around the labouring sailors to make sure there were no unwelcome visitors.

Fowlar had discovered two native fireplaces almost immediately. But they were decayed and scattered, and it seemed unlikely that anyone had been near them for months. Nevertheless, as he paused to watch over the progress of each party, Bolitho was conscious of a feeling of menace. Of hostility, which was hard to define.

On his way inland to the stream yet again he had to stand aside as a heavy sledge, hauled by some two dozen blaspheming seamen, careered past him, shaking the undergrowth, and making several, great red birds flap between the trees, squawking discordantly. Bolitho watched the birds and then stepped back on to the crude trail. It was good to know something was alive here, he thought. Beneath the trees, where the sky was hidden from view, the air was heavy, and stank of rotting vegetation. Here and there, something clicked and rustled, or a small beady eye glittered momentarily in filtered sunlight before vanishing just as swiftly.

Penn gasped, "Might be *snakes,* sir!" He was panting hard, his shirt plastered to his body from his exertions to keep up.

Bolitho found Davy beneath a wall of overhanging rock, marking his list as yet another cask was sealed by Duff for the bumpy ride to the beach.

The second lieutenant straightened his back and observed, "Going well, sir."

"Good." Bolitho stooped and cupped his hands into the stream. It was like wine, despite the rotten looking roots which sprouted from either bank. "We will finish before dark."

He looked up at a patch of blue sky as the trees gave a stealthy rustle. It was unmoving air below the matted branches, but above and to seaward the wind was holding well.

"I am going up the hill, Mr. Davy." He thought he heard Penn sigh with despair. "I hope your lookouts are awake."

It was a long hard walk, and when they moved clear of the trees for the final climb to the summit, Bolitho felt the sun searing down on his shoulders, the heat through his shoes from the rough stones, like coals off a grate.

But the two lookouts seemed contented enough. In their stained trousers and shirts, with their tanned faces almost hidden by straw hats, they looked more like castaways than British seamen.

They had rigged a small shelter with a scrap of canvas, behind which lay their weapons, water flasks and a large brass telescope.

One knuckled his forehead and said "'Orizon's clear, Cap'n!"

Bolitho tugged his hat over his eyes as he stared down the hill. The coastline was more uneven than he had imagined, water glittering between the thick layers of trees to reveal some inlet or cover not marked on any chart. Inland, and towards a distant barrier of tall hills, there was nothing but an undulating sea of trees. So close-knit, it looked possible to walk upright across the top of them.

He picked up the telescope and trained it on the ship. She was writhing and bending in a surface haze, but he saw the boats moving back and forth, very slowly, like tired water-beetles. He felt grit and dust under his fingers, and guessed the telescope had spent more time lying on the hillside than in use.

He heard Penn sucking noisily at a water flask, and could sense the lookouts willing him to leave them in peace. Theirs might be a thirsty job, but it was far easier than hauling casks through the forest. He moved the glass again. All those men, sledges and casks, yet from here he could see none of them. Even the beach was shielded. The boats, as they drew near the shore, appeared to vanish into the trees, as if swallowed whole.

Bolitho turned to his right, the movement making the men stir with alarm. In the telescope's lens the trees and slivers of trapped water grew and receded as he continued his search. Something had touched the corner of his eye, but what? The lookouts were watching him doubtfully, each caught in his own attitude as if mesmerised.

A trick of light. He blinked and rubbed his eye. Nothing.

He began another slow scrutiny. Thick, characterless forest. Or was that merely what he *expected* to see? And therefore . . . He stiffened and held his breath. When he lowered the glass the picture fell away into the distance. He waited, counting seconds, allowing his breathing to steady.

The lookouts had begun to whisper again, and Penn was drinking as before. They probably imagined he had been too long in the sun.

He lifted the glass very carefully. There, to the right, where he had already noticed a faint gleam of water, was something darker, at odds with the forest's greens and browns. He stared at it until his eye watered so painfully he could not continue.

Then he closed the glass with a snap and said, "There is a ship yonder." He saw Penn gaping at him, transfixed. "To the south'rd. It must be some sort of inlet which we did not see earlier."

He shaded his eyes, trying to estimate the distance, where it lay in relation to *Undine* and the beach where he had come ashore.

One of the lookouts exclaimed, "Oi never saw nothin', sir." He looked frightened, and worse.

Bolitho stared past him, trying to think.

"Take this glass and make sure you can see it *now!*"

He knew the seaman was more frightened of his captain, or what might become of him because of his negligence, than anything this discovery might mean.

Bolitho's mind recorded all these reactions as he said, "Have you found it?"

"Aye, sir!" The man bobbed unhappily. "'Tis a mast, right enough."

"Thank you." Bolitho added dryly, "Keep your eye on it. I do not want it to vanish again!"

Penn dropped the flask and scuttled after him as he strode down the hill.

"Wh-what might it mean, sir?"

"Several things." He felt the trees looming around him, a small relief from the sun's torment. "They may have sighted us and are lying low until we weigh. Perhaps they are intent on some other mischief, I am not certain."

He quickened his pace, ignoring creepers and fronds which plucked at his body. But for that brief flaw in the len's picture he would have seen nothing, *known* nothing about the other vessel. Perhaps it would have been better that way. Maybe he was worrying to no purpose.

He found Davy as before, lounging in the shade of the hillside, his features relaxed as he watched his men filling the casks.

"Where is Mr. Fowlar?"

Davy came out of his torpor with a jerk. "Er, on the beach, sir."

"Damn!"

Another hard mile before he could examine Fowlar's chart and Mudge's notes. He looked up at the sky. Hours yet before sunset, but when it did come it would be quick. Shutting out the light like a curtain.

"I have discovered a ship, Mr. Davy. Well hidden, to the south'rd of us." He saw the carpenter emerge from the undergrowth, a saw glinting in one fist. "Take charge here, Mr. Pryke." He beckoned to Davy. "We are going to the beach."

Pryke nodded, his fat face glowing like a ripe apple. "Aye, sir." He looked at Duff. "There be only five more casks, by my reckonin'."

"Well, speed the work. I want our people mustered as soon as the last one is filled."

Davy hurried along at his side, his handsome face puzzled. "Do you think this ship may be an enemy, sir?"

"I intend to find out."

They completed the journey in silence, and Bolitho knew that Davy, like the lookouts, thought he was making too much of it.

Fowlar listened to him calmly and then examined his chart.

"If it is where I believe, then it is not marked here. So it must lie somewhere 'twixt this beach and the next bay." He made a mark. "About there, I would suggest, sir."

"Could we reach it before dark? Overland?"

Fowlar's eyes widened but he answered, "It looks close enough, sir. No more'n three mile or so. But that is four times as much in the jungle." He dropped his eyes from Bolitho's gaze. "You *might* be able to do it, sir."

Davy asked, "But if we wait until tomorrow, sir? We could have *Undine* anchored nearer this vessel you have found."

"It would take too long. She may have weighed and gone overnight. And if they are aware of our presence and purpose, a boat attack would be useless in daylight, and in a confined inlet. You should know that, Mr. Davy."

Davy looked at his shoes. "Yes, sir."

Another heavy cask lurched down the beach, the men panting like animals running from the hounds.

Soames, who had trudged up the beach to listen, said suddenly, "She might be a slaver. In which case she will be well armed." He rubbed his chin and nodded. "Yours is a good plan, sir." His thick forefinger scratched over the chart. "We could cross the bottom of the hill where it reaches for the sea and strike south. If we travel lightly we should be at the inlet before dark." He looked at Davy, his eyes hard. "I'll pick some good men. Ones who won't falter when the passage gets rough."

Davy said nothing, he was obviously smarting because Soames had offered a course of action rather than an unthinking suggestion.

Bolitho looked towards the ship. "Very well. We will rest the hands for half an hour. Then we will begin. Forty men should be sufficient if we are careful. It may be a complete waste of time." He thought of the silent jungle. *Watching.* "But to be anchored so dangerously inland? I doubt it."

He beckoned to Penn. "I will write my orders for the first lieutenant, and you will take them across directly. *Undine* will send her boats tomorrow morning and pick us up from seaward. By then we should know." He glanced at Davy. "One way or the other."

He saw Keen coming out of the trees, a pistol hanging casually from his belt. As he turned towards the sea he halted and raised one arm to point. It was the jolly boat, darting across the water at full speed, the oars winking in the sunlight like silver.

Eventually it ground on to the beach, and without waiting for it to be made fast, Midshipman Armitage leapt over the gunwale and then fell face down on the sand.

Allday, who had been watching critically, exclaimed, "God damn me, Captain! That young gentleman will stumble on an acorn!"

Armitage hurried up the beach, his cheeks scarlet as he dashed past the groups of grinning seamen.

He stammered, "Mr. Herrick's respects, sir!" He paused to wipe sand from his chin. "And we have sighted some small craft to the north of here." He pointed haphazardly into the trees. "A whole party of them. Mr. Herrick thinks they may come this way, although . . . ," he stopped, screwing up his face as he usually did when passing a message, ". . . although they have vanished for the present." He nodded, relieved, as he recalled the last part. "Mr. Herrick suggests they have gone into another beach for some purpose."

Bolitho gripped his hands behind him. The very thing he had been expecting had happened. It could not have come at a worse time.

"Thank you, Mr. Armitage."

Davy said quietly, "That has put paid to the venture, sir. We cannot be divided if hostile natives are about."

Soames said scathingly, "A plague on that, Mr. Davy! We have enough powder and shot to scatter a thousand bloody savages!"

"That will do!" Bolitho glared at them, his mind struggling with the problem. "Mr. Herrick is probably correct. They may have gone ashore to hunt, or to make camp. Either way, it makes our mission all the more urgent." He watched Soames thoughtfully, seeing the mixture of anger and triumph in his deepset eyes. "Select your men at once."

Davy asked stiffly, "What will *I* do, sir?"

Bolitho turned away. In a hand-to-hand struggle Soames would be the better man. If things went against them, Herrick would need brains rather than brawn if he was to continue the voyage on his own resources.

"You will return to the ship with the last of the shore parties."

He scribbled a note on Fowlar's pad. "And you will convey my . . . ," he hesitated, not seeing the desperation which clouded Davy's face, ". . . my ideas to him as best you can."

Davy said tightly, "I am senior to Soames, sir. It is my right to take part in this!"

Bolitho looked at him calmly. "I will decide where your duty lies. Your *loyalty* I take for granted." He watched Soames marching up and down a double line of men. "Your turn will come, be sure of that."

A shadow fell across Fowlar's chart and Bolitho saw the Spanish lieutenant, Rojart, watching him, his face as sad as ever.

"Yes, *Teniente?*"

He must have come ashore in one of the other boats.

Rojart said, "I arrive to offer my services, *Capitan*." He looked at Davy and Allday, his face very proud. "Don Luis 'as instructed me to do all I can to 'elp you."

Bolitho sighed. Rojart had already shown himself to be somewhat of a dreamer. Or perhaps his cruel experiences in the shipwreck had made him as he was. But one more officer, Spanish or not, would be useful. He also provided an excuse.

He said to Davy, "So you see, Mr. Herrick will need your services more than ever now?"

To Rojart he replied, "I accept your offer, *Teniente*, thank you."

The Spaniard gave a flashing smile and bowed. "Your *servant, Capitan!*"

Allday grinned and murmured, "God help us all!"

Another cask was being manhandled on to the beach, and Duff puffed out of the trees, folding his spectacles as he shouted, "That be the last 'un, sir!" He beamed at the onlookers. "A full load!"

Soames tightened his swordbelt and said, "Ready when you are, sir." He pointed to the assembled seamen. "All armed, but without any unnecessary gear to drag 'em back." He ignored Davy.

Keen and his pickets were gathering at the end of the beach, and by the shallows Pryke stood guard over an odd pile of timber which his mates had collected for him.

Davy touched his hat formally. "I wish you luck, sir."

Bolitho smiled. "Thank you. I hope we will not need it just yet."

He glanced at Fowlar. "Lead the way and make notes as we go. Who knows, we may come here again some day."

Then he turned his back on the sea and strode up the beach towards the trees.

"We will rest now."

Bolitho dragged his watch from his breeches pocket and peered at it. Its face was harder to see than the last occasion. When he looked up at a gap in the trees he thought the sky was already duller, the trees touched with purple instead of gold. Around him the seamen dropped wearily on their knees or leaned against the trees, trying to gain relief after their forced march. The first part had not been too difficult. With axes swinging to carve a trail, they had made good time, but as they drew closer to where Bolitho and Fowlar estimated the inlet lay, they had stopped using axes, and had fought their way through the brush and creeper with bare hands.

He looked at them thoughtfully. Their shirts were ripped and torn, faces and arms bloody from encounters with treacherous branches and thorns. At their backs the intertwined trees had grown blacker, and seemed to shiver in the vapour of dead vegetation as if in a wind which could not be felt.

Soames was wiping his face and neck with a rag. "I've sent scouts ahead, sir." He knocked a water bottle from a man's mouth. "*Easy,* damn you! That may have to last awhile yet!"

Bolitho saw him with different eyes. Like the men Soames had selected as scouts, for instance. Not the toughest or the most seasoned seamen as a lieutenant of his background might be expected to choose. Both scouts were from *Undine's* newest recruits and had never been to sea before. One had worked on a farm, and the other had been a Norfolk wildfowler. Excellent choices both, he thought. They had gone off into the trees with hardly a sound.

Allday muttered, "What d'you think, Captain?"

His sturdy figure, familiar and reassuring, made Bolitho relax slightly.

He replied, "I think we are very near now."

He wondered how Herrick was managing, and whether he had sighted any more native craft. He shivered. Like most of his men, he felt out of place here. Cut off.

Fowlar hissed, "Stand to, lads! Someone's a'comin'!"

Muskets moved blindly in the gloom, and a few men started to draw their cutlasses.

Soames snapped, "A scout!" He strode towards the shadow. "By God, Hodges, that was quickly done."

The man stepped into the small clearing and looked at Bolitho.

"I found the ship, sir. She be about 'alf a mile away." He stretched out one arm. "If we veers a piece we should be able to reach 'er within the hour."

"What else?"

Hodges shrugged. He was a lean man, and Bolitho could well picture him as a wildfowler, creeping about in the Norfolk marshes.

He said, "I didn't stray too near, you'll understand, sir. But they're anchored close in. There's more of 'em ashore in a clearing. I 'eard someone," he faltered, "sort of moanin'." He shuddered. "It made me flesh tingle, I can tell you, sir."

Soames said harshly, "As I thought. Bloody slavers. They'll have a camp ashore. They collect the poor devils and sort 'em into groups. Girls in one party, men in t'other. They weigh 'em, then decide who will last the voyage to wherever the cargo is bound."

Fowlar spat on the dead leaves and nodded. "The rest they leave behind. Cut their throats to save powder and shot."

Bolitho looked at the scout, trying to shut Fowlar's blunt

comment from his thoughts. Everyone knew it happened. Nobody seemed to know how to deal with it. Especially when many influential persons reaped a rich profit from the trade.

"Are there guards about?"

"I saw two, sir. But they seem well content. The ship 'as two guns run out."

Soames grunted. "No doubt. A bellyful of grape or canister if anyone tries to free those bastards!"

The Spanish lieutenant moved amongst them. Despite the rough passage through the trees he managed to remain very elegant in his ruffled shirt and wide cuffs.

"Per'aps we should continue towards the shore, *Capitan.*" He shrugged eloquently. "There is no sense in arousing this ship if she is a mere slaver, yes?"

Soames turned away, saying nothing. But Bolitho guessed that like most sailors he was disgusted that Rojart could accept slavery as a natural state of affairs.

"We go forward, *Teniente.* In any case, our boats will not come for us until tomorrow."

He looked at Soames. "Take charge. I am going to see for myself." He beckoned to Midshipman Keen. "You, too." As he felt his way out of the clearing he added, "The rest of you, be ready to follow. No talking, and hold on to each other if you fear getting separated. Any man who fires a musket by whatever means or accident will feel my anger!"

Hodges pushed ahead saying, "My mate, Billy Norris, is keepin' a weather eye on 'em, sir. Follow close. I've marked the way."

Bolitho took his word, although he could see no marks anywhere.

It was amazing how near they had been. It seemed no time at all before Hodges was tapping his arm and gesturing for him to take cover amidst some sharp-toothed scrub, and here, opening up like a theatre, was the inlet. And how much lighter it seemed, the sunlight still lingering on the trees, and painting the sluggishly moving water with rippling reflections.

He eased himself forward, trying to ignore the painful jabs in his hands and chest. Then he froze, forgetting all the discomfort and uncertainty as he saw the ship for the first time.

Behind him he heard Allday voicing his thoughts.

"By God, Captain, it's the one which lured the Dons on to that reef!"

Bolitho nodded. The brigantine appeared larger in the confined inlet, but there was no mistaking her. He knew he would not forget her for many a year to come.

He heard the same pitiful moaning Hodges had described, and then the sharp clatter of steel on the far side of the inlet.

Allday whispered, "Putting manacles on the wretches."

"Yes."

He wriggled forward again, seeing the brigantine's anchor cable, a boat alongside, the glow of light from her poop. As before, no flag. But there was no doubting her watchfulness. Two guns already run out, muzzles depressed to rake any attacker.

A boat glided from the shore, very slowly, and Bolitho tensed as a woman cried out, the sound dragging at his nerves as it echoed around the trees.

"Taking slaves aboard." Allday ground his teeth. "They'll be off shortly. That's my guess."

Bolitho agreed.

To Keen he said, "Fetch the others. Tell them to take care." He sought out the crouching shape of the second scout. "You go with him."

To Allday he said quietly, "If we can seize her, we'll know for sure who was behind *Nervion*'s destruction."

Allday had his cutlass in both hands. "I'm for that, Captain!"

More thuds and sounds from alongside the brigantine, and another shrill cry rising to a scream until it was swiftly silenced by a blow.

Bolitho tried to estimate how far this point was from the sea. The slaver's master would need to be able to slip away as quietly as he had entered. He would require stealth. As little noise as possible until he was clear. It seemed incredible to be watching this same vessel. While *Undine* had waited to search for *Nervion*'s survivors, and had then taken wide detours to avoid land and other ships, the slaver had pushed on with his own affairs. As if nothing had happened. It took iron-hard nerves for that. There were more sharp cries. Like animals at slaughter. Slavers had no nerves. No pity.

He heard furtive noises behind him and Soames's voice, flat, unemotional.

"Young Keen was right then. It is the same vessel." He squinted at the tree-tops beyond the brigantine. "Not much time left, sir. It'll be as black as a boot in an hour. Maybe less."

"What I believe, too." Bolitho looked at the clearing where the slaves were being gathered. A few wisps of smoke from fires. Probably for a blacksmith to work on the manacles. But it was the weakest point. "Take twenty men and move around the camp. At the first sign of alarm you open fire with everything you have. Create panic if nothing else."

"Aye. Makes sense."

Bolitho nodded, his mind chilling with excitement. A kind of madness which always came at such moments.

"I'll want ten men who can swim. If we can board her while the slaves are being loaded, we might be able to hold the poop until you rush the boats and join us."

He heard Soames rubbing his chin.

"A wild plan, sir, but it's now or never, it seems to me."

"It's settled then. Tell Rojart to keep a few hands here to protect our flank. For this is the way we must go if all fails."

Soames started to crawl away, hissing his orders into the forest until he appeared satisfied.

Other figures rustled and grunted nearby, and Keen said, "Our party is ready, sir."

"*Our* party?"

Keen's teeth looked very white in the fading light. "I am an excellent swimmer, sir."

Allday muttered anxiously, "I hope there are none of those damned serpents in the water."

Bolitho looked around at their faces. How well he had got to know most of them. He saw it all in these last moments. Fear, anxiety, wildness to match his own. Even brutal eagerness.

He said shortly, "We will slide into the water below the bushes. Leave your shoes and everything else but your weapons." He sought out Allday. "See that the pistols are well wrapped. It should keep them dry for a while."

He studied the sky. It was darkening swiftly, and only the treetops still held the gentle glow of sunlight. In the inlet and around the anchored brigantine the water was dull. Like liquid mud.

"*Now!*"

He caught his breath as the water came up to his waist and then his neck. It was very warm. He waited a few more seconds, expecting to hear a shout or the sound of a musket. But the muffled cries from the camp told him he had chosen the time well. They were too busy to watch everywhere at once.

The others were in the water behind him, their weapons held high as they paddled slowly away from the bank.

Keen was overtaking him, his arms moving smoothly. He whispered, "I'll make for the cable, sir." He was actually grinning.

Further, and further still, until they had passed the halfway, and Bolitho knew if they were discovered now they would be lost. The masts and yards stood high overhead, the furled sails sharp against the sky, the lantern light shining more brightly in the descending gloom. Feet thudded on deck and a man laughed wildly. A drunkard's laugh. Perhaps you needed extra rum for such work, he thought.

And then, as if by magic, they were all together, clawing the rounded hull below the starboard cathead, the current dragging at their legs, folding them against the rough timbers as they fought to stay concealed.

Allday gasped, "The boats'll never see us here. We're safe for a bit."

At that very instant a terrible cry floated across the water and for a moment Bolitho imagined someone had been killed.

But the seaman at his side was floundering and pointing towards the bank which they had just left.

Even in the dying light it was easy to recognise Rojart's ruffled shirt. He was standing in the open, his arms held out as if to seize the inlet and everything it contained. He yelled again and again, waving his fists, stamping his feet, as if he had gone raving mad.

Rojart's sudden appearance had brought a complete hush to the brigantine's deck, but now as voices babbled and shouted and more feet thudded along the planking, Bolitho knew any hope of surprise was gone.

Keen had been clinging to the bobstay below the bowsprit, but now allowed himself to drift down towards him.

He gasped wretchedly, "Nobody told Rojart it was the ship which sank *Nervion*. He must have just discovered—"

The sound of the shot was deafening and seemed to come from almost overhead. The smoke gushed and eddied across the swirling water, making more than one man duck his face to avoid a fit of coughing.

Before it hid the bank Bolitho saw Rojart hurled away by a full charge of canister. A bloody rag. Not a man at all.

He clung to the line which Allday had bent on to the bobstay and tried to clear his mind. The unexpected and unforeseen.

He winced as another shot crashed out from further aft, the hull shivering under his fingers as if alive. A ball this time, he heard it smashing through the trees and then fading away completely.

And it was then, from beyond the hidden camp, that Soames's men opened fire.

7

HERRICK'S *D*ECISION

THE SPORADIC bang of musket fire was almost drowned by the mingled cries and screams from the terrified slaves. Bolitho heard men tumbling into a boat on the opposite side of the brigantine, and confused yells which were probably to encourage their companions in the camp.

He gestured to Allday. "Now! Over the bows!"

His limbs were like lead as he hauled himself up and across the small beakhead, his heart pounding his ribs, hearing the gasps and frantic whispers from the men below him.

As they climbed on to the forecastle he saw groups of manacled natives, their naked bodies crowded together while they watched what was happening on the land. Two armed seamen stood beside a swivel gun, but as the boat pulled away from the side they were unable to fire without hitting their comrades.

Allday bellowed, "At 'em, lads!" Then he was flying along the deck, his heavy cutlass taking a man across the neck and felling him without even a cry.

The second guard dropped on one knee and aimed a musket as more and more of Bolitho's party scrambled aboard. Faces lit up in the flash, and Bolitho felt the ball whine past, the sickening sound as it smashed into flesh and bone.

More of the brigantine's crew were dashing wildly from the poop, firing as they came, regardless of the screaming slaves who fell dying in their path.

A naked girl, her body shining with sweat, was trying to reach one of the fallen slaves, her arms pinioned by a length of chain. Husband? Brother? Bolitho had no time even to guess as one of the crew hacked her down with his cutlass in order to bar the way aft.

Bolitho felt his sword jerk in his hand as he crossed blades with the girl's killer. He saw the hatred on the man's bearded face, the madness in his eyes as they pressed forward and apart, feet sliding in someone's blood, bodies balanced to withstand each parry.

All round the deck others were fighting and slashing in the shadows with only an occasional pistol shot to throw light on friend and enemy.

Bolitho pushed the man against the main mast, forcing him backwards over the spider-band while their hilts stayed locked below his throat. He could feel the other man's anger giving way to fear, saw the sudden anguish as he jerked the hilt free and struck him hard across the mouth with it. As he fell away, gasping for breath, Bolitho turned and thrust. The man gave one shriek, lifting an arm as the blade drove under his shoulder and deeper still.

Allday dashed to his side and gasped, "Well done, Captain!" He rolled the man away with his foot. Then he snarled, "And another, by God!"

The seaman had jumped from the shrouds. To take them by surprise from above, to escape the unexpected attack, Bolitho did not know. All he heard was Allday's quick breathing, the swish of his blade as he slashed the man down and then finished him with one more terrible blow.

"Two boats comin', sir!"

Bolitho ran to the bulwark, and then ducked as a ball slammed hard into the rail by his fingers.

He yelled, "Train that swivel on them!"

Someone scuttled past him firing a pistol as he fled from Allday's cutlass. Bolitho spun round, sobbing as the pain lanced into his thigh. But when he felt his leg and the jagged tear in his breeches there was no blood, no agonising splinter of broken bone.

The man who had fired had inadvertently run too close to the yelling slaves. Chains swung like serpents, and he vanished beneath a struggling heap of screaming, shining bodies.

Allday threw his arm around Bolitho's waist. "Where are you hit, Captain?" His anxiety was clear even amidst the din of shouting and screaming.

Bolitho pushed him aside, gasping between his teeth, "Hit my watch, damn his eyes!"

Allday grinned and ducked after him. "I think *his* time has stopped, too!"

Bolitho only glanced at the thing which had rolled away from the panting slaves. They had literally torn him to pieces.

He dragged Allday clear. "Stray too close and you will follow him!"

"Ungrateful dogs!"

Bolitho reached the abandoned swivel and swung it towards the nearest long boat.

"Probably think we are a different lot of slavers."

He jerked the lanyard, feeling the hot breath from the muzzle as the canister exploded across the crowded boat. Screams and curses, bodies splashing in the water, and others still firing from the sternsheets.

He twisted round, trying to see where Soames had reached on the shore. But it was impossible to be certain. Shots stabbed and whimpered over the inlet, and once he thought he heard, steel on steel.

Then he turned and looked inboard. "How many?" He caught Keen's wrist as he lurched past, a dirk gleaming in one hand, an empty pistol held like a club in the other.

Keen stared at him dazedly. "We seem to have lost five of our people, sir. But the slavers have either been killed or have jumped overboard."

Bolitho strained his ears for the sounds of more oars, the one thing which would tell him Soames was coming to his aid.

There was a loud thud from aft, and he guessed that another boat was grappling in readiness for boarding. He peered at his little party. Five dead, one obviously wounded. It was not enough.

Allday shouted hoarsely, "We can manhandle one of the guns to the hold and put a ball through her bottom! If we can hold 'em on the poop while—"

Bolitho shook his head, pointing at the slaves. "They are held by more than one chain. They would go down with the ship."

He could feel the fight dying in his surviving men, like fire under heavy rain. Most of them were staring aft, each unwilling to be the first to challenge this new attack.

They did not have long to wait. The poop doors burst open and a group of men charged along the littered deck, their voices yelling wildly in what seemed like a dozen different languages.

Bolitho balanced himself on the balls of his feet, the sword angled across his body.

"Cut the cable! We'll let her drift ashore in the shallows!"

A ball shrieked above his head, and he turned to see one of his men sprawled headlong, blood gushing from his throat. He had been struck by a marksman somewhere in the shrouds.

Allday yelled, "Stand fast, you bastards!"

But it was useless, the remaining seamen were clambering forward again, dropping their weapons in their frantic haste to get away.

Only Keen remained between him and the beakhead, his arms at his sides, his young body swaying with exhaustion.

Allday said, "Come *on*, Captain! It's no use!" He fired a pistol into the advancing shadows, and grunted with satisfaction as a man screamed in agony.

The next seconds were too blurred to understand. One moment Bolitho was astride the bowsprit, and the next he was swimming towards the black wall of trees. He could not remember diving or regaining the surface, although his lungs were raw from shouting, from keeping alive.

Feathers of spray spurted nearby, and he heard feet stampeding along the brigantine's deck as more men climbed from boats or swam out from the shore. Shots whimpered above his head, and there was one short cry as a seaman was hit and disappeared beneath the surface.

"Keep together!"

It was all he could do to speak, and the foul-tasting water was slopping again and again into his mouth.

He saw a white figure splashing down the beach, and when he groped for his sword he stumbled headlong, his feet stubbing against sand and stone beneath him.

But it was Soames, his chest heaving from exertion, his hair wild as he pulled Bolitho to dry land.

Bolitho gasped at the air. They had failed. They had lost several good men. For nothing.

Allday was hauling Keen from the water, and two more figures lay on the sand like corpses, only their fierce breathing telling otherwise. There were no others.

A gun banged out from the brigantine, but the ball went wide, splintering through the trees to a chorus of shrieks from birds and slaves alike.

Soames said harshly, "I could only capture one boat, sir. The slaver had a large party ashore." He sounded angry. Despairing. "When they fired at that damn Spaniard my lads started to attack. It was too soon. I'm sorry, sir."

"Not your fault." Bolitho walked heavily along the water's edge, searching for one more swimmer. "How many did you lose?"

Soames replied indifferently, "Seven or eight." He gestured to several dark shapes along the beach. "But we took a dozen of the others!" He added with sudden fury, "We could have taken that damn ship! I *know* we could!"

"Yes." Bolitho gave up his search. "Muster our people and lead me to the boat. We must pick up Mr. Fowlar and his party while it's dark. The slaver will be ready for us by dawn, I'm thinking."

It was not much of a boat, and leaked badly from a couple of stray musket balls.

One by one the weary seamen clambered into it, hardly looking at each other, or even caring where they were. If they were called on to fight now they would fail completely.

Bolitho watched them anxiously. Vaguely he recalled Herrick's words all those weeks back. *Different in peacetime.* Perhaps they were.

The wounded men were sobbing quietly, and he pushed Keen towards them. "See to them." He saw the youth draw back, knew that he, too, was close to breaking. He reached out and squeezed his shoulder. "Hold on, Mr. Keen."

To Soames he said quietly, "Mr. Fowlar's party can take the oars. They'll be in better shape."

He turned as a new sound intruded from the trees. Like one huge beast stamping its feet, while a combined chorus of yells echoed and re-echoed around the inlet.

Allday muttered, "What in the name of God is that?"

"The slaves at the camp." Soames was standing beside Bolitho as the boat edged away from the land. "They know something we don't."

Bolitho swayed as the overloaded craft rocked dangerously in the current. The slaves must realise that, despite the brigantine's presence, and the power of her guns, they would not now be taken as captives to the other side of the world. Not this time anyway. He thought of the native craft Herrick had sighted. They might be here already.

He snapped, "Easy there! I can see Mr. Fowlar!"

The master's mate peered into the boat with obvious dismay. "I'll never get my party in, too, sir!"

Soames jerked his thumb towards the trees.

"You will if you wish to stay alive!"

Allday took the tiller and checked each man as he climbed into the boat. Somehow they all got in, barely leaving the oarsmen room to pull, and with the hull so low in the water there was hardly six inches of freeboard.

"Shove off!"

He winced as a gun banged out, the long orange flame of fire darting from the vessel's side like a vicious tongue. The ball hissed astern of the boat and pounded into the sand.

Bolitho called, "Easy now! Watch the stroke, lads!"

Too many splashes and the gunners would have an aiming mark.

Keen whispered, "One of them has just died, sir." He added hoarsely, "Hodges."

"Heave him over the side. Watch the trim, lads. Keep her steady."

Poor Hodges. He would not walk in the marshes again. Never feel the North Sea on his face, or see the ducks in flight. He shook himself angrily. What was the matter with him?

The corpse drifted clear, and another man shifted along the thwart.

Soames observed, "They've ceased firing. Probably licking their wounds, like us."

"Most likely."

Bolitho felt the bitterness rising again. The slaver had lost several men, but had still enough captives to make his visit profitable whether he retrieved the rest from the camp or not. Whereas . . . He tried not to face the fact that they had failed. His men had fallen back, probably because they had lost whatever faith they had held in him.

Nervion's attacker was as much a mystery as before. A slaver's crew was usually made up from the sweepings of many ports and many tongues. Perhaps Davy had been right after all, and he should never have attempted to capture the brigantine.

His head was aching to match the bruise on his thigh. He was barely able to think any more.

Fowlar said, "Mr. Mudge has explained it to me, sir. The ship will have to stand well out tomorrow because of the shoals hereabouts. The slaver's master doubtless knows a better passage, but . . ." He left the rest unsaid.

"Very well." Bolitho saw an overhanging clump of trees reaching out across the water like a partly demolished bridge. "We will make fast here. Rest the men, and share out the last of our water and rations."

Nobody replied, and some of them appeared to be sleeping where they sat or crouched like so many bundles.

He tried not to think about the brigantine. But for his action she would be in ignorance of *Undine*'s presence. It was obvious they had not seen her, nor had they understood who had attacked and tried to capture their ship. After all, it was not unknown for one slaver to prey upon another for extra profit.

But now, because of his persistence, her master would recognise *Undine* as soon as he stood out to sea. *Undine* would be unable to venture too close inshore, and a long chase would prove just as fruitless. So, if he had been involved in delaying Puigserver's mission, he would now know that *Undine* at least was on her way.

He clenched his fingers around his sword until the pain steadied him. But for Rojart they would have succeeded. How many battles had been lost by a single, stupid oversight? Poor Rojart. The ship which had destroyed his *Nervion* was the last thing he had seen on earth. Then she had murdered him just as brutally.

The bowman called, "I can see a beach to larboard, Cap'n! Looks safe enough!"

Allday glanced at Bolitho's shoulders, feeling his despair as if it were his own.

Bolitho said, "Take her there, Allday." He pushed his other thoughts aside with something like physical force. "We will work in three watches. Two hours at a time." He tried again. "Post sentries, and keep a good lookout."

The bowman leapt over the stem and waded into the shallows, a line across his ragged shoulder like a halter. The boat nudged on to hard sand, tilting drunkenly to the current and the sudden shift of men as they staggered ashore.

Bolitho listened to Soames as he picked out his sentries for the first watch. Had he been in charge of the boarding party, would he have hesitated? He doubted it. Soames would have done what he saw as his duty, helpless slaves or not, and put a ball through the brigantine's bottom or touched off her magazine. In this climate she would have been gutted in minutes, leaving the slavers isolated and easy to capture at leisure.

Because he had not been able to destroy the slaves, Bolitho had gained nothing. And he had lost nearly a third of his original party as well.

Allday slumped down beside him and handed him a water flask.

"I've secured the boat, Captain." He yawned hugely. "I just hope we don't have to pull too far in it, that's all." Then he said, "Don't you fret, things aren't that bad." When Bolitho remained silent he added, "We've seen an' done much worse in our time. I know some of our people took to their heels instead of rallying when they were most needed, but times are different, or seem so to many of 'em."

Bolitho looked at him dully, but could not see his expression. "How so?"

Allday shrugged. "They don't see the sense in getting killed for a few slaves, or a ship they know nothing about. In the old *Phalarope* it was different, y'see. A flag to follow, an enemy you could recognise."

Bolitho laid back against a tree and closed his eyes, hearing the jungle coming alive for the night. Squeaks and roars, groans and rustlings.

He said, "You mean that they do not care?"

Allday grinned. "If it was a *proper* war, Captain, a real one like the last, we'd soon make 'em into fighters."

"So, unless they are threatened personally they will not fight for those less fortunate?" Bolitho opened his eyes and studied the stars overhead, "Before this voyage is done, I fear that some of them may come to understand otherwise."

But Allday had fallen asleep, his cutlass across his chest like a dead knight.

Bolitho stood up quietly and walked to the boat to see how the wounded man had settled down for the night. He saw the stars reflected on the sluggish water, and was surprised to discover he was feeling less despairing.

He looked back at the trees, but Allday's shape was lost in darkness. By accident or design he did not know, but it had often happened with Allday. He seemed to hit upon the very thing which was troubling him in his simple, open manner. Not dispel it completely, but stand back from it and keep it in its proper perspective.

When he reached the boat he found the seaman sleeping heavily, his rough bandage very white against the planking.

Keen looked up, startled. "Sorry, I did not see you, sir."

Bolitho replied, "Rest, easy, Mr. Keen. We are snug here for the night."

As he walked away, Fowlar, who had been washing his face and hands in the water, moved to the boat and said admiringly, "What a man, eh? Never a one to weep an' wail when things go hard."

Keen nodded. "I know. I hope I'm like him one day."

Fowlar laughed, the sound bringing more cries from the forest. "Bless you, Mr. Keen, I'm sure he'd be flattered to know that!"

Keen turned back to watch the wounded seaman. Under his breath he said fervently, "Well, I *do,* and that's an end to it!"

In the pale glow of morning both sea and sky were joined by a filtered, milky haze. As the overcrowded longboat moved ponderously away from the trees and tiny beaches which lined both sides of the inlet, Bolitho watched for some sign of life or movement which might betray an ambush. A few birds floated overhead, and far beyond the last jutting spit of land he saw open water, colourless in the strange light.

He turned his attention to the men in the boat. Their brief rest seemed to have had little effect. They looked tired and anxious, their clothes filthy with dirt and dried blood, faces dark with stubble. There was little to associate them with a King's ship.

Soames was standing upright beside Allday, peering ahead, watching the men who baled away the seeping water, keeping an eye on the remaining wounded sailor. His eyes were never still.

Keen was right forward, squatting on the stemhead, his bare legs and feet dangling in the water while he watched the nearest bank, his body sagging as if from a great weight.

The hull lifted and dipped as the first inshore swell rolled into the inlet. Some of the men croaked with alarm, but most merely stared listlessly in front of them, beyond caring.

Bolitho said, "We will turn to larboard when we get into open water. It will make our meeting with *Undine*'s boats all the quicker."

Soames glanced at him. "Could be hours before they come. It'll be like a damned oven today, I'm thinking."

Bolitho groped for his watch and winced as his fingers touched the bruise. When he lifted the watch from his pocket he stared at it for several seconds, seeing where the ball had lanced from it, smashing both shield and mechanism to fragments, but saving him from injury. But for it, he would probably be dying now, or at best a prisoner aboard the brigantine.

Soames said quietly, "Made short work of that, sir."

Bolitho nodded. He could remember exactly when his mother had given it to him. He had just been commissioned lieutenant. The watch had meant a lot to him, partly because it reminded him of her, of her gentleness and forbearance over losing her family to the sea.

The boat tilted, and several voices shouted in protest, and he saw Keen struggling back into the hull, his face shocked as he yelled, "Ahead, sir! Larboard bow!"

Bolitho stood up, one hand on Allday's shoulder as he stared at the two low shapes which were emerging around the last spit of land. They were moving quite fast, the long paddles plunging and rising in perfect unison as they headed purposefully into the inlet.

Fowlar said harshly, "War canoes. I seen plenty of 'em in my time. There'll be more close by, if I'm not mistaken." He dragged out his pistol and fumbled with a powder horn.

Soames slitted his eyes to watch the two low canoes, his face like a mask.

"God's teeth, there must be thirty men in each of 'em!"

One of the seamen shouted wildly, "It ain't fair! We got no reason to fear 'em, lads! We ain't no slavers!"

"Silence, that man!" Fowlar cocked the pistol and rested it on his forearm. "To them we're all the bloody same, so hold your noise!"

Bolitho said, "Speed the stroke. They may let us pass."

Allday kept his eyes on the oars. "If you say so, Captain."

Another man called, "Astern, sir! I can see the brigantine's tops'ls!"

Bolitho turned carefully to avoid unsettling the oarsmen. The man had not been mistaken. Far astern, and moving at a snail's pace above some low trees, was a limp square of sail. The slaver must have taken stock of his position and got under way before dawn. The lifeless canvas told Bolitho that the ship was being warped downstream with the aid of her boats. But once in open water she would be free and away. He glanced again at the advancing canoes. Whereas he and his men would stay here and die. If they were lucky.

Soames asked, "What can we do, sir? We can't outpace those canoes, and they'll not let us get near enough to grapple." He was fidgeting with his sword-hilt, showing anxiety for the first time.

Bolitho called, "Check the powder and shot."

There would not be much left. What with the confused battle ashore and his own boarding party leaving their weapons behind, he could hope for very little.

Fowlar reported, "Bare enough for one shot per man, sir."

"Very well. Send the two best marksmen aft. Give them all the powder you have." To Soames he added softly, "We might hold them off until our own boats come for us."

The canoes had stopped, their paddles glinting as they backed at the water, holding the slim hulls motionless like a pair of pike.

Bolitho wished he had a telescope, but that too lay somewhere in the jungle. He could see the natives clearly enough, their skins very black, their bodies angled to the paddles in readiness to move at a second's notice. In the stern of each hull was a tall man wearing a bright head-dress, his body hidden by an oval shield. He thought of the slaves in the clearing. The girl who had been killed on the brigantine's deck. These silent watchers would show no mercy for anyone. He saw the spears glinting in the growing sunlight. Only blood would satisfy them.

Nearer and nearer, until less than half a cable separated them from the poised canoes. Bolitho looked at the two muskets in the sternsheets. Fowlar had one, and a scar-faced seaman held the other. Between them the pile of powder and shot seemed even smaller now.

"Bear to starboard, Allday." He was surprised how unemotional he sounded. "They will have to move soon."

As the longboat swung heavily towards the centre of the opening both canoes came alive, the paddles darting into the water at a great pace, the air suddenly filled with the beat of a drum and the animal cry of a single warrior in the prow of the leading craft.

Bolitho felt the boat thrusting ahead beneath his feet, saw the sweat on the oarsmen's faces, the eyes which turned to watch the oncoming canoes widening with fear.

He shouted, "Take care! Keep the stroke! Eyes in the boat!"

Something hit the water alongside and threw spray over his leg. It must have been a heavy stone, for immediately a whole volley of them rained down on the heads and backs of the struggling seamen, knocking some of them unconscious. The stroke was failing, and one oar had drifted away as still more jagged stones plunged amongst them.

Bolitho said, "Open fire!"

Fowlar squeezed his trigger, and cursed as the ball went astray.

The other musket banged out, and one of the natives screamed and pitched from his canoe.

Soames yelled, "Keep baling!"

He fired his pistol abeam, and swore with satisfaction as another black figure plunged into the water.

Both canoes were swinging round in a wide arc to follow astern, one on either quarter. They were cut off now from each side of the inlet, and ahead the sea was opening up to greet them, mocking them with its emptiness.

Fowlar fired again, and had better luck, bringing down a plumed figure who was apparently beating out the time for the paddles.

The seamen were all so busy at the oars, or peering fearfully astern, that hardly any of them saw the real threat until it was almost too late.

Bolitho yelled, "Get forrard, Mr. Fowlar! Fire when you can!"

He stared fixedly at the canoes which had suddenly swept around the green hump of land, spreading out like a fan as they surged towards him. A dozen at least, all filled with whooping, screaming savages. The first shot made them falter, but only for minutes. Then they came on again, the canoes cutting through the inshore swell like sword-blades.

Some of the seamen were whimpering and pulling haphazardly at their oars, others tried to stand up, while a few began to gather fallen stones to defend themselves.

Fowlar yelled, "That is my last ball, sir!" He cursed as a heavy stone, hurled at extreme range by a sling, glanced off the gunwale and cut open the back of his hand.

The leading canoe was drawing very near, the din of chanting and the drum almost deafening.

Bolitho drew his sword and shouted, "Ready, lads!" He looked at his cowering men. "Close quarters!"

But it was not to be. Instead, another volley of stones clattered over the boat, striking one seaman so badly that he fell overboard.

The man with the musket fired and brought down two savages with one shot. The canoe swung away, some of the paddles being dropped so that the floundering seaman could be hauled up into their midst.

Bolitho watched, sickened, as they dragged the man to his feet, pinioning his arms and holding him so that he faced the slow-moving longboat. He could see the blood on his neck where the stone had hit him, imagine his screams which were drowned by the yelling figures who held him. One, with a high head-dress, waved a knife above his head, back and forth, back and forth, so that the captured seaman followed it with his eyes as if watching a snake, his mouth like a black hole as he continued to scream.

The knife came down very slowly, the blood shining in the sunlight and making several of the seamen retch and groan with horror.

Allday said tightly, "Jesus Christ, they're skinning him."

Bolitho seized the man's shoulder, feeling him jump as if he was dying with the man in the canoe.

"Do what you can." He had to force the words out.

When he looked astern again he saw that the man was still alive, writhing like a soul in hell as the knife did its work.

The musket bucked against the sailor's shoulder, and Bolitho turned away, fighting back the nausea.

Soames said thickly, "The only way, sir. I'd not let a dog suffer like that."

Fowlar shouted, "Brigantine's away, sir!"

The slaver had slipped into deeper water almost without any-one noticing her. Boats hoisted inboard, and already her foresail set and drawing well as she rode clear of the protecting land.

The canoes were forming into two arrowheads again, the drums getting wilder as they manoeuvred for the final attack.

Bolitho held his sword towards the hazy horizon. "Pull, lads! We'll not go under without a fight!"

It was an empty speech, but it was better than merely

standing and watching them overwhelmed, tortured and killed without lifting a finger.

Allday whispered, "Here they come." He held the tiller between his legs and drew his cutlass. "Keep close, Captain. We'll show the bastards."

Bolitho looked at him. They were outnumbered ten to one, and his men were already fit to drop, the fight gone out of them.

He said simply, "We will, Allday." He touched his thick forearm. "And thank you."

A great yell made him turn, and as the boat swayed dangerously to the sudden shift of bodies he saw the crisp topsails and jib, the figurehead shining in the milky glare like pure gold, as *Undine* tacked around the headland, her starboard battery run out in a line of black teeth.

Soames bellowed, "Sit down! You'll have us in the sea otherwise!"

Allday said hoarsely, "Now, there is a *sight*, Captain."

Fowlar called, "She's going about, sir! In God's name, she's a'comin' through the shoals!"

Bolitho could barely breathe as he watched *Undine's* graceful outline shortening, her sails in momentary disarray until the yards had been trimmed again. If she struck now she would share *Nervion's* fate, and worse, when the survivors were taken by the war canoes.

But she showed no hesitation, and he could see the blood-red coats of the marines along the quarterdeck nettings, and even imagined he could discern Herrick and Mudge beside the wheel as the frigate heeled heavily to the wind, her gunports almost awash.

Keen was yelling, "*Huzza! Huzza*, lads!" He was cheering and weeping, waving his shirt above his head, the closeness of danger forgotten.

The brigantine had already changed tack, clawing clear of a dark smudge below the surface while she set more sail to carry her to the south.

Fowlar said with disbelief, "She's goin' after the slaver! They must be mad!"

Bolitho did not speak, just watching his ship was enough. It told him what Herrick was thinking and doing, as if he had shouted it aloud. Herrick knew he could not engage all the canoes in time to save Bolitho and his small party. He was going to stop the brigantine and so distract the war canoes in the only way he knew.

As the realisation came to him, *Undine* opened fire. It was a slow, carefully-aimed broadside, the guns belching smoke and flame at regulated intervals while the frigate swept further and further amongst the hidden shoals.

Someone gave a cracked cheer as the brigantine's foretopmast shuddered and then curtsied down into the sea alongside in a tangle of rigging and canvas. The effect was immediate, and within seconds she was paying off to the wind, her hull broadside on as another volley crashed and ricocheted all around her. One twelve-pound ball struck the sea near her quarter and shattered into fragments, so near was the shoal to the surface.

"She's struck!"

Everyone was yelling and screaming like a madman, hugging each other and sobbing with disbelief. Bolitho dragged his gaze from the brigantine which had slewed round either on a shoal or a sandspit, her canvas in pandemonium while she continued to drive ashore.

He held his breath as *Undine* shortened sail, the tiny figures on her yards like ants, her copper glinting brightly as she thrust round again on the opposite tack. Another half a cable and she would have been aground.

Allday shouted, "She's hove-to, Captain, an' there's a boat be-ing dropped!"

Bolitho nodded, unable to answer.

The canoes were paddling furiously towards the helpless brig-antine, and more canoes had appeared around the headland, the latter very careful to stay clear of *Undine's* bared guns. The frigate's big launch was speeding across the choppy water, and when one of the canoes turned towards it the crash of its swivel gun was enough to make the yelling natives join their companions elsewhere.

Davy stood in the sternsheets, very erect and proper. Even his oarsmen seemed totally unreal against the tattered, cheering remnants of Bolitho's landing party.

The captured longboat was already sinking, more planks having been stove open by stones, and Bolitho doubted if they could have lasted another half-hour even without the attacking canoes.

As the launch grappled alongside, and hands dragged the gasping survivors to safety, he turned to watch the listing brigantine. Even at this distance it was possible to hear the muskets, the baying chorus from the canoes as they surrounded her for the final attack. Revenge or justice, the slaver's end would be terrible indeed.

Davy took his wrist and helped him into the other boat.

"Good to see you again, sir." He looked at Soames and grinned. "And you, of course."

Bolitho sat down and felt his limbs beginning to quiver uncontrollably. He kept his eyes on the ship as she grew and towered above him, very conscious of his own feelings for her, and those who had risked their lives for him.

Herrick was waiting to greet him, his anxiety matched only by his relief as he took Bolitho's hands and said, "Thank God you're safe!"

Bolitho fought for time, looking at the loosely flapping sails, the watching marines, the gun crews who had paused in their swabbing to look at him and grin. Herrick had taken a terrible chance. It had been sheer lunacy. And he could tell from Mudge's expression, beaming and nodding by the compass, that his was an equal share.

But there was something new here, which had been lacking before. He tried to name it.

Herrick was saying, "We heard the shooting, sir, and guessed you might be in trouble. Instead of sending boats, we came in strength, so to speak." He let his glance move along the busy figures at the guns and waiting by the braces. "They did well. They were glad to be here."

Bolitho nodded, understanding. *Pride.* That was it. To find it had cost them dear, and it could have gone much worse.

He said, "Get the ship under way, if you please. Let us stand away from this damnable coast." He paused, searching for the words. "And, Thomas, if you ever doubt your ability to command again, I will remind you of today. You handled her to perfection."

Herrick looked at Mudge and almost winked. "We have a good captain, sir, and are beginning to feel the benefit of his drills and exercises."

Bolitho turned aft, suddenly spent. "I shall not forget."

Then he walked to the cabin hatch with Allday at his heels.

Mudge ambled to Herrick's side. "A near thing, Mr. 'Errick. If you 'adn't given the order, I don't know if I'd 'ave 'ad the will to persist through them shoals."

Herrick looked at him, remembering Bolitho's expression, the guard no longer hiding his thoughts.

"Well, Mr. Mudge, I reckon it was well worth it."

He stared at the misty shore line and at a growing plume of smoke. The brigantine must have caught fire, he thought. For a while longer he held on to the picture of the battered, listing boat, with Bolitho upright in the sternsheets, that old tarnished sword in his hand. If he had not disobeyed Bolitho's order to put the ship's safety before all else, he would indeed be in command now, and Bolitho back there, dying in agony.

"Get the hands to the braces!" He walked to the rail with his speaking trumpet. "And God bless lady luck!"

Below the cabin hatch, Bolitho heard Herrick laugh, and then the clatter of blocks as the seamen went to their stations for getting under way again.

Allday asked quietly, "Can I fetch you some wine, Captain? Or something a mite more powerful?"

Bolitho leaned against the mizzen mast trunk and felt it vibrating urgently to the pressure of wind and canvas high overhead.

"D'you know, Allday, I think that after all the trouble we went through to get it, I would like a glass of fresh water."

8

*M*ADRAS

BOLITHO stood very still by the quarterdeck rail and watched the vast spread of land which reached away on either bow. In the morning sunlight the countless white buildings seemed to rise tier upon tier, the uneven skyline decorated at irregular intervals by tall minarets and plump golden domes. It was breathtaking, and he could tell from the quiet way the seamen were moving around the decks that they were equally impressed.

He turned and looked at Herrick. Very tanned, and strangely unreachable in his best uniform.

"We did it."

Bolitho raised his telescope and watched some high-prowed dhows scudding abeam, their gaunt sails like wings. Even they were part of the magic.

Mudge said, "Ease off a point." Then he, too, fell silent as the wheel squeaked over.

Perhaps he was satisfied, and so he should be, Bolitho thought. Madras, the name itself was like one great milestone for what they had achieved together. Three months and two days after weighing anchor at Spithead. Back there, Bolitho had seen disbelief on Mudge's heavy face when he had suggested they might make the voyage in one hundred days.

Herrick said quietly, "Aye, sir. Since we quit the African coast lady luck came with us for certain." He grinned broadly.

"You and your lady luck." But he smiled all the same.

It had seemed much as Herrick had described. Within a few days of leaving the land, the dead and dying far astern, the wind had risen from the south-west, the fringe of the monsoon which on this occasion had acted as a friend. Day after day, with all sail set, *Undine* had bounded along, freely, recklessly, her forecastle never clear of bursting spray, while dolphins and other strange fish had stayed close in company. It was just as if that terrible confrontation with the war canoes, seeing the seaman being flayed alive, and all else had been one last great challenge.

He glanced up at the gently flapping topsails and forward to the solitary jib, the power barely enough now to carry them into the wide anchorage and between that impressive spread of shipping.

Madras, the most important British station on the south-east coast of another continent. A stepping-stone to advancement elsewhere, to trade and further discovery. Even the names were like fresh challenges. Siam and Malacca, south-east to Java, and beyond to a million unknown islands.

He saw a towering merchantman spreading more sail as she tacked heavily into a pale bank of sea-haze. With her chequered gunports and impeccable sail drill she could have been a man-of-war. But she was one of the East India Company's ships, and three months back Bolitho would have given his right arm for just a few of her seamen. Well trained and disciplined, they were far superior to the Navy's companies in many respects. The Company could and did afford better pay and conditions for its people, while the Navy still had to depend on what it could get by other means, and in time of war that usually meant relying on the pressgangs.

Bolitho had often considered the unfairness of the system. One day, perhaps in his own life, he hoped to see the change come. When the Navy could offer the same fair inducements.

The big Indiaman's flag dipped from her peak, and Bolitho heard Keen calling to his signalling party to return the salute.

Then he looked again at his own company, knowing he would not willingly change them now, merely because it would make life easier. Browned by the sun, toughened by hard work and regular drills with sails and weapons, they were a far cry from that motley assortment at Spithead.

He glanced towards the Indiaman and smiled. Perfect or not, she had had to dip her flag to a King's ship. His *Undine.*

Mudge blew his nose and called, "'Bout five minutes now, sir."

Bolitho raised his hand and saw the master's mate with the anchor party acknowledge. It was Fowlar. A man who had proved his worth, and his loyalty. Who had already earned promotion whenever an opportunity came.

Captain Bellairs was inspecting his marine drummers, and looking even more like a toy soldier in the blazing sunlight.

Davy and Soames were on the gun deck with their separate divisions, and the ship had never looked better.

He heard voices behind him and turned to see Don Puigserver and Raymond speaking together by the taffrail. Like him, they were probably eager to discover what awaited them here in Madras. Puigserver was surprisingly elegant. His clothing consisted of a lieutenant's dress-coat which had been taken apart and refashioned by Mrs. Raymond's maid, aided willingly by Jonas Tait, *Undine*'s sailmaker. Tait had one eye, but was very skilful, even if he was the most villainous looking man aboard. The maid seemed to find him fascinating.

"Well, Captain, you must be pleased with yourself today?"

Mrs. Raymond stepped from the cabin hatch and crossed to his side. She walked easily, so used had she become to *Undine*'s motions and behaviour in every sort of sea. She, too, had altered. Still aloof for much of the time, yet lacking the old veil of disinterest in shipboard life which had first irritated Bolitho. Her large stock of personal delicacies which had come aboard at Santa Cruz had long been consumed, and yet she had taken to the cabin's simple fare with little complaint.

"I am, ma'am." He pointed towards the bows. "You will soon be able to shed the smells and sounds of a small frigate. I have no doubt that an English lady reigns like a queen out here."

"Perhaps." She turned her head as if to watch her husband. "I hope to see you when you come ashore. Here, after all, you are king?" She laughed lightly. "In many ways I am sorry to leave the ship."

Bolitho watched her thoughtfully. He remembered when he had arrived aboard after the running battle with the canoes. Spent, almost asleep on his feet as weariness replaced the will to fight, and memory pushed aside his immediate relief at his own survival. She had guided him to a chair, rapping out orders to her maid, to a startled Noddall, and even to Allday as she had taken charge. She had told someone to fetch the surgeon, but when Bolitho had said harshly, "I'm not hurt! The ball hit my damned watch!" she had thrown back her head and laughed. The unexpected reaction had angered him, then as she had gripped his hand, quite unable to stop her laughter, he had found himself joining in. Perhaps that, more than anything else, had steadied him, had released all the anxiety he had been forced to conceal until that moment.

Some of it must have shown on his face as he remembered, for she said softly, "Can I share them?"

"My thoughts?" He smiled awkwardly. "I was thinking of something. My watch."

He saw her lip begin to tremble again, and wondered why he had not noticed the fine shape of her chin and throat. Until now. When it was too late. He felt himself flushing. For what?

She nodded. "It was cruel to laugh so. But you looked so angry, when anyone but you would have been grateful."

She turned her face away as Herrick called, "Ready, sir!"

"Carry on, Mr. Herrick."

"Aye, sir." But his eyes were on the woman. Then he hurried to the rail yelling, "Man the lee braces! Hands wear ship!"

Undine swung easily into the wind, her anchor splashing down into water so blue it looked like satin.

Puigserver pointed at a small procession of boats which were already moving towards the ship and said, "A time for ceremony, *Capitan*. Poor Rojart would have enjoyed this part."

He was a different man now. Steely eyed, impatient to move again. To get his plans into order.

Behind him, Raymond was watching the oncoming boats with a look of apprehension rather than excitement on his face.

With the anchor down, and all sails neatly furled, *Undine*'s decks were bustling with life as her company prepared to take on stores, visitors, or whatever they were ordered to do. Above all, to be ready to sail again within hours, should it be required.

Bolitho knew he would be needed for a dozen things at once. Even now he could see the purser hovering to catch his eye, and Mudge, waiting to suggest or ask something.

He said, "Perhaps I will see you on land, Mrs. Raymond." The others were listening, and he could feel their glances, their interest. "It has not been an easy passage for you, and I would wish to thank you for your, er," he faltered, seeing her lip quiver very slightly, "forbearance."

Equally gravely she replied, "And may I thank you in turn, Captain, for your companionship."

Bolitho made to bow to her, but she held up her hand and said, "Until the next time, Captain."

He took her hand and touched the back of it with his lips. He felt her fingers give his just the merest squeeze, and when he glanced at her face he knew it was no accident.

Then it was all over as he was caught up in the turmoil of receiving visitors from the governor and handing his despatches to the officer of the guardboat.

As a brightly canopied launch pulled clear of *Undine*'s black shadow he saw his passengers looking astern towards him, growing smaller with each sweep of the oars.

Herrick said cheerfully, "I expect you'll be glad to have the cabin to yourself, sir. You've waited long enough."

"Yes, Thomas. Indeed I will."

"Now, sir, concerning extra hands . . ."

Herrick had seen the lie in Bolitho's grey eyes, and decided it was prudent to change the subject immediately.

It was late afternoon when Bolitho received a summons to report in person to the governor. He had begun to think that his part of the mission had been cancelled, or that in Madras his status had shrunk so much he would merely stay at arm's length and do as he was bid whenever it might suit the proper authority.

Accompanied by Herrick and Midshipman Keen, he was carried ashore in *Undine*'s gig, despite a haughty equerry's insistence that a local boat would be more fitting and comfortable.

An open carriage was waiting to convey them to the governor's residence, and for the whole of the short journey they barely exchanged a word. The bright colours, the surrounding press of chattering people, the whole strangeness of the town took their complete attention. Bolitho found the people very interesting indeed. How different their skins were, ranging from pale brown, no darker than young Keen's tan, to those who were as black as the warriors he had seen in Africa. Turbans and flowing robes, cattle and dejected goats, all milled across the winding streets, in and around the curtained shops and bazaars in an unending panorama of noise and movement.

The governor's residence was more like a fort than a house, with slits in the walls for weapons, and well guarded by Indian troops. The latter were most impressive. Turbaned and bearded, yet they wore the familiar red coat of British infantry set off with baggy blue pantaloons and high white gaiters.

Herrick gestured to the flag which drooped, barely moving, from a high staff and murmured, "That, at least, is familiar."

Once through the gates and into the cool shadows of the house it was another world again. The noise of the streets was sealed off as if by a great door, and all around was an air of watchful elegance. Fine rugs and heavy brass ornaments, bare-armed servants who moved noiselessly like ghosts, and tiled passageways which led away in every direction as in a maze.

The equerry said smoothly, "The governor will see you at once, Captain." He eyed the others without enthusiasm. "Alone."

Bolitho looked at Herrick. "Mr. Keen will remain here in case I need to pass a message to the ship. You can make good use of your time as you will." He turned to hide his face from the equerry. "Don't forget to keep an eye open for extra hands."

Herrick grinned, relieved perhaps at being spared yet another set of questions and answers. The visitors to the ship had kept him on his feet since the anchor had been let go. The sight of an English frigate seemed to attract far more interest than the comings and goings of merchantmen. A link with home. Some word or hint of what these people had left behind in their search for empire.

He said, "Good luck, sir. This is a far cry from Rochester!"

The equerry watched him leave and then glanced at Keen. To Bolitho he said, "I'll send the young gentleman to the troops' quarters if you wish."

Bolitho smiled. "I am sure he will be happier here."

Keen met the man's stare calmly and replied, "Indeed I will, sir." He could not resist adding, "My father will be glad to learn of your hospitality when next I write."

Bolitho turned away. "His father owns quite a large portion of your trading agency here."

The equerry said no more, but led the way down the grandest of the passages. He opened some double doors and announced with as much dignity as he still retained, "Captain Richard Bolitho of His Britannic Majesty's Ship *Undine*."

Bolitho already knew the governor's name, but little else about him. Sir Montagu Strang was almost hidden behind a great desk, the sides of which appeared to be made of ebony, with feet fashioned of massive silver claws. He was a frail, grey-haired man, with a pallid complexion which told its own story of some past fever. Hooded eyes, a thin, unsmiling mouth, he was studying Bolitho's approach along a strip of blue carpet as a hunter might examine a possible victim.

"Welcome, Bolitho." The thin mouth turned upwards a fraction, as if it hurt him to make the effort.

It was then and only then Bolitho realised that Strang's attitude was not one of disdain, for as he moved around the desk he saw that the governor had been standing to receive him, and not in a chair as he had first thought.

"Thank you, sir."

Bolitho tried not to show surprise, or worse, pity. Down to his waist Sir Montagu was a normal if slight figure. Beyond that his legs were tiny, those of a dwarf, and his neat hands hung seemingly to his knees.

Strang continued in the same crisp tone, "Please select a chair. I have a few things to say before we join the *others*." He let his gaze move over him before adding, "I have read your report, and those of certain onlookers. You did well, and have made a fast passage. Your action in trying to save *Nervion*'s people, your attack on the slave-ship, if only partly successful, are the two better pieces of news today."

Bolitho sat down on the edge of a throne-like chair and then realised for the first time that the great overhead fan was being worked by a tiny Indian who was squatting in a far corner, apparently asleep, his bare foot jerking a cord to keep it in regular motion.

Strang returned to his desk and sat down. Bolitho guessed he always behaved in this manner with a new visitor. To get it over with and avoid embarrassment. He had heard that Strang had spent many years in India, as a representative of government, as an adviser on trade and native affairs. A very important man. No wonder he had chosen power out here rather than suffer the constant humiliation of gaping eyes in London.

He said calmly, "Now, Bolitho, to business. I have been waiting too long for despatches, wondering if my original suggestions
have been accepted. *Nervion*'s loss was a serious blow, but your
apparent determination to continue with the voyage without further advice cancels it out in some ways. You have Don
Puigserver's admiration, it seems, although whether that is good
or bad remains to be seen." His hooded eyes flashed angrily. "The
Spaniards lost great opportunities in Teluk Pendang. As a race
they are stealers rather than builders. The sword and the crucifix
are about the most they can offer."

Bolitho gripped his hands together and tried not to let his
mind drift on Strang's words. So the mission was still in being.
Undine would be going to Teluk Pendang.

Strang said sharply, "I can see that you are ahead of me,
Bolitho! Allow me to fill in a few small chinks, eh?" Then he
smiled. "But it is refreshing to find one still able to *think* at all."

Beyond the cool room Bolitho heard the distant call of a bugle.
It sounded strangely sad.

Strang saw his expression and said, "We were hard put during the war. Hyder Ali, the ruler of Mysore, and one with a real
hatred for us, had plenty of support from the French. But for the
Navy, I fear the Fleur de Lys and not the Union Flag would fly
above here today." He continued in an almost matter-of-fact
tone. "But that is not your concern. The sooner we can install a
British governor in Pendang Bay the better I will be pleased.
Since the end of the war, the Spanish garrison there, which com-
prised mainly of native soldiers, has been in a state of confusion.
Fever and some sort of mutiny made their work impossible. I am
hardly surprised that the King of Spain is so willing to rid himself of the station." His voice hardened.

"However, under our protection it will prosper. The local native ruler is harmless enough. He must be, to allow the Spanish
garrison to be alive. But further to the west is a vast area, almost
uncharted, and plundered by another, less charitable *prince*,

Muljadi. If we are to extend our gains, he must be contained, is that understood?"

"I think, so, sir." Bolitho frowned. "Yours is a great responsibility."

"Quite. The wind always shakes the top of the tree, Bolitho."

"I am not certain what I will be required to do, sir. I would have thought a fresh garrison of soldiers would be a better force than mine."

"I know otherwise." His voice was scathing as he added "Native troops for the most part, with British officers whose minds have become numbed by heat and other, er, local attractions. I must have mobility. Your ship, in fact. The French, as you are now aware, are very interested. They have a frigate somewhere in those waters, and that, too, you know. Which is why I cannot afford open conflict. If we are to succeed, we must be in the right."

"And if this Muljadi opposes us, or those showing friendship, sir?"

Strang walked to a wall tapestry and touched it lightly. "You will crush him." He swung round with surprising agility. "In the King's name."

He picked up a small bell and shook it impatiently. "I am arranging a transport for the troops, and all the stores required. The East India Company will provide a suitable vessel in due course. The rest will be up to you. Under the new governor's hand, that is. Rear Admiral Beves Conway has made many of the arrangements." He darted a quick glance at him. "You know him then?"

"Why, yes, sir." Bolitho's mind grappled with a dozen memories at once. "He commanded the *Gorgon*, seventy-four. My second ship." He smiled, despite Strang's set features. "I was sixteen."

"It will be an interesting reunion, no doubt." Strang glared at the open door where a servant stood watching him anxiously.

"Take the captain to the chamber. And next time I ring this bell I want you here *at once!*"

As Bolitho made to leave, Strang added, "You saw a Company ship leaving harbour as you entered today?"

"Yes, sir."

"Homeward bound. A rich cargo for England." He smiled gently. "No, I am not full of regrets or pining for the homeland, which in any case is Scotland. I merely wished you to know that the vessel's crew had a long night's celebration, too much to drink, a way sailors have." He turned his back. "Some twenty of her hands were too drunk to return on board. They are in the care of my officers. They have enough to do without the trouble of drunken oafs who had they been in a naval vessel, would no doubt have been flogged for desertion. I do not wish to know about it further, but should your lieutenants care to take over the *responsibility*, I am certain you could make better use of some extra men."

Bolitho smiled. "Thank you, sir."

"I will join you shortly. Now go and take wine with my staff."

Bolitho found Keen in the entrance hall, and passed the news to him without delay.

The midshipman's eyes widened and he said, "I'll tell Mr. Davy, at once, sir. Though I doubt if 'John Company' will thank you for taking hands from an Indiaman." He chuckled. "Nor will they, sir!"

Bolitho hurried along the passage where he had seen the servant waiting for him, his mind returning to Strang's other news. Beves Conway, then the captain of a two-decker, had always been something of a hero to him. Cold and remote in many ways, but a superb seaman, and not one given to undue harshness, even with his midshipmen.

He had left the *Gorgon* before Bolitho, having held the command for several years. After that he had disappeared completely, which was unusual in the Navy. Faces, like ships, came and went repeatedly, like the sea and wind which governed their lives. With Conway in control of things there would be little tolerance for failure, he thought.

He was ushered into the vaulted room described as the chamber, and was surprised to find it filled with a variety of people, including a number of women.

He saw Puigserver, still dressed in his makeshift clothes, and Raymond in close conversation with a heavy-jowled major. Raymond left his companion immediately, and with barely a nod of recognition, guided Bolitho around the chamber, making introductions, hardly able to hide his impatience if someone asked about England, or what the latest fashion was at home. "Home" was somewhat vague, but for the most part seemed to be London.

Raymond paused while Bolitho took a glass of wine from a bowing servant.

"Like a lot of damned farmers!" He smiled at a lady as she passed, but added savagely, "But they live well enough here!"

Bolitho watched him curiously. Raymond had tried to show his contempt, but had sounded only envious.

Then he heard a familiar voice, and when he turned observed Mrs. Raymond talking with someone he had not so far met.

She saw him immediately and called, "Come and join us!" Her smile faded slightly as she noticed her husband. "We have been talking about local customs."

Raymond said abruptly, "Rear Admiral Conway, the new governor of Teluk Pendang."

Conway had been standing with his back to Bolitho. He was dressed in a dull bottle-green coat, his shoulders sloping badly so that he seemed to be leaning forward. He turned to face Bolitho, his eyes moving rapidly, noting all that they saw.

Bolitho said, "It is good to see you again, sir."

He did not know how to continue. If he had met Conway in Plymouth or anywhere else he would have walked past him. Could anyone change so much in twelve years? He looked thin and very intense, with two deep lines running from his hooked nose to his jaw, so that the mouth appeared to be suspended between them. Only the eyes were familiar. Cool, calculating.

Conway held out his hand. "Richard Bolitho, eh." The handshake, like his tone, was dry. "And a post-captain, no less. Well, well."

Bolitho tried to relax. It was like seeing someone looking through a mask. A rear admiral, but seniority apart, he was only one rank higher than himself. And no title, no proud knighthood to mark his climb to success.

He said quietly, "I have been very fortunate, sir."

Mrs. Raymond touched Conway's sleeve with her fan. "He is too modest by far. I have had good opportunity to watch the captain at his duties, and listen to his past exploits."

Conway's glance darted between them. "Did he relate them *well*, ma'am?"

"I heard them from others." Her eyes regarded him coldly. "To drag self-praise from the captain is to try and open an oyster with a feather!"

Conway picked a thread from his waistcoat. "I am relieved to hear it."

Raymond said, "It seems I am to accompany you to the new station, sir." He did not hide his haste to distract Conway's attention from his wife's sudden anger.

"That is so." Conway looked at Bolitho. "The captain will tell you I am not one to tolerate mistakes. I require everyone connected with the handover of governorship within reach." He glanced at the chattering people around him. "Not here, living in spoiled unreality."

Behind his shoulder Mrs. Raymond looked at Bolitho and pouted.

Conway said, "I must go and speak to the military." He bobbed his head. "If you will excuse me, ma'am."

Raymond waited just a few seconds, then exploded. "Do you *have* to make a scene, Viola? In God's name Conway could be important to me. To us!"

She looked at Bolitho. "He is a pompous . . . ," she sought for a word, ". . . bore!" To her husband she added, "And it makes me sick the way you grovel to his kind. You always seem to throw yourself after the failures."

Raymond stared at her. "He is the new governor! What are you suggesting?"

She flashed a smile to someone across the room. "You do not know anything. He is a failure. You have only to look at him!"

Strangely enough, Raymond appeared relieved. "Is that all? I thought you had heard something." He stared after Conway. "I had better go to him. Sir Montagu Strang has instructed me to give all my experience to aid him."

She held her fan across her lips and whispered, "That should take very little time." She slipped one hand through Bolitho's arm. "And now, Captain, you can escort me, if you will."

Bolitho was still thinking of that rapid exchange between them. Most of all of Conway, and what he had become.

She squeezed his arm. "I am waiting."

"An honour." He smiled at her impatience. "And thank you for your defence just now." He shook his head. "Although I cannot imagine what has happened to Conway."

Her fingers dug into his arm. "One day, some stupid officer will say that about you." She tossed her head. "Anyway, it was true. The pompous old bore!"

Bolitho saw the heavy-jowled major watching him and then turning to murmur to a fellow soldier.

"There will be talk, ma'am, if we walk about like this."

"Good." She looked at him calmly. "Do you care?"

"Well, no."

She nodded. "And my name is Viola. Please use it in the future."

True to his word, Sir Montagu Strang lost no time in putting his long-standing plan into operation. Two days after *Undine*'s arrival at Madras the *Bedford*, a heavy transport wearing the flag of the East India Company, dropped anchor nearby and began to take in stores and equipment for the new station.

After his first visit to the governor's residence, Bolitho had had no time for relaxation. So little was known of Teluk Pendang, except by those who had been engaged with local trade there, that it was some while before he was satisfied with his calculations. Mudge, who knew the waters well, gave his cautious approval, and when Bolitho had paid a visit to the *Bedford*'s captain, he had been quick to praise not merely his work, but also his readiness to consult an officer of the Company.

"Not like a King's officer!" He had been greatly amused. "Most of 'em would rather drive aground than enquire from the likes of us!" Bolitho wondered what his attitude might have been had he known about the twenty extra seamen he had poached from the all-powerful E.I.C.

Before he had left the transport he had caught his first sight of the troops who were being sent to replace the Spanish garrison. They looked as if they intended to make their new station a permanent home, for they were accompanied by as many wives and children, varied livestock, and a great mass of pots and pans, which made him wonder where they could all be stowed. *Bedford*'s captain was unimpressed, so he guessed it was the normal way of doing things out here.

He was in his cabin writing his readiness report when Herrick arrived to announce that a launch was approaching. Its only passenger was Rear Admiral Beves Conway.

Bolitho hurried on deck, half wondering why Conway had stayed away from him since *Undine*'s arrival, and partly concerned at the lack of notice.

To his surprise he saw that Conway was still dressed in his green coat, devoid of decorations or sword. He was not even wearing his hat as he stepped through the entry port and bowed curtly to Bellairs's guard of honour and to the quarterdeck at large.

"Taut ship, Bolitho."

The eyes flitted this way and that, and Bolitho tried to dispel his sudden resentment at Conway's attitude. Perhaps he had always been like this, even in the *Gorgon* when Bolitho had watched his regular appearances on the quarterdeck with something like awe.

"Dismiss the side party. This is in informal visit."

Conway walked to a six-pounder and ran his hand across the breech. Then he looked aloft where some hands were blacking down the rigging, making it shine like ebony.

He nodded. "She looks well enough."

He turned his attention to the *Bedford,* at the booms which swayed back and forth above the boats and lighters moored around her.

Bolitho was able to watch him less cautiously, and saw the thinness of his hair, which was completely grey.

Without turning Conway asked, "What is your estimated time of arrival at our destination?"

"Given fair winds, sir, and in accordance with all I have discovered, I hope to make a landfall in eighteen days. Three weeks at the most. I have already been told that I am to sail ahead of the transport."

"My idea." Conway turned and looked at him searchingly. "No sense in dragging our feet with that damned hulk."

"Then you will be coming in *Undine,* sir?"

"Disappointed?" Conway shrugged. "Of course I shall. I have made arrangements for my baggage to be sent out this afternoon."

Bolitho's picture of his cabin faded. He had thought of it often since arriving at Madras. Somewhere he could examine his mistakes and assemble his advantages. Puigserver was one thing. Conway another entirely. It would be like being Conway's junior officer again.

He said, "I will inform my first lieutenant at once, sir."

"Herrick?" He sounded indifferent. "No need!"

Bolitho stared at him. That was not like Conway.

He tried again. "At least we shall have a rear admiral's flag at the mizzen when we reach Teluk Pendang, sir."

The effect was startling. Conway spun round, his features working with sudden anger.

"Was that slur intended? Does it give you some twisted pleasure to sneer? If so, I will damn soon break you for your insolence!"

Bolitho kept his voice calm, aware of Herrick watching nearby with obvious concern. "I am sorry, sir. I meant no disrespect!"

Conway took a deep breath. "No flag, Bolitho. I am the governor-elect of Pendang Bay, a place neither you nor most of the world has ever heard of until now." The bitterness had put a new edge to his voice. "To all intents I am out of naval service. What respect I receive at your hands will be arranged accordingly!"

Bolitho stared at him. It was suddenly all too clear. Conway had been putting off this moment, not out of haughtiness or from any sort of envy at Bolitho's steady promotion since their first meeting, but because he was a broken man.

"Then it will be done well, sir. That I can promise you." He looked away. "I have been fortunate in the Navy; in many cases I have been aided by sheer chance, or luck, as my first lieutenant would say. But I have never forgotten where I first gained the value of experience, and the patience of my own captain."

Conway fumbled with his waistcoat, apparently oblivious to the sun across his neck and shoulders.

"That was kindly said." He looked at his hands and then thrust them behind his back. "May we go below?"

In the cabin he moved about restlessly, touching the furniture, peering into corners without saying anything.

Then he looked at one of the wooden quakers and snapped, "This was done for that woman, eh?"

"Yes, sir. But I will see that they remain until you are settled in your new command." He had meant to say residence, but the word just slipped out.

Conway watched him, his thin face expressionless. Then he said, "No. Have the guns replaced. I need no bloody pampering. I want this ship ready for anything. A few missing guns might make a world of difference." He did not explain, but asked in the same abrasive tone, "That woman? Mrs. Raymond. How did she stand up to three months in a fifth-rate, eh?"

"Better than I had expected."

"Hmm." He studied Bolitho grimly, his features in shadow. "Watch yourself with her. She is three years older than you, but the gap in experience is immeasurably wider."

Bolitho said hastily, "Might I ask when sailing orders will arrive, sir?"

"Tomorrow probably, but I can tell you now. You will weigh the day after you receive your orders. No delays. Maximum haste. We will have company on the passage."

"Sir?"

Bolitho was certain that Conway's thoughts were elsewhere, even though his ideas came out in perfect order.

"Brig. Don Puigserver has chartered her for his own use. Partly my suggestion. It is too close to the war for me to take a Don as a friend."

"I see, sir."

"You don't. But no matter."

He walked to the stern windows and stared at the shoreline, at the countless tiny craft which jostled the waterfront like busy insects.

"I would like to stay aboard, Bolitho."

"Until we weigh, sir?"

Bolitho looked around the cabin. Tiny compared with the residence ashore.

"Yes." He swung away from the windows. "D'you object?"

Just for a second it was there again. The same voice which Bolitho still remembered.

"No, sir." He smiled. "I have been waiting to broach some wine I have brought from London, I—"

"London?" Conway sighed. "That cursed place. I've not set foot there for five years. A plague on it and its selfishness!"

"Perhaps it has changed since—"

"People do not change, Bolitho." He touched his breast. "Not here, inside. You, of all people, should know that. When I learned who commanded my *transport,* I knew you would be as you are. Not so merry-eyed and trusting perhaps, but you've not altered."

Bolitho stayed silent, watching the emotions on the other man's face, each one perhaps representing a memory.

"*Gorgon* seems in eternity back in time. The best moments were with her, although I did not realise it was so."

Bolitho said carefully, "Your new post will probably make you believe otherwise, sir."

"You think that?" Conway smiled, but no humour touched his eyes. "It is given to me because I will succeed. I must. There is nothing else left. When you make a slip, Bolitho, you sometimes get one final chance to redeem yourself." He pounded one hand against the other. "And I intend to succeed!"

There was a tap at the door and Allday stepped into the cabin.

"Who is this fellow?"

"My coxswain, sir." Bolitho had to smile at the incredulous look on Allday's face.

"I see."

Allday said, "Mr. Herrick's respects, and could you come on deck to receive *Bedford*'s captain."

Bolitho excused himself to Conway and followed him from the cabin.

Allday muttered, "*Fellow,* Captain? He was a trifle hard, I thought."

Bolitho grinned. "I am sure that when he knows you better he will call you by your first name!"

Allday faced him guardedly and then chuckled. "No doubt, Captain." He lowered his voice. "A message has been sent aboard." He held out an engraved card, tiny in his broad palm.

She had written across the back, *Eight o'clock. Please come.*

Bolitho stared from it to Allday's masklike face.

"Who gave you this?"

"A servant, Captain." His eyes did not even flicker. "The lady knows she can trust me."

Bolitho turned away to hide his expression. "Thank you."

Allday watched him hurry up the quarterdeck ladder and grinned. "It will do him good." He saw the marine sentry watching him and snapped, "Who are you gaping at?" He grinned again. "My good fellow?"

9

GIFT FROM A *L*ADY

ONE HOUR before the morning watch was relieved Bolitho came on deck to enjoy the most peaceful time of the day. With his shirt open to his waist he crossed to the weather side and studied the set of each individual sail before going aft to consult the compass. Madras lay twelve days astern, but the wind, which had begun so promisingly, had lulled to a gentle breeze, so that even with all sails set it was unlikely they could maintain more than four knots.

Fowlar was scribbling on the slate beside the wheel, but straightened his back as Bolitho approached.

He touched his forehead and reported, "East by south, sir. Full an' bye."

Bolitho nodded and shaded his eyes to watch the sails again. The wind, such as it was, came from the south-west, and *Undine*'s yards were braced well round, laying her over to the starboard tack. About a mile abeam the brig *Rosalind* had no difficulty in maintaining station on her heavier consort, and Bolitho found himself tempted to take a telescope and examine her more closely.

Fowlar seemed to think that he was expected to add something to his report and said, "Might pick up before nightfall, sir. Mr. Mudge seems to think the wind'll freshen when once we enter the Malacca Strait."

"Er, yes."

Bolitho tried to compose himself. From *Rosalind*'s deck *Undine* must make a beautiful sight under full canvas. But for once this gave him little consolation. He wanted to drive his ship faster to become involved with his mission. Ghosting along like this, even if idyllic for poet or artist, gave too much time for other thoughts.

He saw Davy hurrying towards him, frowning as he said, "I beg pardon for not seeing you come on deck, sir." He gestured towards the main mast "I was dealing with a complaint from a marine." He added swiftly, "Nothing important."

"You are officer of the watch, Mr. Davy. You should know by now I don't interfere in your affairs merely to excite attention." He smiled. "A fine day, is it not?"

"Yes, sir."

Davy followed his gaze over the nettings. The sea was very blue, and apart from the low-hulled brig there was not a speck of land or another ship to break the emptiness, its sense of vastness.

Davy asked casually, "Is it true this sort of mission often leads to permanent appointments in the realm of colonial government, sir?"

Bolitho nodded. "Rear Admiral Conway's appointment is such."

He watched Davy's tanned features gravely. He was worried about something. It was showing now, just like the time when he had selected Soames and not him for the raiding party.

"I was thinking . . ." Davy faltered. "I am of course well content with life as a King's officer. It is what I want. I am the first in my family to follow the sea. My father was a city merchant and had no use for service life. He was loath to allow me to enter the Navy."

Bolitho wished he would get on with it. He said encouragingly, "Mr. Herrick is like you. The first sailor in his family."

"Yes." Davy looked suddenly desperate as Soames emerged from the cabin hatch, yawning and consulting his pocket watch. "Well, it is not *exactly* what I meant, sir."

Bolitho turned and faced him. "Mr. Davy, I would be obliged

if you would come to the point. In an hour it will be an oven again. I would like to take my walk before breakfast, and not wait until after dinner tonight."

Davy bit his lip. "I am sorry, sir." He nodded firmly. "Yes, I will try to explain." He lowered his eyes. "May I speak of your brother, sir?"

Bolitho tensed "My *late* brother?"

"I did not mean to offend." Davy looked up and allowed the words to come out in a flood. "I heard somewhere that he quit the Navy."

Bolitho waited. Always it seemed to catch up with him. Now even his second lieutenant was risking a rebuke to satisfy his own curiosity. But he was wrong in Davy's case.

Davy said quietly, "It was because of his gambling I was told?"

He looked so strained, so pleading, that Bolitho forgot his own bitterness and asked, "Is that what bothers you? Gambling?"

"Yes, sir. Like a fool. I tried to win back my losses in London. With my father dead I am responsible for my mother's welfare, and that of the estate." He looked away. "In time of war I might have gained early promotion, and all the prize-money which went with it."

"You could have just as easily been killed." Bolitho added gently, "Am I to be told how much you owe?"

"Twenty, sir."

Bolitho stared at him. "In God's name, you could pawn your dress-coat for more, man!"

Davy gritted his teeth. "Twenty *thousand,* sir."

Bolitho ran his fingers through his hair. "*Undine* and the brig yonder would cost about that sum. And I thought you had more sense."

"Perhaps I should have kept my secret, sir." Davy was shamefaced. Wretched.

"No. It is better shared. At least you are safe from your creditors out here." He watched Davy grimly. "But twenty thousand. It is a small fortune."

Soames clumped past and beckoned to a bosun's mate. "Have the watch piped aft, Kellock." He was careful to keep to the lee side of the deck.

Davy hurried on, well aware that Soames was waiting to relieve him. "You, see, sir, I thought that on a voyage such as ours I might gain some new standing."

"I see. However, this is a mission of protection, not of discovery, or the capture of Spanish gold." He nodded to Soames and added softly, "But I will keep it in mind."

He began to pace the deck while the two lieutenants conversed over the compass.

Undine had gathered all sorts within her slender hull. It was not only the lower deck which sported its fortune-hunters, it seemed. He saw Midshipman Keen walking along the larboard gangway with Armitage, and prayed he would never be left in Davy's predicament, or in one such as his brother Hugh's.

In family background Davy and Keen were similar. Both had wealthy parents who had gained promotion in trade rather than in the King's service. Davy's father had died leaving his son and heir totally unprepared for the temptations which he had managed to overcome. Keen on the other hand had been sent to sea *because* of his father's riches and influence. Herrick had said that Keen had confided in him during a night watch in the Indian Ocean. *To make a man of me.* It had seemed to amuse him, Herrick had said. But Keen's father must be a remarkable man, Bolitho thought. There were not many who would risk a son's life or limb for such a goal.

He saw Noddall scurrying aft along the gun deck with a can of boiling water from the galley. Conway must be up and about, waiting to be shaved. It was surprising how little Conway's presence aboard had interfered with daily life. He had explained it himself. *Informal.* That did not mean he was disinterested. Quite the reverse. Whenever a ship had been sighted, or the hands had been called to reef or make sail, he had been there, watching. Once, when becalmed for half a day, the seamen had streamed a seine net in the hopes of getting some fresh fish, just a few flounders, and some flatheaded fish which Mudge had knowingly described as "foxes" were the entire result of their efforts, but Conway could not have been more pleased if they had caught a whale.

It was as if he was living out every hour, like a prisoner awaiting sentence. It was not pleasant to watch.

Bolitho was not quite twenty-eight years old, but as a post-captain with two previous commands behind him he had learned to accept, if not agree, with many of the Navy's judgements.

Conway's experience had come out at dinner, one evening. It was the second day out of Madras, and Bolitho had told Noddall to fetch some of his special wine to make it an occasion. It was madeira, the most expensive he had ever purchased in his life. Conway hardly seemed to notice. Had he been offered cider, Bolitho doubted if he would have remarked on it. But he had become very drunk. Not slowly, or by accident, or even out of bravado. But with the firm determination of one who has been too often alone, and wishes to blur the realisation without delay.

It had all happened two years back in these same waters, when the French admiral, Suffren, had captured Trincomalee and very nearly toppled Britain's power in India for good. Conway had started to tell his story as if Bolitho had not been there. As if he just wanted to make sure he could still remember it.

He had been in command of an inshore squadron and employed on the protection of supply ships and military convoys. A sloop had brought news of a French squadron off the coast of Ceylon, and without ado he had set off to engage or cripple the enemy ships until help arrived to complete the victory.

Unbeknown to Conway, another sloop was already searching for him, sent by the Commander-in-Chief with new orders for the defence of Trincomalee. Conway reached the area where the French had been sighted, only to find them gone. Fishermen informed him they had sailed towards the very position he had just left, and with an anxiety which Bolitho could only imagine, he had put his ships about once again. He managed to find and bring the French rear to a brief but unsatisfactory action before losing contact in the night. When dawn united his small squadron again, Conway found the supply ships which he had been guarding had been captured or destroyed, and when the admiral's sloop contacted him, she, too, had fresh news to cancel all previous instructions. Trincomalee had been taken.

In the silence of the cabin Conway's voice had risen suddenly, like a dying man's cry.

"Another day and I'd have brought them to grips! Not Suffren, nor any other admiral, could have got us out of Ceylon then!"

Bolitho looked up as the first working parties swarmed aloft for the constant round of repairs, splicing and stitching. It was all too plain. Conway could have emerged a hero. Instead, he was seized upon as a scapegoat. He must still have influence somewhere, he thought. A governorship, no matter where it was, represented reward rather than a continuance of disgrace.

He halted in his stride, his mind suddenly very alert. But suppose there was a second, more devious reason? Another scapegoat perhaps?

He shook his head. What would be the point of that?

Bolitho turned as Allday walked along the quarterdeck towards him.

"Breakfast's ready, Captain." He squinted his eyes towards the brig. "Still with us then?" He smiled calmly at Bolitho's steady gaze. "That's good."

Bolitho watched him and wondered. It was the same look he had given when he had brought the gig for him at Madras.

"Thank you." He added coldly, "And *what* is amusing you now?"

Allday shrugged. "Hard to put a name to it, Captain. It's a sort of glow I get inside sometimes." He massaged his stomach. "Comforting."

Bolitho strode past him towards the hatch. His morning had been badly interrupted.

As he stepped into the cool shadows between decks he imagined Viola Raymond just a mile abeam in the brig. Her husband would be watching her. *Mister Pigsliver* would be watching both of them.

It was still hard to know what she really thought about him, or if she saw his attraction as some sort of game. There had been several visitors staying at the residence, soldiers, Company officials, but she had been determined to keep him to herself. It had not been anything she had actually said. It had been more of an excitement, a sense of recklessness. A dare which he found impossible to ignore.

She had no longer stayed at arms' length, and several times had allowed her hand to linger on his, even when Raymond had been close by.

When he had made to return to the ship she had followed him on to a shaded terrace below the inner wall, and had held out a small box.

"For you."

She had made light of it, but he had seen the hot eagerness in her eyes, the thrust of her breasts beneath her gown as he had opened the box.

It was a gold watch.

While he had turned it over in his hands she had gripped his, arm and had whispered, "I will always remember your face that day . . ." But she had not laughed that time. "Do not refuse my little gift, *please.*"

He had taken her hand and kissed it, his mind grappling with what he was doing, seeing all the dangers, and yet dismissing them.

"It is as well you are sailing in another ship, Captain!" She had laughed and then had pulled his hand below her breast. "See how my heart beats now! A week, a day even, and who can say what might occur!"

Bolitho walked past the sentry and into the cabin, his mind still hanging on to that moment.

Conway was spreading thick treacle on a biscuit, his wispy hair ruffling in the breeze from the stern windows.

"What time is it, Bolitho?"

"Time, sir?"

Conway eyed him wryly before taking a mouthful.

"I observed that you had your, er, new watch in your hand and assumed that time was of some importance?"

Bolitho stared at him, the midshipman in front of his captain again.

Then he grinned. "It was a memory, sir, that was all."

Conway sniffed. "That I can well believe!"

"It makes a fine sight, Thomas."

Bolitho lowered the telescope and wiped his forehead with the back of one hand. The noon sun was merciless, but like most of the men around him, or standing high in the shrouds, he was momentarily unaware of it. Fifteen days out of Madras, and in spite of the wind's perversity, *Undine* had done well. Bolitho had made many landfalls in his time, but the sight of any shore after the hazards and doubts of navigation never failed to move him.

And now, just visible through the glare of sea and sky, he could see a smudge of green across the larboard side, and felt a fresh excitement and satisfaction. The narrowest part of the Malacca Strait. To starboard, hidden even to the masthead lookout, was the great scimitar-shaped island of Sumatra, poised as if to squeeze the strait shut and leave them sailing in a wilderness forever.

Herrick said, "It seems a mite too narrow for comfort, sir."

Bolitho smiled at him. "It is wider than the English Channel even here, Thomas. The master assures me it is the safest course to take."

"Perhaps." Herrick shaded his eyes again. "So that is Malacca, eh? It is hard to believe we have reached this far."

"And in five days or so, with God's good grace, we'll anchor in Pendang Bay." He paused, seeing the doubt in Herrick's blue eyes. "Well, come on, Thomas, let us see that smile again!"

"Yes, sir, I *know* it is a good and fast passage, and I am well satisfied, as you are." He fidgeted with his belt buckle. "But I am more concerned with something else."

"I see."

Bolitho waited, knowing what was coming. He had seen the worry mounting in Herrick's face over the past fifteen days. Having to spend much of his time with the admiral, Bolitho had had little chance of enjoying Herrick's company. A walk together before dusk, a pipe of tobacco and a glass of wine.

Herrick said bluntly, "Everyone knows about it, sir. It's not my place to speak on your behaviour, but . . ."

"But that is exactly what you are about to do?" Bolitho smiled gravely. "It is all right, Thomas, I am not going to snap your head off!"

Herrick would not relent. "It is no joke, sir. The lady is the wife of an important government official. If this sort of tale ever reached England, you would be in real danger, and that's the truth."

"Thank you for your concern." He glanced ahead where far beyond the gently spiralling bowsprit he saw *Rosalind* leading the way through the shallows and sandspits as she had no doubt done many times before. "But it is something I do not wish to discuss. Even with you if you are to disagree with everything I say."

"Yes, sir, I'm sorry." But Herrick added stubbornly, "I can't stand by and see you in irons because of others, sir, not without trying at least to help."

Bolitho gripped his arm. "Then we will say no more of the matter, Thomas. Agreed?"

"Aye, sir." Herrick regarded him, unhappily. "If it is the way you want it."

A seaman left the galley and darted down an open hatch below the forecastle. He was carrying a bucket and swab.

Herrick said wearily. "The surgeon is sick again. That man must be going to clean out his quarters."

Bolitho looked at him. "Drunk, I suppose?"

"It would seem so. But there is little to occupy him, sir, and our people have been remarkably free of illness."

"That is just as well." Bolitho felt unreasonably angry. "What in hell's name am I to do with him?"

"He has a lot on his mind, sir."

"So have many others."

Herrick kept his voice even. "He saw his young brother hanged for a crime of which he was later proved innocent. Even if he had been guilty it would still have been a terrible thing to watch."

Bolitho swung round from the rail. "How did you discover this?"

"At Madras. He came aboard drunk. I was a mite harsh with him and he started to rave about it. It is destroying him."

"Thank you for telling me, even if it is somewhat late."

Herrick did not flinch. "You have been rather busy, sir. I did not wish to trouble you."

Bolitho sighed. "I take your point. But in future I would like to hear everything. Most ship's surgeons are no more than butchers. Whitmarsh has been something more, but as a drunken sot he is a menace to everyone aboard. I am sorry for his brother; I for one can appreciate his feelings." He looked steadily at Herrick. "We will have to see what we can do to put things right for him, whether he likes it or not."

Herrick nodded gravely. "I agree, sir. The one afflicted is not always the best judge of his own malady." He tried not to grin. "If you see what I mean, sir."

Bolitho slapped his shoulder. "By God, Thomas, you go too far! I am not surprised your father sent *you* to sea!"

Then he walked up the tilting deck to the weather side and left Herrick to supervise his watch.

So they knew all about it, did they? He touched the bulge in his breeches pocket. What would Herrick say if he saw the inscription inside the watch-guard, he wondered?

"We will wear ship directly, Mr. Herrick." Bolitho strode to the compass and peered over Mudge's untidy shoulder. "Steer nor' nor'-east."

Herrick touched his hat. "Aye, aye, sir." He was equally formal.

It was five days since they had discussed Viola Raymond and the doctor's personal problem, and in that time Bolitho had never felt better. The ship had settled down to a regular, unhurried routine, and even the drills had passed off without complaint. At gunnery *Undine*'s company still had a lot to learn, but at least they moved as a team and not a stumbling, confused rabble.

He raised his glass and studied the new shapes and patterns which parted sea from sky. Mudge had assured him that Pendang Bay lay some five miles distant, but it was difficult to accept that they had all but arrived at their destination. Over fifteen thousand miles. Another world. A different life.

"Hands wear ship! Man the braces there!"

Shoes scraped on the planking, and Bolitho turned to study Conway's reaction as he came on deck. It was early morning, and for a few seconds he thought he was imagining what he saw.

Conway was wearing his rear admiral's uniform, complete with laced cocked hat and sword. The latter he held like a pointer, as if unsure of his reception.

Bolitho said, "Good morning, sir."

He saw Herrick staring at them, his speaking trumpet in mid-air.

Conway joined him by the rail and raised his head to watch as the great yards creaked round in unison, while the straining seamen hauled and panted at the braces.

"Well?" His tone was wary. "What do you think?"

"I think you look right for the occasion, sir."

He saw the quick tightening of Conway's mouth, the lines on either side deepening still further. It was moving, if pathetic, to see Conway's gratitude, for that is what it was.

"It is a bit creased of course. I was merely trying it on to see if it required alteration." He added sharply, "If I am to be governor, I'll land as I intend to continue, damn their eyes!"

Midshipman Armitage was watching the brig as she trimmed her yards to take station off *Undine*'s lee.

He remarked nervously, "Thunderstorm, sir."

But Bolitho was already snatching a telescope.

"Not this time, Mr. Armitage." He looked at Herrick. "Shorten sail, if you please, and then beat to quarters."

He saw them all gaping at him. Like total strangers.

"That *thunderstorm* is of a kind I have come to respect!"

10

*A*NOTHER FLAG

"SHIP CLEARED for action, sir." Herrick watched Bolitho's face anxiously.

Bolitho moved the telescope slowly from bow to bow, trying to avoid the overlapping mesh of shrouds and stays as he stared fixedly at the shore. Because of the glare which filtered through the morning haze it was impossible to fix any proper mark or to take an accurate bearing.

He replied, "Too long, Mr. Herrick. I want the time cut to twelve minutes." He was speaking merely to give himself another moment to gather his thoughts.

The distant gunfire had stopped, but there had been at least a dozen shots. Sharp and loud, despite the range. Probably small pieces.

He swung the glass further to starboard, seeing the low-lying wedge of land reaching out to lie parallel with their slow approach. The eastern headland of Pendang Bay. There was no room for further doubt.

Something dark intruded into the lens, and he saw the brig tilting to the low breeze, her yards alive with tiny figures as she finished reefing. A huge Spanish flag had been hoisted to her peak, blinding white in the glare, and he found time to wonder how *Rosalind*'s master was reacting to Puigserver's show of national pride.

Almost without intending to speak aloud he said, "I wish the Don was here with us. I think combined thought and action may be called for."

He heard Conway grunt. "Unnecessary. Ours is the ship of war, Bolitho. I want no damned Spaniard under my feet today."

Herrick asked quietly, "What d'you make of it, sir?"

Bolitho shook his head. "An attack on the settlement maybe. But I understand the place is well defended and—"

Conway interrupted harshly, "All this fuss over a few bloody savages!"

Herrick was standing beside Mudge and whispered, "I expect that is what poor Captain Cook said!"

Bolitho turned sharply. "If you've all nothing better to do than make stupid remarks . . ." He swung away and added, "Two good leadsmen in the chains immediately. Begin sounding!" To Mudge he snapped, "Let her fall off a point."

The edge in his tone was having the right effect. Men who seconds earlier had been chatting and gossiping about what might be happening ashore were now silent and alert, standing to their guns, or grouped at halliards and braces for the next command.

The wheel creaked, the sound very loud in the sudden stillness, and the helmsman called, "Nor'-east by north, sir!"

"Very well."

Bolitho glanced at Conway's profile, the glassy intentness in his eye.

From forward came the leadsman's cry, "No bottom, sir!"

Bolitho looked at Mudge, but the master's heavy face was expressionless. He probably thought it was a waste of time to take soundings. The chart, and all available information, told them the water was deep until the last cable or so. Or maybe he thought his captain was so nervous that he was afraid to leave anything to chance.

Another single crack echoed out from the mist-shrouded coast and died away very gradually.

Bolitho tugged out his new watch and stared at it. At this speed it would take near on an hour to close the land. But it could not be helped.

"No bottom, sir!"

He said, "Pass the word for Captain Bellairs. I'll want a full landing party. Tell Mr. Davy to prepare the boats for lowering once we have anchored. He will take charge of them."

Conway said briefly, "Good beach, I'm told. The settlement and fort are on a slope to the western side of the bay."

Herrick strode aft and touched his hat. "Shall I order the guns to load, sir?" He sounded guarded.

"Not yet, Mr. Herrick."

Bolitho trained his glass across the larboard bow. Settlement, fort, they could have been imagination. The blurred green outline of the land looked totally deserted.

He heard the marine sergeant bellowing orders, the stamp of boots as his men were divided and sub-divided in readiness to disembark. Bellairs was watching them from the starboard gangway, his face completely blank, but his eyes missing nothing.

"By the mark twenty!" The leadsman sounded triumphant.

Mudge nodded gloomily. "About right. Twenty fathoms hereabouts."

Some small birds darted across the sea's face and circled above the braced yards. Bolitho watched them, recalling the swifts flying about the grey stone house in Falmouth. It would be fine there today. Sunshine, bright colours. The hills dotted with sheep and cattle. The town itself busy with farmers and sailors, each depending on the other, as it had always been.

He saw Herrick nearby and said quietly, "Forgive my anger just now."

Herrick smiled. "No matter, sir. You were right. We have been caught unawares already on this venture. Trouble will not fade away merely because we turn our backs on it."

"*Rosalind*'s settin' 'er fores'l again, sir!"

They turned to watch as the brig dipped to the wind and gathered way.

Conway snarled, "By God, the Don intends to lead us inshore, blast him!"

"It is his right, sir." Bolitho trained his glass on the other vessel, seeing the busy figures above and below, the great slash of her ensign with its crowned shield bright in the sunlight. "It is still the territory of the Spanish Royal Company until he says otherwise."

Conway scowled. "That is mere formality." He stared hard at him. "Fire a warning shot, Captain!"

Bolitho looked at Herrick. "Pass the word forrard. One ball. But mind it drops well clear of the brig."

The leadsman called again, "Deep eighteen!"

Bolitho shut his ears to the squeak of gun trucks as the foremost twelve-pounder was run out. The gun captain was peering along the muzzle, and as the light touched him Bolitho saw that one hand was a metal hook. Turpin.

Herrick shouted, "Ready, sir!"

"As you will then."

The gun crashed out, and seconds later a thin waterspout rose like a feather far beyond the brig's bowsprit.

Bolitho said, "Well, at least they will know we are coming, sir."

Conway snapped, "Savages. I'll soon get to the bottom of this little matter."

Bolitho sighed as the brig fell off slightly, her foresail already being brailed up in response to his rough signal. The thought of having a poorly armed brig lying between an enemy and his own artillery was a worry he could not afford. And she was aboard *Rosalind*, too.

He turned round sharply, angry with himself for allowing his thoughts to drift. Right now he needed to be completely clear. His mind like steel.

"Mr. Mudge, d'you know much of this place, other than you have already told me?"

The master shrugged. "Very few people 'ave seen inland, sir. 'Ead 'unters, warrin' tribes there are a'plenty, I'm told. But the natives are often sailors, pirates from the north of Borneo. Sea-Dyaks they calls 'em. Many a good ship 'as been overrun at anchor by them devils." He shook his jowls. "Then it's snip, snip with their long knives, an' poor Jack is no more!"

At that moment a seaman beside a six-pounder pointed aloft as the masthead pendant licked out with renewed energy.

Like a long, low curtain the sea mist began to move and shred itself, vanishing into the land, and laying bare endless stretches of beach, thick jungle, and finally the overlapping hills beyond.

Herrick lowered his telescope and exclaimed, "And is *that* the settlement, sir?"

Bolitho steadied his own glass, not daring to look at Conway's face. What he had first taken to be a heap of lopped and piled trees was shaping itself into long, spiked palisades, supported and guarded at regular intervals by squat, timbered blockhouses. As the mist slipped away he saw what must be the governor's residence. It had to be, for it was the largest building in sight. Again, it was built entirely of timber, with an upper and lower rampart and one spindly watchtower in its centre, above which the Spanish flag lifted occasionally in the sea breeze.

Conway said thickly, "In God's name!" The words were wrung from his throat.

Bolitho watched the distant fort for some sign of life other than the flag. The place looked crude, but was well sited, easy to defend. There must be settlements like this all over the world, he thought. But what about *before?* Someone had first to wade ashore from a boat, or march through swamp and jungle to plant a flag. To claim the land for his own country. He had heard of islands in the Pacific which were regularly claimed and re-claimed by half a dozen nations, sometimes out of the genuine desire to colonise, but often merely because their ships paused there for no other reason than to find water and firewood.

"By the mark ten!"

He looked at Herrick. "We will anchor in eight fathoms." He saw Allday scrambling over the gig on its chocks. "Then boats away as fast as you can."

He turned his attention to the cruising wavelets which had risen to enjoy the freshening breeze. It was a large but well-sheltered bay. It was said that the Spanish Royal Company had claimed it years earlier almost by accident. They had intended to place their settlement further north, to gain access for trade with the Philippines. But fever, losses in ships and resources had found them here instead. It was easy to understand why the Spaniards had lost heart, easier still to realise how much more important it would be to the British. Within reach of both India and the vast, barely-tapped resources of the China Seas, it could be a vital link, given time and skilful handling. With the French and Spaniards gone from the area, only the power of the Dutch East Indiamen offered any sort of competition. He glanced quickly at Conway's stiff features. But was he the one to begin it, he wondered?

Fighting men rarely saw much further than the strategy and tactics of the moment. And one made bitter and desperate by past mistakes would be less inclined to compromise.

"People leaving the palisade, sir!"

Bolitho raised the glass again. Twos and threes, some carrying muskets, others limping down the sand towards the water's edge and a long, partly-constructed pier of rough timber and piles.

Most of them were so dark-skinned they could be natives, but the uniforms were Spanish well enough.

Not one of them waved. They merely stood or sat dejectedly watching the frigate's careful approach.

Herrick said under his breath, "God, they look like scarecrows!"

"What did you expect, Mr. Herrick, *sir?*" Unseen and unheard, the surgeon had appeared on the quarterdeck, his face and neck like raw meat.

Bolitho watched him impassively. "You are recovered, it seems, Mr. Whitmarsh?"

The surgeon turned his gaze on him. His eyes were red-trimmed with strain, so that they looked too hot for their sockets.

He muttered vaguely, "We have arrived, I see, sir." He reached out for support and, finding none, almost fell headlong. He mumbled, "Pattern never changes. First they hand over their power of protection to us. With ships and men if needed to give power to that *protection*. When all is safe the traders will come, and the Company's flag will be supreme."

Bolitho asked coldly, "And then what?"

Whitmarsh regarded him emptily. "The place will become a colony, a possession. Or if we have cleaned it out like an empty shell, we will simply . . . ," he retched, ". . . discard it. Cast it away!"

Conway seemed to hear him for the first time. "Get off this deck, you drink-sodden creature!" His face was working with despair, a need to release his anger. "Or by heaven you will be sorry!"

The surgeon gave an awkward bow. "But I *am* sorry, believe me! Sorry for you, sir, at being given this wretched task." He swayed towards Bolitho. "For the good captain, who will eventually be made to stand between justice and tyranny. And more sorry perhaps . . ." He pitched forward in an untidy heap and lay completely still.

"By the mark eight!"

The leadsman's call brought Bolitho back to reality.

He snapped, "Have him taken to his quarters."

As some seamen seized the inert surgeon and carried him to the ladder, he caught the sour odour of vomit and spilled wine. The stench of a man's decay.

Conway was still staring at the deck. "Another second and I'd have had him in irons!" He glared at Bolitho. *"Well?"*

"There was something in what he said, sir. What is on a sober man's mind is often on a drunkard's tongue."

Herrick called, "Close enough, I think, sir."

Bolitho hurried to the quarterdeck rail, glad to be free of Conway's mood. He studied the lie of the smaller headland to larboard, the great eastern one on the opposite beam, thrusting out to sea, and already a delicate green in the early sunlight.

"Signal our intention to *Rosalind,* and then wear ship, if you please." He waited until the anchor party had assembled above the cathead. Then he added, "Tell Davy to keep our people together once we are ashore. I want no plague raging through *Undine.*"

"D'you think there is fever here, sir?"

For just a moment there was fear in Herrick's eyes. Like most seamen he could accept blood and broadside, as well as the harsh discipline which guided his daily life. But the unknown, the terror of plague which could render a whole ship useless, turn her into a floating tomb, was entirely different.

"That we will discover directly."

"*Rosalind*'s acknowledged, sir!"

Keen seemed his usual carefree self. Even Armitage was watching the land with something like expectancy.

"Wear ship!"

"Man the lee braces!"

Bolitho saw the helm going over, and moved to Conway's side to avoid the rush of seamen across the quarterdeck as the frigate turned slowly into the wind.

"Will you wait for Don Puigserver, sir?"

Conway looked at him, a nerve jumping in his throat, as

the anchor plunged into the clear water in a mighty cascade of spray.

"I suppose so." He peered towards the brig which was already swinging easily to her cable. "I wish you to accompany me."

"An honour, sir."

"You think so?" Conway removed the gold-laced hat and ran his palm over his grey hair. He smiled bitterly. "We shall see."

Noddall came on deck with Bolitho's sword, but quailed as Allday rasped, "Here, give me that!"

He hurried to Bolitho's side and carefully buckled the scabbard into place, muttering, "The very idea!"

Then he straightened his back and stared at the boats which were being swayed up and over the nettings.

"A long way we've come together, Captain." He turned to watch the brig's boats being lowered into the water. "It's not a happy place, I'm thinking."

Bolitho did not hear him. He watched the marines clambering out and down into the swaying boats, their coats very red, their boots slipping and clattering as they always did. Captain Bellairs was studying each and every one of them, especially the young corporal who carried the sheathed Union Flag which would soon be planted on foreign soil.

Like many sea officers, Bolitho had often thought about such moments, but the mental picture had always been grander and vaster. Endless lines of men, bands playing, cheering people, and the anchored ships looking splendid and secure at the sea's edge.

Now he understood differently. It was only a beginning. Small, but no less impressive because of that.

Conway said, "Well, we had best begin. I see the Don is already on his way."

The brig's boats were indeed moving inshore, one bearing the Spanish flag, the others that of the Company.

Bolitho was thankful Viola Raymond was remaining aboard the *Rosalind*.

Conway followed him into the gig, and with the armed and crowded boats fanning out on either beam they started towards the nearest beach.

Bolitho could smell the jungle long before they were within hail of the people by the frothing surf, like incense, heady and overpowering. He gripped his sword-hilt tighter and tried to compose himself. It was a moment he must always try to remember.

He glanced quickly at Conway for some sign or reaction. He looked remote and sadly stern.

The new governor of Teluk Pendang had arrived.

Lieutenant Thomas Herrick walked a few paces across the quarterdeck, his movements restless as he watched Bellairs's marines and some seamen below the nearest palisade. It was just past noon, with the sun blazing down on the anchored ships with savage intensity. Most of the unemployed hands were sheltering by the guns beneath the gangways, but Herrick felt unable to leave the deck, even though his head was swimming, his shirt plastered against his body like a wet rag.

Tugging at her cable, the *Undine* had swung her stern towards the long, pale beach, and with the visibility sharp and clear, it was easier to see the extent of Conway's new command. Larger than he had first imagined, it had obviously been planned and constructed by a military engineer. Even the unfinished timber pier looked neat and strong, but like the rest of the place, was in a state of bad neglect.

As he had paced the quarterdeck, or peered across the taffrail, Herrick had seen Bolitho and some of the landing party moving along the wooden ramparts, or exploring the ground between the two separate palisades which guarded the approaches to the fort and its surrounding buildings. The boats lay like dead fish on the beach, exactly where they had ground ashore some four hours earlier. He had watched some marines hauling the swivel guns towards the fort, others, harried by the massive Sergeant Coaker, had manned the ramparts, or could now be seen patrolling near the pier. The handful of Spanish soldiers had withdrawn into the fort, and of the enemy, or whatever the garrison had been firing at, there was not a sign.

He turned as a heavy step fell on the tinder-dry planking and saw Soames shading his eyes with one hand, and munching a biscuit with the other.

"Any sign yet, sir?" Soames eyed the distant settlement without enthusiasm. "What a place to end your years, eh?"

Herrick was worried. Something should have happened by now. There were supposed to be some three hundred Spanish soldiers and followers in the settlement, and God alone knew how many local natives. From what he had seen there were hardly any. The same old thought crossed his mind. Plague perhaps? Or something even more terrible.

He replied, "They appear to be examining the inner defences. I am not surprised the Dons wish to be rid of it." He shuddered. "From here it looks as if the damned jungle is pushing the whole lot back into the sea."

Soames shrugged and pointed his half-eaten biscuit at the gun deck. "Shall I dismiss the gun crews? There seems to be little here to excite action."

"No. There are only five of them manned. Change 'em round and send the others below for a spell."

He was glad when Soames walked away. He needed to concentrate, to decide what to do if he was suddenly required to act without Bolitho at his elbow. It had been different the last time. A sort of wild recklessness had come over him, prompted as ever by the need to dash to Bolitho's aid in the only way he knew.

But here were no yelling savages, no darting canoes which a few bursts of canister could scatter. Silence, and depressing immobility.

Midshipman Penn called in his shrill voice, "One of the boats is being launched, sir!"

Herrick felt his heart lift as the distant figure thrust *Undine's* green-painted gig into the shallows. He saw Bolitho's tall figure striding down the beach, pausing to say something to Davy before swinging his legs over the gunwale.

At last. Soon they would know what was happening. Only four hours, but to Herrick it felt an age.

"Muster the side party. Stand by to receive the captain!"

Bolitho looked strained and thoughtful as he climbed up through the entry port, his coat covered with sandy dust, his face damp with sweat. He glanced at the motionless side party but did not seem to see them.

He said, "Have the surgeon and his mates sent ashore to report to Mr. Davy. When the other boats arrive I want powder and shot, food and fresh fruit sent over, too." He peered towards the anchored brig and at another boat which was pulling quickly towards her. "I have sent word for *Rosalind* to assist in every way she can." He looked at Herrick's round face and smiled for the first time. "Easy, Thomas. It is not the end, though it was nearly so. Come to my cabin when you have dealt with my orders. Allday has a list of things required."

When Herrick finally joined Bolitho in the sterncabin he found him stripped to the waist and drinking a large tankard of lemon juice.

"Sit down, Thomas."

Herrick sat, aware that although Bolitho sounded controlled and level, there was something else, something familiar which told him his mind was busy along another tack.

"When the war ended there was a garrison of about three hundred here." It was as if he was drawing a picture, just as it had been painted for him. "The commandant, the King of Spain's trusted controller, was Colonel Don José Pastor, a dedicated soldier to all accounts, and one well used to building such settlements. He gained some trust from the natives, and by barter and other inducements, as well as the usual Spanish use of force, he was able to create a strong defence line, as well as clear much of the surrounding land. There is even a road of sorts, although that now is overgrown. A wilderness."

Herrick ventured, "Fever?"

"That, of course, but no more than you might expect in such a place." He studied Herrick for several seconds, his eyes very grey in the reflected light. "The settlement has been under almost constant attack for over a year. At first they thought it was only the work of marauding tribesmen, Dyak pirates maybe who were becoming worried by the spread of Spanish influence in their midst. Colonel Pastor had set up a Catholic mission above the settlement. The monks were found terribly mutilated and headless." He did not see Herrick's expression of horror. "Then others died when the fresh-water pools were poisoned. The garrison had to fall back upon its own little stream within the walls. But for it, the fight would have ended long ago. Think of it, Thomas, if you had been an officer here. Trying to hold up morale, fighting an unseen enemy, while day by day your strength is dwindling. Each dawn you would be watching the horizon, praying for a ship, any vessel which could bring relief. Only one came in the whole of that time, but would not land its people for fear of the plague. She merely dropped despatches and left. God knows I can understand that. They are like living skeletons over yonder." He looked round as a boat pulled clear of the hull. "Let us hope our surgeon will find others to help and think less of himself."

Herrick asked quietly, "What will Admiral Conway do, sir?"

Bolitho closed his eyes, remembering the small gathering in the room at the top of the wooden fort, hearing Puigserver's emotional voice as he had translated the report of the settlement's one remaining officer, Captain Vega.

The attacks had gone on and on, and when once an armed picket had been ambushed, the fort's defenders had nearly been driven mad by the screams and pitiful cries as their comrades had been tortured to death within sight of the walls.

Bolitho said, "To the west of us is a small cluster of islands. The Benua Group."

Herrick nodded, unable to understand. "Yes. We passed them a day back."

"They lie astride the strait between Borneo and the islands of Sumatra and Java." His tone hardened. "This self-styled prince, Muljadi, has his stronghold there. The Dutch built a fortress in one of the isles many years ago, but abandoned it when disease killed most of the garrison." He looked through the stern windows, his eyes grave. "Not like Conway's new domain, Thomas. It is built of stone."

Herrick attempted to shift Bolitho from his mood of passive despair. "But a few ships and men would soon destroy this damned Muljadi, surely?"

"Once, perhaps." Bolitho drained the glass and stared at it. "This morning there was a final attempt to overthrow the defences here. I expect the attacker saw *Undine* pass through the strait yesterday and knew they must make haste. Now they are gone into the jungle. Captain Vega of the garrison says they will head west to the marsh district, where they will be taken by sea to Muljadi's stronghold." He gave a great sigh. "Of all the men at the settlement, there are but fifty survivors. Poisoned darts, musket balls, for they have our weapons, too, and fever have wrought a terrible price from them. There was even a mutiny, when Vega's men fought with their own native soldiers, most of them too crazed with drink and despair to know what they were about."

Herrick stared at him. "What of Colonel Pastor, sir? Is he also killed?"

Bolitho sat down and massaged the white scar above his ribs. "I am coming to that part. Weeks back, a ship *did* finally arrive. Not to bring help, or to offer relief to people from their own part of the world. She was the *Argus*, Thomas." He swung round, the weariness falling away like a cloak. "Of forty-four guns, under the hand of Capitaine Le Chaumareys. He landed himself and met with Colonel Don Pastor. He brought a message from Muljadi. *Personally.*" He gripped the desk with both hands. "And required him to lower the flag, to relinquish all claims on the settlement in the name of Spain."

"My God."

"Indeed. Apparently the colonel told of help which would soon arrive, but Le Chaumareys laughed at him. Said there would be no relief, no ships coming to his aid."

"Then the French do have a hand in this, sir?"

"A big one." His face lit up. "Cannot you see it, Thomas? Le Chaumareys was instructed to force the Spanish to surrender their rights here. He knew better than most that *Nervion* or *Undine,* or both, would be delayed by any means available. With the settlement handed over to Muljadi, and a written agreement from Pastor, who after all is his King's representative here, there would be nothing we or anyone else could do. I have no doubt Le Chaumareys had further orders to recognise Muljadi's rule in the name of France, and to offer him whatever he needed to control his alliance." He looked towards the beach, at the seamen who were unloading two of the boats. "But we did come, Thomas. Too late for Colonel Pastor, for he left in the *Argus* to parley for his men with Muljadi. I pity him, even if I admire his courage."

Herrick nodded slowly, his eyes clouded. "And when he had gone, the last attack began. No governor, few defenders. Dead men have little to say."

Herrick thought of their slow approach that morning, the mist on the water distorting the sounds of cannon fire. No wonder the remaining, ragged defenders had not been able to wave or greet them. *Undine* must have seemed like a miracle.

Bolitho said, "Don Puigserver is our one red card. He can act in the name of Spain and assure Conway of his country's confidence—"

"How did *he* react to the news?"

Bolitho thought of the Spaniard's face as he had listened to

Vega. Anguish, shame and then fury. He had seen it all. Only Conway's attitude still remained in shadow. He had said little, and not even argued with Raymond when he had started off on what Parliament would or would not support. Only one thing was certain. The affair had to be contained. No build-up of additional force, no acceptance that there had been a change in rulership, here or anywhere else. As Raymond had explained more than once, the Dutch were too busy recouping their losses caused by the war to want another conflict in their midst. If France thrust more naval might into the area, then Spain, too, might change her views about her untried allegiance with Britain. It could be war, all over again.

Only when Bolitho had made to leave for his ship had the rear admiral drawn him into a corner.

He had said very calmly, "Politics, a need for furthering trade or colonial power, all are attitudes. Only one thing is properly clear to me, as it must be to you, Bolitho." He had held his gaze, searching for a reaction before adding, "Every puzzle must have a key. This one has two. *Undine* and *Argus*. Governments may try to use more power later on, but by then it will be too late for us all. If *Undine* is lost, so are we. Be sure that Le Chaumareys is already well aware of it!"

When Bolitho had made to question him further he had said, "He is a good officer, make no mistake. Our squadrons had cause to damn his eyes in the war. France has loaned Muljadi their best, as I hope England has aided me in the same manner!"

Much of his thoughts Bolitho had spoken aloud, for Herrick exclaimed, "But it is not war, sir! No Frenchman will cross swords for fear of starting one!"

Bolitho watched him and was glad he was here. "Le Chaumareys will have a letter of marque. He is far from a fool. When he runs out those forty-four guns it will be Muljadi's flag at his peak, not the Fleur de Lys of France." He stood up and moved vaguely about the cabin. "But behind each breech will be an experienced crew, the cream of his navy. While we . . ." He half turned, his face suddenly drained again. "But that is enough. Battles are not won or lost on daydreams."

Herrick nodded. "And what will we do now, sir?"

Bolitho tugged the shirt over his head, the same stained one as before.

"We will weigh when the tide is right. If Muljadi has vessels in the area we must close with them. Show him we mean to continue what we have begun."

He pulled Herrick towards the stern windows as a bugle wailed sadly across the glittering water. Above the fort there was Conway's new flag, the little group of marines beneath it glowing like tiny red insects.

"See, Thomas, there is no drawing back. Not for Conway. Not for any of us."

Herrick watched the little tableau doubtfully. "Better await the *Bedford*, surely? With troops and more cannon we would stand a better chance."

"That is what Le Chaumareys will be thinking." He smiled, his face suddenly very young. "At least, I *hope* that is so!"

Herrick groped for his hat, glad of something to occupy his mind and to hold back the apprehension Bolitho's news had brought.

"Will we leave Bellairs and his marines?"

"Half of them. There is much to be done. With corpses lying unburied, the place is a dunghill. The defences are stout, but in need of good men to patrol them. *Rosalind* will remain also under the protection of the battery, such as it is. I think her master is eager to get clear of this place, but Conway is more than a match for him."

Herrick moved towards the door. "It is not what I was expecting, sir."

"Nor I. But like it or not, we have a duty. If Muljadi and his threat is to be overcome, then he must be seen as a common pirate." He ran his hands along the desk top. "*Argus* or no!"

Herrick hurried out, his thoughts tugging in several directions at once. He found Mudge in the wardroom staring gloomily at a plate of salt beef.

The master asked, "Are we off again, Mr. 'Errick?"

Herrick smiled. Fact soon grew from rumour in a small ship. "Yes. The *Argus* is busy here, it seems. As a privateer, and not openly in the name of France."

Mudge yawned. Unimpressed. "Nothin' new. We used to do the same for the Company in India. A few ready muzzles always seemed to impress a doubtin' rajah if a little strength was called for."

Herrick looked at him and sighed. "So the Frogs will back an armed uprising, and we will support the protection of trade. But what of the people in between, Mr. Mudge?"

The master pushed his plate away with disgust. "Never asked 'em!" was all he said.

II

*L*UCK OF THE GAME

BOLITHO studied the masthead pendant and then walked aft to the compass. North-west by west. It was mid-afternoon, and despite the sky's unclouded, relentless glare there was sufficient wind to make it easier to endure. *Undine* had been made to lie at anchor in Pendang Bay almost until dusk the previous day, the set of the coastal currents and the wind's determination to remain from the south-west making a night passage too dangerous even to attempt. But in the last moments the wind had backed considerably, and with her sleek hull tilting to its pressure, *Undine* had beaten out of the bay, losing the settlement and its grim memories in purple shadow.

But if the wind had remained fresh it was still necessary to hold the ship close-hauled, the yards braced round to keep each sail drawing and steer *Undine* clear of the land. Should the wind veer without warning, and she lay too close to that undulating pattern of green coast, *Undine* could easily find herself hard upon a lee shore, and in real danger.

Herrick asked "How much longer will we continue, sir?"

Bolitho did not reply immediately. He was watching the tiny triangular sails of *Undine's* cutter as it tacked daintily around a small clump of rocky islets.

Then he shifted his gaze to the maintop where Midshipman Keen sat with one bare leg dangling over the barricade, a telescope trained on the distant boat. Davy had the cutter, and would signal the moment he sighted anything. There was no sense in taking the ship too close when good visibility remained.

He said, "We are off the south-western cape, or as near as I can calculate. There are marshes and swamps aplenty, according to Mr. Mudge and Fowlar. If Captain Vega's information is correct, the Muljadi's vessels may be close by."

He turned his face into the wind, feeling the sweat drying on his forehead and neck.

"The Benua Islands are about a hundred miles to the west'rd of us. A goodly piece of open water, if we get the chance to run these pirates down."

Herrick watched him doubtfully, but was comforted by Bolitho's apparent optimism.

"What do we *know* of Muljadi, sir?"

Bolitho walked up the slanting deck to the weather rail and tugged the sticky shirt clear of his ribs.

"Little or nothing. Originally he came from somewhere in North Africa, Morocco or the Barbary Coast, it is said. He was taken as a slave by the Dons and chained in one of their galleys. He escaped and was recaptured."

Herrick whistled quietly. "I imagine the Dons were hard with him."

Bolitho thought suddenly of the elderly Colonel Pastor and his impossible mission.

"The Dons lopped off a hand and an ear and left him marooned on some desolate beach."

Herrick shook his head. "Yet somehow he reached the Indies, and can now strike fear into his old masters."

Bolitho regarded him impassively. "Or whoever stands between him and his final goal, whatever that may be."

They both stared up as Keen yelled, "Deck there! Cutter's signalled, sir! Mr. Davy points to the north'rd!"

Bolitho snatched a glass. "Of course! I should have realised!"

He trained it on the cutter, and then beyond to the gently sloping cape. Tiny islets, crumbling ridges and rocks, and everywhere the unbroken backcloth of green. Any small vessel could work her way through there, as Davy's cutter was now doing.

Herrick slammed his fists together. "Got 'em, by God!"

Bolitho said crisply, "We will remain on this tack for the present. Hoist the recall signal for Mr. Davy and then beat to quarters." He smiled, if only to ease the mounting excitement. "In *ten* minutes maybe?"

Herrick waited until Keen had shinned down a backstay to rejoin his signal party and then yelled, "Beat to quarters! Clear for action!"

A solitary drummer-boy did the best he could, his sticks blurring in double-time as the tattoo brought the hands tumbling from hatchways and gratings.

"That might frighten 'em off, sir."

Mudge was by his helmsmen, his jowl working on some meat or a quid of tobacco. There was little to choose between them, Bolitho often thought.

"I believe otherwise."

Bolitho watched the bare-backed seamen dashing to their guns, casting off the lashings and groping for the tools of their trade. A reduced detachment of marines, under the command of a solitary corporal, was parading across the quarterdeck, while a handful more clambered aloft to the foretop and its swivel gun.

The cutter had already turned bows-on, her sails lowered, and thrusting through the inshore swell under oars alone.

"They will not have met with many frigates, I'm thinking. Their leader will try to reach open sea and outreach us, rather than face a blockade or the risk of our landing marines at his back." He touched Mudge's arm impetuously. "He'll not know how unused we are to such affairs, eh?"

Mudge pouted. "I only 'ope that bugger Muljadi is 'ere, too! 'E needs to be taught a lesson, an' double quick, in my reckonin'!"

"Deck there!" The lookout at the masthead waited until the scamper on the gun deck stopped. "Sail on th' lee bow!"

"By heaven, so there is!" Midshipman Keen gripped a seaman's arm and added excitedly, "Schooner by the cut of her!"

The seaman, pigtailed, and with ten years in the Navy, glanced at him and grinned.

"By God, I envy you young gentlemen your learnin', sir!"

But his sarcasm was lost in the excitement of the moment.

Herrick held up his hand as the last gun captain faced aft towards him. From the break below the quarterdeck a bosun's mate shouted, "All cleared aft, sir!" Herrick swung round and saw Bolitho examining his new watch.

"Cleared for action, sir."

"Twelve minutes, *exactly*." Bolitho glanced up at the masthead. "But for the lookout's hail, I believe you may have done it in less." He let the mock formality drop. "Well done, Mr. Herrick, and pass the word to all hands."

He walked back down the angled deck and trained his glass across the nettings. Two raked masts with big dark sails. Like wings. They appeared motionless, the hull still hidden beyond one more probing spit of land. It was an illusion. She was edging around the last dangerous point. After that she would be up and away. But it would take her a good while yet.

He swung round. "Where is that damned cutter?"

Mowll, the master-at-arms, and easily the most unpopular man aboard, called, "Comin' up fast, sir!"

"Well, signal Mr. Davy to make haste. I'll have to leave him astern otherwise."

"Deck there! 'Tis another sail on th' lee bow!"

Herrick watched in silence until he had discovered the second pair of sails in his glass.

"Another schooner. Probably Company ships taken by these pirates."

"No doubt."

Bolitho turned to watch the cutter swinging round to drive beneath the main chains with a shuddering thud. Curses and clattering oars, all were finally quenched by Davy's angry voice and the more patient tones of Shellabeer, the boatswain, who was studying the whole manoeuvre from the gangway with obvious disgust.

Allday had been standing behind Bolitho and whispered, "Should have had young Mr. Armitage in charge, Captain. He'd have driven right through into the spirit store, cutter an' all!"

Bolitho smiled and allowed Allday to buckle on his sword. He had not seen his coxswain since breakfast, just after dawn. Yet the moment of danger, a hint of action, and he was here. Without fuss, and hardly a word to betray his presence.

"Maybe."

He saw Midshipman Armitage with Soames below the foremast, checking a list of gun crews which Soames had reallotted on passage from India. He found a moment to wonder what Armitage's mother would think if she saw her adored boy now. Leaner, and well tanned, his hair too long, and his shirt in need of a good wash. She would probably burst into tears all over again. But in one way he had not changed. He was still as clumsy and as lacking in confidence as his first day aboard.

Little Penn, on the other hand, who was strutting importantly beside the starboard battery of twelve-pounders and waiting to assist Lieutenant Davy, had no such handicap. If anything, he was prone to attempt tasks which were several spans of experience beyond his twelve years.

Davy came struggling aft, ducking beneath a swinging shadow as the cutter was hoisted inboard and on to its chocks above the gun deck. He was soaked in spray, but very pleased with himself.

Bolitho said, "That was well done. By making a quick sighting report, you have given us an edge on those two vessels."

Davy beamed. "Some prize-money perhaps, sir?"

Bolitho hid a smile. "We will see."

Herrick waited for Davy to join his gun crews and then said, "Just the two schooners. Nothing else in sight." He rubbed his hands noisily.

Bolitho lowered the telescope and nodded. "Very well, Mr. Herrick. You may load and run out now." He glanced at the masthead pendant for the hundredth time. "We will make more sail directly, and show these pirates what they are against."

"Both schooners are keeping well inshore, sir." Herrick lowered his telescope and turned to watch Bolitho's reactions. "With that rig they can sail really close to the wind."

Bolitho walked to the compass, the picture of the two other vessels sharp in his mind. For over half an hour they had worked slowly and methodically between a small crop of islets, and were now following the coastline towards a sloping spur of headland. Around that there was yet another bay, with more jutting spits of land, but the schooners would choose their moment most carefully. Go about and dash for the open sea, separate perhaps, and so lessen *Undine's* chances of conquest.

They were both well-handled vessels, and through his glass he had seen an assortment of small cannon and swivels, and an equally varied selection of men.

Mudge watched him gloomily "Wind's backed a'piece, sir. *Might* 'old."

Bolitho turned and stared along his ship, weighing the risks and the gains. The green headland was reaching down towards *Undine*'s starboard bow, or so it appeared. In fact, it was still some three miles distant. The two schooners, black against the lively wave crests, seemed to overlap into one ungainly craft, their great sails etched across the land.

He said firmly, "Get the t'gallants on her, and alter course two points to starboard."

Herrick stared at him. "It'll be close, sir. If the wind veers we'll be hard put to beat off the shore."

When Bolitho did not reply he sighed and lifted his speaking trumpet.

"Man the braces!"

From further aft the helmsmen spun their spokes, the senior one squinting at the flapping canvas and at the tilting compass bowl until even Mudge was satisfied.

"Nor'-west by north, sir!"

"Very well."

Bolitho studied the headland again. A trap for the two schooners, or a last resting place for *Undine,* as Herrick seemed to think.

Herrick was watching the topmen, waiting until the topgallant sails were freed and then brought under control like bulging steel breastplates. *Undine* was moving swiftly now, for with the wind sweeping tightly across her larboard quarter, and with topsails and topgallants braced to best advantage, there was little doubt the range was falling away.

Mudge asked worriedly, "D'you think they'll try to go about, sir?"

"Perhaps." Bolitho shivered as a curtain of spray lifted and burst across the weather rail, soaking him to the skin, adding to his rising excitement. "They'll try and weather the headland as close as they dare and use the next bay to change tack. Or, if one or both loses his head, we'll rake 'em as he goes about on this side of the headland."

He peered at the gun deck, at the figures beside each twelve-pounder. One good broadside would be more than enough for any schooner. The second might strike without risking a similar fate. He shut it from his mind. The fight was not even begun yet.

He pictured Conway back there in his remote kingdom. He would know better than Puigserver or Raymond what was at stake. With any luck *Undine* might settle Conway's security long enough for him to demonstrate what he could do.

A faint crack echoed across the water and a white feather of spray showed itself for just a few seconds, well away from the starboard bow. It brought a chorus of jeers from the waiting gun crews.

"Run up the Colours, Mr. Keen."

Bolitho saw the handful of marines in the foretop adjusting their swivel gun. Some more were already cradling their long muskets along the hammock nettings, their faces stiff with concentration.

"One of 'em's making a run for it, sir!"

Bolitho caught his breath as the sternmost schooner tilted at a steep angle, her great mainsail sweeping above her deck like a huge wing while she altered course hard to larboard.

Somebody yelled, "By Jesus, she's in irons! Look at th' bugger!"

The schooner's captain had mistimed it very badly, for as his command pounded round to cross the wind's eye and find sea-room elsewhere, the sails flapped and rippled in hopeless confusion.

Bolitho shouted, "We'll take him first! Stand by, the larboard battery!"

He saw Soames hurrying down his line of guns, the captains crouching like athletes behind each breech, trigger lines taut as they peered through the open ports for a first sight of the target.

Bolitho straddled his legs and tried to hold his telescope on the nearest vessel. She was falling awkwardly down-wind, her narrow deck clearly visible as her crew fought to bring her back under control. *Undine* was overhauling her so rapidly that she was already lying some two cables from the larboard bow, and seemed to swell in size even as he watched. He saw the strange flag at her peak, black, with a red emblem in its centre. A prancing beast of some sort. He closed the glass with a snap and saw Keen flinch at the sound.

Allday grinned. "Two minutes, Captain. Just right." He nodded towards the opposite bow where the other schooner was holding steadily on course towards the headland. "He seems content to let his mates go under."

Soames was peering aft, his curved hanger glittering in the bright sunlight as he raised it slowly above his head. The glare was making him grimace so badly that he appeared to be grinning like a madman.

Bolitho looked at Mudge. "Let her fall off another point." He forced a smile. "Not a moment longer than necessary, I promise."

He pulled out his sword and held it casually across his shoulder. Through his crumpled shirt it felt like ice.

The helmsman yelled hoarsely, "Nor', nor'-west it is, sir!"

There was no time to perfect the set of the yards, no time for anything now as with barely a stagger *Undine* turned even further towards the shore, the movement dragging the labouring schooner into the view of the eager gun captains.

Bolitho shouted, "As you bear, Mr. Soames!"

Soames bellowed, "Stand by!" He came loping aft, pausing at each gun to peer along its muzzle. Satisfied, he jumped aside and yelled, *"Fire!"*

Bolitho tensed as the uneven broadside belched and shuddered along his ship's side. Soames had done well. To an extra puff of wind which had pushed the frigate over to leeward, he had judged it perfectly, taking the enemy ship on the uproll, raking her savagely from end to end.

Bolitho grasped a stay, his eyes blinded with smoke as the wind funnelled it back through every port. Men were coughing and swearing in the thick brown fog, but urged on by shouts and threats they were still managing to sponge out and reload for another broadside when needed.

He stared with amazement at the schooner as the smoke cleared away from the quarterdeck. Dismasted, almost buried under a chaos of fallen spars and ripped canvas, she seemed a total wreck.

"Bring her back to nor'-west by north, Mr. Mudge."

He did not see the master's face, his look of relief and admiration. His ears were still ringing to the thunder of cannon fire, the sharper, probing cracks of the quarterdeck six-pounders. He hoped the less experienced men had found time to tie their scarves over their ears. Caught at the wrong angle, it only took one shot to deafen a man. Often permanently.

"Run out!" Soames was peering at his crews as gun captain after captain raised a powder-blackened fist to show his weapon was loaded.

Herrick shouted, "Now for t'other one!"

He waved to Davy at the starboard battery, the gesture impulsive, unnoticed by himself. Davy waved back, his movement jerky, like a puppet. As they swept after the second schooner Midshipman Penn moved slightly to place his lieutenant between him and any possible damage.

Herrick laughed aloud. "By God, young Penn has the right idea, sir!" He peered up at the streaming pendant. "The wind is still kind, and this is putting new heart into our people."

Bolitho watched him gravely. Later they would talk about it. But when it was happening, to you, to those around you, it was pointless to discuss anything. You never really knew the man in action. Pride, anger, insanity, it was there, and more. Even on Herrick's homely face. His own, too, no doubt.

He said, "We will run him as close as we can to the headland. After that it will be up to him. Strike or fight."

He moved the sword-blade on his shoulder. The ice was gone. Now it was like a heated gun-barrel.

Mudge remarked, "That master is a fool. 'E should 'ave gone

about sooner. I would 'ave done so. Crossed *Undine*'s bows afore we could blast 'im." He sighed. "'E'll not get a second chance, I'm thinkin'."

Bolitho looked at him. Mudge was right of course. *Undine* was playing a dangerous game to drive so bravely towards a lee shore, but the schooners had taken even more of a chance.

Herrick was saying, "Prize crew on one, and take the other in tow, eh, sir? We should get good recompense for two schooners, even if one of 'em is little more than a hulk."

Bolitho watched the schooner without answering. Was Muljadi aboard her? Or in the other one, dying or already dead with some of his men? Better so, he thought, than fall into Puigserver's hands.

"Deck there!" The cry was almost lost above the chorus of spray and booming canvas. "Ship on the larboard quarter!"

Bolitho swung round, imagining for a moment that the look-out had been too long in the sun. For an instant he could see nothing, and then as his vision cleared he saw the forecourse and topsail of another ship standing around the last headland, the one they had rounded so carefully in pursuit of the schooners.

Herrick gasped, "What is she?" He stared at Bolitho. "The *Argus*?"

Bolitho nodded grimly. "I fear so, Mr. Herrick."

He tried to keep his tone level when his whole being was screaming at him to act, to do the impossible. And how easy he had made it for them. He had allowed the schooners to draw him, like a fox after two rabbits. *Argus* must have been following them along the coast, waiting for the trap to be sprung, reading Bolitho's mind without even being able to see him.

Herrick exclaimed, "Then, by God, we'll tell Mr. Frenchman to sheer off! This is none of his affair!"

Keen called, "She's overhauling us, sir."

Bolitho looked past him. The *Argus* was already beating well out on their larboard quarter, taking the wind-gage, doing exactly what he had attempted to do to the schooners. Now *Undine* was in the trap. Run aground, or try and claw to windward? He saw the sunlight flashing down the big frigate's exposed side, the small moving shadows above the creaming water as she ran out her whole broadside.

He thought of the man behind those guns. How did he feel at this moment?

Herrick said quietly, "Eighteen-pounders, I'm told, sir?" He watched his face, as if hoping for a denial of *Argus*'s strength.

"Yes."

He drew in a long breath as a flag broke from the Frenchman's peak. Black and red, like the ones which had flown above the schooners. *Letter of marque.* Hired by a foreign power, the flag merely to keep up a pretence of legality.

Keen lowered his telescope and said quickly, "She's almost to the dismasted schooner, sir." He was managing to sound calm, but his hands were shaking badly. "There are some men in the water. I think they were thrown outboard when the masts came down."

Bolitho took the glass and watched, his mind cold as he saw the frigate ride through and over the men in the water. The captain had probably not even seen them. All he saw was *Undine*.

He raised his voice, hoping the others would not despair at its strangeness. "We will alter course directly." He ignored the unspoken protest on Mudge's heavy face. "Get the t'gallants off her, Mr. Herrick. The Frenchman will expect us to do so if we are about to fight." He looked at Mudge again. "Without so much canvas we may be able to gain a little room to give an account of ourselves."

Mudge replied harshly, "It'll mean crossin' 'er bows, sir!" Even if we gets round without 'avin' the sticks torn out of us, what then? The *Argus* will overreach us and put a full broadside through our stern as she passes!"

Bolitho regarded him bleakly. "I am relying on his desire to retain the wind-gage, for without it he might change places with us." He saw no agreement in Mudge's tiny eyes. "Or would you have me haul down our colours, eh?"

Mudge flushed angrily. "That ain't fair, sir!"

Bolitho nodded. "Neither is a battle."

Mudge looked away. "I'll do me best, sir. Lay 'er as close to th' wind as she's ever bin." He tapped the compass bowl. "If th' wind 'olds, we should be able to steer almost due west." He strode to the wheel. "God 'elp me."

Bolitho turned and saw the topmen sliding down to the deck again, felt the more sluggish motion as *Undine* plunged ahead on topsails and forecourse. A glance at the other ship told him that her captain was doing likewise. He had no need to worry. *Undine* would have to stand and fight. There was no room left to run away. He walked slowly back and forth, stepping unseeingly over the six-pounder tackles, his knee brushing against a crouching seaman as he passed. *Argus*'s captain would be watching his every move. The advantage, if there was one, would last only seconds, a few minutes at best. He looked at the headland. It seemed very close now, extending far out beyond the larboard bow, like a great arm waiting to snatch them whole.

Then he strode to the quarterdeck rail and called, "Mr. Soames! I will want a broadside as we put about. You have small chance of hitting him, but the sudden challenge may have an effect." He let his gaze move slowly along the upturned faces. "You will have to reload and run out quicker than ever before. The *Argus* is a powerful ship and will endeavour to use her heavier iron to full advantage. We must get to close quarters." He felt the grin frozen to his lips like a clamp. "Show him that our lads are better, no matter what damn flag he wears!"

A few raised a cheer, but it was not much of a rally.

Herrick said quietly, "Ready when you are, sir."

It seemed very quiet. Bolitho looked aloft yet again. The pendant flicked out as before. If the wind backed further it would be some small help. If it veered it would be disaster. Then he looked at Soames as he clumped heavily aft and disappeared below the quarterdeck. To supervise the sternmost twelve-pounders, which would bear first once they had altered course. Davy was by the foremast, sending some of his own gun crews across to assist the larboard battery. If *Argus's* eighteen-pounders got to grips they would need plenty of replacements, he thought grimly.

He faced Herrick and smiled. "Well, Thomas?"

Herrick shrugged. "I'll tell you what I think when it's over and done with, sir."

Bolitho nodded. It was an unnerving feeling. It always was, of course, and yet you imagined that each time was worse than the one before. In an hour, in minutes, he could be dead. Thomas Herrick, his friend, might be fighting a battle not of his choosing, or screaming out his life on the orlop deck.

And Mudge. Hand-picked because of his vast store of knowledge. But for this commission he would have been discharged now. Living with his children, and his grandchildren, too, in all probability.

He snapped, "So be it then! Put the helm down!"

"Man the braces. Lively there!"

Shuddering and groaning in protest, *Undine* slewed round to the thunder of wind and wildly flapping canvas. Bolitho saw spray bursting through the open ports as she swayed further and further to the violent change of tack. From the corner of his eye he saw the *Argus's* topsails lifting above the hammock nettings, her shape shortening as *Undine* swung round across her bows. A gun banged out, and the ball whimpered somewhere overhead. Someone must have fired too soon, or perhaps the French captain had already guessed what they were trying to do.

Soames was ready and waiting, and the first crash of gunfire shook the deck violently, the smoke swirling up and over the nettings in a writhing pall. Gun by gun down the side, from stern to bow, the six-pounders joining in as the *Argus* crossed each black muzzle. Bolitho saw her foresail jerk and throb to the onslaught, holes appearing like magic as Soames's gun crews fired, reloaded and fired again.

When he peered forward Bolitho saw that the headland had eased back to starboard, the schooner already tiny as she scuttled around it and into the next bay.

Mudge yelled, "West by north, sir! Full an' bye!" He was mopping his eyes with his handkerchief, clinging to the mizzen mast pike rack to hold himself upright.

He gestured towards the gaff where the red ensign streamed almost abeam. "Close as we can get, sir!"

Bolitho winced as the six-pounders barked out again, and saw the nearest one bounding inboard until caught and held by its tackle. Its crew was already sponging out and groping for fresh charges and another ball from the shot garland, eyes white and staring through the grime, voices lost in the crash and roar of cannon fire, the squeal of trucks as like angry hogs the heavy guns were run out towards the enemy.

The *Argus* had at last followed Bolitho's lead. She was swinging round, her yards braced almost fore and aft, to hold the wind and keep *Undine* under her lee.

Even as he watched Bolitho saw the long orange tongues flashing from her ports, the bombardment unhurried and carefully aimed as gun by gun she fired through the swirling curtain of smoke and spray.

A ball screamed above the quarterdeck and slapped through the maintopsail before dropping far abeam. Others were hitting the hull, above or below the waterline, Bolitho had no idea. He heard someone screaming through the choking smoke, saw men dashing hither and thither like prisoners in hell as they rammed home the new charges and threw their shining, blackened bodies to the tackles again and again.

Above the din he heard Soames's deep voice rallying and cursing as he kept his men at their guns. A swivel banged out from the top, and he imagined the marines were firing more to ease their own fears than with much hope of hitting anything.

A quarterdeck gun port seemed to explode in a great burst of flame, and Bolitho saw men, and pieces of men hurled in all directions at once as a ball tore splinters from the bulwark and transformed them into hideous darts.

One marine ran sobbing from the nettings, his hands clawing at what remained of his face. Others stood or knelt by their fallen companions, firing, reloading, firing, reloading, until it seemed life itself had stopped.

A down-draught of wind swirled the smoke away, and Bolitho saw the other frigate's yards and punctured sails barely fifty yards abeam. He saw the filtered sunlight touching pikes and cutlasses as the enemy prepared to board, or to fight off their attempt to do likewise. He gasped as another line of bright tongues darted through the smoke, felt the planks buck under his feet, the crash and clatter of a gun being overturned or smashed to fragments.

When he peered upwards he saw that the maintopsail was little better than a rag, but every spar was still intact. A wounded seaman clung to the mainyard, his blood running down one leg unheeded to the deck far below. Another seaman managed to reach him and drag him to safety, and together they crouched below the maintop, caught in the severed ratlines like two broken birds.

Herrick was yelling, "He's trying to cripple us, sir! Take us as a prize!"

Bolitho nodded and stopped to drag an injured man clear of a six-pounder. He had already guessed *Argus*'s intentions. Another ship for Muljadi's use, or perhaps to replace *Argus* so that she could return to France.

The thought seemed to drive into his heart like a knife.

"We'll put the helm hard down! Swing the bows right into him!" He did not recognise his own voice. "Tell Davy to get ready to grapple!" He seized Herrick's arm. "We *must* grapple! He'll pound us to splinters at this rate!"

He felt the blast of a ball past his head, heard it strike the opposite bulwark and send a mass of wood splinters scything across the deck like arrows.

Herrick was yelling to Mudge and the men at the braces, and through the smoke Bolitho saw *Argus*'s shadowy outline loom above the forecastle, the sudden movement of figures in her bows as the two ships drove together.

Above the din of gunfire and shouting he heard the sails jerking and banging, the wind lost to them, the ship already falling sluggishly abeam.

Herrick staggered in some blood and gasped, "No use! Can't grapple!"

Bolitho stared past him. The enemy was already edging ahead and across *Undine*'s larboard bow, a few guns firing as she went, holding the wind and changing course very slightly while *Undine* floundered helplessly, her remaining sails almost aback.

She was going to rake *Undine* with every available gun, but give Bolitho time to haul down his colours before she reached his stern and finished what she had begun.

He felt Herrick tugging his arm.

"What now?"

Herrick pointed up through the smoke, where the sunlight was making a small path through the drifting smoke.

"The lookout, sir! He's reported a sail to the west'rd!" His eyes were shining with hope. "The Frenchman's making off!"

Bolitho looked at him dully. It was true and he had heard nothing. Deafened by gunfire, or fogged in his own despair, he did not know. But the *Argus* was already spreading her mainsail and was driving down-wind with gathering power towards the open strait.

Bolitho said, "Hands to the braces, Mr. Herrick. Lay her on the larboard tack again. If we can signal this newcomer we may still be able to give chase."

He heard a small cry, and when he turned he saw two seamen

kneeling beside Keen's body. The midshipman was trying to reach down to his stomach, but one of the seamen was gripping his wrists while the other slit open his bloodstained breeches with a dirk and threw them aside. A few inches above the groin there was something like a broken bone, but Bolitho knew it was far worse. A wood splinter blasted from the deck, and probably held tight by its own barbs.

He knelt down and touched it with his fingers, seeing the blood pulsing across the youth's thigh, hearing his sobs as he tried not to scream.

Bolitho thought of Whitmarsh, far away in Pendang Bay, helping to heal the sick and wounded from the garrison.

One of the seamen said, "'E'll not last, sir, without 'elp. I'll fetch a surgeon's mate."

Allday was kneeling beside him and said, "No. I'll do it."

Bolitho looked at him, seeing the determination on his face.

Then he turned and said, "Easy, Mr. Keen. You'll be about again soon."

He felt the rising anger and despair pricking his eyes. What had he brought them all to? He touched the midshipman's bare shoulder. It was smooth like a woman's. He had not even begun to live yet.

He snapped, "Are you sure, Allday?"

The coxswain eyed him calmly. "I'm as good as those other butchers."

Davy came hurrying aft and touched his hat. "Masthead has reported the other ship to be the *Bedford*, sir. The Frenchman must have thought her to be a man-of-war."

He looked at Keen's wound and said hoarsely, "My God."

Bolitho stood up slowly, watching the midshipman's fingers opening and closing like trapped animals in the seaman's strong grip.

"Very well, Allday. Take him aft to the cabin. I'll be down myself as soon as I've attended to things here."

Allday looked at him. "Don't you fret, Captain. It's the luck of the game. Our turn will come." He nodded to the two seamen. "Pick him up."

Keen gave a sharp cry as they moved him to the cabin hatch, and before he vanished below Bolitho saw that his eyes were fixed unwinkingly on the sky above the tattered sails. Trying to hold on to it? So that by keeping the picture in his mind he might retain his life itself.

Bolitho bent and picked up the midshipman's dirk from the stained deck. He handed it to Davy and said, "We will make contact with the *Bedford*. There is nothing more we can do for the present but return to the settlement."

Herrick said, "The old *Bedford*." He sounded bitter. "A bloody storeship from Madras full of seasick soldiers and their womenfolk."

Bolitho watched the helmsman bringing *Undine* carefully back on course, the skilful way they were allowing for the punctured sails' loss of power.

"If *Argus* had known that, she'd have done for both of us." He saw the surprise and sudden concern and added simply, "But not before we had rendered *her* equally useless."

He glanced aloft at the masthead pendant. How many times had he done that? He took out his watch and flicked open the guard. Remembering. The whole sea-fight had taken less than two hours, and already *Argus* was almost lost in the offshore haze which marked the coming of evening. He shaded his eyes to look for the *Bedford*, and saw her topsails on the horizon like small yellow shells.

Then he looked around at the splintered planking, the small line of corpses which had been dragged below the weather gangway. There was much to do, and he must not give way for an instant if his men were to keep the will to fight again if the time came. He saw another corpse being carried up from the forehatch, and knew he would have to deal with the reports of damage, arrange for replacements and repairs. And burials.

He heard another sharp cry through the cabin skylight, and thought of Keen being spreadeagled there while Allday tried to extract the splinter.

He said, "I am going below, Mr. Herrick. Deal with reports on damage and casualties." He saw him nod. "Thank you."

As he hurried below Herrick said quietly, "No. Thank *you.*"

Bolitho brushed past the sentry at his door and then stopped. It was very quiet in the cabin, and when he saw Keen's naked body lying on the deck he thought he was too late.

Allday said, "All done, Captain! He held up the jagged red lump in some pincers. "I think he did very well, for a lad!"

Bolitho looked down at Keen's ashen face. There was blood on his lips where one of the seamen had held a strap between his teeth to prevent him from biting through his tongue. Noddall and the other seamen were finishing tying the dressing around the wound, and there was a thick smell of rum in the air.

Bolitho said quietly, "Thank you, Allday. I never knew you understood such things."

Allday shook his head. "Did it to a sheep once. Poor thing fell down a cliff on to a broken sapling. Very much the same really."

Bolitho walked to the stern windows and sucked in a lungful of air. "You must tell Mr. Keen that when he is well again." He turned and watched him gravely. "Do you think he will fully recover?"

Allday nodded. "Yes. Another inch or so and it might have been the end." He forced a grin, seeing the strain on Bolitho's face. "For the ladies, anyway!"

The door opened and Herrick said, "We are within signalling distance of *Bedford,* sir."

"I'll come up." He paused and looked down at Keen. Even a glance told him his breathing was easier. "Casualties?"

Herrick dropped his eyes. "Ten killed, sir. Twenty wounded. It's a miracle we didn't lose far more. The carpenter and his mates are below, but it seems most of the holes are above the waterline. She's a *lucky* ship, sir."

Bolitho looked from him to Allday. "I'm the lucky one." Then he walked from the cabin.

Allday shook his head and sighed, releasing more rum into the smoky air.

"My advice is to leave him be, Mr. Herrick, sir."

Herrick nodded. "I know. But he has taken this setback badly, though I know of no captain who could have done better."

Allday dropped his voice. "But one captain *did* do better today. And ours'll not rest until he's met with him again, I'm thinking."

Keen gave a soft moan and Allday snapped, "Come on, you idlers! Basin to his head! I've poured so much grog into his guts he'll spew all over the cabin when he comes to the surface again!"

Herrick smiled and walked out towards the ladder, seeing the men replacing the lashings on the guns, glancing at him and grinning as he passed.

One of them called, "We showed the bastards, eh, sir?"

Herrick paused, "That we did, lads. The captain was proud of you."

The seaman grinned more, broadly. "Aye, sir. I seed 'im in the thick of it walkin' about like 'e was on Plymouth 'Oe. I knew then that we was go'in to be all right."

Herrick climbed towards the sunlight and stared up at the torn sails. If only you knew, he thought sadly.

He found the other lieutenants and warrant officers already assembled on the quarterdeck giving their various reports while Bolitho leaned against the mainmast trunk.

When he saw Herrick he said, "There is still a good span of daylight left. We'll put the hands to replacing canvas and running-rigging while it lasts. I have ordered the galley fire to be lit, and we'll see that our people get a good meal." He gestured towards the labouring storeship which was now less than a mile away. "We might even poach a few extra hands from *her*, eh?"

Herrick saw the others watching Bolitho dully, their bodies almost limp with exhaustion and delayed shock. He guessed that this other Bolitho, cool, confident, filled with ideas again, was the one the seaman on the gun crew had pictured throughout the battle.

The fact that he knew the real Bolitho behind the shield made him feel suddenly privileged and restored.

12

IN FOR A *B*LOW

REAR ADMIRAL Beves Conway made a dark silhouette against the window's colourful rectangle, but Bolitho could recognise his impatience even though his back was turned. Beyond him, still and peaceful above their own varying shadows, the anchored ships shone in the late sunlight.

Undine lay apart from the heavy transport and the little brig *Rosalind,* and it was impossible to see the damage she had received from the French frigate's eighteen-pounders. Occasionally, when there was a lull in the voices, Bolitho heard the echoes of thudding hammers, the rasp of saws to show that only distance made *Undine's* trim appearance a lie.

The air in the big, timbered room was cool after the open bay, and although the various figures sitting around it looked as if they had barely moved since his last visit, Bolitho noticed that the place itself had changed considerably in so short a time. More furniture, some rugs, and a whole array of gleaming decanters and glasses made it look lived in, rather than a fortress under siege.

Don Luis Puigserver sat on a brass-bound chest, sipping wine, while James Raymond, tight-lipped and unsmiling, faced him across a littered table. The brig's master, Captain Vega of the original garrison and two red-coated soldiers from the *Bedford* made up the rest of the gathering. One of the latter, a heavy-faced man introduced briefly as Major Frederick Jardine, and who commanded the soldiers brought from Madras, Bolitho instantly recognised as the one he had seen there when he had been escorting Viola Raymond. He had a fat, belligerent face, and his small, piggy eyes had hardly left Bolitho since he had arrived. The other soldier, a Captain Strype, was his second-in-command, and a complete opposite. Tall and stick-thin, with a black moustache, he spoke with a lisp, and had a short, barking laugh. He was probably rather stupid, Bolitho thought, but was obviously much in awe of his superior.

Conway said sharply, "Naturally I am very distressed to learn of *Argus's* attack, Captain Bolitho."

Raymond said, "*Unwarranted,* too."

Conway turned lightly on his heels, his hair yellow in the sunlight. "But not unexpected, Raymond. Not by me, that is. It was obvious from the beginning that the French were implicated. They have to be, for their own interest's sake. We are lucky that *Bedford's* arrival put paid to their intention to take Captain Bolitho's ship from him." He shifted his gaze, his tone incisive. "And he would have done so, eh?"

Bolitho felt all their eyes on him. "I believe so, sir."

Conway bobbed his head. "Good. Good, Bolitho. I wanted the truth and, believe me, I know what it cost you."

Raymond tried again to put his point of view. "I think, sir, that we should despatch the brig to Madras without delay. Sir Montagu Strang may consider that further operations here might be imprudent." He ignored Conway's stiffening shoulders. "Later, perhaps, some new plan may be conceived. Until then, we must take this affair as a warning."

Conway rasped, "A *warning?* Do you imagine that for one instant I will let some damned pirate work off his wrath on me and so imperil the very task I have just undertaken?" He stepped closer. "Well, *do you?*"

Raymond paled but replied stubbornly, "I am here on behalf of the government, sir. As an adviser. The French must realise that you are out-manoeuvred before you have begun. If this Muljadi is allowed to plunder and ravage these waters, then there is no chance of using Pendang Bay as a new and flourishing station for trade. No shipping master would risk it." He turned towards the brig's captain. "Is that not so?"

The man nodded glumly. "We need more protection, sir."

Raymond sounded triumphant. "Exactly! Which is what the French intend. If we ask for more men-of-war to patrol the area, they, too, will even the balance by sending additional consorts for *Argus*."

Conway stared at him. "Then so be it!"

"No, sir. It would mean war. *Argus* is protected by her letter of marque. Muljadi is protected by his own power and backed up by big French friends. There are a thousand Muljadis in the Indies, some who are genuine rulers, and some who reign over fewer people than Captain Bolitho does at present. We all want to extend our trade and influence, to China if need be, and beyond. There are riches we can only dream of, lands where people have never heard of King George, or Louis either, for that matter."

Bolitho said quietly, "You are advising the governor to admit defeat, sir. Do I understand correctly?"

Raymond smiled calmly. "As you have done, eh?"

Bolitho walked to the window and stared down at his ship. It gave him time. Allowed the sudden blinding anger to depart. In the lower enclosure he saw Midshipman Keen sitting with one of the ship's boys rescued from the *Nervion*. He had been detailed to look after Keen, to assist him, if only by making him rest. It was still not possible to be sure he would recover from his wound. Was it really only the day before yesterday? The smoke and noise, the aftermath of hard, heavy work to put their ship to rights. The sea-burials, each corpse heavily weighted to ensure it went straight down to avoid the prowling sharks.

He said, "I take it, Mr. Raymond, you have never borne arms for your country?" He did not wait for an answer. "Had you ever worn the King's coat you would have known that one defeat, if admitted, is not the end of a battle."

He heard Captain Strype say in his thin voice, "By Gad, that's not much of an argument, what?"

Bolitho turned swiftly, his tone hard. "I was addressing Raymond, sir, not some damned mercenary who because of his rank imagines himself to be a solider!"

Don Puigserver brought his glass down to the table with a loud bang. "Gentlemen! I know that Vega and I are no longer involved here. I also believe that both Señor Raymond and the governor," he bowed slightly to Conway, "are both right. With Muljadi free to use his ruthless power and so influence other *friendly* rulers in the Indies, you can make no advances. With more military strength you would only excite a hostile reaction and further French involvement." He paused and gave an eloquent shrug. "Which I doubt my own country could ignore."

Bolitho nodded towards him, grateful for his interruption. Another second and he knew he would have said too much, and Conway, even had he wanted to, would have been unable to help him.

Major Jardine cleared his throat. "Despite what the gallant captain has said," he did not look at Bolitho, "I believe my force will be sufficient. I have two hundred sepoys and a mule battery. All experienced." He had a thick voice, and sweated badly, despite the room's comparative coolness.

Puigserver regarded him gravely. "If *Nervion* had been here, none of this could have happened. An additional ship, the men, and the showing of our flag to the *Argus* would certainly have delayed, if not defeated, Muljadi's intentions."

Conway said, "But she is not here. Only the *Undine*."

Jardine said thickly, "And she does not seem to have acquitted herself too well." He turned to Bolitho, his small eyes like steel.

"Even as a mere soldier, a *mercenary,* I can see that neither of the schooners lies at anchor, and as far as we know, the *Argus* still flies Muljadi's colours. What say *you,* Captain?"

Bolitho faced him. "The first schooner turned turtle and sank. The other took advantage of *Argus's* presence to escape." He could feel little emotion now. Words and taunts were inevitable. It was better to get it over with. Clear the air.

"Indeed, yes." Jardine leaned back in his chair, his polished boots squeaking. "And then the *Bedford* arrived to give you help. The poor, much-maligned Company's own ship was the one to drive *Argus* away."

"Had you been there, Major—"

Jardine spread his plump hands. "But I was not, sir. I am a soldier. I am supposed to be able to leave such matters to our Navy, surely?"

Conway said coldly, "I have heard enough. I will brook no more hostility here. Not from you, Bolitho," he looked at Jardine, "nor from anyone else!" He thrust his hands behind him, making his sloping shoulders droop even further. "Had *Undine* been beaten in open combat I would have removed Captain Bolitho from command. He knows that well enough, and so should the rest of you. The Navy is too often expected to fight greater forces than itself possesses, and has been so successful in the past that victory against ridiculous odds is now taken for granted. By the empty-minded men of politics, and those who care more for quick profit than lasting security! As it is, Captain Bolitho will be required to sail without further delay, other than completing *necessary* repairs, for Muljadi's own territory in the strait." He looked at Bolitho calmly. "You will make contact with *Argus's* captain, under flag of truce, and convey a message which I will give you."

Raymond said quickly, "May I suggest, plead with you, sir, that you allow Don Puigserver to go with Captain Bolitho? He has the right to demand the freedom of Spain's last governor here, Colonel Pastor. He could explain his displeasure at such—"

Conway shouted, his voice bounding back from the timbered walls. "I have been appointed governor, Raymond! I don't need your apron strings, nor do I need the help of the King of Spain, d'you understand?"

Raymond's defiance wilted under Conway's sudden anger. He said nothing.

Puigserver stood up and walked slowly towards the door, followed gratefully by Capitan Vega.

He paused and looked back at them, his eyes very dark. "I would have accompanied Capitan Bolitho with pleasure, of course." He smiled briefly. "I have a great admiration for his courage, his . . ." he searched for the word, ". . . his integrity. But I have much to do. My task is to embark the remaining Spanish soldiers and their dependents on to the *Bedford*." He glanced at Conway, his smile fading. "As you remarked this morning, the flag of Spain no longer has authority here."

Bolitho watched him stride out. He had sensed the tension as soon as he had arrived. It could not have been easy for Conway. Fretting over lack of news, waiting for supplies and troops to arrive. But he was wrong to antagonise Puigserver. If things went badly here, Conway would need all the references he could get, even in Spain.

Jardine remarked vaguely, "I'd better be off then. Settle the sepoys in their company lines, and replace the marines as sentries and pickets."

No thanks, no admiration for what Captain Bellairs and his marines had achieved in so short a time. Bolitho glanced through the window again. The encroaching brush and creeper cleared away, and corpses buried. The place used as a hospital had been cleaned and painted, and even Whitmarsh had been full of praise for their efforts.

Conway nodded. "I will meet you here after sunset, Major."

Bolitho waited until the two soldiers had left the room and

then said, "I am sorry about my outburst, sir. But I have had my bellyful of his kind."

Conway grunted. "Perhaps. But you will hold your tongue in future. If Jardine commanded only a handful of crippled beggars I would say the same. I need every man I can get."

Raymond stood up and yawned. "This damned heat. I think I'll take a nap before dinner."

He, too, walked out. He did not look at Bolitho.

Conway said softly, "He disliked your remark about bearing arms, you know." He chuckled. "His wife has been singing the praises of sea-officers in general during your absence, and you in particular." He frowned. "I seem to be plagued with those intent on disruption."

"Is she well, sir?" He could not face him. "I have not seen her since my return."

"She's been assisting that sot of a surgeon with the sick and wounded." His eyebrows mounted. "*Surprised?* By God, Bolitho, you've much to learn about women!" He nodded sharply. "But you'll see, all in good time."

Bolitho recalled her refusal to help tend the injured aboard *Undine* after Puigserver had been carried aboard more dead than alive. And her reasons? He sighed. Perhaps Puigserver and Conway were both right. He had much to learn.

He replied, "I will return to the ship, sir. There will be a lot to arrange."

"Yes." Conway watched him thoughtfully. "And remember. When you meet *Argus*'s captain, keep your personal feelings to yourself. He is doing his own work as best he can. You would do the same if so ordered. If Le Chaumareys is still in command, and not killed by one of your guns, he will be eager to meet you also. He is older than you, but I think you may have something in common." His lines deepened as he added dryly, "A disrespect for your superiors, if nothing else!"

Bolitho picked up his hat. You could never be sure about Conway. Where the warmth ended and the steel began.

Conway said, "Please come ashore tonight and dine with the rest of . . ." he waved one hand around the room, ". . . the cast-aways."

Bolitho recognised the dismissal and walked from the room.

Beyond the palisades the jungle was as thick and as overpowering as ever, and yet already the place felt familiar, lasting.

He found Allday lounging in the shade below the main entrance. He was watching some native women who were washing clothes in a large wooden trough. They were small and olive-skinned, and although well covered, displayed supple charm which Allday apparently admired greatly.

He straightened his back and said, "All done, Captain?" He saw Bolitho's glance and nodded. "Fair little wenches. We will have to watch our people, Captain."

"Only the people?"

Allday grinned. "Ah, well now . . ."

At that moment Bolitho saw the surgeon emerge from the makeshift hospital, wiping his hands on a rag and squinting into the slanting sunlight.

He saw Bolitho and nodded. "Two of the men wounded in your battle can return to work, sir. Two more died, as you know, but the rest stand a good chance of survival." He looked away. "Until the next time."

Bolitho considered his words. A total of twelve had died because of *Argus*. Despite the luck at there being few in comparison to the fierceness of the battle, it was too many. He sighed. Perhaps Herrick had got some more "volunteers" from the other ships.

Whitmarsh said, "Your coxswain did a good job, by the way. The boy should have died by rights." He looked at Allday. "Wasted. You should make something of your life!"

Bolitho said quietly, "I am glad you thanked him for his efforts on Mr. Keen's behalf. But I am sure he will decide his own future."

Allday could have been stone-deaf for all the notice he paid to their comments.

Whitmarsh said, "Well, anyway, sir, I've cleaned up a bit here. Most of them will heal, although a few more will die before they reach Spain. Disease mostly, of course."

"Of course?"

Whitmarsh looked him full in the eyes. "Rotten with it just as they have given it to these poor ignorant savages, too. If any one of your sailors comes to me with that damned pox, I'll make him wish he'd never touched a woman in his life!"

"They are your sailors, too, Mr. Whitmarsh."

Bolitho regarded him searchingly. Despite his usual attitude where naval matters were concerned, he looked a great deal better. Or perhaps there was little to drink here? Either way, he was nothing like the drunken hulk who had tumbled aboard in England.

"So *there* you are, Captain!"

He turned and saw her watching him from the entrance. She was almost covered by a white smock, and wore the same straw hat she had brought from Santa Cruz. Her eyes were in shadow, but there was no doubting the warmth of her smile.

He replied, "I am grateful for what you have done, ma'am."

Whitmarsh nodded. "She is the one who took charge here. Organised the whole hospital from top to bottom." His admiration was genuine.

She smiled at Allday and then slipped her hand through Bolitho's arm.

"I'll walk with you to the beach, if I may. It is so refreshing to have you back again."

Bolitho could feel Whitmarsh and Allday watching them.

He said, "You are looking, er, very well."

Her hand tightened very slightly. "Say Viola."

He smiled. "Viola."

"Better."

When she spoke again her voice was different. "I saw your ship dropping anchor and was half mad with anxiety. I wanted James to take me out to her by boat. He refused. He would. Then I saw you with a telescope. It was like being there with you. And today I have spent a little time with Valentine."

"Valentine?" Bolitho looked at her profile. "Who is that?"

She laughed. "Of course, you would never remember a thing like a mere name. Why, I am speaking of your Mr. Keen." The mood changed again. "The poor boy. He looks so ill, yet can speak of no one but you." She gripped his arm hard. "I am almost jealous!"

Bolitho looked past her to where the gig lay beached on the sand, the small breakers hissing and receding around it. The boat's crew were engaged in noisy conversation with some seamen from the brig, and it was plain they were describing what they still saw as their victory over the *Argus* and the schooners.

He smiled, despite his earlier bitterness and disappointment. Perhaps they were right. To remain alive under such circumstances could well be seen as a victory.

She was looking at him, standing slightly apart as if searching for something.

"You smile, Captain? At me? At my boldness perhaps."

He reached out and took her hand. "Not that. Never."

She tossed her head. "That is better, Captain."

He heard Allday's shoes on the sand, the sudden silence from the gig.

"The name is Richard," he said gravely.

Allday heard their combined laughter and felt suddenly worried. This was a danger he could recognise well enough, far better than his captain, he thought.

He removed his hat as Bolitho walked, down the beach towards the gig, and heard him say, "I will be ashore later, ma'am!"

She held the hat brim to shade her eyes. "Until then, Captain!"

But Allday had seen the look on her face before it was hidden in shadow. That, too, was something he could recognise. He glanced quickly at the tower above the fort and took a deep breath.

Squalls ahead, he decided, and not too far away.

Bolitho looked it him. "Well?"

Allday's face was rigid. "So it would appear, Captain!

Three days after returning to Teluk Pendang His Majesty's frigate *Undine* weighed anchor again and put to sea. By late afternoon of that day she stood well out in the glittering expanse of the Java Sea with not even a cormorant for company.

To any casual observer who might have watched her departure there was little to betray her mauling from *Argus's* cannon, but as Bolitho came on deck he was well aware of it.

Shrouds and stays which had been cut by grape and canister shone brightly in their fresh tar. Deck planking, hastily replaced, looked duller than the well-tried and holystoned wood which had been in the ship since she had been built. The sailmaker and his mates had been busier than most, and even now, as he walked slowly along the weather side, Bolitho saw Jonas Tait squatting with some helpers, his one eye gleaming watchfully as with needles and palms they continued with their patching.

Fowlar, who was master's mate of the watch, touched his forehead and reported, "South-west by south, sir." He gestured abeam. "A bit of a swell, and Mr. Soames has gone forrard to check the gun lashings!"

Bolitho glanced at the compass and then the set of each sail by turn. He had already noticed the steep, sickening motion, but it was too early to gauge its importance. The barometer was unsteady, but that was usual in these latitudes, and when he had consulted Mudge he had chosen his words carefully.

"Could be in for a storm, sir. You never know in these waters!"

He nodded to Fowlar and walked to the quarterdeck rail, feeling the sun lingering on his shoulders and face. It was a fair wind, he thought, but sultry, and somehow depressing.

He saw Herrick speaking with Soames by the starboard twelve-pounders. The boatswain was there, too, pointing out various repairs yet to be done, and through the main hatch he heard the lively sounds of a jig from the ship's fiddler. Normal, everyday sights and noises. He shifted wearily and begin to pace up and down the weather side.

From one corner of his eye he saw Soames climb from the gun deck, make as if to approach him, and then return to the opposite side of the deck. Bolitho was relieved. Soames had proved himself a tower of strength in a fight, but as a conversationalist he was heavy and limited.

And Bolitho needed to be left alone. To think. To examine the rights and the wrongs of what he had done. With the land left far astern, and once more abandoned to his own resources, he could view everything much more clearly. Now, as his shadow bobbed and swayed above the black six-pounders, he decided there were far more wrongs than rights.

Inevitable? Something which either of them could have stopped in a second merely by a word, a hint even? He recalled the way she had watched him across the table while the others had talked and chattered the night away. Capitan Vega had entertained them with a song so sad it had brought tears to his eyes. Puigserver had spoken of his adventures in the South Americas and the West Indies before the war. Raymond had become steadily drunk after getting into a fruitless argument with Major Jardine on the possibilities of a lasting peace with France.

Conway had remained terribly sober, or if not, Bolitho thought he must be a better actor than he had imagined.

When then, had the actual moment of decision arrived?

He had found himself on the upper rampart with her at his side, leaning over the rough timber to look at the anchored ships in the bay. They had made a fine picture. Tiny lights reflected on the uneasy water, the pale splash of oars as a guardboat patrolled monotonously around its heavier charges.

Without looking at him she had said, "I want you to stay on shore tonight. Will you?"

Perhaps that had been the moment? He had felt reckless, dangerously so.

"I'll send a message to my first lieutenant!"

He turned to stare along the deck. Herrick was still talking to Shellabeer, and he wondered if he had guessed what had occurred.

He could remember the room exactly. More like a cell, with fewer luxuries than a lieutenant's cabin in a man-of-war. He had lain on the bed, his fingers locked behind his head, listening to the strange noises beyond the walls and the rapid beats of his own heart.

Cries from the jungle, the occasional call of a picket challenging one of the sergeants of the guard. Wind murmuring around the square tower without response from deck or rigging which was his normal life.

Then he had heard the sound of her footstep in the passageway, a quick whisper to her maid before she opened the door and shut it quickly behind her.

It was becoming harder to remember in perfect sequence. The continuity was confused. He could recall holding her tightly against his body, the warmth of her mouth on his, the overwhelming, desperate need which threw all last sudden caution to the winds.

There had been no light in the tiny room, but that from the moon. He had seen her only briefly, her bare shoulder and thigh shining like silver before she had climbed on to the bed, pulling him down and down, until at last, spent and gasping with the extent of their desire they had lain together as one.

He could not remember sleeping at all. Just holding her, needing her, tortured by the realisation it could not last.

Once during the night and towards dawn she had whispered in his ear, "Do not reproach yourself. It is not a question of honour. It is a part of life." She had put her lips to his shoulder and had added softly, "What a lovely smell you have. Of the ship. Salt and tar." She had giggled quietly. "I must have it, too."

Then the nervous tap on the door, the quick scramble to put on her gown as her faithful maid warned of the coming of another day.

But for Bolitho it had been different from all other days. He felt totally unlike anything he had been before. Alive, yet restless. Replete, but needing more.

He heard steps on the deck and saw Herrick watching him.

"Yes, Mr. Herrick?"

"Wind's freshening again, sir. Shall I call the hands to reef tops'ls?" He ran his eyes across the ship. "Rigging's straining a'piece by the sound of it."

"We'll give her her head a while longer. Until eight bells if possible, when we change tack and run to the west'rd. No sense in tiring the hands when one operation will suffice." He leaned back, hands on hips as he stared at the main topgallant masthead, the long pendant undulating in the wind. "She's a lot of power to offer us yet."

"Aye, sir." Herrick sounded tired.

"Is anything wrong?"

Bolitho walked to the weather rail and out of earshot of Soames and two seamen who were splicing halliards.

Herrick said quietly, "You know already, sir. I've said my piece. What's done is done."

Bolitho watched him gravely. "Then let us leave it well alone."

Herrick sighed. "Very well, sir." He looked at the helmsmen. "I'm sorry I could only get four extra hands. Neither *Bedford* nor the *Rosalind* were eager to part with any more. And those I did obtain are troublemakers by the cut of them." He gave a slow smile. "Although Mr. Shellabeer assures me they will change their ways before another dawn."

Midshipman Armitage ran up the ladder and touched his hat.

To Herrick he stammered, "Mr. Tapril's respects, sir, and would you join him in the magazine."

Herrick asked, "Is that all?"

The boy looked uncomfortable. "He said you'd *promised*, sir."

"And so I did, Mr. Armitage."

As the midshipman hurried away Herrick said, "I was going to arrange to have the powder casks inspected and marked again. No sense in losing good powder." He lowered his voice "Look, sir, are you sure you cannot see the folly of what you are doing? There is no telling what damage it might do to your career."

Bolitho swung towards him and then saw the anxious concern on Herrick's face.

He replied, "I am relying on your lady luck, Thomas!"

He walked towards the cabin hatch, adding for Soames's benefit, "Call me the moment there is a change."

Soames watched him go and then walked aft to the compass.

Fowlar watched him warily. Once back in England, he, too, would get the chance to obtain a commission as lieutenant. The captain had said as much, and that was good enough. But if he did make that first all-important step up the ladder, he hoped he would be happier about it than Lieutenant Soames appeared to be.

Soames rasped, "Mr. Fowlar, your helmsmen are wandering off a point or so! Damn my eyes, I don't expect that from you!"

Fowlar watched him move away and smiled to himself. There was nothing wrong with the helm, and Soames knew it. It was part of the game.

He said, "Watch your helm, Mallard."

Mallard transferred a plug of tobacco from one cheek to the other and nodded.

"Aye, Mr. Fowlar, sur."

The watch continued.

Before the last dog watch had ran its course it was obvious the rising wind made it necessary to reef topsails.

Bolitho gripped the hammock nettings and faced along his ship's length as he watched the petty officers checking their men in readiness for going aloft, while Shellabeer and his own hands were already busy scrambling about the boat-tier with further lashings.

Herrick shouted above the wind, "A second reef within the hour, sir, if I'm any judge!"

Bolitho turned aft and felt the spray as it hissed freely above the weather quarter. The wind had backed rapidly and now blew lustily from the south-east, making the motion both violent and uncomfortable.

He replied, "We will steer due west once we have reefed. On the larboard tack she will be steadier."

He watched the great, steeply banked swell, like serried lines of angry glass hills. When the wind got up further, those rounded rollers would break into heavy waves.

Bolitho heard Mudge shout, "We're in for a blow right enough, sir!" He was clinging to his misshapen hat, his small eyes watering in the wind. "The barometer is poppin' about like a pea on a drum!"

Davy shouted, "All mustered, sir!"

"Very well. Hands aloft." Herrick held up his hand. "Keep them from racing each other, and stop the bosun's mates from using their ropes'-ends." He glanced at Bolitho. "One slip, and a man would go overboard without a chance of recovery."

Bolitho agreed. Herrick always remembered things like that.

He said, "I hope this doesn't last too long. If we have to ride it out it will upset Admiral Conway's other arrangements, I have no doubt."

He looked up as faint shouts and curses told him of the struggle the topmen were having with the violent, unruly canvas. Fisting and kicking, pitching this way and that, with the deck far below, the very sight of their efforts made him feel queasy.

It took the best part of an hour to master the sails to Herrick's satisfaction, and by then it was time to take in yet another reef. Spray and spindrift whipped across the weather side, and every timber and stay seemed to be groaning in a protesting chorus.

Bolitho shouted, "Lay her round another point, Mr. Herrick! We will steer west-by-south!"

Herrick nodded, his face running with spray. "Afterguard to the mizzen braces!" He shook his speaking trumpet angrily. "Keep together, damn you!"

A marine had slipped and fallen in a scarlet heap, knocking several of his comrades into confusion.

Bolitho pointed abeam, to the first glitter of white crests as the wind did its work.

"She's steadier, Mr. Herrick!" He relaxed as the experienced seamen rushed aft to help the marines and less skilled hands on the mizzen braces. "And not a man hurt by the looks of it!"

Undine had paid off stiffly to the wind, her shrouds and ratlines shining jet-black against the rising swell. But with her yards comfortably braced, and canvas reduced to topsails and jibs, she was making the best of it.

Davy panted on to the quarterdeck, his shirt wringing and sodden.

"All secure, sir!" He lurched backwards, tottered and then reeled against the nettings, adding savagely, "By the Lord, I'd forgotten what a real gale felt like!"

Bolitho smiled. "Dismiss the watch below. But tell the boatswain to make regular inspections. We can't afford to lose precious gear for want of a good lashing." He turned to Herrick. "Come below with me."

Despite the din of sea and strained timbers it seemed warm and inviting in the cabin. Bolitho watched the spray making diagonal patterns across the stern windows, heard the rudder grinding and squeaking while the helmsmen held the frigate on her new course.

Noddall pattered into the cabin, his small body steeply angled as he fetched goblets for the two officers.

Herrick wedged himself in a corner of the bench seat and regarded Bolitho questioningly.

"If we have to run before the wind, would it make so much difference, sir?"

Bolitho thought of his written orders, Conway's brief but lucid instructions.

"It might." He waited until they both had goblets and said, "To what we can achieve, Thomas!"

Herrick chuckled, "I'll share *that* toast!"

Bolitho sat at the desk, feeling the deck tilting and then sliding into yet another trough.

He was glad he had insisted that Keen and some of the other wounded had been left at Pendang Bay. Too much of this sort of motion would burst open even the finest stitches.

He said, "Admiral Conway intends to let *Bedford* put to sea as soon as we are on our way to the Benua Islands. I think he wishes to get rid of the Spanish troops and dependents as soon as possible."

Herrick watched him. "Bit risky, isn't it, sir? With the damned *Argus* still at large?"

Bolitho shook his head. "I think not. I am certain the French or Muljadi will have agents watching Conway's settlement. They will have seen us weigh anchor. *Argus* will know we are coming well enough."

Herrick looked glum. "They are as clever as that, eh?"

"We must assume so. I think Conway is right. Better to get *Bedford* away with her passengers and despatches for Madras before things get any worse."

"If there's a real storm, it'll put paid to everything!" Herrick cheered up somewhat. "The Frogs don't like bad weather!"

Bolitho smiled at Herrick's confidence. "This one may not care. He has been in these waters a long time, I believe. He is not one of the hit-and-run kind who used to dash out of Brest or Lorient and flee for home again at the sight of an English ship!" He rubbed his chin. "This Le Chaumareys interests me. I would like to know more of him than his record in battle."

Herrick nodded. "He appears to know a lot about you, sir."
"Too much."

A steep roller cruised beneath the quarter, holding the ship up
and tilting her forward at a steeper angle before freeing her again
to sidle into the next rough. Beyond the closed door they heard the
marine sentry slip and fall, his musket clattering away while he
cursed and fought to regain his composure.

Bolitho said slowly, "When we meet with *Argus*'s captain we
must keep our eyes well opened. If he agrees to parley, we may
learn something. If not, we must be ready to fight."

Herrick frowned. "I'd rather fight, sir. It's the only way I know
how to be at ease with a Frenchman!"

Bolitho thought suddenly of that room at the Admiralty, the
calm features of Admiral Winslade as he had given a brief outline
of *Undine*'s mission. Four months back. A time of peace, yet ships
had foundered, and men had been killed or crippled for life.

But even the lordly power of admiralty, the guile and experience of politics were useless out here. A solitary, wind-swept
frigate, minimum resources, and no guiding hand when one might
be needed.

Herrick took Bolitho's quiet mood as a signal. He placed his
goblet inside the table fiddles and rose carefully to his feet.

"Time to do my rounds, sir." He cocked his head to listen as
water gurgled and sluiced along the quarterdeck scuppers. "I have
the middle watch, and may snatch a cat-nap before I face the
breeze."

Bolitho pulled out his watch and felt Herrick looking at it.

"I will turn in now. I have a notion we may all be needed
before long."

In fact, it felt only minutes after his head had touched the
pillow that someone was clinging to the cot and tapping his shoulder. It was Allday, his shadow rising and falling like a black spectre
as the cabin lantern swung violently from the deckhead.

"Sorry to wake you, Captain, but it's getting far worse up top."

He paused to allow Bolitho's brain to clear. "Mr. Herrick told me to pass the word!"

Bolitho stumbled out of the cot, instantly conscious of a new, more uneven motion. As he pulled on his breeches and shoes and held out his arms for a heavy tarpaulin coat he asked, "What time is it?"

Allday had to shout as the sea thundered against the hull and surged angrily along the upper deck.

"Morning watch is about to be called, sir!"

"Tell Mr. Herrick! Call them *now!*" He gripped his arm and together they lurched half across the cabin like two tipsy sailors. "I want all hands directly! I'm going to the chart space."

He found Mudge already there, his lumpy figure sprawled across the table while he peered at the chart, blaspheming quietly as the lantern went mad above his head.

Bolitho snapped, "How is it?"

He glanced up at him, his eyes red in the feeble glow.

"Bad, sir. We'll 'ave the canvas in shreds unless we lie to for a bit."

Bolitho peered at the chart. Plenty of sea-room. That was the only consolation.

He hurried towards the quarterdeck ladder and almost fell as the ship swayed and corkscrewed in two separate motions. He fought his way to the wheel, where four helmsmen, their bodies lashed firmly to prevent their being caught unawares by an incoming wave, were fighting the spokes, their eyes glowing in the flickering compass light.

Herrick shouted, "I've called all hands, sir! And I've put extra ones on the pumps!"

Bolitho peered at the jerking compass card. "Very well. We will lie to under shortened maintops'l. Get Davy to put the best men aloft at once!"

He turned as a sound like gunshot echoed above the shriek of wind and sea, and saw the mizzen topsail rip itself apart, the fragments tearing yet again into ragged streamers, pale against the low, scudding clouds.

He could hear the dismal clank of pumps, hoarse cries as men blundered to their stations, dodging below the gangways as more frothing water flooded amongst them.

Fowlar shouted, "The sailmaker has only just repaired that cro'jack, sir!" He was grinning, in spite of the confusion. "He'll not be pleased!"

Bolitho was watching the black shapes of the topmen as they climbed cautiously up the vibrating ratlines. The wind flattened them occasionally against the shrouds, so that they hung motionless before starting up again for the topsail yards.

Mudge yelled, "Th' quarter boat 'as carried away, sir!"

No one paid any heed, and Herrick spluttered in spray before saying, "There goes the foretops'l, sir! Those lads are doing fine."

Something dropped amongst the taut rigging before falling to the gun deck with a sickening thud.

Herrick shouted, "Man from aloft! Take him to the surgeon!"

Bolitho bit his lip. It was unlikely he could live after such a fall.

Fighting every yard of the way, *Undine* came round into the wind, her hull awash from quarterdeck to beakhead, and with men clinging to tethered guns or stanchions as each wave surged and broke across her reeling deck.

Mudge bellowed hoarsely, "She'll ride it out now, sir!"

Bolitho nodded, his mind cringing from the onslaught, the very vehemence of the storm.

"We'll set the spanker if the tops'l carries away. Tell the boatswain to have his hands ready, there'll not be time for regrets if that one goes!"

He felt a bowline being bent around his waist, and saw Allday's teeth bared in a grin.

"You look after us, Captain. This'll take care of you."

Bolitho nodded, the breath knocked out of him. Then he clung to the dripping nettings, peering through the painful needles of spray as he watched over his command. A lucky ship? Perhaps he had spoken too soon. Tempted fate.

Herrick gasped, "Could be over by first light, sir."

But when dawn did come, and Bolitho saw the angry, copper-coloured clouds reflected upon the endless, jagged wavecrests, he knew it was not going to give up so willingly.

High above the deck, torn and broken cordage floated to the wind like dead creeper, and the solitary braced topsail looked so full-bellied that it could follow the fate of the other at any second.

He looked at Herrick, seeing the angry sores on his neck and hands where the blown salt had done its work. The other crouching, battered figures nearby were no better. He thought of the other frigate, probably snug in a protected anchorage, and felt the anger welling up inside him.

"Get some hands aloft, Mr. Herrick! There's work to be done!"

Herrick was already clawing his way along the nettings towards the rail.

Bolitho wiped his face and mouth with his arm. If they could weather this one, he thought, they would be ready for anything.

13

NO *Q*UARTER

"Some more 'ot coffee, sir?" Noddall held his pot above Bolitho's mug without waiting for a reply.

Bolitho sipped it slowly, feeling the scalding liquid running through him. A taste of rum, too. Noddall was certainly doing his best.

He eased his shoulders and winced. Every bone and fiber seemed to ache. As if he had been in actual battle.

He studied the weary figures who were moving about the upper deck, made curiously ghostlike and unreal by the heavy vapour which rose from sodden planking and clothing alike.

It had been just that, he thought gravely. A battle, no less than if cannon had been employed. For three days and nights they had fought it out, their confined world made even smaller by the great roaring expanse of wavecrests, their minds blunted by the ceaseless shriek of the wind. Like him, the ship seemed to have had the breath knocked from her. Now, under barely drawing topsails, her littered decks steaming once more beneath an empty sky, she was thrusting only slowly above her reflection. In places paint had been pared away to display wood so bare it could have been the work of a carpenter. Everywhere men were at work, marlin spikes and needles, hammers and tackles, endeavouring to restore the ship which had carried them through such a frenzy that even Mudge had admitted it was one of the bitterest he had endured.

He came across the deck now, his coat steaming gently, his jowls almost hidden in white stubble.

"Accordin' to me reckonin', sir, we've overreached the Benua Group by a fair piece. When we checks the noon sights I'll be 'appier." He squinted upwards towards the flapping pendant which had lost almost half its length in the storm. "But the wind's veered as I thought it might. I suggest we 'old your new course, nor' nor'-east until we gets a better fix of our position." He blew his nose loudly. "An' I'd make so bold as to say 'ow well you 'andled 'er, sir." He puffed out his cheeks. "A couple o' times I thought we was done for."

Bolitho looked away. "Thank you."

He was thinking of two men less fortunate. One had gone during the second night. Swept away without a sound. Nobody had seen him go. The other had slipped from the larboard cathead where he had been working feverishly to repair chafing lashings around the anchor stock. A solitary wavecrest had pulled him from his perch almost casually, so that for a while longer he had still imagined he would be saved. Willing hands reached out for him, but another wave had flung him not outwards but high in the air like a kicking doll before hurling him against the massive anchor with savage force. Roskilly, a bosun's mate, had insisted he had heard the man's ribs cave in before he had been dragged screaming into the frothing water alongside.

Including the man who had fallen from aloft, that made three dead, with some seven others injured. Broken bones; fingers torn raw by bucking, sodden canvas; skin inflamed by salt, by wind, and by lines snaking through clutching hands in pitch darkness made up most of the surgeon's list.

Herrick strode aft and said, "I'm having a new jib bent on now, sir. The other's only fit for patching." He took a mug from Noddall and cradled it gratefully to his mouth. "Heaven help the poor sailorman!"

Bolitho looked at him. "You'd not change it."

Herrick grimaced. "A few times back there I wondered if I'd get the choice!"

Davy, who had the watch, joined them by the rail.

"What are our chances of a landfall, sir?"

He looked older, less assured than he had before the action with the frigate. During the storm he had behaved well, so perhaps he still believed the only real menace came from a cannon's mouth.

Bolitho considered his question. "That will depend on fixing our position. Allowing for our drift, and the shifting of the wind, I'd say we might sight the islands before nightfall."

He smiled, the effort making him more conscious of the strain he had been under.

Herrick said dourly, "The damned Frog will be laughing at us. Sitting in harbour under that bloody pirate's guns."

Bolitho looked at him thoughtfully. The same idea had only left him occasionally, and that when he had needed all his thoughts elsewhere. To parley with the French captain was one thing. To accept that he was serving under Muljadi's flag meant far more. It would be an open admission of failure. An acceptance that Muljadi's sovereignty did exist. If Conway agreed to the latter, every other European power which had trading and protection rights in the Indies, especially the powerful Dutch East India Company, would see it as England's move to take all the advantages for herself. Which was exactly what the French would like.

What should he do if the French captain refused to be moved by Conway's message? Patrol up and down outside the islands and draw *Argus* into combat? It would be a one-sided affair. Le Chaumareys was an old hand in these waters, knew every islet and cove where he had once hidden to avoid British frigates in time of war. Equally, he would be well advised to lie at anchor, living off the land, until *Undine* was made to withdraw.

He felt his tiredness putting an edge to his anger. If only the politicians were here to see what their ideas of world strategy actually represented in flesh and blood, in wood and canvas.

"Land ho! Fine on th' starboard bow!"

Davy rubbed his hands. "Nearer than you thought, sir."

Mudge said quickly, "Never!" He fumbled with his slate and made some rapid calculations. "There's a small islet, some forty miles to the south'rd of the Benuas, sir." He peered round until he had discovered Midshipman Penn's diminutive shape by the taffrail. "Aloft with ye, Mr. Penn, an' fetch the big glass for company." He eyed him fiercely. "Take a look, an' make me a sketch just like I taught you!"

He waited until the boy had scampered for the main shrouds and chuckled. "Cap'n Cook 'ad the right idea, sir. Sketch an' describe every damn thing you see. Time'll come when every man-o'-war will 'ave a complete set o' pictures to study." He watched Penn's progress. "Not that some'll 'eed 'em, o' course."

Bolitho smiled at Herrick. "Better than I had expected. We'll have a man in the chains and begin soundings as we pass this islet of the master's. The chart describes some nineteen fathoms hereabouts, but I'd prefer to be certain."

Twenty minutes later Penn returned to the deck, his brown features sprinkled with sweat. He held out his grubby pad and stood back to watch Mudge's reactions.

Over his shoulder Davy said, "Looks like a whale to me."

Mudge eyed him coldly. "So it does." To Penn he said, "Fair work. It is 'ow I recalls it." His small eyes returned to Davy. "Exactly like a great rocky *whale*." The merest pause. *"Sir."*

"Anything there?"

Bolitho took a glass and trained it above the gun deck. As yet he could see nothing but the same, painful glare. He wondered momentarily where the storm had gone, how it could vanish after showing so much fury.

"Bless you, no, sir." Mudge beamed at Davy's discomfort. "Just a fistful o' rocks, like the tip of some undersea ridge, as no doubt it was one time. But I suppose it could be used as shelter in a full gale."

Bolitho watched some seamen hauling a new length of hemp along the larboard gangway. Tired and unshaven perhaps, but there was something else, too. The way they worked together. Confidently.

He said, "We will alter course a point, Mr. Davy, and take a look at your whale."

Davy hurried to the rail. "Mr. Penn! Pipe the hands to the braces!"

Herrick watched him, smiling easily. "Any reason, sir?"

Bolitho shrugged. "More of a feeling."

He watched the men thronging along the decks, where the steamy vapour continued to drift amongst them. From forward he saw real smoke, as Bogle, the cook, got busy with the first hot meal they would have eaten since the storm had come and gone.

He saw the yards swinging to the pull of the braces, heard the helmsman cry, "Nor'-east by north, sir!"

Davy hurried past to consult the binnacle and the set of the sails. "Another pull on the weather mainbrace, Mr. Shellabeer!" He dabbed his streaming face. "Now belay!"

COMMAND A *K*ING'S SHIP   233

Bolitho smiled. When Davy was irritated he always performed his duties better, for some reason.

He said, "Put another good lookout aloft, if you please. I want that islet watched until we are up to it."

He glanced at the sun's blinding patterns beyond the gently pitching bowsprit.

"I am going below to shave and to bribe Noddall into finding a clean shirt."

Later, as he lay back in a chair while Allday busied himself with his razor, he found time to wonder what he would do if or when he met with *Argus's* captain.

The hastily heated water, the skilful movement of the blade against his skin was making him relax, muscle by muscle, and he could feel the air from the open stern windows across his bare shoulders like a soothing embrace.

All around the world the King's captains were going about their affairs. Fighting scurvy and disease, carrying despatches for an admiral or some lonely outpost not marked on any schoolboy's map. Or pondering behind a cabin bulkhead in dread of mutiny, or planning some diversion to prevent one. Fighting maybe, with some dissident ruler who had attacked the King's subjects, defiled the flag, butchered men and women. He smiled. And some would be like himself. A tiny extension to a half-formed plan.

Through the open skylight he heard the lookout's cry, "Deck there! Ship at anchor close inshore!"

He jumped to his feet, seizing the clean shirt and using it to dab away the soap from his chin.

Allday stood aside and grinned admiringly. "By God, Captain, you must have more wiles than a farmyard cat! How did you know there was a ship?"

Bolitho was tucking the crumpled shirt inside his breeches. "Magic, Allday!"

He hurried for the door, and then forced himself to wait until Midshipman Penn appeared in the entrance.

"A ship, sir! Mr. Davy's respects, and he believes it may be a schooner."

"Thank you, Mr. Penn." It was all he could do to appear calm. "I will come up when I have completed dressing. My compliments to the first lieutenant, please ask him to meet me on the quarterdeck.

He turned and saw Allday hiding a smile.

"Is something amusing you?"

"Why, no, Captain." Allday watched him gravely. "But I am always ready to see my betters at their affairs."

Bolitho smiled. "Then I hope you learn from it."

He walked into the passageway and made for the ladder.

Herrick greeted him excitedly. "A schooner, sir! The man in the foremast crosstrees is my best lookout, and I had a glass sent aloft to him." He stared at Bolitho with open astonishment. "It is uncanny!"

Bolitho smiled shortly. "A fair guess, if the truth be told. But it was a bad storm, and when the master suggested this small isle as a place for shelter I began a'thinking."

He took Penn's telescope and trained it towards the bows. There was the islet now, an uneven blob of grey/blue. The masthead would be able to see much more.

"Where is the wind?"

Davy said, "From the south-west, sir."

Bolitho let his mind move accordingly. "Alter course and lay her on the larboard tack." He crossed to the binnacle, seeing the helmsmen watching him curiously. "We will steer nor' nor'-west."

He waited as a bosun's mate dashed to pipe the hands to the braces again.

Then to Herrick and Davy he added slowly, "This way we will keep the isle between us and the other vessel and hold our advantage to wind'rd. Get the courses on her, but keep the t'gallants furled for the present."

Herrick understood at once. "Aye, sir. The less canvas we

display, the less likely they are to sight us."

Bolitho glanced at Mudge, who had appeared with Fowlar beside the helm.

"You put the thought in my mind. I have always wondered why Muljadi has good warning of our movements. I think we shall soon know his methods." He looked at the washed-out blue sky above the tapering masts. "But for the storm we would have approached from the east'rd. Thanks to the weather's rough mood we have gained something for once."

Herrick asked softly, "What of the admiral's instructions, sir?" Then he grinned. "I can see from your expression that you intend to choose your own moment, sir."

Bolitho smiled. "One cannot bargain if one is a beggar. I have learned that long since."

He looked up as with sails cracking and shivering to the new tack *Undine* tamed purposefully to larboard, the small, humped islet moving away from the weather bow as if released from an anchor.

"Nor' nor'-west, sir. Full an' bye!"

Bolitho beckoned to Davy. "Get the courses on her now." To Mudge he called, "How long, by your consideration?"

Mudge pouted. "Two hours, sir."

"Good. Then once the sails are drawing well we can send both watches for their meal."

He watched the scurrying figures clawing along the yards, others standing below on deck ready to sheet home the great fore and main courses.

Herrick nodded approvingly. "Bit different from when they came aboard, sir."

Bolitho found he was desperately hungry. "I think that applies to most of us."

He strode to the cabin hatch, knowing that the unknown vessel might be harmless, or an old wreck long abandoned. Or one more trick to delay or deceive him.

Noddall watched him warily. "It's salt beef again, sir."

"That will be excellent." He ignored the amazement on Noddall's rodent features. "And I'll take some claret to wash it down."

He leaned over the sill and stared at the frothing wake below the counter.

Chance, luck, call it what you will, he thought. It was all they had, and he intended to make good use of it.

"By th' mark seventeen!" The leadsman's cry rose easily above the sounds of flapping canvas as *Undine,* her courses again brailed up to the yards, glided steadily towards the islet.

Bolitho saw Shellabeer touch the leadsman's shoulder and reach out to feel the tallow arming in the bottom of weight before calling, "Rocky bottom, sir!"

Bolitho nodded. As Mudge had described it, the small islet was more like an isolated rock pile than part of the sea-bed.

"Prepare to anchor, Mr. Herrick."

He took a glass from Penn and moved it slowly over the ragged outline. They were five cables offshore, but it was close enough to see that the first smooth impression of a surfaced whale had changed severely. The rocks were blue-grey, like Cornish slate, and cut by wind and tide into massive steep gullies, as if some giant had hacked the islet into slices. Apart from a few clumps of gorse or rock flowers, it looked bare and unwelcoming, but there were plenty of sea-birds perched in little clefts, or circling busily above the highest point, which he estimated to be some three hundred feet above the water.

He heard Herrick shouting his orders, the creak of rigging as *Undine* dipped and rose again in a sudden swell. The water looked deep, but it was an illusion. He could see some narrow, stony beaches at the foot of the nearest cliff, and guessed that the safest anchorage was on the opposite side where the other vessel lay hidden. There was surf, too, steep and angry as it licked and spluttered around the one visible landing place.

"Helm a'lee!"

He moved his glass in time with the ship as she turned easily into the wind, watching for any sign of life, the merest movement to show their approach had been seen.

"Let go!"

The sound of the anchor hitting the water seemed unusually loud, and he imagined he could hear it echoing back from those desolate cliffs.

Herrick shouted, "Lively, lads! Secure those lines!" To Davy he added, "Lowering parties, man the tackles!"

Bolitho said, "Have the leadsman watch his line now and see that the anchor is holding fast. If we begin to drag because of the rocky bottom we will veer more cable directly."

"Aye, sir."

Herrick hurried away, his face totally absorbed in his own duties.

With the ship swaying and pulling lazily to her cable, it was even quieter, and Bolitho saw some of the birds quitting their precarious perches to fly and circle above the mastheads.

Herrick returned, breathing heavily. "We seem safe enough, sir. But I've told the anchor-watch to keep alert." He squinted towards the shore. "It looks like a graveyard."

"We will need two boats." Bolitho spoke his thoughts aloud. "Gig and cutter will suffice. They will have to run smartly through that surf. The beach is steep by the look of it. So put a good cox'n in the cutter."

He saw Allday signalling with his fist as the gig rose jerkily from its chocks, the guy-ropes tautening to swing it round and above the gangway.

He added with a smile, "I think my boat is in safe hands."

Herrick looked at him anxiously. "Are *you* going, sir?"

"It is not for want of glory, Thomas." He lowered his voice, watching the chosen hands as they mustered by the arms' chests. "But I need to know what we are against, if anything."

Herrick sounded unconvinced. "But if the other craft is one of the pirate's, sir, what then? Surely you'll want to sweep round and rake the devil as he slips his cable?"

"No." He shook his head firmly. "He will be safely anchored yonder. In shallower water than I'd dare enter close enough to rake him. Once clear he could lead us a merry maypole dance, and I fear we would never match his agility in these conditions." His tone hardened. "Besides which, I want to *take* him!"

"Boats lowered alongside, sir." Davy came aft, a curved hanger dangling from his belt.

Bolitho touched his own sword-hilt and saw Captain Bellairs watching the boats with visible irritation at being left behind.

He called, "Captain Bellairs, I would be obliged if I could have three of your very best sharpshooters in each boat!"

Bellairs brightened considerably and snapped at Sergeant Coaker, "Well, lively, Sar'nt! Although they should *all* be excellent marksmen, what?"

Herrick grinned. "That was thoughtful, sir."

"Perhaps." Bolitho shifted the glass again to watch some birds landing delicately along the clifftop. They would never do that if men were close by. "But if seamen are better at scaling cliffs, there is no beating a well-aimed ball at the right moment!"

He nodded to Davy. "Man your boats." To Herrick he added casually, "If things go wrong, you will find the admiral's orders in my cabin."

"You can rely on me, sir." Herrick was looking troubled again. "But I'm certain that—"

Bolitho touched his arm and smiled. "Yes. But just bear it in mind. If you have to, act upon them, as *you* see fit."

He walked slowly towards the entry port, seeing the watching seamen and marines as he passed. Familiar now, he could put a name and a value on all of them.

Midshipman Armitage was looking confused and embarrassed. "Sir! The sharpshooters will not remove their coats, sir!" He blushed as some of the oarsmen in the boats nudged each other and chuckled.

Bellairs snapped, "Can't have my fellows tramping about like damn vagrants, what?" He saw Bolitho and added quickly, "I mean, can we, sir?"

Bolitho slipped out of his blue coat and tossed it to Noddall who was hovering by the quarterdeck ladder.

"It is all right." He nodded to the unsmiling marines. "If I can shed a little authority, I am certain your men can." He saw the sergeant gathering up the red coats and shakos, honour apparently restored. He added, "And it will be a rough climb, with who knows what at the end of it."

He paused above the swaying boats, trying to think of something he might have missed or forgotten.

Herrick said quietly, "Good luck, sir."

Bolitho ran his glance along the crowded gangway and up to the men in the shrouds.

"And you, Thomas. Have the people stand-to, watch and watch about. You know what to do."

He saw Armitage staggering between the oarsmen in the gig. It was almost cruel to take him. A liability. But he had to begin somewhere. It was a marvel he had ever got to sea at all with a mother like his. If Keen had been here, he would have taken him. He saw Penn peering wistfully from the gun deck. He would have gone with the boats like a shot. He smiled to himself. No wonder the seamen called him "The Tiger."

Then he climbed down into the gig. No ceremony this time. As the boats shoved away from the side he was conscious of sudden tension.

"Take the lead, Allday."

He watched the rocky cliffs rising higher and higher with each pull of the oars, and could feel the strong undertow as the inshore swell frothed and mounted into seething lines of breakers. When he glanced astern he saw the cutter's stem lifting and plunging through the flashing spray, Davy's head and shoulders swaying above the oarsmen while he, too, peered at the land. What was he thinking about? Being killed in this Godforsaken place? Taking a step nearer that badly needed prize-money? Bolitho wiped the spray from his face and concentrated on the swift approach. There was more chance of being drowned than of anything in the immediate future.

He glanced at Allday who was standing in a half crouch, one fist gripping the tiller-bar, as he peered from bow to bow, gauging the set of the angry surf, the diagonal lines of breakers as they hurried noisily into the shadows below the cliffs. No need to warn him. Any suggestion at all might have the opposite effect and bring disaster.

Allday remarked, "Very steep beach, Captain." His sturdy figure swayed with the hull. "Go in fast, put her bow round at the last moment t'wards the surf and beach her broadside-to." He glanced down at him quickly. "Does that sound fair, Captain?"

Bolitho smiled. "Very fair." It would also give them time to scramble ashore and help the cutter as she followed them in.

He felt a sudden chill and realised that the shadows had finally reached out to cover them, and he heard the slap of water, the creak of oars in rowlocks echoing back from the cliffs, as if there was a third and invisible boat nearby.

They almost planed across the last of the surf, the oars desperately keeping with the stroke until Allday yelled, *"Now!"* And as he slammed the tiller hard round he added, "Back-water to larboard!"

Floundering and tilting dangerously the gig came to the beach almost broadside, the keel grinding across loose pebbles and weed in a violent, protesting shudder.

But men were already leaping into the spray, holding the gunwale, guiding the gig to safety with sheer brute-strength.

"Clear the boat!"

Allday steadied Bolitho's arm as with Armitage and the others he waded, reeled and finally walked on to firm beach.

Bolitho ran to the foot of the cliffs leaving Allday to supervise the business of getting the gig safely secured.

He waved his arm towards the three marines. "Spread out! See if you can find a way to the top!"

This, they understood, and with barely a glance towards the onrushing cutter they loped up the first crumbling rock-slide, their muskets primed and held ready.

Bolitho waited, staring up at the jagged clifftop, the pale blue sky above. No heads peering down. No sudden fusillade of musket balls.

He breathed more evenly and turned to watch the cutter as it edged round and plunged wildly before driving on to the beach and amongst the waiting seamen.

Davy staggered towards him, gasping for breath, but loading his pistol with remarkably steady fingers.

Bolitho said, "Muster the men, and send your three marines after the others."

He looked for Armitage, but he was nowhere to be seen.

"In God's name!"

Davy grinned as the midshipman came round a large boulder, buttoning his breeches.

Bolitho said harshly, "If you must relieve yourself at such times, Mr. Armitage, I would be obliged if you would remain in sight!"

Armitage hung his head. "S-sorry, sir."

Bolitho relented. "It would be safer for you, and I will try and hide any embarrassment you might cause me."

Allday crunched over the loose shingle, chuckling as he, too, loaded a brace of pistols with fresh, dry powder.

"Bless me, Mr. Armitage, but I can understand how you feel!"

The youth stared at him unhappily. "You can?"

"Why, once, I was hiding in a loft." He winked at the cutter's coxswain. "From the bloody pressgang, believe it or not, and all I could think of was pumping my bilges!"

Bolitho said to Davy, "That seems to have helped his mind a little."

He forgot Armitage's troubles and said, "We'll leave four hands with the boats."

He saw *Undine* swaying like a beautiful model; her stern windows flashing in the sunlight, and imagined Herrick watching their progress. He could send aid to the beached boats if trouble arrived. He looked up at the cliffs again. Damp, clammy, deceptively cool. That would change as soon as they reached the top and the waiting sun.

Bolitho waited for Davy to rejoin him. "Best be moving off."

He examined his landing party carefully as Allday waved them towards the cliffs. Thirty in all. Apart from Davy and Armitage, he had brought a master's mate named Carwithen, knowing the man would have resented being left behind after Fowlar's previous involvements. A dark, unsmiling man, he was, like Bolitho, a Cornishman; and hailed from the fishing village of Looe.

He waited while they checked their weapons. His chain of command. Ship or shore, it made no difference to them.

Carwithen said, "I hope they've a drop to drink when we gets t'other side."

Bolitho noticed that hardly anybody smiled at his remark. Carwithen was known as a hard man, given to physical violence if challenged. Good at his work, according to the master, but little beyond it. How different from Fowlar, Bolitho thought.

"Lead your party to the left, Mr. Davy, but allow the marines to set the pace." He looked at Armitage. "You keep with me."

He saw a marine waving from a high ledge, indicating the path up the first section of cliff.

It was strange how sailors always hated the actual moment of leaving the sea behind. Like having a line attached to your belt, dragging you back. Bolitho eased the sword further around his hip and reached out for the nearest handhold. Smoothed away by timeless weather. Stained with droppings from a million sea-birds. No wonder ships avoided the place.

As he moved carefully up the fallen boulders he felt a small pressure against his thigh, the watch she had given him in Madras. He thought suddenly of that moment when she had offered him far more. And he had taken it without even a smallest hesitation. How soft, how alive she had felt in his arms.

He grimaced as his fingers slipped in a pile of fresh droppings. And how quickly circumstances could change, he thought grimly.

The passage across the small islet was to prove harder and more exhausting than anyone could have expected. From the moment they topped the first cliff and the sun engulfed them in its searing glare, they realised they must climb immediately into a treacherous gully before they could begin scaling the next part. And so it went on, until they were finally tramping across an almost circular depression which Bolitho guessed was the central part of the islet. It held the heat and shielded them from any sea-breeze, and their progress was further delayed by the clinging carpet of filth which covered the depression from side to side.

Allday gasped, "Will we rest up once we get to the far side, Captain?" Like the others, his legs and arms were caked with muck, and his face masked in a fine film of dust. "I am as dry as a hangman's eye!"

Bolitho refrained from looking at his watch again. He could tell from the sun's angle that it was late afternoon. It was taking too long.

He peered across to the other side of the unsheltered depression, seeing Davy's straggling line of men, the marine sharpshooters walking like hunters through a cloud of pale dust, their muskets over their shoulders.

He replied, "Yes. But we must go carefully with the water ration."

It was like being on top of the world, the curving sides of the depression hiding everything but the sun and open sky. One of the long, slanting shadows behind him faltered and then sprawled in the inches-deep bird droppings, and without turning he knew it was Armitage.

He heard a seaman say hoarsely, "Give us yer 'and! Gawd, you do look a sight, beggin' yer pardon, sir!"

Poor Armitage. Bolitho kept his gaze fixed on the pale breeches of the marine directly ahead of him, his body smoking in haze and dust. There were rocks beyond the marine, probably marking the end of the depression. They could take a rest. Find brief shelter while they regained their senses.

He turned and sought out the seaman who had helped Armitage to his feet. "Can you raise the breath to carry a message to the scouts ahead, Lincoln?"

The man bobbed his head. Small and wiry, his face was disfigured by a terrible scar from some past battle, or in a tavern brawl. A surgeon had made a bad job of it, and his mouth was drawn up at one side in a permanent, lopsided grin.

"Aye, sir." The man shaded his eyes.

"Tell them to halt at those rocks."

He saw Lincoln hurry ahead of the column, his tattered trousers flapping and stirring up more choking dust.

It took another hour to reach those rocks, and Bolitho had the impression he was taking two paces backwards for every one he advanced.

Davy's party arrived amongst the tall rocks almost at the same time, and while the men threw themselves down into the small patches of shade, gasping and wheezing like sick animals, Bolitho called the lieutenant aside and said, "We will take a look." He saw Davy nod wearily, his hair bleached so much that it was like corn in the sunlight.

They found a marine on the far side of the rocks, his eyes slitted with professional interest as he stared at the gently sloping hillside which continued without a break towards the sea. And there, cradled inside the narrowest sweep of the islet, the "whale's tail," was the schooner.

She was so close inshore that for an instant longer Bolitho imagined she had been driven aground in the storm. Then he saw the drifting smoke from a fire on the beach, heard the muffled tap of hammers, and guessed her crew were carrying out repairs. They might even have had the schooner careened to put right some damage to her bilge or keel, but at first glance she looked well enough now.

Tiny figures moved about her deck, and there were several more on the beach and scattered amongst the rocks. The heaviest part of their work was apparently completed.

Davy said, "They're looking in rock pools, sir. After shellfish or the like."

Bolitho asked, "How many, d'you reckon?"

Davy frowned. "Two dozen, at guess."

Bolitho fell silent. It was a long way down the hillside, and no cover at all. His own men would be seen long before they could get to grips. He bit his lip, wondering if the schooner intended to wait another day, or longer.

Carwithen had joined them and said hoarsely, "They'm not ready to quit yet, sir." He was whispering, as if the schooner's crew were a few feet away. "They've got their boats hauled well up the beach."

Davy shrugged. "I expect they feel very safe."

Bolitho took a small glass and trained it carefully between the rocks. One false move, and the sunlight would throw a reflection from the telescope which would be seen for miles.

A lookout. There must be at least one on the shore. A man so placed that he could watch over the tiny cove and see everything but the far side of the island where *Undine* now lay at anchor. He smiled grimly. It was hardly surprising they had found no sentries when they had landed when he thought of their exhausting trek from the beach.

He stiffened, seeing a small movement on a ridge, almost in line with the motionless schooner. He adjusted the glass very slowly. A white, floppy hat, the darker blob of a face underneath.

"There's a lookout on that ridge. The one with the rock pools directly below it."

Carwithen said, "Easy. From the sea, no, but I could take him from behind with no trouble at all." He sounded brutally eager.

The crash of a shot made them crouch lower, while from behind Bolitho heard the sudden clatter of weapons as his men dived for cover.

Something white and flapping fell from the sky and lay quite still on the beach. The searching sailors from the schooner paid very little attention as one of their number walked over to it and picked it up.

Carwithen, said, "One of 'em's shot a booby. They make fair eatin' if you've nothin' better."

The marine said, "Then 'e must be a bloody good shot, sir."

Bolitho looked at him. His own thought exactly. It would make a frontal assault virtually fatal for all of them.

He said, "I'll send a message back to the ship. We must wait until dark." To the marine he added, "Take this glass, but keep it well shielded." No need to add a warning or a threat. The marine had just proved he could think as well as shoot.

They found the others relaxed again amidst the rocks, and Allday said, "Take a drink, Captain." He held out a flask. "Tastes like bilge water."

Bolitho scribbled on his pad and handed it to one of the seamen. "Take it back to the beach and give it to the petty officer there." He saw the despair on his face and added gently, "You need not return. You will have earned a rest by the time you reach *Undine*."

He heard another shot, muffled this time by the rocks, but it was followed by a different sound, a soft thud.

Carwithen was on his feet in a second. "'Nother bird, sir!"

Bolitho followed him to where they had left the marine. He

was staring with amazement at the big booby which had dropped almost at his feet, wings outspread, its breast clotted with bright blood.

Davy said harshly, "Now, how in the name of hell did—"

But Bolitho held up his hand, freezing them all to silence.

Faintly at first, and then more insistently, he heard the scrape and clatter of loose stones as someone hurried up the hillside to collect the dead sea-bird.

He looked round swiftly. You could not hide thirty men amongst these few rocks. He saw Allday signalling everyone to remain quite still, saw the anxiety in Armitage's eyes as he stared transfixed at the last barrier where the sea's edge shone against the sky and rocks like the top of a great dam.

The sounds were much louder, and Bolitho could hear the man's heavy gasps as he struggled up the last part of the hill.

Nobody moved, and he saw the marine staring at his musket which was two feet away from his fingers. The slightest sound and they were done for.

It was then Carwithen acted. He was closest to the rock barrier, and with barely a sound he reached out and gathered up the dead bird, holding it just a few inches below the top of the nearest rock. His free hand he held under his short blue coat, and Bolitho could see his fingers moving beneath the cloth, trying to free something, while all the time his eyes were fixed unblinkingly on the bird.

It seemed to take an eternity before anything else happened. When it did, it was all too fast to follow.

The man's dark face gaping down at them, his eyes flicking from the bird to Carwithen even as he groped forward to retrieve his prize. The master's mate dropped the booby, the movement so swift that the man was thrown off balance, his hand groping at his belt and the gleaming butt of a pistol.

Carwithen murmured, "Not so, my pretty one!" It was said quietly, almost gently.

Then the other hand came out of his coat, a boarding axe twisting in his fingers as he brought the rearmost end, with its short, savage barb, hard down in the man's neck. With a great heave he gaffed him bodily over the rocks, withdrawing the axe, turning it again just as swiftly before hacking him full across the throat with its blade.

Armitage fell against the marine, whimpering and retching, blood spurting over his legs as the axe jerked free, hesitated and cut down again.

Bolitho seized Carwithen's arm, seeing the axe quivering above the bulging eyes and that great gaping wound. He could feel the pent-up hatred and madness in his biceps, the effort to shake him away and drive the axe again and again into the choking, bubbling thing at his feet.

"Easy! *Enough*, damn you!"

There was another terrible silence while they stared at each other or at the corpse which was sprawled across the dead booby.

Carwithen whispered hoarsely, "That bugger'll never raise hell again!"

Bolitho forced himself to examine the victim. Probably Javanese. Dressed in little better than rags, but the pistol was inscribed with the crest of the East India Company.

He heard Carwithen say, "Took it off some poor sailor, the bastard!"

Nobody looked at him.

Bolitho knelt by the rocks and studied the beach with the glass. Carwithen had acted quickly and efficiently. But he had enjoyed it. Relished it.

He watched the distant lookout in his rocky ledge, the small figures still searching aimlessly amongst the pools.

He said quietly, "They saw nothing."

Davy looked at the sobbing midshipman and asked quietly, "Will this change things for us, sir?"

Bolitho shook his head. "Only when this man is missed by his companions." He looked at the slanting shadows from the rocks. "So we must bide our time and hope for darkness to come."

He saw Carwithen wiping his boarding-axe on some cloth he had just cut from the dead man's smock. His face was devoid of anything but satisfaction.

Davy gestured to the others. "Take this thing away and cover it with stones." He swallowed hard. "I'll not forget this day in a hurry."

Bolitho gripped the midshipman's shoulder and pulled him away from the rocks. "Listen, Mr. Armitage." He shook him roughly, seeing the youth's eyes as he stared at the red smudge left by the corpse. "Get a grip on yourself! I know it was a foul thing to witness, but you are not here today as a mere onlooker, d'you understand?" He shook him again, hating to see the pain and the revulsion in his eyes. "You are one of my officers, and our people will have to look to you!"

Armitage nodded dazedly. "Y-yes, sir. I'll try to—" He retched again.

Bolitho added gently, "I'm sure you will." He saw Allday watching him over the midshipman's quivering shoulders, the almost imperceptible shake of his head. "Now be off with you, and check that my message has been sent."

Allday said quietly, "Poor lad. He'll never get used to this sort of thing."

Bolitho looked at him gravely. "Did you? Did I?"

Allday shrugged. "We learned to hide what we thought, Captain. It's all a man can do."

"Perhaps." He saw Davy kicking dust across the drying blood. Then he looked at Carwithen's dark features as he examined the dead man's pistol. "Although there are some who have no feelings at all, and I have always found them to be less than men."

Allday followed him back into the shade. Bolitho's mood would soon change at a hint of action, and for the present it was best to leave him to his thoughts.

14

THE BRISTOL *Sailmaker*

"Time to move, is it, sir?" Davy watched Bolitho as he craned over the rocks, his shirt pale against the darkening sky.

"I believe so. Tell Carwithen to muster the hands."

He shivered as the sea-breeze explored his body. Once the sun had dipped over the hills at his back it grew cool, even cold, in minutes. They had been too long in the heat, plagued by sun and thirst, and a multitude of flies which had appeared as if by magic. He watched the anchored schooner's outline, the soft glow of lights from poop and forepeak. The fire on the beach had died to a blotch of red embers, and he could see nobody near it, but guessed the lookout was still in his refuge beyond the pools.

Allday whispered, "All ready, Captain." He held his cutlass clear of the rocks. "Mr. Davy's making sure they all know what to do."

Bolitho nodded without answering, trying to gauge the distance they must cover. Surprisingly, it seemed greater in the growing darkness, but he was reassured by the occasional snatches of voices from the vessel to show they had given no heed to their missing comrade.

Davy slithered down beside him. "I've sent Carwithen's party away, sir." He looked at the sky, the isolated puffs of light cloud. "Wind's steady enough."

"Yes." Bolitho checked his pistol and tightened his belt. "Follow me. Single file."

Like ghosts they topped the last rock barrier, the sounds of loose stones and rubble seemingly very loud in the gloom. But as Davy had observed, the wind held steady, and was making a lively chop along the beach and narrow spur of headland. Noisy enough to drown any small sound they might be making.

Once, as they followed the curve of the hillside they all froze in their tracks as two dozing sea-birds rose flapping and screaming almost from under their feet.

Bolitho waited, listening to his heart, to the sharp breathing of the men at his back. Nothing. He lifted his arm and they began to move forward and downwards again.

When he looked across his shoulder he saw the rough edge of the rock barrier, where they had waited fretting for sunset, far above his slow-moving party. They were almost down to beach level now, and he heard a man curse quietly as he slipped in the first of the small pools. Davy's party were having to wade in the shallows to his right, and he hoped none of them would fall headlong into one of the rock pools there, now hidden by the rising tide.

He thought momentarily of the ship, anchored on the other side of the islet. The familiar sounds and smells. Herrick waiting anxiously for news of success or disaster. If it was to be the latter, he could do nothing to help this time. His would be the task of contacting the "enemy" and making what he could of it. It was easier to think of them as the enemy. It never helped to picture them as men. Flesh and bone like himself.

Allday touched his arm urgently. "Boat coming inshore, Captain!"

Bolitho held up his hand and brought both parties to a shuffling silence. The boat must have come around the schooner's hidden side. He could see the splash of oars, the lively froth of the stem as it bounced across the first leaping surf.

He thought of Carwithen and his handful of men who were creeping up and around the solitary lookout. They should have been there by now. He recalled Carwithen's brutal madness with the boarding axe, and wondered if he had been the one to strike the luckless lookout down.

A voice echoed suddenly in the darkness, and for an instant Bolitho imagined Carwithen had been delayed, or that the lookout was calling in alarm. But the voice came from the boat, louder this time, and despite the strange tongue, Bolitho knew the man was calling a question. Or a name perhaps.

Allday said, "They've come alooking for their mate, Captain." He dropped to one knee to keep the grounding boat framed against the surf. "Six of 'em."

Bolitho said quietly, "Stand fast, lads. Let them come to us."

He heard a man clicking his jaws together. Tense, nervous. Probably terrified in these unfamiliar surroundings.

Allday said, "One of 'em's going up the cliff to the lookout."

Bolitho drew his sword very carefully. Of course. It would be the first place a searcher would go. Ask if the missing man had been seen.

He watched the other five strolling up the beach, swinging their weapons casually, chatting as they approached.

Bolitho glanced behind him. His men were barely visible as they crouched or knelt amongst fallen rocks, or squatted in the sea itself. He turned to study the oncoming shadows. Twenty yards, fifteen. Surely one would see them soon.

A terrible cry tore the stillness apart, hanging above the ridge long after the man had died.

Bolitho saw the five shadows turn in confusion, knew the dying scream must have been the man sent to the lookout.

He yelled, "At 'em, lads!"

Without a shout or a cheer they were all up and rushing after the five figures who had turned back towards the surf.

One of them slipped and fell headlong, tried to rise, but was slashed into a sobbing heap by a seaman's cutlass as he dashed past.

The others had reached the boat, but deprived of two of their strength, were unable to shift it. Steel gleamed in the shadows, and as the seamen charged amongst them the fight became confused and deadly. A seaman caught his foot in the boat-rope and before he could recover his balance was pinned bodily to the shingle by a long sword. His killer died almost simultaneously. The remaining two threw down their weapons and were instantly clubbed into unmoving heaps by the maddened sailors.

Davy snapped tersely, "One of ours is dead, sir." He rolled the man over on to his back and dragged the cutlass from his fingers.

Bolitho eased the sword back into its scabbard. His legs felt shaky from running, from nervous tension. He looked at the anchored schooner. No shouts, no calls to arms. He thought he heard the same sing-song voice chanting above the seething surf, remote and vaguely sad.

Davy said hoarsely, "Damned poor lookout, sir."

Bolitho watched his men gathering around the two boats. The one which had been there all day was furthest up the shingle and would need the more men to move it.

He replied, "Would *you* have expected trouble, in their place?"

Davy shrugged. "I suppose not."

Carwithen came hurrying down from the ridge, his helpers hard put to keep up with him.

He said savagely, "That bloody fool Lincoln was too slow with his dirk!" He glared at the watching men around him. "I'll see to him later!"

Bolitho said, "Boats in the water." He sought out the six marines. "You take the second one. You know what to do."

One, the man who had first sighted the schooner, grunted. "We knows, sir. We holds the boat where we can see the poop, an' pin down anyone who tries to pass the lanterns there."

Bolitho smiled. "Captain Bellairs was right about you."

Allday whispered, "This way, Captain."

He felt the surf engulfing his legs and waist, the boat's scarred planking as Allday reached down to drag him over the gunwale.

"Shove off!"

Bolitho restrained the urge to watch the frantic oars, the efforts to steer the boat clear of the surf. Just one blast of canister would be enough to nip his flimsy plan in the bud.

The boat lifted and then surged heavily forward, the blades

taking control as the hull freed itself from the strong undertow. Bolitho saw the schooner's tall masts rising to greet him, the tracery of rigging and shrouds almost lost against the sky.

Allday stood straddle-legged and wary, the tiller bar held lightly in his fingertips.

"Easy all!" He craned forward as if to impress them more. "Bow-man, ready!"

Astern Bolitho heard the regular splash of oars as the other boat pulled hastily towards the schooner's bows.

Allday said quickly, "It's now or never, Captain!" His teeth were bared with concentration so that some men in the forward part of the boat thought he was smiling.

Bolitho stood up beside him and reached out to fend off the overhanging quarter, as like a moving object it loomed right above the boat.

"*Now!*"

There was a yell and a quick clatter as the bow-man hurled his grapnel up and over the bulwark. With a jerking, grinding crash the boat came alongside, some men falling in confusion, while others climbed eagerly over their sprawled bodies and entangled oars as if using a living bridge to reach the vessel's main deck.

Figures were already dashing from the forecastle, but as a man ran wildly from aft there was a muffled bang, the well-aimed musket ball hurling him round like an insane dancer, his agony clearly silhouetted against the poop lanterns.

Bolitho felt rather than saw a figure coming at him from the scuppers. Something hissed above his head even as he ducked round and struck for his attacker with his sword. The swaying figure backed and came on again, and Bolitho realised he was holding a huge axe, swinging it from side to side as he advanced.

Carwithen exclaimed, "A plague on that bastard!" and fired his pistol full in the man's face. To Bolitho he snarled, "That'll teach him!"

Another of the crew had climbed frantically into the foremast shrouds and was being pursued by a yelling seaman. Once again a musket stabbed the darkness from the other boat, and with a faint cry the man fell headlong to the deck where he was promptly despatched by a waiting cutlass.

Allday yelled, "Most of 'em have gone below, Captain!" He ran to a hatchway and fired his pistol into it. "The fight's gone out of 'em now, I'm thinking!"

Bolitho peered aft at the poop lanterns. "Call the other boat to give assistance!"

It was suddenly very quiet on the schooner's deck, and as Bolitho walked slowly towards the small cabin hatch just forward of the wheel he was conscious of his own footsteps and the feeling the fight was not yet over.

He moved warily around the outstretched corpse which had been the first to fall to a marine sharpshooter, its face shining in the lantern light, the lower jaw broken away as if by an axe stroke.

Allday said, "Stand aside, Captain!"

But a seaman was already clambering over the hatch coaming, his face suddenly screwing up in terrible agony as a pistol exploded beneath him.

A shadow darted through the pluming smoke, and Bolitho saw it was the scarfaced seaman called Lincoln, his eyes like stones as he allowed his lean body to drop straight through the hatch, using his dead companion to cushion the fall. His feet thudded into the corpse, and as he turned he whipped a knife from between his teeth, hitting out twice in the darkness, the second blow bringing a scream of pain.

More men were swarming down after him, and Bolitho yelled, "Bring a lantern! Drag those men clear!"

Feet pounded over the planking, and he heard Armitage calling anxiously from the boat alongside.

Carwithen was already down on the cabin deck, knocking a seaman aside even as he made to finish the wounded pirate with his dirk.

Bolitho paused on the ladder, searching for Davy, his mind still able to grapple with the realisation that Allday had saved his life. But for his warning, he and not that poor seaman would be lying there dead.

"Mr. Davy! Hoist both boats inboard once you have secured our prisoners!"

"Aye, aye, sir!" He sounded jubilant.

"And mount a guard on them. I want no fanatic opening the bilges to the sea before we can even make sail!"

He followed Allday down the ladder, the sea-noises suddenly muffled and lost.

A seaman kicked open the cabin door and darted inside with a levelled pistol.

"Nothin', zur!" He swung round as a shadow moved beyond an upended chair. "Belay that, zur! There's another rascal 'ere! I'll get 'im for 'ee!"

Then he fell back in horror. "By Jesus, zur! 'E's one of us!"

Bolitho stepped into the cabin, ducking low between the deck-head beams. He could appreciate the seaman's shocked rise. It was a small, cringing wreck of a man. He was on his knees, fingers interlocked as in prayer while he swayed bark and forth in time to the ship's motion.

Bolitho sheathed his sword stepping between the quivering creature and his fierce-eyed seaman.

"Who are you?"

He made to move closer and the man threw himself bodily at his feet.

"Have mercy, Captain! I done nothin sir! I'm just an honest sailorman, sir!"

He gripped Bolitho's shoes, and when he reached down to pull him to his feet Bolitho saw with horror that every nail had been torn from his fingers.

Allday said harshly, "On your feet! You are speaking to a King's officer!"

"Easy." Bolitho held up his hand. "Look at him. He has suffered enough."

A seaman dropped his cutlass and lifted the man into a chair. "Oi'll get 'im a drink, Cap'n."

He dragged open a cupboard and gaped as the little man screamed wildly, "Don't touch! 'E'll flay you alive if you dare lay yer 'ooks on it!"

Bolitho asked, "Who will?"

Then he seemed to realise what was happening. That it was not part of another in a whole procession of living nightmares. He stared at Bolitho's grave features, tears running unheeded down his sunken cheeks.

"*Muljadi!*"

Carwithen muttered, "What, here?"

The creature peered around Bolitho, his terrified eyes searching the crowded passageway, the dead seaman below the hatch.

"There! 'Is *son!*"

Bolitho turned swiftly and stooped above the man brought down by Lincoln's knife. Of course, he should have seen it. Instead of congratulating himself on being spared a horrible death.

The man was still alive, although the seaman's blade had laid open his neck and shoulder in a great, gaping wound. Must have missed the artery by a whisker and no more.

He was naked to the waist, but his loose trousers, now blotchy with his own and the seaman's blood, were of the finest silk. His eyes were tightly shut, his chest moving in quick, uneven thrusts.

Carwithen said, "Let me finish the bastard, sir!" He was almost pleading.

Bolitho ignored him. The man was not aged much more than twenty, and around his throat he wore a gold pendant in the form of a prancing beast. Like the one on Muljadi's flag. It was just possible.

He snapped, "Bind his wound. I want him to live."

He turned to the ragged figure in the cabin. "My men will take care of you, but first I want—"

The figure edged nearer the door. "Is it really over, sir?" He was shaking violently and close to collapse. "It's not a cruel trick?"

Allday said quietly, "This is Captain Bolitho, matey. Of His Majesty's Ship *Undine.*"

"Now tell us who *you* are?"

The little man sank down to the deck again. Like a cowed dog.

"I was sailmaker, sir. In the Portuguese barque *Alvares.* Took on in Lisbon when I lost me own ship. We was carryin' a mixed cargo from Java when we was attacked by pirates."

"When was this?" Bolitho spoke carefully, very aware of the other man's confusion.

"A year back, sir. I think." He closed his eyes with the effort. "We was taken to Muljadi's anchorage, wot there was left of us. Muljadi's men killed most of 'em. Only kept me 'cause I was a sailmaker.

"I tried to escape once. Didn't know I was bein' 'eld on an island, y'see. They caught me before I'd been free an hour. Put me to torture." He was shaking more violently now. "All of 'em sat there watchin'. Enjoyin' it. Laughin'." He lurched to his feet and threw himself towards the door, snatching up a cutlass as he screamed, "Pulled out all my nails with pincers, an' worse, the *bloody bastards!*"

Lincoln caught his wrist and turned the cutlass away from the unconscious figure in the passageway.

"Easy, mate! You could cause a mischief with that, eh?"

The man's cheerful voice seemed to steady him in some way.

He turned and looked at Bolitho very steadily. "Me name's Jonathan Potter once of Bristol."

Bolitho nodded gravely. "Well, Jonathan Potter, you can be of great service to me. It will not bring back your friends, but it may prevent others suffering in the same manner." He glanced at Allday. "Look after him."

He walked from the cabin, grateful for the clean air which greeted him on deck, the sense of purpose as Davy's men prepared to get under way. Potter had probably been the only Englishman aboard the Portuguese barque. For that, and no other reason, had his life been spared. Kept like a slave, a downtrodden creature less than a man. From what he had heard of Muljadi, it seemed a far more truthful reason.

Davy crossed to his side. "I am about ready to weigh, sir." He paused, sensing Bolitho's mood. "That poor devil must have suffered terribly, sir. He is scars and scabs from head to toe. Little more than bones."

Bolitho studied his pale outline thoughtfully. "Something kept him alive, Mr. Davy. Fear of death, a need for revenge, I know not which." He grasped a stay as the deck swayed restlessly in the swell. "But whatever it was, I intend to use it to good purpose."

"And the schooner's master, sir?"

"If he is really Muljadi's son we have a catch indeed. But either way I want him kept alive, so pass the word to that effect." He thought of Carwithen's eyes. "To *all* hands."

He peered abeam at the small islet where so much had happened. The craggy distortions were lost in deep shadow. It was a whale once again.

"We will run to the sou'-east directly and gain sea-room. I am not yet acquainted with these waters. By dawn we should be able to come about and make contact with *Undine*." He looked at the men hurrying about the schooner's deck. "She's a fine little prize."

Davy stared at him and then at the vessel, the realisation coming to him apparently for the first time.

"I see, sir. A *prize*." He nodded happily. "Worth a good price, I'll be bound."

Bolitho walked to the opposite side. "I thought that might interest you, Mr. Davy." He added, "Now, have the capstan manned and break out the anchor while the wind holds." He thought of Herrick. "We are no longer beggars."

Davy shook his head, not understanding. Then he looked at the helmsman and at the others gathering at the capstan bars and grinned broadly.

A prize at last. Perhaps the first of many.

Noddall hovered by the cabin table and bobbed his head with satisfaction as Bolitho pushed his empty plate aside.

"More like it, sir! A man works the fairer on a full belly!"

Bolitho leaned back in his chair and let his eyes move slowly around the cabin. It felt good to be back aboard *Undine,* and with something to show for their efforts.

The lantern above the table seemed much dimmer, and when he glanced through the stern windows he saw that dawn had already given way to an empty sky, the horizon slanting across the thick, salt-stained glass like a thread of gold.

In the captured schooner he had rejoined *Undine* at almost the same hour as this, the previous day, the strain and tension of their short, bitter fight lost momentarily in the cheers from the watching seamen and marines.

Herrick had been almost beside himself with pleasure, and had insisted that Bolitho should go to his cabin without delay and rest.

The schooner had once been under the flag of the Dutch East India Company, although it was impossible to tell how long she had been in the pirates' hands. But from her filthy condition and disorder between decks it seemed likely it had been a considerable while since Dutch sailors had manned her.

He let his mind drift as he listened to bare feet padding overhead, the sluice of water and the clank of a pump as the decks were washed down for another day.

Noddall was right, he had eaten a good breakfast. Thinly sliced fat pork, fried pale brown with biscuit crumbs. Always his favourite. Helped down with strong coffee and some treacle.

Herrick tapped on the door and entered the cabin.

"Wind's holding steady from the sou'-west, sir." He looked alert and clear-eyed.

Bolitho smiled. "Good, Thomas. Have some coffee."

It was always strange how Herrick relaxed once there was a set plan to perform. If he really guessed how hazy it was in his captain's mind he gave no sign.

"Mr. Mudge informs me that we are logging some ten knots, sir." Herrick took a mug from the servant and grinned. "He's up there beaming away as if he's just won a fortune at the tables."

Bolitho frowned. "That means we should make a landfall at any time now. If yesterday's wind had been more than a snail's pace we could have been there now." He spread his arms, feeling the touch of a clean shirt against his chest and back. "But there was plenty to do."

Herrick smiled. "Mr. Davy's well on his way to Pendang Bay by now."

Bolitho replied, "Aye. He'll be feeling like a post-captain, if I'm not mistaken."

When he had put Davy in charge of the schooner, and had sent him back to Conway, he had seen his face come alight, as if from within. He must have looked like that himself once, he thought. He had been put in charge of a prize when he had been a lieutenant, far younger than Davy. The first step to real command was said to be the greatest, so perhaps it would work for Davy, too.

He looked up at the open skylight as a voice pealed, "Deck there! Land on the lee bow!"

Bolitho smiled, feeling the chill on his spine. "If the *Argus* is elsewhere, I will have to think again."

The door opened slightly and Midshipman Armitage reported, "Mr. Soames's respects, sir. Masthead has sighted land on the lee bow."

Bolitho said, "Thank you, Mr. Armitage."

He saw the deep hollows around his eyes, the nervous way his fingers twitched against his patched breeches. Unlike any of the others who had returned, he was unable to hide his real feelings. His fear. His knowledge that he could no longer contain it.

"My compliments to Mr. Soames. Tell him we will exercise both watches at gun drill in half an hour." He hesitated and added,

"If there is anything troubling you, it would be as well to confide in the first lieutenant here, or myself, if you feel it might help."

Armitage shook his head. "N-no, sir. I am better now." He hurried away.

Bolitho looked at his friend and asked quietly, "What are we to do about that one?"

Herrick shrugged. "You cannot carry them all, sir. He may get over it. We've all had to go through it at one time or another."

"Now then, Thomas, that does not sound like you at all!" He smiled broadly. "Admit you are concerned for the lad!"

Herrick looked embarrassed. "Well, I was thinking of having a word with him."

"I thought as much, Thomas. You haven't the right face for deceit!"

Another knock at the door announced the surgeon had arrived.

"Well, Mr. Whitmarsh?" Bolitho watched him framed in the doorway, the early sunlight from the cabin hatch making a halo around his huge head. "Is our prisoner worse?"

Whitmarsh moved through the cabin like a man in a prison, ducking under each beam as if seeking a way of escape.

"He is well enough, sir. But I still believe, as I told you when you returned to the ship, that he should have been sent back to the settlement in the schooner."

Bolitho saw Herrick's jaw tighten and knew he was about to silence the surgeon's aggressive outburst. Like the other officers, Herrick found it hard to cover his dislike for him. Whitmarsh was little help in the matter either.

Bolitho said calmly, "I cannot answer for a prisoner if he is there and we are here, surely?"

He watched the beads of sweat trickling down the man's forehead and wondered if he had taken a drink this early. It was a wonder it had not killed him already.

Above his head he heard the regular stamp of boots, the

click of metal, as the marines mustered for morning inspection.

He made himself say, "You must trust my judgement, Mr. Whitmarsh, as I do yours in your own profession."

The surgeon turned and glared at him. "You are admitting that if you'd sent him back to Pendang Bay he would have been seized and hanged!"

Herrick retorted angrily, "Damn, your eyes, man, the fellow is a bloody pirate!"

Whitmarsh eyed him fiercely. "In *your* opinion, no doubt!"

Bolitho stood up sharply and walked to the windows.

"You must live in reality, Mr. Whitmarsh. As a common pirate he would be tried and hanged, as well you know. But if he is the son of Muljadi he is something more than a cat's-paw, he could be used to bargain. There is more at stake here, more lives in peril than I feared. I'll not falter because of your personal feelings."

Whitmarsh siezed the edge of the table, his body hanging over it like a figurehead.

"If you'd suffered as I have—"

Bolitho turned on him, his voice harsh. "I know about your brother, and I am deeply sorry for him! But how many felons and murderers have you seen hanging, rotting in chains, without even a thought?" He heard someone pause beside the open skylight and lowered his voice. "Humanity, I admire. Hypocrisy, I totally reject!" He saw the fury giving way to pain on the surgeon's flushed features. "So take care of the prisoner. If he is to be hanged, then so be it. But if I can use his life to advantage, and in doing so save it, then amen to *that!*"

Whitmarsh moved vaguely towards the door and then said thickly, "And that man Potter you brought from the schooner, sir. You have put him to work already!"

Bolitho smiled. "Really, Mr. Whitmarsh, you do not give up easily. Potter is with the sailmaker as his assistant. He will not be worked to death, and I think that keeping busy will be a quicker cure than brooding over his recent sufferings."

Whitmarsh stalked from the cabin, muttering under his breath.

Herrick exclaimed, "What impertinence! In your shoes I'd have laid about him with a belaying-pin!"

"I doubt that." Bolitho shook the coffee pot, but it was empty. "But I feel that I'll never win his confidence, let alone his trust."

Bolitho waited for Noddall to bring his dress coat and best cocked-hat, feeling rather ridiculous as the servant fussed and tugged at cuffs and lapels.

Herrick said bluntly, "I think it's a bad risk, sir."

"One I'll have to take, Thomas." He saw Noddall pull a long strand of hair from one of the buttons. Her hair. He wondered if Herrick had noticed. He continued, "We have to trust the French captain. All the rest is so much supposition."

Noddall had taken the old sword from its rack on the bulkhead, but held it across his arm, knowing by now it was more than his life was worth to usurp Allday's ritual.

Bolitho thought of Whitmarsh's anger, and knew that much of it had good foundation. Had the prisoner been sent back in the schooner he would doubtlessly have been taken by Puigserver, if he was still at the settlement, or held in irons until he could be sent to the nearest Spanish authority. Then, if he was lucky, he would certainly be hanged. If not, his fate hardly bore thinking about. Like father, like son.

As it was, the schooner's surviving crewmen, a savage-looking collection of half-castes, Javanese and Indians, would meet a swift fate before much longer.

How many lives had they taken, he wondered? How many ships plundered, crews murdered, or broken into husks like Potter, the Bristol sailmaker? The bargain was probably one-sided.

He walked from the cabin, still pondering the rights and wrongs of instant justice.

On deck it was remaining fresh, the day's heat yet to come, and he took a few paces along the weather side while there was still

time. In the heavy dress coat he would be dripping unless he held
to the sails' curved shadows.

Fowlar touched his forehead and said awkwardly, "May I thank
you, sir?"

Bolitho smiled. "You have earned it, Mr. Fowlar, have no fear."

He had made the master's mate an acting-lieutenant to fill the
gap left by Davy. Had young Keen been aboard, it would have been
his chance. Another would be put in Fowlar's place. And so it went
on, as in all ships.

Herrick took Fowlar aside and waited until Bolitho was pacing
again.

"A word of warning. *Never* interrupt the captain when he is
taking his walks." He smiled at Fowlar's uncertainty. "Unless in real
emergency, of course, which does not include your promotion!" He
touched his shirt. "But congratulations, all the same."

Bolitho had already forgotten them. He had seen the dark
smudge of land which just topped the glittering horizon, and was
wondering what he might find there. It looked at this distance like
one great spread of land, but he knew it consisted of a crowded
collection of islets, some even smaller than the one where they had
captured Davy's schooner. The Dutch had originally occupied
them because of their shape and position. Ships anchored amidst
the surrounding islets would have the advantage of using any wind
to put to sea, the use of several channels to avoid delay. The fortress
had been built to protect the place from marauders, such as the one
who now commanded it and challenged all authority and every
flag. The Dutch still listed the Benuas as one of their possessions.
But it was in name only, and they were no doubt glad to be rid of
it and its unhappy history.

He saw the sailmaker speaking with Potter below the forecastle, and wondered if he would ever really recover from his
suffering. It could not be easy for him to be drawing so near to
Muljadi's stronghold again. But of all the people aboard, he was
the only man, apart from the prisoner, who had seen what lay

beyond the protective reefs and sandbars where he had endured so much.

He shivered slightly in spite of his heavy coat. Suppose he had misjudged his opponents? He, too, might become another Potter, a pitiful, broken thing which even his friends and his sisters in England might wish to think of as dead.

And Viola Raymond? How long would she take to forget him?

He shook himself out of his mood and said, "Mr. Soames! You may beat to quarters and clear for action now!" He saw the ripple of excitement run through the men on the gun deck. "Exercise the larboard battery first."

Allday walked up the slanting deck and turned the sword over in his hands before buckling it to Bolitho's belt.

"You'll be taking me, of course, Captain."

He spoke calmly, but Bolitho saw the anxiety in his eyes.

"Not this time."

Calls shrilled along the berth deck, and the marine drummer boys ran breathlessly to the quarterdeck rail, pulling their sticks from their white crossbelts to begin their urgent tattoo.

Allday said stubbornly, "But you'll be *needing* me, Captain!"

"Yes." Bolitho looked at him gravely. "I will always do that . . ."

The rest of his words were lost in the rattle of drums, the stampede of feet as the *Undine*'s people ran to quarters once again.

15

*F*ACE TO FACE

BOLITHO levelled his telescope across the hammock nettings and studied the overlapping islets in silence. All morning and into the forenoon watch, while *Undine* had cruised steadily towards them, he had noted each unusual feature, and had compared his findings with what he already knew. The main channel through the islets opened to the south, and almost in the centre of the approach was one stark hump of rock upon which stood the old stone fortress. Even now, with the nearest spurs of land less than two miles distant, it was impossible to see where the fortress began or the craggy hilltop ended.

"We will alter course again, Mr. Herrick." He lowered the glass and dabbed his eye with his wrist. "Steer east nor'-east."

He saw the men by the larboard twelve-pounders peering through their open ports, the guns already shimmering in the sunlight as if they had just been fired.

Herrick shouted, "Hands to the braces! Alter course two points to larboard, Mr. Mudge!"

Bolitho sought out the frail figure of Potter amongst the unemployed hands below the forecastle, and when he glanced up beckoned him aft.

He slipped out of his heavy coat and handed it with his hat to Allday, saying as calmly as he could, "I will go aloft myself."

Allday said nothing. He knew Bolitho well enough to understand what it was costing him.

Potter hurried on to the quarterdeck and knuckled his forehead.

"Sir?"

"D'you think you could climb to the maintop with me?"

Potter stared at him dully. "If you says so, sir."

Herrick called, "East nor'-east, sir!"

He looked from Bolitho to the mainyard stretching athwartships and vibrating to the great press of canvas below it.

Bolitho unbuckled his sword and gave it to Allday. "I may need your eyes today, Potter."

Feeling every man watching him, he swung out on to the weather shrouds and begin to climb, his fingers locking so tightly around each ratline that the pain helped to steady him. Up and up, with his gaze fixed on the futtock shrouds which leaned out and around the sturdy maintop where two marines were studying his progress with unblinking curiosity.

Bolitho gritted his teeth and fought the urge to look down. It was infuriating. Unfair. He had first gone to sea at the age of twelve. Year by year he had studied and matured, had replaced his child's infatuation for the Navy with a genuine understanding which had amounted almost to love. He had overcome seasickness, and had learned to hide his loneliness and grief from his companions when his mother had died while he had been at sea. So, too, his father was buried while Bolitho had been fighting Frenchman and American in and around the Caribbean. He had watched men suffer horribly in battle, and his body bore enough scars to show the narrow margin between his own survival and death. Why then, should he be cursed with this hatred of heights?

He felt his shoes scrabbling on the ratlines as he hauled himself out and around the futtock shrouds, his body hanging in space and supported only by fingers and toes.

A marine said admiringly, "By God, sir, that was a fair climb!"

Bolitho arrived beside him, his chest heaving painfully. He watched the marine to see if he was disguising his sarcasm, but saw it was the same sharpshooter who had discovered the anchored schooner just two days back.

He nodded and allowed himself a glance at the ship far below.

Foreshortened bodies moved about the quarterdeck, and when he looked forward he saw the leadsman in the chains, the blur of his arm as he hurled the heavy weight deftly beyond the bows.

He relaxed, and waited for Potter to scramble up beside him.

For a moment longer he toyed with the idea of forcing himself up the next length of quivering shrouds to the maintopsail yard, but rejected it. Apart from proving something to himself, or showing his capability to those who might be watching from below, it would serve for little. Potter was exhausted by the climb, and if Herrick needed him urgently on deck he would look even more foolish if he fell headlong from his perch.

He unslung the telescope from his shoulder and trained it on the channel between the islets. In the time it had taken him to climb from the deck and regain his wind *Undine* had cruised over a cable, and it was possible to see the next overlapping islet behind the central hill with its forbidding fortress and steep, sunbaked cliff.

Potter said, "I never bin to the east'rd side, sir. There's a good channel there, too, I'm told." He shuddered. "They used to bury the corpses in the sandbars at low water. What there was left of 'em."

Bolitho stiffened and momentarily forgot the deck far beneath him. He saw the blacker silhouette of a ship's masts and yards almost hidden around the curve of the inner channel. A frigate.

Potter saw his interest and added dolefully, "Best place to anchor, sir. The battery on the fortress can protect two channels at once, an' any craft wot chooses to lay there."

Something pale flapped and broadened against the furthest islet. A small boat hoisting its sail.

Bolitho glanced quickly at the foretopmast where Herrick had run up a big white flag. One way or another they would soon know.

There was a hollow boom, and after what seemed like an age, a tall waterspout shot skywards about a cable off the larboard beam. He trained the glass quickly towards the fortress, but the smoke had already fanned away so it was impossible to gauge the angle of the shot.

He shifted the glass again and saw the boat moving more quickly around a litter of broken rocks, the sail braced back like the fin of a great shark.

He let out a long breath as he saw a white flag flapping from her masthead. His request to parley was accepted. The single shot from the battery was a warning.

Bolitho slung the telescope across his shoulder. "You stay here, Potter. Keep an eye on everything, and try to remember any item which might be of use. It could well save lives one day." He nodded casually to the two marine marksmen. "I hope you'll not be needed!" He slung a leg over the low barricade and tried not to lower his eyes. "*Argus* intends us to do all the sweating!"

The men grinned and nudged each other, as if he had just given them access to some priceless and vital information.

Bolitho swallowed hard and began to make the journey to the deck. When he reached the point where he could see the nettings on the opposite side again he allowed himself to look at the group which awaited him by the bulwark. Herrick was smiling, although whether from relief or amusement it was hard to tell. Bolitho jumped down to the deck and glanced ruefully at his fresh shirt. It was dripping with sweat, and bore a black streak of tar across one shoulder.

He said, "Never mind. The coat will hide that." In a brisker tone he added, "A boat is coming out, Mr. Herrick. Heave-to, if you please, and prepare to anchor."

He glanced up at the great yards again. It had not been quite so bad as he had imagined that time. Then he thought of the ideal conditions as compared with a screaming gale, or making the same climb in pitch darkness, and changed his mind.

Bolitho allowed Herrick to shout his orders before asking Mudge, "What did you make of that shot?"

The master regarded him dubiously. "Old gun, I'd say, sir. From where I was standin' it sounded like a bronze piece."

Bolitho nodded. "As I thought, too. It would be likely that they'd still have the original cannon." He rubbed his chin, thinking aloud. "So they'd be loath to use heated shot for fear of splitting them." He grinned at Mudge's mournful expression. "Not that it matters much, I daresay. If they fired solid rock, they could scarcely fail to hit a ship trying to force the channel!"

Fowlar shouted, "The boat has an officer aboard, sir." He grinned. "Most o' the hands are the colour of coffee, but he's a Frog if ever I saw one."

Bolitho took a glass and watched the oncoming boat. Locally

built, with the familiar high prow and lateen sail, it was moving fast and well on a converging tack. He saw the officer in question, standing easily below the mist, his cocked hat pulled down over his forehead to shade his eyes from the fierce glare. Fowlar was right. There was no mistaking this one.

He made himself walk a few paces away from the side, as with her courses brailed up and her topsails in booming confusion *Undine* turned noisily into the wind to await her visitors.

Bolitho gripped the rail and watched in silence as the boat surged round and under the main chains, where some of *Undine's* seamen and Mr. Shellabeer waited to secure her lines and, if necessary, fend off any risk of collision.

He said, "And now, Mr. Herrick, we shall see."

He walked along the swaying gangway to the entry port and waited for the officer to scramble aboard. He stood quite alone framed against the cruising ranks of small whitecaps, his eyes exploring *Undine's* gun deck, the watching seamen and marines above and below him. Seeing Bolitho, he removed his hat with a flourish and gave a small bow.

"Lieutenant Maurin, *m'sieu.* At your service."

He bore no marks of rank, and his blue coat showed plenty of evidence of patching and repairs. He was tanned to the shade of old leather, and his eyes were those of a man who had been at sea for most of his life. Tough, self-assured, competent, it was all there on his face, Bolitho decided.

Bolitho nodded. "And I am Captain Bolitho, of His Majesty's ship *Undine.*"

The lieutenant gave a wry smile. "My *capitaine*'as been expecting you."

Bolitho glanced briefly at the cockade on Maurin's hat. It bore the small red beast instead of a French insignia.

He asked, "And what is your nationality, Lieutenant?"

The man shrugged. "I am employed in the service of Prince Muljadi." He shrugged again. "Naturally."

Bolitho gave a wry smile. *"Naturally."*

He added sharply, "I wish to meet your captain, and without delay. I have certain matters to discuss."

"But of course, *m'sieu.*" The lieutenant was looking at the men on deck. His eyes were always moving. Calculating. He continued, "Capitaine Le Chaumareys is prepared for me to remain aboard as 'ostage to ensure your, er, good 'ealth!"

Bolitho hid his relief. Had Le Chaumareys been killed or replaced he might have had to alter his tactics.

He said calmly, "It will not be necessary. I have every faith in your captain's honour."

Herrick exclaimed, "But, sir, you cannot mean it! Keep him, I say! Your life is too valuable to risk on a Frenchman's word!"

Bolitho looked at him and smiled. "If Le Chaumareys is the callous brute you describe, do you imagine he would care about losing a lieutenant if it were to gain him a better bargaining point?" He touched his arm. "I have made some notes in my cabin. They may help you to pass the time in my absence." He touched his hat to the quarterdeck and said to Maurin, "I am ready."

For a moment longer he stood in the port, looking down into the boat alongside. There were about a dozen men aboard, naked but for a few scraps of rags, but armed to the teeth, and with the looks of men prepared to kill without question.

Maurin said quietly, "You will be safe with me, *m'sieu.*" He lowered himself swiftly on to the boat's gunwale, adding, "For the moment."

Bolitho jumped the last few feet and steadied himself against a crude backstay, very conscious of the acrid stench of sweat and filth which floated unheeded in the bilges.

"You choose strange allies, Lieutenant."

Maurin signalled for the boat to be cast off, one hand resting casually on his pistol.

"Lie with a dog and you arise with fleas, *m'sieu.* It is quite common."

Bolitho glanced at his profile. Another Herrick perhaps? Then as the sail billowed and cracked to the wind, and the slim hull began to gather way, he forgot Maurin, even the anxious faces on *Undine*'s quarterdeck, as he considered what he was about to do.

Bolitho clung to the backstay as the boat scudded dangerously close to a line of black-toothed rocks and then went about to enter the main channel. He noticed that the current was strong and at odds with the incoming sea, and felt the hull leap and stagger as it straightened up for the final leg of the journey. When he looked astern he could see nothing of his own ship. She was already hidden by a wedge of land, the side of which lay deep in shadow.

Maurin asked suddenly, "Why d'you take such risks, *m'sieu?*"

Bolitho looked at him impassively. "Why do you?"

Maurin shrugged. "I obey orders. But soon I will be going 'ome again. To Toulon. I 'ave not seen my family for . . ." He smiled sadly. "Too long."

Bolitho glanced across the lieutenant's shoulder and studied the grim fortress which was slipping past the port beam. It was still difficult to see the extent of its buildings. A high wall, undulating with the edge of the clifftop. The spaced windows were little more thin black slits, like mournful eyes, while above on the weather-worn battlements, he could see the muzzles of several large guns, just visible through their individual embrasures.

Maurin said, "A foul place, is it not? But they are not like us. They live like crabs in the rocks." He sounded contemptuous.

Bolitho saw several small boats bobbing at anchor, and a schooner similar to the one they had captured moored to a stone pier.

Maurin did not try to stop him looking at everything, to prevent his interest in the many figures which moved about the pier and up the sloping track to the fortress gates. Bolitho decided he was being brought by the main channel by careful design. So that he should see the growing strength of Muljadi's private army. And it was impressive. To think that a pirate, an alien to the Indies, could muster this force, and instil such discipline, was enough to impress anyone. Even a pompous fool like Major Jardine.

He turned as the boat's crew began to shorten sail, and saw the anchored frigate lying directly across the bows. Close to in a confined space she seemed even larger. Far bigger than *Undine*. Even his last command would have been reckless to match her deadly broadside of eighteen-pounders.

He remarked, "A fine ship."

Maurin nodded. "The best. We 'ave been together for so long we even think alike!"

Bolitho saw the activity around the entry port, the gleam of sunlight on fixed bayonets where a guard awaited his arrival. A very carefully staged performance, he thought. He noticed that boarding nets were furled along the gangways where they could be spread without delay. Fear of a cutting-out attack? More likely he was taking no chances with his new "ally." It was the only promising thing Bolitho had seen so far.

A small fishing dory drifted abeam, and he saw some natives standing in it shaking their fists at him and baring their teeth like wild beasts.

Maurin said simply, "They probably think you are a prisoner, eh?" It seemed to depress him.

Bolitho pushed him from his thoughts as the boat swung heavily towards the frigate's main chains. Capitaine Paul Le Chaumareys, a man about whom many tales had been told. Battles won, convoys harried and settlements destroyed. His record in the war had been formidable, just as Conway had described. But as an individual he was a mystery, mostly because he had spent much of his service far away from his own beloved France.

He ran his eyes the full length of the ship's side. *Argus*, the hundred-eyed messenger of Hera. Very appropriate for a man as elusive as Le Chaumareys, he thought. Sturdily built, and showing the scars and blemishes of hard service, she was a ship he would have been proud to command. She lacked *Undine*'s grace, but had a heavier toughness which could not be ignored.

The boat had made fast to the chains, and the crew stood grouped by the mast as Bolitho climbed up to the gunwale. Nobody attempted to assist him. Then, a young seaman jumped down from the chains and held out his hand.

"*M'sieu!*" He grinned broadly. "*A votre service!*"

Bolitho seized his wrist and levered himself towards the entry port. The French seaman could have been one of his own.

He removed his hat to the broad quarterdeck, and waited while the calls shrilled a salute and a guard presented muskets. Not crisply like Bellairs's marines would have done, but with a familiar jauntiness. Of long practice. Like the upper deck itself, he thought. Not dirty, but not gleaming and in perfect order either. Well used. Ready for anything.

"Ah, *Capitaine!*" Le Chaumareys stepped forward to greet him, his eyes fixed on Bolitho's face.

He was quite unlike anyone he had expected. Older. A good deal so. Perhaps in his middle forties. And one of the largest men he had ever met. Taller than six feet, with shoulders so broad that his bared head seemed tiny by comparison, especially as he wore his hair very short, like a convict.

"I welcome you to my ship." He waved his hand around the deck. "To my world, as it has been for so long." He smiled, the effect lighting up his face in an instant. "So come below to the cabin." He nodded to Maurin. "I will call for you when it is time."

Bolitho followed him to the cabin hatch, seeing the eyes watching from both deck and gangways, the way they studied his every move, as if to discover something.

Le Chaumareys said casually, "I hope Maurin took good care of you?"

"Very, thank you. His English is excellent."

"Yes. One of the reasons I chose him for my ship. He is married to an Englishwoman," he chuckled. "You, of course, are *not* married. So why not a French bride for you, eh?"

He threw open the door and watched Bolitho's reactions. The cabin was large and well furnished, and like the rest of the ship, vaguely untidy. Lived in.

But Bolitho's attention was immediately drawn to a table which was laden with food.

Le Chaumareys remarked, "Much of it is locally obtained." He jabbed a large joint with his finger. "Like this. It is very much the same as smoked ham. You must eat your fill, while you can, eh?" He chuckled, the sound rising from what Bolitho now saw to be a large belly.

He replied, "I am here to present—"

The other captain wagged a finger. "You are aboard a French ship, *m'sieu*. First we drink."

He shouted a brief command and a servant hurried from the adjoining cabin with a tall crystal jug of wine. It was extremely good, as cool as spring water. Bolitho glanced from the jug to the table. Genuine? Or was it one more trick to show they were superior, even in their supplies and comforts?

A chair was brought for him, and when he was seated Le Chaumareys seemed to relax.

He said, "I have heard of you, Bolitho. You had a fine record in the war for one so junior." His eyes did not flicker as he added, "It was difficult for you. The unfortunate affair of your brother."

Bolitho watched him calmly. Le Chaumareys was a man he could understand. Like a duellist. Relaxed one moment, making a thrust the next.

He said, "Thank you for your concern."

The small head bobbed back and forth. "You should have been in these waters during the war. Independence, an ability to work beyond the reach of some admiral, eh? I think it would have fitted you well."

Bolitho felt the servant refilling his glass. "I have come to speak with Muljadi."

He tightened his grip on the glass. It had come out just like that, as if the words had been lying in his mind for months instead of seconds.

Le Chaumareys stared at him with amazement. "Are you insane? He would have you screaming for death in a moment, and I could not help you. No, *m'sieu,* it would be a lunatic thing even to think of."

Bolitho said, "Then I will return to my ship."

"But what of your Admiral Conway? His despatches? Is there nothing from him for me?"

"It would be pointless now." Bolitho watched him warily. "Besides which, you are not here as a French captain, but as a subordinate to Muljadi's authority."

Le Chaumareys took a deep swallow from his glass, his eyes slitted against the reflected sunlight from the windows.

He said abruptly, "Listen to me. Curb your impatience. As I have had to do, when I was your age, eh?" He looked around the cabin. "I have my instructions. I obey them, as you must yours. But I have served France well, and I am near finished in the Indies. Perhaps I made my services too valuable to be allowed home earlier, but that is as may be. I *know* these seas like my own face. During the war I had to live off the islands for food and shelter, for repairs, and to glean intelligence about your patrols and convoys. When I was told to continue in these same waters I resented it, but I suppose I was flattered also. I am still needed, eh? Not like many who fought so bravely and are now without bread." He looked at Bolitho sharply and added, "As in your country, too, no doubt?"

Bolitho replied, "Yes. It is much the same."

Le Chaumareys smiled. "Well then, my impetuous friend, we must not fight again! We are too much the same. Needed one minute, expendable the next!"

Bolitho said coldly, "Many have died because of your actions. But for our arrival at Pendang Bay all the garrison would have been killed, and you must know it. A Spanish frigate was destroyed to delay our arrival, to allow this *Prince* Muljadi to give his piracy some sort of repute, to make him an ally of France, and a constant threat to peace."

Le Chaumareys's eyes widened. "Well said. But I had no part in *Nervion*'s destruction." He held up one large fist. "Of course I *heard* about it. I hear many things I do not like. That is why I brought the Spanish commandant here to parley for his garrison's safety. He was still the representative of his own King. He could agree to terms which but for your intervention would have given Muljadi certain rights in Pendang Bay." He became very grave. "I did not know an attack would be launched the very moment I had left the bay! You have my word, as a French officer!"

"And I accept it."

Bolitho tried to remain calm, but could feel the blood tingling in his veins like ice water. It was exactly as he had imagined. A set, calculated plan which had begun perhaps in Europe, in Paris and London, even Madrid, and which had almost worked. But for his decision to take *Undine* and the *Nervion*'s few survivors to their destination, and Puigserver's arrival in Pendang Bay, the matter would be settled, and Le Chaumareys probably on his way home at last, his work done, and done well.

He heard himself say, "I have come to take the commandant back to his own kind. Don Luis Puigserver, the King of Spain's representative, will be expecting his return." He hardened his tone. "Is Colonel Pastor still alive? Or is his death another thing you know of but did not approve?"

Le Chaumareys stood up and moved heavily to the quarter window.

"He is here. A prisoner of Muljadi's. In that ruin on the hill. He will never allow you to take him, dead or alive. His presence can still give legality to his demands. Can show that England is unable to honour her word and protect the rights and citizens of Spain. A hard story to believe? But time and distance can make truth a mockery."

"Then why would Muljadi fear to see *me?*" Bolitho watched him as he moved away from the window, his face lined and grim. "I'd have thought he would have been eager to throw his power in my face."

Le Chaumareys walked across the cabin, the deck creaking under his corpulent frame. He halted by Bolitho's chair and looked directly into his eyes.

"It is I who fear for *you*, Bolitho. Out here, in my *Argus*, I am Muljadi's arm, his reach. To him I am not merely a sea captain, but a symbol, a man who can spring his plans into reality. But beyond these timbers I cannot answer for your security, and that is the truth." He hesitated, his eyes still on Bolitho's face. "But I see I am wasting time. You are determined, no?"

Bolitho smiled gravely. "Yes."

Le Chaumareys added, "I have met many Englishmen in war and peace. Some I liked, many I hated. Few did I respect." He held out his hand. "You I admire." He smiled sadly. "A fool, but a brave one. *That* I can admire."

He rang a bell and then gestured to the table. "And you eat nothing."

Bolitho reached for his hat. "If what you say is true, then it would be wasted, eh?" He smiled, despite his tumbling thoughts. "And if not. I will have to content myself with salt pork in the future."

A tall, lank-haired officer entered the cabin, and Le Chaumareys spoke to him swiftly in French. Then he picked up his own hat and said, "My senior lieutenant, Bolitho. I have changed my mind. I am coming with you." He shrugged. "Curiosity, or to prove my original beliefs, I know not which. But without me you are a dead man."

When they reached the quarterdeck Bolitho saw there was a boat already alongside, and that the gangways were filled with silent spectators. Having a good look, he thought grimly. A one-way journey, if he had miscalculated.

Le Chaumareys held his arm. "Listen to me. I am older, and, I expect, wiser than you. I can have you taken back to your ship. You will suffer no disgrace. In a year all this will be forgotten. Leave politics to those who daily dirty their hands without remorse."

Bolitho shook his head. "In my position, would *you?*" He forced a smile. "Your face tells me what I need to know."

Le Chaumareys nodded to his watching officers and then led the way to the entry port.

Bolitho glanced quickly along the gun deck, noting the fresh repairs to timbers and cordage. Where *Undine* had made her own challenge, and when he had felt the battle was nearly lost. It was an uncanny feeling to be walking with *Argus's* captain. More like compatriots than men who had so recently tried to destroy each other. If they met again after this, there could be no more truces.

The boat pulled steadily across swirling water towards the pier below the fortress, the French seamen watching Bolitho the whole time. Curious? Or merely seeing the face of an enemy?

Le Chaumareys spoke only once on the short crossing.

"Do not lose your temper with Muljadi. One sign and he will have you seized. He is without pity."

"And what about your position here?"

The Frenchman gave a bitter smile. "He *needs* me, *m'sieu.*"

Once alongside the pier Bolitho gained a new understanding of the hatred he had seen earlier. With the French seamen surrounding him as an escort he was made to hurry up the steep slope towards the fortress, while on all sides voices rose in shouts and curses, and it was obvious that without Le Chaumareys's massive presence even the sailors would have been set upon.

The lower part of the fortress was little more than an empty shell, its courtyard littered with rushes and rags which the defenders and Muljadi's growing army of followers used for bedding. He looked up at the blue sky above the ramparts and saw the guns. Old but powerful, each with balls nearby, and long ropes which trailed carelessly to the courtyard, and some crude baskets which presumably were used to haul fresh powder and shot when required.

More rough steps, the sun probing across his shoulders, then sudden shadows making his body feel chilled and damp.

Le Chaumareys grunted, "You will wait here."

He led Bolitho into a roughly hewn room no bigger than a cable tier and strode towards an iron-studded door at one end. It was guarded by some heavily armed natives, who faced the French seamen as if hoping for a fight.

Le Chaumareys seemed to sail right through them, like a three-decker breaking the line of battle. Supreme confidence, or a well-practised bluff. Bolitho did not know.

He did not have to wait long. The door was dragged open and he saw a large room, a chamber, which seemed to span the whole breadth of the upper fortress. Against the dull stone and smoky walls the dais at the far end made a fine splash of colour.

Muljadi was arranged on a pile of silk cushions, eyes fixed on the door, his body completely at ease.

He was naked to the waist, and wore only white baggy trousers and red leather boots underneath. He had no hair, so that in the sunlight from the slitted windows his head seemed pointed, and his single ear very prominent and grotesque.

Le Chaumareys was standing to one side of the dais, his face stern and alert. Around the walls were some of the dirtiest and cruellest-looking men Bolitho had ever seen in his life, although the quality of their weapons marked them as leaders or lieutenants in Muljadi's command.

He walked towards the dais, half expecting one of the onlookers to rush forward and cut him down, but nobody moved or spoke.

When he was within a few feet of the cushions Muljadi said flatly, "That is close enough!"

He spoke good English, but with a strong accent which was probably Spanish.

He continued, "Before I have you killed, *Captain,* is there anything you wish to say?"

Bolitho wanted to lick his parched lips. He heard the rustle of expectancy behind him, saw Le Chaumareys watching him with despair on his tanned face.

Bolitho said, "On behalf of His Britannic Majesty, King George, I have come to demand the release of Colonel Don Jose Pastor, subject of Spain, and under my country's protection."

Muljadi sat bolt upright, the stump of his severed wrist pointing like a gun.

"*Demand?* You insolent dog!"

Le Chaumareys stepped forward hastily. "Let me explain, *m'sieu.*"

Muljadi screamed, "You will address me as *Highness!*" To Bolitho he added savagely, "Call on your God for help! I will make you *plead* for death!"

Bolitho could feel his heart pumping against his ribs, the sweat pouring down his spine and gathering around his waist like ice-rime. Deliberately he reached into his pocket and pulled out his watch. As he flicked open the guard he heard Muljadi leap to his feet, the gasp of disbelief as he threw himself from the dais to seize Bolitho's wrist in a grip like a manacle.

He screamed into Bolitho's face, "Where did you get *that?*"

He jerked up his wrist and the watch, upon which the prancing gold beast dangled like a fob.

Bolitho forced himself to keep his voice level. To stop his gaze from falling on the similar pendant which hung on Muljadi's chest.

"From a prisoner." He added sharply, "A pirate!"

Muljadi twisted his wrist slowly, his eyes like fires as he snarled, "You lie! And you will suffer for it! *Now!*"

Le Chaumareys called, "In God's name, do not *make* him kill you!"

Bolitho kept his eyes on Muljadi's, feeling his power, his hatred, but something more. Anxiety?

He said, "If you take a telescope, you will be able to see my ship. You will also see there is a halter at the mainyard. If I do not return before dusk, your son will hang there, you have my word on it! I took this from his neck when I captured him and his schooner some forty miles to the south'rd of where we are standing."

Muljadi's eyes seemed to be bulging right out of his head. *"You lie!"*

Bolitho eased his wrist from Muljadi's grasp. The fingers had left marks like rope burns.

He said quietly, "I will exchange him for your prisoner." He looked at Le Chaumareys's astonished face. "The *capitaine* can arrange it, I am certain."

Muljadi ran to a window and snatched a telescope from one of his men.

Over his shoulder he said hoarsely, "You will stay as hostage!"

Bolitho replied, "No hostages. A fair bargain. You have my word, as a King's officer."

Muljadi threw the telescope to the ground, shattering the lens in all directions. His chest was heaving violently, and his shaven head was glittering with tiny jewels of sweat.

"King's officer? Do you think I care for you?" He spat on the stones by Bolitho's shoes. "You will suffer, that I promise you!"

Le Chaumareys called, "Let it be done!" He hesitated. "Highness!"

But Muljadi was almost beside himself. Like a madman. He suddenly grasped Bolitho's arm and propelled him to the opposite end of the chamber and thrust him against the window.

"Look down there, *Captain!*" He was spitting out each word like a pistol ball. "I will give you your colonel, but it is too late to save you now!"

Bolitho stared down at the glittering water which snaked around and amongst the next cluster of islets. Anchored in a bend of the channel, her decks alive with hurrying figures, was a frigate.

He felt Muljadi's hatred turning to a wild jubilation as he shouted, "Mine! All mine! Well, my *King's officer*, are you still so confident?"

Le Chaumareys said harshly, "Why did you have to do that?"

Muljadi whirled round on him, his eyes wild. "Do you think I have to be told what to do? That I am a child? I have waited long enough. The waiting is over now."

A door grated open and Bolitho saw the Spanish commandant, supported on either side by an armed pirate, his eyes blinking in the light as if he was almost blind.

Bolitho strode past Muljadi and his men. "I have come to take you home, *Señor*." He saw the filth on his torn clothing, the shackle marks on his thin wrists. "It was a brave thing you did."

The old man peered blearily at him, his beard quivering as he said jerkily, "I do not understand?"

Le Chaumareys said, "Come. Now." Under his breath he added, "Or I will not answer for your safety!"

It was like a dream. Down the sloping track to the pier and into the boat, and for most of the way pursued by Muljadi's voice, which had lapsed into another language, although the threat was no less evident.

Bolitho said coldly, "The frigate. She was English."

Le Chaumareys nodded wearily. "Yes. Damaged in battle in '82, she was beached near here and her company removed by another vessel. We have been working on her for two years almost. Putting her to rights. I was ordered to hand her to Muljadi ready for use, before I am allowed to return home."

Bolitho did not look at him. He was supporting the Spanish commandant against his knees, feeling his sobs and his misery.

"Then I hope you are proud of your work, *m'sieu*. And what it may mean when Muljadi puts her to work."

The French frigate's yards loomed above the boat, and Bolitho followed the other captain up to the entry port.

Le Chaumareys said abruptly, "Maurin will attend to the transfer."

He looked searchingly at Bolitho for several seconds.

"You are still young. One day you might have understood.

Now that is past." He thrust out his hand. "When we meet again, as I fear we must, it will be for the last time."

He turned on his heel and strode to the cabin hatch.

Bolitho pulled out his watch and examined the gold pendant. If he had been mistaken, or Potter had given him wrong information . . . He stopped his train of thought there and then. It did not bear even conjecture.

Then he thought of the captured frigate. But for Muljadi's flare of anger he would never have known of it. The knowledge was little help, but it was better than nothing, he decided.

Maurin said cheerfully, "I will take a boat away to your ship, *m'sieu*. They will be surprised to learn of your safety, as I am."

Bolitho smiled. "I was well protected, thank you." He glanced at the cabin hatch, but was uncertain what he meant.

16

NO BETTER, NO *W*ORSE THAN MOST

BOLITHO walked slowly along the upper rampart at the inland side of the settlement, watching the steamy haze rising from the jungle, the afternoon sunlight playing on the dripping leaves and fronds nearest the palisade. *Undine* had anchored shortly before noon below an empty blue sky, and yet during their slow approach towards Pendang Bay he had seen the land dark under the weather, and had almost envied the isolated downpour. He sighed, smelling the thick, heady scents from the jungle, the drowsy aromas of rotting leaves and roots hidden in deep shadow below the trees.

For the last two days *Undine* had been plagued with opposing wind, and when at last it had changed in their favour there had been little more than a breath to bring life to the sails.

He watched some red-coated sepoys working beyond the palisade, and two native women approaching the gateway with heavy bundles on their heads. At a glance it seemed nothing had changed, but now as he waited to confront Conway for the second time within the hour he knew everything was different.

He continued his walk to the next corner of the crude timber rampart and saw *Undine* riding easily to her cable, the captured schooner close abeam. As he looked towards the shallows where he had last seen the brig *Rosalind* when *Undine* had set sail for Muljadi's stronghold, it was all he could do to stop himself from cursing aloud. Like the transport *Bedford,* she had gone. Back to Madras, to carry despatches and Raymond's own appreciation of the situation to Sir Montagu Strang.

Bolitho had been shocked by Conway's appearance when he had reported ashore within thirty minutes of dropping anchor. Wild-eyed, more shrunken than ever, he had been almost beside himself with anger and despair.

He had shouted, "You dare to stand here and tell me that you actually chose to ignore my orders? That despite the importance of my instructions you made no attempt to parley with Le Chaumareys?"

Bolitho had stood very still, his eyes on Conway's distorted features. An empty decanter lay on the table, and it was obvious he had been drinking heavily for some time.

"I could not parley, sir. To do so would have been to recognise Muljadi. Which is exactly what the French want."

"Are you telling me something I do not already know?" Conway had gripped the table violently. "I ordered you to tell Le Chaumareys to return Colonel Pastor unharmed! The Spanish government would have raised a savage argument against England if we had allowed him to remain a prisoner, *and right under my nose!*"

Bolitho recalled his own voice. Taut and flat. Not daring to arouse Conway's fury any more than it was.

"When I found I had captured Muljadi's son I knew I *could*

bargain, sir. There was a good chance I would succeed. As it turned out, we arrived in time. I fear that Pastor would have died in a few more days."

Conway had screamed, "Pastor be damned! You took Muljadi's son, and you dared to release him! We could have had that bloody pirate crawling at our feet, pleading for his son's life!"

Bolitho had said abruptly, "There was a frigate lost in these waters during the last months of the war."

Conway had been taken off guard. "Yes, yes. The *Imogene*, Captain Balfour." He had squinted against the sun's glare from a window. "Twenty-eight guns. Had been in battle with the French and then got caught by a gale. Drove aground, and her people were taken off by one of my sloops. What the *hell* does she have to do with it?"

"Everything, sir. But for my meeting with Muljadi I would never have known until we were totally unprepared. The frigate, the *Imogene*, is there, sir, in the Benuas, and from what I saw, about ready to weigh anchor."

Conway had lurched against the table, as if Bolitho had actually struck him.

"If this is some trick, some ruse to deter my—"

"She is there, sir. Refitted and repaired, and I have no doubt well trained by Le Chaumareys's officers." He could not conceal his bitterness. "I had hoped the brig would still be here. You could have sent word. Demanded help. There is no choice in the matter now."

The next part had been the worst. Conway walking unsteadily to the sideboard and fumbling with another decanter, and muttering, "Betrayed, right from the start. Raymond insisted on sending the brig to Madras. She's a Company vessel, and I could hold her no longer. He had all the arguments. All the answers, too." Claret had slopped over his shirt like blood as he had shouted, "And me? Nothing but a cat's-paw! A tool for Strang and his friends to use as they please!"

He had smashed a goblet with the decanter and groped hurriedly for another, adding, "And now you, the one man I trusted, tells me that Muljadi is ready to attack my settlement! Not merely content with showing me to be incompetent, Raymond will now tell his damned superiors that I cannot even hold this territory under the British flag!"

The door had opened noiselessly and Puigserver had moved into the room. He had glanced briefly at Conway and had said to Bolitho, "I stayed until your return. My men have sailed in the *Bedford*, but I could not leave also without offering my gratitude for securing Don Pastor's release. You seem to make a habit of risking your life for others. I trust that this time it will not go unrewarded." His black eyes had moved to Conway again. "Eh, Admiral?"

Conway had stared at him vaguely. "I must think."

"We all must." The Spaniard had settled in a chair, his eyes still on Conway. "I heard some of it through the door." He had shrugged. "Not spying, you understand, but your voice was somewhat forceful."

Conway had made a new effort to control himself. "Conference. Immediately." He had fixed Bolitho with a bleary stare. "You wait outside. I must *think*."

Now, as he looked emptily at the small figures below the palisade, Bolitho could feel his returning anger, a sense of urgency.

"Richard!"

He swung round and saw her at the corner of the square tower. She was well covered against the sun, and wore the same wide-brimmed hat as before. He hurried to her and seized her hands.

"Viola! I was wondering—"

She shook her head. "Later. But listen." She reached up and touched his cheek very gently, her eyes suddenly sad. "It has been so long. Eleven days, but they were years. When the storm came I worried about you."

He tried to speak, to break the pain in her voice, but she

hurried on, "I think James suspects. He has been very strange lately. Probably my maid let slip something. A good girl, but easily flattered into words." She studied him searchingly. "But no matter. He will do nothing. It is *you* I am concerned for." She dropped her head. "And it is all my fault. I wanted him to be something in this world, mostly, I suspect, for my own gain. I drove him too hard, too fast, wanting him to be the man he could never be." She squeezed his hand. "But you know all this."

Voices echoed below the parapet and Bolitho thought he heard footsteps.

She said huskily, "James will have sent his own report to Sir Montagu. He knows now that Conway is not the man for this appointment, and will use this knowledge to his own advantage. But you, my darling Richard, will be included in his report. I know him so well, you see. To get at you, to use his petty revenge, he will also blame you for the inability to destroy an ignorant pirate, French aid or no!"

He replied quietly, "It is worse than that. Muljadi has many men at his back. When once he has overthrown this settlement the whole area will rise to support him. They have little choice. The pirates will become saviours, the protectors the invaders. It is not uncommon."

She turned her head quickly and he saw a pulse jumping in her throat.

"Listen to me, Richard. Do not become further involved. You are valuable to your country and to all who look up to you. Do not, I implore you, continue to look up to those who are unfit even to lick your boots!" She cupped his face in her hands. "Save your ship and yourself, and damn *their* eyes, I say!"

He held her wrists very gently. "It is no longer so simple." He thought of Le Chaumareys, encouraging him to quit, to get away and still retain his honour. "And I wish to God you had sailed in the brig. Muljadi has more strength now, and when he comes . . ."

He let his gaze move outward and down towards the anchored

frigate. How small she appeared in the harsh glare.

"There is only *Undine* between him and these walls."

She stared at him, her eyes wide and suddenly understanding. "And you intend to fight *all* of them?"

Bolitho prised her hands away as a sepoy corporal rounded the tower and said, "Captain Bolitho, *sahib*, the governor will meet you, please."

Bolitho looked at her and said, "Now we will see, Viola." He tried to smile. "The battle's not done yet."

He found Conway seated behind the table, his stained shirt covered by his heavy dress coat. Puigserver had not moved, and Raymond was standing with his back to a window, his face hidden in black shadow. Major Jardine and his second-in-command made up the conference.

Conway said sharply, "I have told them, Bolitho. Word for word as you described it to me."

"Thank you, sir."

Bolitho looked at Raymond, knowing it would come from him.

"You took a great deal upon yourself, Captain. More, I suspect, than the governor intended?"

"Yes, sir. But I was taught to use initiative, especially when beyond the fleet's apron strings." He saw Puigserver examining one shoe with sudden interest. "The fact is, Muljadi intends to attack this settlement. It is all he can do now that he has lost his hostage, and understands that we are informed of his additional frigate. It has changed everything."

Jardine said harshly, "If he comes, my men can hold him off until help arrives. When the brig reaches Madras they'll soon send a force to finish this ruffian! Even when the Navy is apparently incapable of so doing, what?"

Bolitho waited, watching Raymond's hands on the window sill.

"Well, Mr. Raymond? Is the gallant major right?" He saw the hands take a firmer grip and added, "Or did you suggest in your report to Sir Montagu Strang that Pendang Bay is, in your opinion, *no longer an asset?"*

Jardine bared his teeth. *"Rubbish!"* He hesitated and asked, "Well, sir?"

Raymond sounded very calm. "I told the truth. No ships will be sent, other than transports to remove the Company's soldiers and their dependents."

Jardine exploded, "But I can manage, sir! You should have told me first!"

Bolitho said, "You cannot *manage,* Major. Muljadi will have more than a thousand men when he comes. His stronghold is crammed to capacity, that I *did* see. You may have been able to hold the walls until help was forthcoming from Madras. Without it, your only chance is a forced march through dense jungle to the east'rd to contact the Dutch East India Company base and find safety." His tone hardened. "But through dense jungle, and at this time of the year, I doubt if many would survive, even without attack from those who will want to impress Muljadi with their loyalty."

Raymond said thickly, "No blame can fall on my shoulders! I reported what I knew! I had no knowledge of this other frigate!" He tried to recover his original calm. "Any more than you did!"

Conway stood up very deliberately, each movement an effort of will.

"But you could not wait, *Mr.* Raymond. You used your authority to seek your own ends and despatched the brig even after I requested she be held here until *Undine's* return."

He walked to the opposite side of the room and stared unseeingly at the close-knit jungle.

"So what can we do? How best can we prepare ourselves for slaughter?"

He turned with the speed of light and yelled, "Well, Mr. Raymond? Will you explain, for indeed it is beyond me!"

Major Jardine stammered, "Surely it cannot be that hopeless?"

Puigserver was watching Bolitho. "Well, *Capitan?* You have been *inside* the lion's den, not us."

Bolitho looked at Conway. "May I suggest something, sir?"

The admiral nodded, his wispy hair in disorder. "If there is anything left to say."

Bolitho walked to the table and moved the heavy silver inkwells into a pattern.

"The Benuas are much as they appear on our charts, sir, although I suspect some of the smaller channels between the islets are silted and shallow. The fortress stands high on a central islet, a rock-pile, if you like." His fingers made a sweeping gesture down the front of one inkwell. "The seaward face of the islet is sheer, and what I first took to be reefs at its foot I now believe are fragments of cliff which have fallen away over many years of wear."

He heard Captain Strype say gloomily, "That rules out any hope of a scaling attempt. It *is* hopeless."

Conway glared at him and then snapped, "Continue. What about this cliff?"

Bolitho looked at him calmly. "If we attack at once, sir." He ignored the gasps. "Before Muljadi is ready. We might nip his whole plan in the bud."

Conway exclaimed, "Attack? When you have just finished destroying our hopes even of staying alive!"

"The main gun battery is on the seaward rampart, sir. Bring it down and the ships at anchor will be without immediate protection."

Conway was rubbing his chin in quick, nervous movements. "Yes, I can see that. But how?"

Jardine sneered, "An act of God maybe?"

"The schooner, sir." Bolitho kept his gaze fixed on Conway's lined forehead, seeing all the doubts and apprehension gathering like a storm. "We could use the prevailing wind, sail her straight on to the fallen rocks at the foot of the cliff, filled to the deck beams with powder and a goodly fuse. The explosion would, I believe, bring down more of the cliff." He hesitated, feeling the sudden tension around him. "And the battery."

Captain Strype was staring at the inkwell as if seeing the actual explosion. "It might well work, sir! A damn fine idea!"

Jardine growled, "Hold your tongue! What sort of fool would do such a thing anyway?"

He fell back as Conway snapped, "Be still!" To Bolitho he added, "And you think this is a reasonable risk?"

"I do. The schooner would be lightly manned, and her crew could get clear in their boat once the final course was laid. A long fuse would allow them time enough." He kept his eyes steady. "The moment the charge explodes I will force the channel in *Undine* and take the anchored frigates before they can recover. After an explosion like that, they will not be expecting a further intrusion."

Puigserver nodded grimly. "Fair justice, too."

Conway glared at him. "It is the wildest plan I have ever discussed."

Bolitho said quietly, "I must argue that point, sir."

"*What?*" Conway swung on him. "Are you questioning me again?"

"I recall a certain captain, sir. Years back, when I was a stupid midshipman. He took a fair chance or so when he considered it necessary."

Conway reached out and gripped his wrist. "Thank you for that." He looked away, patting his pockets as if searching for something. "I'd forgotten."

Bolitho said, "The troops will have to remain here, of course."

He thought he saw relief on Jardine's heavy face, resentment on his aide's. Strange, he thought, that the one who appeared the weaker was the stronger after all.

He added, "If this plan fails, and we must face that possibility, it will be up to the sepoys to evacuate the settlement as best they can. But please take my word for this. No parley with Muljadi, for to him victory means only one thing. Extinction for all those who have represented his enemies throughout his entire life." He pointed towards the window. "And once through those palisades, there will be no time left for regrets."

Conway returned to the table, his face very composed.

"I agree." He glanced at Jardine. "Set your men to work transferring powder to the schooner, every barrel and cask from our magazine, if that is what is needed."

He looked at Bolitho. "And who will command the schooner, have you thought of that?"

"I am not decided, sir." He smiled gravely. "Yet."

He turned as Raymond walked around the table, showing his face at last in the sunlight.

Raymond said, "I acted as I thought fit."

Conway nodded, his eyes contemptuous. "If we survive this affair, you may yet share the advantages, if there are any." His tone was like ice. "If we fail, you will probably receive the knighthood you covet so dearly." He paused as Raymond hurried to the door. "Posthumously, of course!"

When he faced the table again Conway seemed about ten years younger.

"Now that I am decided, Bolitho, I cannot wait!"

Bolitho nodded. He could feel his muscles and bones aching as if from physical effort, and could barely realise what he had done, what he had committed himself and his ship to.

He said, "I will return aboard now, sir. I need fresh water and fruit if there is any."

Faces flashed across his thoughts. Carwithen with his axe embedded in the pirate's neck. Davy's pride at being given command of the schooner. Fowlar's genuine pleasure with his temporary promotion. And Herrick most of all. What would he say to this pathetic, desperate plan? Smile? Shake his head? Accept that at last his captain had made the one fatal mistake? For all of them.

Conway was saying, "You are a sly-boots, Bolitho, more than I ever suspected." He made as if to reach for the new decanter but changed his mind. "If I am to lose my head, then it had better be a clear one, eh?"

Puigserver was touching one of the silver inkwells with a spatulate finger.

"When will it be, *Capitan?*"

"Early." Bolitho watched him thoughtfully. Puigserver, too. He had been in the story from the very beginning. "Dawn attack."

Conway nodded. "And if ever you have prayed for the wind to set fair, then do it from now on."

Bolitho smiled. "Aye, sir. I will bear that in mind."

He made to leave, but halted as the admiral added gruffly, "Whatever the outcome, we will have tried. Done our best."

When he turned towards the sunlight Bolitho was shocked to see the moisture in his eyes.

"Raymond was right, of course. I'm not the man for the appointment, nor do I suppose it was ever intended I should retain it once the settlement had been founded . . . ," he hesitated, ". . . or lost. But we will show them."

He strode to his private door and slammed it behind him.

Puigserver whistled. "The old lion awakes, eh?"

Bolitho smiled sadly. "If you have known him as I once did, *Señor.* If you had seen the people cheering themselves hoarse, with the smoke of battle still thick between decks, then you would have understood."

"Perhaps." Puigserver grinned broadly. "Now away with you. I think you have learned a great deal since we first met. About many things, eh?"

Bolitho walked out past a nodding servant, and then started as someone touched his sleeve. It was Viola Raymond's maid, her face screwed up with fright as she whispered, "This way, sir! Just down here!"

Bolitho followed her quickly, and then saw the pale figure by a door at the far end of the passageway.

He asked, "What is it? We should not meet like this."

She stared at him, her eyes blazing. "You are going to get killed! He just told me!" She threw her big hat on the floor and added angrily, "And I don't care! I don't care what happens to you!" Then she threw herself against him, her voice breaking in sobs as she cried, "It's a lie! I *do* care, my darling Richard! I'll die if anything happens to you! I didn't mean to say those things."

He held her chin in his hand. "Easy, Viola." He pushed the hair from her forehead. It was hot and feverish. "I had no choice."

Her body shook uncontrollably and she gripped his arms even tighter, oblivious to her maid, and the real possibility that someone might walk into the passage at any second.

"And no chance! No chance at all!"

Bolitho held her away and waited until she was calmer.

"I must go! And I *will* take care." He saw her returning anguish and said quickly, "I must not damage my new watch, now must I?"

She tried to return his smile, the tears flowing freely down her face as she said, "I would never forgive you."

He turned and walked towards the stairway, and then stopped again as she called his name. But she did not follow him. Instead she held up one hand, as if he was already a long way off. Beyond reach.

He found Allday waiting by the beached gig and said sharply, "Back to the ship."

Allday watched him curiously. "They're taking powder casks to the schooner, Captain."

"Is that a question?" He glared at him but Allday's face was unmoved.

"I was just thinking. Mr. Davy's not going to be happy about this."

Bolitho clapped his arm. "I know. And I have no excuse for taking out my temper on you."

Allday squinted up at the timbered fort above the palisades, the white figure in one of the windows.

Under his breath he said, "I know just how it feels, Captain."

Bolitho twisted in the sternsheets to watch the boats busying themselves alongside the schooner. It had sounded so simple, so neat. To take two anchored frigates in a confined space was better than matching gun for gun in open waters. But many would curse his name as they died, nonetheless.

He sighed as the gig gathered speed towards the frigate. Puigserver had been right. He had learned a great deal since their meeting at Santa Cruz. Mostly about himself.

"All present, sir." Herrick seated himself beside the cabin door and waited for Bolitho to speak.

Beyond the stern windows it was very dark, but it was possible to see the yellow lanterns moving back and forth between the settlement and the surf as the business of loading the schooner continued without pause.

Bolitho looked at the faces around the cabin. Everyone was here. He let his gaze rest briefly on Midshipman Keen. Even him, although the surgeon had told him he would not be responsible for his condition. Keen looked strained, and whenever he moved it was easy to see the pain on his mouth and eyes. But he had insisted on rejoining the ship.

Mudge and Soames. Fowlar, looking slightly self-conscious at his first important conference. Davy, whose handsome features were still showing some of the dismay remaining from Bolitho's news about the schooner. Captain Bellairs, debonair and bland-faced in the gently spiralling lantern light. The purser, as mournful as ever. Armitage and Penn, like ill-matched brothers, and lastly, below the skylight, Whitmarsh, the surgeon, his face glowing like a great beetroot.

Bolitho clasped his hands behind him. An average wardroom, he thought. No better, no worse than most, yet he was about to ask more of them than would be expected from a veteran company.

"You know me well enough by now to understand that I

dislike speeches. Making or listening to them."

He saw Herrick grin, and Mudge's tiny eyes vanish on either side of the great nose.

"At the beginning of this commission there were many aboard, wardroom included, who thought my methods too hard, my ideals too high for a ship on a peacetime mission. Now all of us know that things have changed, and our experience, our training is the only thing of value we have to protect us, and more to the point, those who are depending on our ability."

He nodded to Herrick. "Open the chart."

As Mudge leaned forward to weigh down Herrick's chart with books and brass dividers he took another glance at their faces. Anxiety, trust? It was too early to know.

He continued, "The schooner will sail directly into the main channel, using the easterly headland for cover until the last available moment. Once on course for the rocks at the foot of the cliff," he paused to lay the dividers on the small cross, "the helm will be lashed, and the crew will take to the boat. They will be recovered later." He made himself smile, although his heart felt strangely heavy. "After we have excised the two frigates while their people are still collecting their wits!"

Penn said, "We'll show 'em, sir!" He quailed under Mudge's withering stare.

"And *we*," Bolitho smiled at the scarlet-faced midshipman, "driven on by Mr. Penn's enthusiasm, will move into the channel, rake both anchored ships, come about and rake 'em again." He looked at Davy. "So tell all gun crews to look alive. The first broadsides will be the telling ones."

Bellairs drawled, "Bit of a chance for the schooner, I'd say, sir. All that gunpowder aboard. One heated ball from the battery, and up she goes." He blinked under Bolitho's level stare and added, "No disrespect to the bold fellows aboard her, of course, but where would it leave *us?*"

Bolitho shook his head. "The battery is old. I am almost

certain that heated shot will not be available, for fear of splitting the guns. Normally they would not need it. With such an arc of fire, the battery can hit any vessel once it is within the two main channels."

He smiled to hide the sudden doubt which Bellairs had laid in his mind. Suppose there was heated shot already simmering in furnaces? But he would have seen them, surely? No baskets could hoist glowing balls to that high rampart.

He said, "And we will know that most of that battery is lying in the sea, where it should have been years ago.

"We will weigh at first light tomorrow. The wind seems to be in our favour, and with luck it will serve our purposes. There remains just one matter . . ." He paused and saw Herrick watching him from across the cabin.

But he must not think of his friend. The best and firmest one he had ever had. He was his first lieutenant, the most competent officer in the ship. Nothing more counted. It must not.

He continued, "Mr. Herrick will command the schooner."

Herrick nodded, his face expressionless. "Aye, sir. I'll take six good hands. Should be enough."

Bolitho held his gaze, the rest of the officers fading around him as he said, "I will leave it to you. If Potter wishes to join with you, then take him." He saw Whitmarsh rising to protest and added harshly, "He knows the channel. We need all we can get."

The door opened slightly and Carwithen thrust his head into the lantern light.

"Beg pardon, sir, but the water casks 'ave been stowed, an' a message 'as been sent to say that the schooner is fully loaded."

His gaze shifted to Fowlar, but there was no recognition. Fowlar's first step to promotion had already marked them apart although it was possible they had never had much in common, Bolitho thought.

"Very well." Bolitho waited for the door to close. "Carry on, gentlemen. You all have your duties to attend." He faltered, wondering why there were never the right words when you needed them most. "We will have little time for discussion until this matter is settled." *Or we are all dead.* "Remember this, and remember it well. Our people will be looking to you, more than they, or you ever expected. Most of them have never been in a real sea fight, and when we last met with *Argus* many still believed we had won a battle rather than secured a retreat. This time there can be no retreat, for us, or the enemy. Le Chaumareys is a fine captain, probably the best ever produced by France. But he has one weakness." He smiled gravely. "One which we have not yet enjoyed. That of supreme confidence in his ship and himself. His belief, and your skill and determination will win the day for us if anything can."

They stood up, silent and grim-faced, as if only just aware of their responsibilities. The finality of their position.

Then as they moved towards the door Bolitho said, "A moment, Mr. Herrick."

Alone together in the gently pitching cabin, Bolitho said, "I had no choice."

"I would have been dismayed, had you selected a junior, sir." Herrick smiled. "So there's an end to it."

Bolitho held out his hand. "May God protect you, Thomas. If I have misjudged this affair, or the enemy outwits us, then pull back at once. If I signal a recall, then abandon your attempt. If die we must, then I want you with me."

Herrick gripped his hand tightly, his blue eyes suddenly concerned.

"Enough of this talk, sir! It is not like you. *Win* we must, and here's my hand on it!"

Bolitho followed him towards the door. Hating the moment. Conscious of the weight which he had caused to fall on his own shoulders. She had seen his danger, as had Le Chaumareys. Perhaps Herrick also.

On deck, in the noise and bustle of preparing for sea, the contact was at last broken.

Herrick said, "I'll go and pick my hands, sir."

Bolitho nodded, his heart aching. "Carry on, Mr. Herrick. The second lieutenant will relieve you forthwith."

As Herrick melted into the shadows Davy crossed the quarterdeck and touched his hat.

Bolitho said, "I am sorry about your schooner. I seem to have little choice in anything at the moment."

Davy shrugged. "It does not seem to matter any more, sir. For once, I cannot see further than the next few days, nor care either."

Bolitho seized his arm savagely and swung him round. "Has nothing I said to you made any sense?"

Davy struggled in his fierce grip and blurted out, "I—I am sorry, sir!"

"You will be if I hear you talking like that again! Your responsibility is to me, the ship and the people you command. Not to your own personal considerations. When a man starts to believe there are no more tomorrows, he is as good as sewn up in a hammock between two round-shot. Think of the tomorrows, believe in them, and the men who depend on your skill, or lack of it, will see their own survival on your face!" He relaxed his hold and added in a steadier tone, "Now be off with you."

He began to pace along the larboard side, his feet stepping automatically over ringbolts and gun tackles, although his eyes saw none of them. He had not been reprimanding Davy, but himself. It was no time for doubt or recrimination, but only for living the role he had adopted, had earned in a dozen battles or more.

"Boat ahoy!" The challenge rang out from the gangway where lanterns glinted on levelled muskets and bayonets.

From the bay itself came the reply, "Don Luis Puigserver wishes to come aboard!"

Davy came hurrying aft. "Is that in order, sir?"

Bolitho smiled, calm again. "I was expecting him, I believe."

The stocky figure rose through the port and hurried across the deck to greet him.

Puigserver said, "I had to come, *Capitan*. *Nervion*'s loss made me a part of this. I cannot withdraw until the matter is settled." He patted the ornate pistols beneath his coat. "And I am an excellent shot, no?"

"I could order you to leave, *Señor*."

"But?" Puigserver tilted his head to one side. "But you will not. In any case, I have left written word to explain my deeds and my reasons. If we survive the battle, I will tear it to pieces. If not . . ." He left the rest unsaid.

"Then I accept your offer, *Señor*. With gratitude."

Puigserver walked to the nettings and stared across at a glittering riding-light. "When will the schooner set sail?"

"Before dawn. She will need all the time available to work into her position to best advantage."

Again the ache. The thought of Herrick sailing his floating magazine into the muzzles of Muljadi's battery.

"I see." Puigserver yawned. "Then I think I will join your offwatch officers for a glass in the wardroom. You will need your solitude tonight, I am thinking."

Some hours later Bolitho was awakened by Allday's hand on his shoulder. He had fallen asleep in the cabin, his head on his forearm across the chart where he had been working.

Allday watched him anxiously. "Schooner's weighed, Captain."

Bolitho rubbed his eyes. Was it almost dawn? He felt suddenly chilled. Desperate for sleep.

Allday added quietly, "Mister Pigsliver's gone, too."

Bolitho stared at him, wondering if he had expected this. Had known it was what Puigserver had wanted from the moment he had outlined his plan.

"Is she well clear?"

"Aye, Captain." Allday stretched and yawned. "Stood round

the headland half an hour back." He added slowly, "He'll be good company for Mr. Herrick, and that's no error."

Bolitho looked at him. "You *knew*, didn't you?"

"Aye, Captain." Allday watched him sadly. "I thought it for the best."

Bolitho nodded. "I expect it is." He walked to the windows as if to see the riding-light still twinkling above the water. "It is a bad thing to be alone."

Allday glanced at the tarnished sword which hung from the bulkhead. For a moment he thought about Bolitho's other cox-swain, who had died protecting his back from French marksmen at the Saintes. They had come a long way together since those times, he thought. Soon now, it might all end. He looked at Bolitho's shoulders as he peered through the stern windows.

But you will never be alone, Captain. Not while I've a breath left.

17

CLOSE *A*CTION

BOLITHO rested his hands on the quarterdeck rail and peered searchingly along his command. In the darkness the decks and gangways made a pale outline against the sea beyond the bows, and only the irregular drift of spray, the swirling white arrowhead from the stem gave any true hint of their progress.

He restrained himself from going aft again to examine his watch by the shaded compass light. Nothing had changed since his last inspection, and he was well aware of the danger of adding to the tension around him.

Three days since they had left the anchorage in Pendang Bay, making good speed with favourable winds for most of the time.

They had stood well clear of the land, even the approaches to the little whale-shaped islet, in case Muljadi or Le Chaumareys had thought fit to place another craft there to warn of any unwelcome sail.

The previous evening, just before sunset, they had sighted Herrick's schooner, a tiny dark sliver on the copper-edged horizon, seemingly motionless as she idled to await *Undine*'s arrival at the arranged point of rendezvous. A brief dipping signal from a lantern before both vessels had lost each other again in darkness.

Bolitho shivered, feeling the cool, clammy air exploring his face and throat. The middle watch had only just run its course, and there was still an hour or so before any lightening of the sky could be expected. But overnight, while all hands had worked to prepare the ship for action, the clouds had gathered and thickened, brushing out the stars so that *Undine* seemed to be sailing remorselessly into a void.

He heard Mudge moving restlessly below the hammock nettings, rubbing his palms together to keep warm. The sailing master seemed unusually preoccupied. Perhaps his rheumatism was troubling him, or like Bolitho, he was thinking of Herrick, somewhere out there on *Undine*'s larboard bow.

Bolitho straightened his back and looked up at the blacker outlines of yards and rigging. The ship was sailing under topsails and jibs, and with only the great forecourse hiding the sea ahead of the bowsprit. It was strange to feel so chilled, when within hours the sun would be back to torment them, to add to whatever else lay in store.

He asked, "How is the wind, Mr. Mudge?"

Mudge was glad to break the silence. "Still sou'-west, sir. By an' large." He coughed noisily. "Under most occasions I'd be grateful for that."

"What are you thinking?"

"Not sure, sir." Mudge moved away from the seamen waiting by the quarterdeck six-pounders. "It's too *uneven* for my tastes."

Bolitho turned to peer forward again. The big forecourse seemed to echo Mudge's doubts. *Undine* was steering almost due north, and with the wind coming across her quarter she should have been making easy-going of it. But she was not. The forecourse would billow and harden, making the stays and shrouds hum and vibrate, holding the ship firm for several minutes. Then it would flap and bang in disorder before falling almost limp against the foremast for another frustrating period.

Mudge added doubtfully, "You never knows in these waters. Not for sure."

Bolitho looked at his untidy outline. If Mudge was worried, with all his experience, how much worse it would be for many of the others.

He called, "Mr. Davy! I am going forrard directly." He saw the lieutenant's shape detach itself from the rail. "Tell Mr. Keen to keep me company."

He slipped out of his tarpaulin coat and handed it to Allday. He had been so occupied with his own thoughts and doubts he had not fully realised how heavily these dragging hours must be affecting his company. He had ordered the ship to be prepared for action as soon as he was satisfied with the final leg of their course towards the Benua islands. Working in almost total darkness, the hands had completed the task almost as quickly as in broad daylight, so familiar had they become with their surroundings. Their home. It was a simple precaution. Sound travelled too easily at sea, and the clatter of screens being torn down, the scrape and squeak of nets being spread above the gun deck and chain slings being rigged to every yard seemed loud enough to wake the dead. But from then on they had nothing to do but wait. To fret on what daylight might bring, or take away.

Keen came out of the darkness, his shirt pale against a black six-pounder.

Bolitho asked, "How is the wound?"

"Much better, thank you, sir."

Bolitho smiled. He could almost feel the pain which was probably showing on Keen's face.

"Then take a stroll with me."

Together they walked along the lee gangway, ducking below the taut nets which Shellabeer's men had rigged to catch falling cordage or worse, seeing the upturned faces of each gun crew, the restless shapes of the marine sentries at hatchways, or powder-monkeys huddled together while they waited to serve the silent cannon.

On to the forecastle, where the squat carronades pointed from either bow like tethered beasts, their crews shivering in the occasional dashes of spray.

Bolitho paused, one hand gripping the nettings as *Undine* sidled unsteadily into a deep trough. Most of the seamen were stripped to the waist, their bodies shining faintly above the dark water alongside.

"All ready, lads?"

He felt them crowd around him, their sudden interest at his arrival. Of necessity, the galley fire had been doused when the ship had gone to quarters. A hot drink now would be worth more than a dozen extra guns, he thought bitterly.

To Keen he said, "Pass the word to Mr. Davy with my compliments. A double tot of rum for all hands." He heard the instant response around him, the murmur of appreciation as it flowed aft along the gun deck. "If the purser complains, tell him he'll have me to reckon with!"

"Thankee, sir! That was right thoughtful, sir!"

He strode to the ladder, turning away in case they could see his face through the darkness, or sense his mood. It was too easy to raise their spirits. So simple that it made him feel cheap, hypocritical. A double tot of rum. A few pence. Whereas within hours they might have given their lives, or their limbs.

Bolitho paced aft beside the main hatch, seeing Soames's great figure towering above that of Tapril, the gunner. He nodded to

Fowlar nearby, and to the larboard crews of the twelve-pounders. All were his men, his responsibility.

He thought suddenly of Rear Admiral Sir John Winslade, all those weeks and months ago in his office at the Admiralty. He had needed a frigate captain he could know and trust. One whose mind he could follow even though it was on the other side of the globe.

He thought, too, of the ragged soldiers below the Admiralty window, one blind, the other begging for the both of them.

All the brave schemes and plans, the lofty preparations for a new world. Yet when it was boiled down, nothing was changed. *Undine* and *Argus* were but two ships, and yet their presence and their needs made them no less important than opposing fleets.

And if *Undine* failed, what would they say in those fine residences in Whitehall and St. James's Square, and in the busy coffee houses where mere rumour grew into fact in minutes? Would they care that men had fought and died for them in the King's name?

Someone gave a hoarse cheer in the gloom, and he guessed the rum had arrived on deck.

He continued aft, hardly aware that he had stopped short in his tracks as his bitterness had given way to anger. How spacious the deck seemed without the boats lying one upon the other across their tier. All were now towing astern, awaiting the moment to be cast adrift, mute spectators of the battle which might come. Which had to come.

It was always a bad moment, he thought. Boats were frail things, but in battle they made an additional menace with their splinters flying like savage darts. Despite the danger, most men would wish them kept aboard. A link, a hope for survival if things went badly.

Keen came back panting hard. "All done, sir. Mr. Triphook was a trifle perturbed at the extra issue!" His teeth shone in the darkness. "Would *you* care for a glass, sir?"

Bolitho disliked rum. But he saw the seamen and marines watching him and exclaimed, "Indeed I would, Mr. Keen."

He raised the glass to his mouth, the powerful stench of rum going straight to his empty stomach.

"To us, lads!"

He pictured Herrick and Puigserver aboard their floating bomb. *And to you, Thomas.*

Then he was glad he had accepted the rum and added, "I can now understand what makes our jacks so fearsome!" It brought more laughs, as he knew it would.

He glanced at the sky. Still without light, or sign of a star.

He said, "I'll go below." He touched the midshipman's arm. "You remain here by the hatch. Call, if I am needed."

Bolitho climbed down into the darkness, his feet less certain here. Anyone could call him when required, but he must spare Keen an unnecessary visit to the surgeon's domain. It might come soon enough. He recalled the great pulsating wound, Allday's gentleness as he had searched out that bloody splinter.

Another ladder. He paused, feeling the ship groaning around him. Different smells abounded on this deck. Tar and oakum, and that of tightly compressed humanity, even though the tiny messes were now deserted. And from forward the reek of the great anchor cables, of bilge water and damp clothing. Of a living, working ship.

A feeble lantern showed him the rest of the way to Whitmarsh's crude surgery. The sea-chests lashed together where terrified wounded would be saved or driven to despair. Leather straps to jam between teeth, dressings to contain the pain.

The surgeon's great shadow swayed across the tilting deck. Bolitho watched him narrowly. There was a stronger smell of brandy in the damp air. To quench pain, or to prepare Whitmarsh for his own private hell, he was not certain.

"All well, Mr. Whitmarsh?"

"Aye, sir."

The surgeon lurched against the chests and braced his knee to the nearest one. He waved one hand around his silent assistants, the loblolly boys, the men who would hold their victims until the work was done. Brutalised by their trade. Without ears for the screams. Beyond pity.

"We are all awaiting what *you* send us, sir."

Bolitho stared at him coldly. "Will you never learn?"

The surgeon nodded heavily. "I have learned well. Oh yes indeed, sir. As I have sawed away at a man's leg, or plugged carpenter's oakum into his empty eye-socket, with nothing to ease his torment but neat spirits, I have come closer to God than most!"

"If that be true, then I pray you get no closer."

Bolitho nodded to the others and strode towards the ladder.

Whitmarsh called after him, "Perhaps I shall be greeting *you*, sir!"

Bolitho did not reply. The surgeon was obviously going completely mad. His obsession with his brother's horrible death, his drinking, and the very way he earned his living were taking their toll. But he had to hang on to what remained of that other man. The one who had spoken of suffering with compassion, of serving others less fortunate.

He thought again of Herrick, and prayed he would get his boat away when the schooner was set upon her final course to destruction. Strange companions he had, too. Puigserver, and the frightened sailmaker from Bristol, finding courage from somewhere to sail back to that place which had broken his mind and body.

"Captain, sir!"

He quickened his pace as Keen's voice came down the next ladder.

"What is it?"

But as he gripped the ladder and turned his face towards the sky's faint rectangle he knew the answer. Slow, heavy drops of rain were falling across the hatchway, like small pebbles dropped from the yards as they tapped on planking or bounced across the gangways.

He dragged himself up the last few steps and hurried aft to the quarterdeck. He was within a few feet of it when the clouds opened and the rain came down in a great roaring, deafening torrent.

He yelled above the deluge, "How is the wind now?"

Mudge was cringing by the binnacle, his hat awry in the fury of the downpour.

"Veerin', sir! Far as I can tell!"

Water hissed and gurgled down decks and scuppers, and the chilled gun crews pressed beneath the gangways and cowered behind the sealed ports to escape the torrential rain.

Bolitho felt Allday trying to throw the tarpaulin coat over his shoulders, but pushed him away. He was already soaked to the marrow, hair plastered over his forehead, his mind ringing to the din of rain and spray. Yet through it all he managed to keep contact with the ship and her affairs. The deck felt steady enough, despite the angry downpour, and above his head he managed to make out the maintopsail's shape flapping and shining wetly as the wind eased round still further.

He snapped, "Hands to the braces, Mr. Davy! We will be full and bye directly!" He heard the men groping and cursing as they lurched to obey the orders, the protesting squeak of swollen cordage being hauled through blocks while yards were trimmed to hold the ship on her larboard tack. He called, "Bring her up a point!"

Men slithered around the big double wheel, and he saw Carwithen punch one of the helmsmen as he bowed under the sheeting rain.

"Nor' by west, sir. Full an' bye she is!"

"Hold her so!"

Bolitho mopped his face with his sleeve. The probing downpour helped to clear his aching mind, to make him accept what was happening. If the wind continued to veer, even if it stayed where it was, Herrick would be unable to place his schooner in position where he could destroy Muljadi's battery. The disastrous change of wind made the rain feel like tears. Tears for all their hopes, their pathetic determination, which minutes ago had made even the impossible seem undaunting.

He lurched to Mudge's side and shouted, "How far now, d'you reckon?"

"Four or five mile, no more, sir." Mudge was staring at the rain with dismay. "This lot'll pass over quick enough. But then . . ." He shrugged.

Bolitho looked away. He knew well enough. A rising wind was most likely once the sun appeared. A wind which would do no service to Herrick, and keep Le Chaumareys in the safety of his anchorage. *Undine* would be helpless. She would be made to stay offshore until the enemy's double strength was prepared and ready to fight on their terms. Or they could turn and run for Pendang Bay with nothing to offer but a final warning.

Davy shouted, "By God, life is hard!"

Mudge glared at him. "Life's a bloody rear-guard action, Mr. Davy, from the day you're born!"

Bolitho swung round to silence both of them and then saw that the master's mate's face was clearer than before. He could even see Carwithen scowling at the same luckless helmsman. The dawn was forcing itself to be taken notice of.

He felt the blood racing in his head as he snapped, "We will attack as before! Pass the word to all hands!"

Davy gaped at him. "Without destroying the battery, sir?"

"It might not have worked anyway." He tried to sound calm. "The enemy will be listening to the rain and thanking God for being at anchor." He added harshly, "Are you deaf, man? Tell Mr. Soames to prepare for loading, once the rain is passed!"

Davy nodded jerkily and hurried to the rail.

Captain Bellairs strode to Bolitho's side and remarked coolly, "Damn risky thing, sir, if you'll pardon my sayin' so."

Bolitho felt his shoulders beginning to sag under the rain, the sudden spark deserting him.

"What would *you* have me do?"

Bellairs turned up his collar and pouted. "Oh, I'd fight, sir, no choice in the matter, what? Pity though, all the same. Waste. Damn bloody waste."

Bolitho nodded heavily. "No argument there."

"Deck there! Land ho!"

Bolitho walked stiffly to the lee side, his shoes squeaking on the puddled deck. A darker blur, reaching out on either bow, deceptively gentle in the feeble light.

A voice said, "Rain's goin'." He sounded surprised.

As if to mark its passing, the dripping forecourse lifted and boomed dully to receive a fresher gust of wind. It made Bolitho shiver and grit his teeth.

"Tell Mr. Soames. Load, and prepare to run out when I pass the word."

He looked around for Keen. "Run up the Colours, if you please."

Another voice muttered, "No chance, mates. They'll do for the lot of us."

Bolitho heard the halliards squeaking as the ensign dashed up to the peak and broke out to the wind, unseen as yet in the clinging darkness.

"As soon as it is light enough, Mr. Keen, have your party make a signal to the schooner. *Discontinue the action.* Mr. Herrick can stand off and retrieve our boats."

Keen said, "Aye, aye, sir, I'll see to it when—"

He turned angrily as a voice murmured from the shadows, "Pick up our bloody corpses, more's the like!"

Keen shouted, "Keep silence there! Master-at-arms, take that man's name!"

Bolitho said quietly, "Easy. If it helps them to curse, then let it be so."

Keen faced him, his fists doubled at his sides. "But it's not *fair,* sir. It's not your doing."

Bolitho smiled gravely. "Thank you, Mr. Keen."

He recalled with sudden clarity his lieutenant in his first command, the little sloop *Sparrow*. An American colonist, he had endured the worst of the war, serving his King, but fighting his own kind at the same time. What would he have replied? *I ain't so sure.* Bolitho could almost hear him, as if he was present at this very moment.

He turned quickly to starboard, seeing the glowing rim of sunlight as it probed above the bare horizon. Very soon now.

He discovered he was dreading the daylight, that which would lay them naked under the guns as they drove into the narrow channel where he had met Le Chaumareys.

Bolitho heard a step behind him and Allday's voice. Firm, unruffled. "Better go below and get out of those wet things, Captain."

He swung towards him, his voice cracking with strain. "Do you think I have nothing else to do?"

The coxswain regarded him stubbornly. "Not just yet, you haven't." He added in the same flat tone, "You remember the Saintes, Captain?" He did not wait for an answer "It was a bad time. All those Frogs, the sea abounding with their damned ships until it was nigh on bursting. I recalls it well. I was right forrard on one of the carronades. The lads were all quaking with fright at what was to come. Then I looked aft and saw you pacing the quarterdeck, like you were going to church instead of to hell."

Bolitho stared at him, his mind suddenly steady. "I remember."

Allday nodded slowly. "Aye. You wore your best uniform."

Bolitho looked past him, recalling another voice. His coxswain who had died that day. *They'll want to see you.*

He replied quietly, "Very well. But if I'm called . . ."

Allday gave a slow smile. "*Immediately*, Captain."

Mudge said hoarsely, "That was fool advice, man! The cap'n'll make a fine target for sharpshooters in 'is gold lace!"

Allday eyed him angrily. "I know. He does, too. He also knows we are depending on him today, and that means *seeing* him."

Mudge shook his head. "Mad. You're all mad!"

"Deck there! Schooner fine on th' weather bow!"

Keen called, "Hoist the signal to recall her!"

Allday was standing with his arms folded, his eyes on the spreading carpet of early light as it reached towards the islands.

"Mr. Herrick won't see it."

Davy glared at him. "It will be light enough very soon now."

"I know, sir." Allday looked at him sadly. "But he'll not see it. Not Mr. Herrick."

Without furniture or fittings the cabin felt strangely hostile, like an empty house which mourns a lost master and awaits another. Bolitho stood by the shuttered stern windows, his arms limp at his sides, while Noddall clucked around him and patted the heavy dress coat into position. Like the boat cloak, it had been made by a good London tailor with some of his prize-money.

Through the wide gap left by the screens, which had now been bolted to the deckhead, he could see straight out along the gun deck, the shapes and restless figures still only shadows in the frail light. Even here, in the cabin where he had found peace in solitude, or had sat with Viola Raymond, or shared a pipe with Herrick, there was no escape. The chintz covers had gone from the twelve-pounder, and had followed the furniture to a safer stowage below the waterline, and by the guns on either beam the crews stood awkwardly, like unfinished statuary, conscious of his presence, wanting to watch him as he completed dressing, yet still held apart by the rigidity of their calling.

Bolitho cocked his head to listen to the rudder as it growled and pounded in response to the helm. The wind was fresher, heeling the ship over and holding it so. He saw the nearest gun captain checking his firing lanyard and noted how his body was angled to the deck.

Noddall was muttering, "More like it, sir. Much more like it." He said it fervently, as if repeating a prayer. "Cap'n Stewart was always most particular, afore a fight."

Bolitho wrenched his mind back from his doubts and misgivings. Stewart? Then he remembered. *Undine's* last captain. Had he felt the same, too, he wondered?

Feet stamped over the deck above, and he heard someone shouting.

He snapped, "That will have to suffice."

He snatched up his hat and sword and then paused to pat Noddall's bony shoulder. He looked so small, with his hands held in front of him like paws, that he felt sudden compassion for him.

"Take care, Noddall. Stay down when the iron begins to fly. You're no fighting man, eh?"

He was shocked to see Noddall bobbing his head and tears running down his face.

In a small, broken voice he said, "*Thankee,* Cap'n!" He did not hide his gratitude. "I couldn't face another battle. An' I'd not want to let you down, sir."

Bolitho pushed past and hurried to the ladder. He had always taken him for granted. The little man who fussed over his table and darned his shirts. Content in his own small world. It had never occurred to him that he was terrified each time the ship cleared for action.

He ran up the last steps and saw Davy and Keen with telescopes trained towards the bows.

"What is the matter?"

Davy turned, and then stared at him. He swallowed hard, his eyes still on Bolitho's gold-laced coat.

"Schooner has not acknowledged, sir!"

Bolitho looked from him to the streaming flags, now bright against the dull topsails.

"Are you sure?"

Mudge growled, "Yer cox'n seems to think she won't neither, sir."

Bolitho ignored him, his eyes exploring the spread of land across the bows. Still lost in deep shadow, with only an occasional lip of light to betray the dawn. But the schooner was clear enough. In direct line with *Undine*'s plunging jib-boom, her canvas looked almost white against the cliffs and ragged hills.

Herrick must have seen the recall. He would have been anticipating it as soon as the wind veered. He peered up at the masthead pendant. God, how the wind had gone round. It must be west-south-west.

He shouted, "Hands aloft, Mr. Davy! Get the t'gallants on her!"

He swung round, seeing them all in those brief seconds. Mudge's doubts. Carwithen behind him, his lips compressed into a thin line. The helmsmen, the bare-backed gun crews, Keen with his signal party.

The calls shrilled, and shadows darted up the ratlines on either beam as the topmen hurried to set more canvas.

Davy shouted, "Maybe Mr. Herrick intends to go ahead with the plan, sir!"

Bolitho looked at Allday, saw the way he was watching the schooner.

He said quietly, "It would seem so, Mr. Davy."

Under a heavier press of sail *Undine* thrust her shoulder into the creaming water with added urgency, the spray hurling itself above the forecastle and nettings in long spectres of foam. The hull shook and groaned to the pressure, and when he peered aloft Bolitho saw the upper yards bending forward to the wind. From the peak the ensign was clearly visible, like the marines' tunics as they stood in swaying lines by the hammock nettings, or knelt in the tops by their muskets and swivels. Like blood.

He heard himself say, "Repeat the signal, Mr. Keen!" He barely recognised his own voice.

Soames stood on the breech of a twelve-pounder, gripping the gangway with both hands as he stared towards the land.

Then he looked aft at Bolitho and gave a brief shrug. In his mind, Herrick was already dead.

Keen said huskily, "It will not work! The wind'll carry the

schooner clear! At best she'll explode in the centre of the channel!"

Penn shrilled from the gun deck. "I heard a trumpet!"

Bolitho wiped his eyes, feeling the salt, raw and smarting. A trumpet. Some sentry on the fortress had left the protection of the wall to look seaward. He would see the schooner immediately, and *Undine* within the next few minutes.

The sea noises seemed louder than ever, with every piece of rigging and canvas banging and vibrating in chorus as the ship drove headlong towards the land, and the pale arrowhead which marked the entrance to the channel.

A dull bang echoed across the water, and a man yelled, "They've opened fire, sir!"

Bolitho reached out for a telescope, seeing the grim faces of the seamen by the nearest guns. Waiting, behind closed ports. Hoping. Dreading.

He trained the glass with difficulty, his legs well braced on the swaying, slippery planking. He saw the schooner's masts swim past the lens, the patch of scarlet which had not been there before. He felt himself smiling, although he wanted to weep, to plead unheard words across those two miles of tossing white-horses. Herrick had hoisted his own ensign. To him, the schooner was not merely a floating bomb, she was a ship, *his* ship. Or perhaps he was trying, with that one simple gesture, to explain to Bolitho, too. To show he understood.

Another bang, and this time he saw the smoke from the battery before it was whisked away. A feather of spray lifted well out beyond the schooner to mark where the massive ball had fallen.

He kept his glass on the schooner. He saw the way the deck was leaning over, showing the bilges above the leaping spray, and knew Herrick could not lash the tiller for the final, and most dangerous, part of the journey.

Davy yelled, "That ball was *over,* sir!"

Bolitho lowered the glass, Davy's words reaching through his anxiety. The fortress lookout must have sighted *Undine* and not

Herrick's little schooner. And by the time Muljadi's men had realised what was happening, Herrick had tacked too close inshore for the gunners to depress their muzzles sufficiently to hit him.

He looked again as a double explosion shuddered across the water. He saw the flashes only briefly, but watched the twin water-spouts burst skyward directly in line with the schooner, but on the seaward side of her.

Captain Bellairs forgot his usual calm and gripped the sergeant's arm and shouted, "By God, Sar'nt Coaker, he's goin' *to sail her aground himself!*"

It took a few more seconds before the truth filtered the length and breadth of the frigate's decks.

Then, as the word moved gun by gun towards the bows, men stood and yelled like maniacs, waving their neckerchiefs, or capering on the sanded decks like children. From the tops and the forecastle others joined, and even Midshipman Armitage, who moments earlier had been gripping a belaying pin rack as if to stop himself from falling, waved his hat in the air and yelled, "Go on! You'll show them!"

Bolitho cleared his throat. "Ask the masthead. Can he see the frigates?"

He tried not to think of the schooner's crammed holds. The fuse, perhaps already hissing quietly in the peace of the lower hull.

"Aye, sir! He can see the yards of the first one around the point!" Even Davy was wild-eyed, indifferent to the fight still to come, overwhelmed by Herrick's sacrifice.

There was more cannon fire now, and he could see splashes all around the schooner's hull. Probably from the nearest anchored frigate, or some smaller pieces on the spit of land which guarded the entrance. Bolitho found he was gritting his jaw so hard it was hurting badly.

The French were at last aware that something was happening, but they would not have guessed the full extent of the danger.

There was a combined groan from the watching hands. Bolitho

raised the glass and saw the schooner's maintopmast buckle and then plunge down in a flailing mass of canvas and rigging.

Half to himself he whispered, "Fall back, Thomas! In God's name, come about!"

Allday said, "She's hit again, Captain. Badly this time."

Bolitho dragged his mind away, knowing he must not think of Herrick. *Later.* But in minutes those guns would be ranging on *Undine* as she made that last desperate dash into the channel.

He drew his sword and held it above his head.

"See yonder, lads!" He only vaguely saw their faces turn towards him. It was like looking through a mist. "Mr. Herrick has shown us the way!"

"She's struck!" Davy was almost beside himself. "Hard and fast!"

The schooner had hit, lifted and then plunged firmly across the litter of broken rocks and stones. Exactly as they had pictured it. Had planned it with Conway's silver inkwells.

Even without a glass it was possible to see some small boats moving from the fortress's pier towards the stranded hull which now lay totally dismasted, the spray leaping over it like some old hulk. Occasional stabs of fire showed where marksmen were firing into the wreckage, and Bolitho prayed that the fuse was still alight, that Herrick would not be captured alive.

The explosion when it came was so sudden, so violent in colour and magnitude that it was hard to face, harder still to gauge. A solid wall of orange flame exploded from the rocks and spread out on either hand like huge fiery wings, engulfing the circling boats, searing away men and weapons and reducing them into ashes.

And then the sound came. When it reached the frigate it was with a steadily mounting roar which went on and on, until men stood clutching their ears, or staring stupefied at the miniature tidal wave which rolled past the frigate's hull, lifting it easily before dissipating itself astern in the last departing shadows.

Then it died away, as did the fires, leaving only tiny, glowing pinpricks of red and orange, like slow-matches, to show where gorse and brush still smouldered on the hillside.

Once again, the sea and wind, the sounds of tackle and canvas returned, and Bolitho heard men talking, almost whispering, as if they had just witnessed an act of God.

He said harshly, "Brail up the forecourse, Mr. Davy!" He walked to the rail, each step like physical pain. "Mr. Shellabeer! Cast all but the quarter boat adrift!" He must keep talking. Get them moving again. Clear that dreadful pyre from his own brain.

He saw Soames watching him and shouted, "Load and run out, if you please!"

His words were almost lost in the flap and thunder of rebellious canvas as the big forecourse was brailed up to its yard. Like a curtain, he thought dully. Pulled away for the final scene. So that nothing should be missed.

He heard the port lids squeaking in unison, and then, as Soames barked his command, the gun crews threw themselves on their tackles, and with increasing haste the black muzzles rumbled towards the daylight, thrusting out above the creaming water on either beam.

Davy touched his hat. "All guns run out, sir!" He looked strained.

"Thank you."

Bolitho kept his eyes on the dark hump astride the channel. No flashes from those great muzzles. It had worked. Even if the garrison managed to manhandle some of the guns from the far side of the fortress it would be too late to fire on *Undine* as she surged into the drifting curtain of smoke.

He shaded his eyes and stared towards the spit of land, the dark lines which marked the masts and yards of the first anchored ship. *Soon. Soon.* He gripped the sword until his knuckles showed white. He could feel the hurt and the anger. The rising madness, which only revenge for Herrick would control.

And there was the sunlight, growing stronger every dragging minute. He climbed into the weather shrouds, heedless of the wind and leaping spray which dappled his coat like bright gems. Abeam he could see *Undine*'s shadow reaching away across the broken water, his own blurred outline like part of the fabric itself.

He looked down at Mudge. "Get ready to alter course once we are past that spit!"

He waited while those at the braces took the strain, each man an individual now as the sunlight found his naked back, or a tattoo, or some extra long pigtail to mark a seasoned sailor. He jumped down to the deck, tugging at his neckcloth, as if it were strangling him.

"Marines, stand to!" Bellairs had drawn his elegant hanger and was watching while his men nestled their long muskets on the closely packed hammock nettings.

At every open port a gun captain crouched with his lanyard almost taut as he watched for the first sign of a target.

The spit of land reached out as if to touch the bilges as the ship swept inshore, her bow wave causing a ripple amongst some jagged rocks which Bolitho remembered from his other visit.

"Braces there!"

Mudge shouted, "Put the wheel to larboard! Lively now!"

Like a thoroughbred, *Undine* heeled round under pressure of canvas and rudder, the yards swinging together as she turned into the sunlight.

"Steer nor'-east by east!" Mudge heaved his ungainly bulk to assist the helmsmen. " '*Old 'er*, you buggers!"

There were several muffled bangs, and a ball cracked through the foretopsail with the sound of a whiplash.

But Bolitho barely noticed it. He was staring at the anchored frigate, the scrambling activity along her yards and deck where her company prepared for sea.

Davy echoed his dismay. "She's not the *Argus*, sir!"

Bolitho nodded. It was the other frigate. The one which had

been abandoned by her crew. He screwed up his eyes, trying to watch every movement, still attempting to accept what had happened.

Le Chaumareys had gone. By chance? Or had he once again proved his superiority, a cunning which had never been outmatched?

Almost savagely he lifted the old blade over his head and yelled, "Starboard battery! As you bear!" The sword caught the glare as it cut down. *"Fire!"*

The broadside roared and flashed along *Undine's* starboard side, gun by gun, each captain taking his aim while Soames strode past every recoiling breech, yelling and peering towards the enemy. Bolitho watched the smoke spouting from the ports and rolling towards the other ship which seemed suspended in the fog, her hull lying almost diagonally across the starboard bow.

Here and there a gun flashed out in reply, and he felt the deck planking jerk under his feet as at least one ball smashed into the side.

The quarterdeck gun crews were all shouting and cursing as they, too, joined in the battle. The stocky six-pounders hurled themselves inboard on the tackles, the wild-eyed seamen sponging out and ramming home fresh charges within seconds.

Overhead, and splashing violently into the channel on either beam, came a fusilade of smaller shot, from fortress or frigate Bolitho neither knew nor cared. As he paced briskly athwart the deck by the quarterdeck rail he saw nothing but the other ship's raked masts, the patch of colour from the prancing beast of her flag, the rising pall of smoke as again and again *Undine's* broadside thundered into her.

Once he chilled as he saw some charred flotsam bobbing past the quarter, a headless corpse pirouetting in *Undine's* crisp bow wave, tendrils of scarlet moving around it like obscene weed.

Herrick had known the *Argus* had gone. He must have seen the anchorage long before anyone in *Undine*. He would never have faltered. Bolitho felt his eyes stinging again, the hatred boiling inside him as the quarterdeck guns cracked out, their sharp detonations making his mind cringe even as their crews scrambled with handspikes to edge their weapons round for another salvo.

Herrick would have accepted it. As he had in the past. It was what he had lived for.

Bolitho shouted aloud, heedless of Mudge and Davy nearby. "God damn them for their plans and their stupidity!"

Keen called, "They've cut their cable, sir!"

Bolitho ran to the nettings, feeling a musket ball punch into the deck by his feet. It was true, Muljadi's frigate was yawing sluggishly in wind and current, her stern swinging like a gate across *Undine's* path. Someone must have lost his nerve, or perhaps in the confusion of the exploding schooner and *Undine's* savage attack an order had been misunderstood.

He yelled, "We'll go alongside her! Stand by the tops'l halliards! Put the helm a'lee!"

As men dashed to the braces again, and topsails flapped and thundered wildly to their sudden freedom, *Undine* turned deliberately to larboard, her jib-boom sweeping round until it pointed to the distant pier and the litter of smouldering craft left by the explosion.

Soames bellowed, "Point! Ready!" He was peering, red-eyed, along his panting gun crews, his sword held out like a staff. "Drag that man away!" He ran forward to help pull a wounded seaman from a twelve-pounder. "Now!" His sword flashed down. *"Broadside!"*

This time, the whole battery exploded in a single wall of flames, the long tongues darting into the smoke, making it rise and twist, as if it, too, was dying in agony.

Someone gave a hoarse cheer. "There goes th' bastard's fore!"

Bolitho ran to the gangway, marines and seamen pounding behind him.

High above the smoke the nimble topmen were already hurling their steel grapnels, jeering at one another as they raced even here to beat their opposite numbers on the other masts. Another cheer, as with a shuddering lurch *Undine* drove alongside the drifting frigate, her bowsprit rising above the poop. While the impetus carried them closer and closer together, the guns still bellowed, louder now as their fury matched across a bare thirty feet of tormented water.

"Boarders away!"

Bolitho waited, gripping the main shrouds, gauging the moment as Soames roared, "Cease firing! At 'em, lads! Cut the bastards down!"

Then he was across, clinging to the enemy's boarding nets, which had been rent in great holes by the broadsides. Muljadi's own plans must have been ready, for there seemed to be hundreds of men surging to meet the cheering, cursing rush of boarders.

Muskets and pistols, while from somewhere overhead a swivel banged out, the packed canister tearing across the enemy's quarterdeck, hurling wood splinters and bodies in all directions.

A bearded face loomed out of the smoke, and Bolitho slashed at it, holding to the nets to keep from falling outboard and being crushed between the hulls. The man shrieked and dropped from view. A marine thrust Bolitho aside, screaming like a madman as he pinned a man with his bayonet before wrenching out the blade and ramming the musket's butt into a wounded pirate who was trying to crawl out of the fight.

Allday ducked under a cutlass and caught his attacker off-balance. He even pushed the man away with his left fist, giving himself room for a proper stroke with his own blade. It sounded like an axe on wood.

Bellairs was striding in the centre of a squad of marines, snapping unheard commands, his elegant hanger darting in and out like a silver tongue as he forced his way aft towards the enemy's quarterdeck.

Another wave of insane cheering, and Bolitho saw Soames leading his own boarding party up and over the frigate's main shrouds, muskets barking point-blank into the press below him, his sword crossing with that of a tall, lank-haired officer whom Bolitho remembered as Le Chaumareys's first lieutenant.

Soames slipped and sprawled across an upended cannon, and the Frenchman drew back his arm for the fatal thrust. But a marine was nearby, the musket ball taking away most of the lieutenant's skull and hurling him from the deck like a rag doll.

Bolitho realised that Allday was shaking him by the arm, trying to make him understand something.

He yelled, "The *hold*, Captain!" He jabbed at the wide hatchways with his cutlass. "The bastards have set her afire!"

Bolitho stared at it, his brain and mind reeling from the screams and cheers, the grate of steel, the madness of close action. The smoke was already thicker. Perhaps Allday was right, or maybe a burning wad from one of *Undine*'s guns had found its way into the hull when Soames had sent his last broadside crashing home. Either way, both ships would be destroyed unless he acted, and at once.

He yelled, "Captain Bellairs! *Fall back!*"

He saw Bellairs gaping at him, blood dripping unheeded from a gash on his forehead.

Then he, too, seemed to get a grip on his own lust of battle and shouted, "Sound the retreat!" He sought out his sergeant whose massive frame had somehow avoided both steel and musket ball. "Coaker! Take that fool's name if he don't do as I ask!"

Coaker gripped a small marine drummer boy, but he was dead, his eyes glazed and unseeing as Coaker wrenched the trumpet from his hands and blew it with all his might.

It was almost harder to discontinue the battle than to board the other frigate. Back and back, here and there a man falling, or being hauled bodily across the gap between the hulls to avoid capture. The pirates had at last seen their own danger, and without the French lieutenant in command they seemed intent only on abandoning their ship as quickly as they could.

The first tongue of flame licked through a hatch, bringing a chorus of shrieks from the abandoned wounded, and within seconds the gratings and surrounding boat tier were well ablaze.

Bolitho gripped the ratlines and took a last look as his men threw themselves on to *Undine*'s gangway. Forward, Shellabeer's men were already cutting the lashing which held the hulls together, and with the topsails once more braced round, and the helm over, *Undine* began to sidle clear, the wind holding the smoke and sparks away from her own canvas and vulnerable rigging.

Mudge panted, "What now, sir?"

Bolitho watched the frigate slipping past, a few crazed men still firing across the widening gap.

He shouted, "A final broadside, Mr. Soames!"

But it was already too late. A great sheet of flame burst upwards through the vessel's gun deck, setting the broken foremast and sails alight and leaping to the mainyards like part of a forest fire.

Bolitho heard himself reply, "Get the forecourse on her, and smartly with it. We'll not be able to beat back the way we came. That ship's magazine will go at any moment, so we will try the eastern channel."

Mudge said, "May be too shallow, sir."

"Would you burn, Mr. Mudge?"

He strode to the taffrail to watch the frigate as the blaze engulfed the poop. An English ship. It were better this way, he thought vaguely.

He turned and added harshly, "Mr. Davy, I want a full report of damage." He waited, seeing the wildness draining from his eyes. "And the bill for all this."

Bolitho saw the yards edging round, the sails, pockmarked and blackened by the fight, hardening to the wind. The channel seemed wide enough. About a cable to starboard, more on the other side. He had managed worse.

"Boat in the water, sir!" Keen was standing in the shrouds with his telescope. "Just two men in it."

Mudge called, "I'll 'old 'er steady, sir. We're steerin' almost nor'-east again, but I dunno—"

The rest of his words were lost as Keen yelled, "Sir! *Sir!*" He stared down at Bolitho, his face shining with disbelief.

Davy snapped, "Keep your head, Mr. Keen!"

But Keen did not seem to hear. "It's Mr. Herrick!"

Bolitho stared at him and then clambered up beside him. The boat was a wreck, and the scrawny figure who was now standing to wave a scrap of rag above his head, looked like a scarecrow. Lying in the bottom of the boat, half-covered with water, was Herrick.

As he held the telescope Bolitho could feel his hands shaking violently, and saw Herrick's face, ashen beneath a rough bandage. Then he saw his eyes open, imagined the other man shouting the news to him, his words as plain as if he could hear them himself.

He said, "Pass the word to the bosun. I want that boat grappled alongside." He gripped the midshipman's wrist. "And tell him to be careful. There'll be no second chance."

Allday had gone below for something. Now he was back, his eyes everywhere, until Bolitho said quietly, "The first lieutenant is coming aboard. Go forrard and bid him welcome for me, eh?"

As the frigate slipped past another shelving hump of land the sun came down to greet them, to warm their aching limbs, to hold the shock of battle at arm's length a while longer. A deep explosion came from the main channel, and more smoke spouted high above the nearest land to show the wind which awaited them in open water, and to sound the other vessel's final destruction.

Muljadi may or may not have been aboard, and the real fight was still ahead.

Bolitho heard shouts from forward, and then a cheer as some seamen clambered into the sinking boat to pluck Herrick and his companion back on board.

But whatever was waiting beyond the green humps of land, no matter how hopeless their gesture might be, they would be together.

18

IN THE *K*ING'S NAME

"ALTER course two points."

Bolitho tried to pace along the littered deck, but was unable to overcome his anxiety. It was an hour since they had edged into the eastern channel, under minimum canvas and with two leadsmen in the chains they had felt their way towards the sea.

An hour of answering demands and listening to reports. Ten killed, fifteen wounded, half of them seriously. Considering what they had done, it was a small enough bill, but as he watched the familiar bundles awaiting burial, or heard occasional cries from the main hatch, he found little comfort in it.

If only Allday would come on deck and tell him about Herrick. He had already questioned the surviving seaman. It had been the little man called Lincoln, the one with the permanent grin made by a grotesque scar.

Bolitho had watched him reliving it as he had stammered out his description, oblivious to his captain and officers crowding around him, and seemingly only half aware he was actually alive.

It had been much as Bolitho had imagined. Herrick had decided to destroy the battery, drive his schooner aground regardless of risk and the inevitability of death. At the last moment, with the fuse lit and the vessel being fired on from a hillside, Herrick had been struck by a falling block from the mainmast. The little seaman had said in a whisper, "Then up comes Mister Pigsliver, as cool as you please. 'Take to th' boat,' he shouts. 'I've an old score to settle,' though 'e didn't say wot 'e meant like. By then there was only three 'ands left. So me an' Jethro lowers Mr. 'Errick into the dory, but t'other bloke, the little sailmaker named Potter, 'e decides to stay with the Don." He had given a great shudder. "So off we goes. Then the schooner blows up like the gates of 'ell, an' poor

Jethro was lost overboard. I just kept paddlin', and prayin' that Mr. 'Errick would stir to 'is senses an' tell me wot to do." He had paused, sobbing soundlessly. "Then I looks up, an' *there she is*, large as life, th' old *Undine*. I shakes Mr. 'Errick and calls to 'im, 'look alive, sir, the ship's a' comin' for us,' an' 'e— well— 'e just looks at me an' says, 'an' wot did you expect?'"

Bolitho had said quietly, "Thank you, Lincoln, I shall see you do not go unrewarded."

The little man had added, "An' you'll not forget to mention a piece about Mister Pigsliver, sir? I—I mean, 'e may be a Don, sir, but, but . . ." Then he had broken down completely.

Now, as he moved restlessly past the six-pounders where the gun captains knelt in the sunlight, checking their equipment, testing the tackles, their bodies stained with smoke and dried blood, Bolitho said to himself, "No, I will not forget."

"Deck there!"

He looked up, his eyes smarting in the glare.

"Open water ahead, sir!"

Shoes scraped by the cabin hatch and he swung round.

"Allday, where the *devil* have you been?"

But it was not Allday.

Bolitho strode across the deck and held out both hands. "Thomas!" He gripped Herrick's hands in his, oblivious to the watching faces on every side. "I don't know what to say!"

Herrick smiled sadly. "I am the same, sir."

"You should remain below until—"

"Deck there! Ship to the east'rd!"

Herrick withdrew his hands and replied quietly, "I am the first lieutenant, sir." He looked slowly around the quarterdeck, at the protruding splinters and the flapping edges of torn hammocks where musket balls had ripped home. "My place is here."

Davy crossed the deck and touched his hat. "Beat to quarters again, sir?"

"Yes."

Davy looked at Herrick and smiled. "It seems you had no better luck in holding on to the schooner than I." He added, "I am relieved you are here, and that's the truth."

Herrick touched the fresh bandage on his head and winced. "If it had not been sworn otherwise, I would have said that Don Puigserver struck me down himself. He was that eager to finish what we had begun."

He fell silent as the drums rattled out their tattoo and the lolling figures by guns and braces stirred themselves into life.

Bolitho was watching the last shoulder of land sliding away, the expanse of blue water and lively wavecrests growing and spreading to reveal an endless, dazzling horizon.

To larboard, her hull and spars black against the glare, lay the *Argus*. She appeared to be moving very slowly, her yards well braced to hold her on a converging tack.

Herrick muttered, "Four miles, I'd say."

"About that."

Bolitho studied the other ship, unable to look away. She reminded him of a wild cat, the way she edged across the busy, white-capped waves. Stealthy, purposeful. Lethal.

He imagined he could hear the squeak of trucks as her smooth sides became barbed by gun muzzles. Le Chaumareys was taking his time. Waiting for Bolitho to make the first move.

He looked away at last, feeling the tension returning, but heavier than before. Perhaps Le Chaumareys had planned it this way, distrusting his ally Muljadi, guessing that Bolitho might bring off a stalemate, if not a victory, if he chose his own method of attack.

The *Undine*'s company had fought hard. He looked searchingly at the shot holes and punctured sails, heard the hammers as Pryke, the portly carpenter, and his mates got busy on repairs in the lower hull, and knew it was asking much of them to fight yet again, and to win against this great, black-hulled veteran of the French navy.

Then he glanced at those nearest him. He needed every bit of skill and experience they possessed, not least their courage.

"Well, Mr. Mudge, what of the wind now?"

"It'll get up, sir." Mudge took out his handkerchief and blew his great nose violently. "Might back a bit." He gestured up at the masthead pendant. It was stiff, like a spear. "I'd suggest, beggin' yer pardon, sir, that you fights under topsails only."

Bolitho turned to Herrick. "What do you say?"

Herrick was watching the other ship, his eyes like slits. "Get to grips, sir. He'll pound us to pieces with those long guns otherwise."

The deck lifted across the first true roller, and spray drifted high above the nettings.

"Let's be about it then." Bolitho licked his parched lips. "Get the forecourse off her." He dropped his voice. "And have those corpses buried directly. It does no good to see where some of us will end this morning."

Herrick watched him calmly. "I can think of better reasons for dying." He glanced at the motionless seamen by the guns. "But no better place for it."

Bolitho walked to the rail and watched the *Argus* for several minutes. Le Chaumareys had a good position. He had probably considered it very carefully. He was over there now, watching him, expecting him to act. To try and take the wind-gage, or to alter course and attempt to cross his stern and cripple him with one good broadside as he passed.

The French frigate dipped to the swell, showing her copper for several seconds. The wind was tight across her exposed side, but Le Chaumareys was holding back, keeping on *Undine*'s larboard bow, barely making headway.

Bolitho bit his lip, his eyes running in the sun's fierce stare. His men would find it hard to shoot well into the blinding sunlight.

When he looked at the gun deck again he saw that the corpses were gone.

Herrick came aft and said, "All done."

He saw Bolitho's intent features and asked quietly, "Is something wrong, sir?"

"I think I am starting to understand Le Chaumareys." He could feel his heart beginning to pound again, the familiar chill at his neck and spine. "I think he *wants* us to have the wind-gage."

"But, sir . . ." Herrick's blue eyes darted to the *Argus* and back again. "Is the sun in our eyes of greater value to him?" Understanding spread across his round face. "It might well be. He can stand off and use his heavy artillery to better result."

Bolitho turned, his eyes flashing. "Well, it's not to be, Mr. Herrick! Get the t'gallants on her directly!" He added, "I am sorry, Mr. Mudge, but if we lose the sticks out of her to your damned wind it may be better than losing them the other way!"

Herrick was already raising his speaking trumpet. "Hands aloft! Loose t'ga'n's'ls!" When he looked at Bolitho again there was little to show what he had so recently endured. "By God, sir, what we miss in weight we can show that bastard in agility today!"

Bolitho grinned at him, his lips painful. "Alter course two points to starboard. We'll run for his bows."

Allday folded his arms and watched Bolitho's shoulders, and then glanced up at the flag as it rippled in the freshening wind.

"And that is *all* the running you'll be doing, I'm thinking."

"East nor'-east, sir!" Carwithen had one hand resting on the polished spokes as the helmsmen concentrated on the compass and the set of the sails overhead. "Steady as she goes!"

Mudge rubbed his hands on his coat. "She's movin' well, sir."

Bolitho lowered his telescope and nodded thoughtfully. The extra power of the topgallants was laying *Undine* firmly in line across the other ship's path. *Argus* had not set any additional sail. Yet. He winced as the sunlight lanced down from the lens. Le Chaumareys still held the best position. He could alter course to lee'rd and present his broadside as *Undine* tried to pass him. Equally, he could allow her to cross his bows, and while she lost time in changing tack, he could take the wind-gage, sun's glare or not, and attack him from the other side.

Herrick said hoarsely, "He's holding the same course. He may have let her fall off a point, but there's nothing in it." He breathed out slowly. "She makes a fair sight, God rot her!"

Bolitho smiled tightly. *Argus* had barely changed her bearing, but that was because *Undine* had altered course to starboard. She was much closer now, a bare two miles, so that he could see her red and yellow figurehead, the purposeful movement of figures about her sloping quarterdeck.

There was a sudden bang, and seconds later a thin waterspout rose lazily amongst the tossing wavecrests, slightly ahead of *Undine*'s path, and half a cable short. Ranging shot, or merely to unnerve *Undine*'s own gun crew. Another of Le Chaumareys's little ruses.

Herrick muttered fervently, "If I know the Frogs, he'll try and dismast us with chain-shot and langridge. Another prize for his bloody ally!"

"You don't know *this* Frenchman, Mr. Herrick." Bolitho recalled Le Chaumareys's face when he had spoken of home, his France which he had been denied for so long. "My guess is he'll want a complete victory."

The word made him feel uneasy. He could even picture *Undine* dismasted and wallowing amongst her own dead and dying before her final plunge. Like the one he himself had just destroyed. Like *Nervion*, and so many he had watched crumble and perish.

The stage was set. Two ships, with not even a seabird to watch their manœuvres, their dedicated efforts to outwit each other.

"There, sir! He's setting his t'gallants!" Carwithen's voice jarred him from his thoughts.

Herrick exclaimed, "He intends to outreach us after all."

Bolitho watched intently as the *Argus*'s upper yards filled with freshly-set, bulging canvas. He could see the instant effect it had around her raked stem as she bit into the waves and thrust forward with sudden haste.

From his position behind the rail it looked to Bolitho as if the other ship's jib-boom was actually touching his own, although she was still over a mile away. Smoke wreathed above her hull, and he held his breath as the bright tongues of fire licked from her exposed ports.

The sea boiled and shot skywards as the heavy balls ploughed into the wind-ruffled water, or ricocheted away far abeam. One ball smashed hard down alongside, the shock transmitting itself to the very mastheads.

"Trying to rattle our wits!"

Herrick was grinning, but Bolitho saw the anxiety behind his eyes.

Le Chaumareys had not seemed the kind of man who wasted gestures on the wind. He was preparing his gun crews, showing them the range, probably telling them right now in his resonant voice exactly what he expected of them.

"By God, the devil's shortening sail again!"

Bolitho saw the topgallants vanishing along the *Argus's* yards, and leaned across the rail.

"Stand by, the larboard battery!"

Perhaps he had found Le Chaumareys's one real weakness. That he *needed* to win and to survive. Bolitho knew that the two did not always walk hand in hand.

"Alter course three points to larboard!"

He heard the rush of feet, the confused shouts as his orders were relayed to the waiting seamen.

Mudge asked, "Is that wise, sir?"

Bolitho waited as the helm went down, and then turned to watch the bowsprit swinging slowly and then more quickly to larboard, the other frigate suddenly enmeshed in the criss-cross of rigging and shrouds.

"Hold her so!"

He waited impatiently while Herrick bellowed through his

trumpet, and the hands on the braces hauled feverishly to retrim the yards.

"Nor'-east by north, sir!" The helmsman sounded breathless.

With the wind sweeping tightly across the larboard quarter, *Undine* swept straight down towards the other ship, as if to cut her in halves. More flashes darted from the Frenchman's side, and Bolitho clenched his fists as metal shrieked overhead, parting rigging, slapping through sails and hurling spray in profusion on either beam.

"Now we shall see!"

Bolitho craned forward, gripping the rail, his eyes stinging painfully in the hazy glare. Another rippling line of flashes, the sounds of the broadside rolling across the water like the thunder of mighty drums. He felt the hull stagger violently, and saw some of the seamen below the quarterdeck exchanging quick, desperate glances.

Argus was still holding her course and speed, lying across *Undine*'s path and growing in size with every agonising minute.

More shots, and a savage jerk below his feet told Bolitho *Undine* was being hit again. But *Argus*'s broadsides were more ragged now, and fewer balls were falling near their target.

Herrick said fiercely, "He'll have to do something!"

Bolitho did not reply, but stared fixedly through his telescope at the cluster of figures on *Argus*'s quarterdeck. He could see Le Chaumareys's powerful bulk, his small cropped head bobbing as he shouted commands to his subordinates. He would be missing his first lieutenant, Bolitho thought quickly. As he would have missed Herrick, but for their unlikely reunion.

He called, "The *wind*, Mr. Mudge?" He dared not look at him.

"Backed a point, sir! From the pendant, I'd say it was near sou'-westerly!"

Herrick shouted, "*Argus* is standing away, sir!"

Somebody gave an isolated cheer, but Bolitho snapped, "Keep

the people quiet!" He added quickly, "Stand by to alter course hard to larboard! I'll want her as close to the wind as you can lay her, Mr. Mudge!"

He watched, barely able to move, as *Argus*'s yards edged round, her outline shortening as she stood off, making a triangle between the two converging ships. She loosed another slow broadside, and Bolitho heard a scream from aloft, then saw a marine fall headlong on to the nets, blood gushing from his mouth and splashing on the gun crew immediately below him.

Le Chaumareys had mistaken Bolitho's headlong charge as an act of empty bravery. He had waited for the right moment before swinging clear to present his full broadside, to cripple *Undine* completely as she attempted to cross the bows.

Bolitho held up his hand, praying that those flashing guns would give him time to act.

"Larboard battery! Fire as you bear!"

Relieved, eager to hit back, the gun crews pounced on their weapons.

"Stand by!"

Davy watched as Soames hurried to the leading gun.

"*Fire!*"

Bolitho felt the hull quiver, and drew breath again as the smoke billowed away from the hull towards the enemy.

"Stand by to alter course!" He held Herrick's gaze. "No, we are not going to embrace him just yet!" He felt the insane grin on his lips. "We'll cross his stern. He has left the door open!"

A heavy ball smashed through the larboard bulwark, upending a twelve-pounder and painting the planking and gratings in bright, spreading scarlet.

Screams and curses were drowned as Soames bellowed, "Stop your vents! Sponge out!" He glared wildly through the smoke. "You, Manners! Take that handspike and *move yourself,* damn you!"

The man in question was gaping at his legs which had been spattered with blood and fragments from the neighbouring crew.

Bolitho dropped his hand. "Now! Helm a'lee!"

To the mounting wind, and the sudden change of direction, *Undine* swayed over and down, the gun crews firing off another uneven salvo before *Argus* was plucked from their open ports.

Bolitho yelled, "Mr. Davy! Starboard battery!"

Men dashed from the still-smoking guns and threw themselves to assist the opposite side. Overhead, spars and blocks strained and bucked in protest, and more than one seaman fell headlong as the ship came thundering up close to the wind, her yards almost fore and aft.

The fore topgallant sail split suddenly and violently, the fragments like streamers in the wind, but Bolitho ignored it. He was watching *Argus*'s black shape sliding out and away from the starboard bow while his own ship turned steeply towards her poop. Shots crashed into hull and rigging alike, and Bolitho watched sickened as two seamen were pulped into offal and broken weapons against the opposite side.

Davy's voice was almost a scream. "Starboard battery! As you bear!"

The order to fire was lost in the first crash from the forward guns, followed instantly along the deck as the *Argus* loomed up and over the nettings like a black cliff.

"*Sponge out! Reload! Run out!*"

The crews had no trouble in running out, for the ship was heeling so steeply to the wind that each gun squealed down the deck like an enraged hog on the rampage.

Bolitho cupped his hands. "Hold your fire!" He gestured to the men by the carronades on the forecastle. Several corpses lay near them, and he guessed Le Chaumareys's marksmen had realised his intention.

A musket ball clanged against a six-pounder, and one of the helmsmen fell kicking and spluttering, his chin shot away by the ricochet.

Bolitho shouted above the din, "Let her fall off a point, Mr. Mudge, you know what I expect today!"

Shadows danced across the decks as pieces of broken rigging, blocks, a musket and other fragments bounced on the nets above.

And here was the *Argus,* plunging heavily to starboard, trying to follow *Undine* round, but losing the chance as the English frigate swept across her stern.

"*Fire!*"

A carronade banged loudly, biting fragments from *Argus*'s stern and smashing her small quarter-gallery to fragments. Gun by gun the twelve-pounders followed its example, the balls slamming into the stern, or scything through the gaping windows to create death and confusion within.

Men were cheering, despite threats and blows from their petty officers, and above the great writhing wall of smoke Bolitho saw the French frigate's masts moving slowly away and beyond the starboard quarter. But it was no time to falter now.

"We will wear ship, Mr. Herrick! Lay her on the starboard tack!"

"Aye, sir!" Herrick wiped his streaming face. Above the stains on his cheeks and mouth his bandage shone in the filtered sunlight like a turban. "It's lively work today, sir!"

"Man the braces! Stand by to wear ship!"

A man screamed as he was dragged from a gun, bleeding badly. As Whitmarsh's mates lifted him he struggled and kicked to free himself, more terrified of what waited below than of dying on deck.

Sails thundering, and spilling wind from countless shotholes, *Undine* changed tack yet again, turning her bowsprit away from the islands and towards the sun.

The sea looked much wilder now, with short wavecrests crumbling to the wind, or throwing sheets of spray above the gangways with hardly a break.

Bolitho wiped his eyes and tried to restrain from coughing. Like his eyes, his lungs were raw with powder smoke, the stench of battle. He watched the other ship as she swam above the leaping spindrift. Willingly or not, Le Chaumareys had the wind-gage, and his ship now stood off *Undine*'s starboard bow, a bare cable's length away. If *Undine* continued to overhaul her, both ships would run parallel, a musket shot apart. *Argus* would get her revenge at such a murderous range.

He glanced quickly at Mudge. He, too, was watching the sea and the masthead pendant, but was it for the same reason?

But to ask him now, to show that he was in need of a miracle and had nothing to replace one, would take the fight out of his men no less than an instant defeat. He saw them at their guns, panting and gasping, tarred hands gripping tackles and rammers, sponges and handspikes. Their naked bodies were streaked with sweat which cut through the powder grime like the marks of a fine lash. Their eyes shone through their blackened faces as if trapped.

The marines were reloading their muskets, and Bellairs was strolling with his sergeant by the taffrail. At the helm another had taken the dead man's place, and Carwithen's coarse face was working on a plug of tobacco, his eyes cold, without expression. There were fewer men on the gun deck, although Bolitho had not seen many fall. Yet they had gone, had died or been maimed without a word from him to give reason for their sacrifice.

He reached out to steady himself as the deck tilted more steeply. When he peered over the riddled hammocks he saw the sea's face forming into short, steep ranks, ranging towards the two ships as if to push them away.

He yelled, "Mr. Davy! *Are you ready?*"

Davy nodded dully. "Every gun loaded with chain-shot, sir!"

"Good." Bolitho looked at Herrick. "I hope to God that the master knows his weather!" In a sharper tone he added, "Get the forecourse on her!"

With the great foresail set and drawing, *Undine* began to overhaul the other ship at a remarkable pace.

Bolitho flinched as more balls crashed alongside from *Argus*'s stern-chasers, one of them hurling the quarter-boat into spinning pieces.

A last challenge. That was what it had to look like. Gun to gun. No quarter until *Undine* was a sinking wreck.

He said, "We will alter course when I give the word."

He waited, aching in every muscle, his mind jumping to each gunshot from the Frenchman's poop. *Undine's* jib-boom seemed to be prodding her larboard quarter like a lance. A few stabs of fire above her shattered stern showed where marksmen had taken fresh positions, and Bolitho saw two of his marines drop like red fruit from the foretop, their cries lost to the mounting wind.

Mudge said worriedly, "We may lose our sticks when we comes round, sir!"

Bolitho ignored him.

"Ready lads!"

He watched the sea rising and breaking against *Argus's* opposite quarter, the mounting pressure against her yards.

"Now!"

He gripped the rail as the helm went over and the bows started to pull towards the enemy. He saw *Argus* trimming her yards, the hull tilting steeply as she followed *Undine's* turn.

Sunlight flashed on her quarterdeck, and then her side exploded in a line of great flashes, the air rent apart with the savagery of her broadside.

Bolitho almost fell as the massive weight of iron crashed into the hull or screamed and tore through the rigging overhead. He was choked by swirling smoke, his mind reeling from the combined noises of screams and yells, of musket fire from all angles.

Somehow he dragged himself up the angled deck and peered towards the *Argus*. Smoke was drifting from her last broadside so fast that *Undine* seemed to be moving abeam to meet her. The illusion told him Mudge had been right, and as he watched *Argus's* sails bellying out towards him, he also saw her gunports awash as the wind thrust her over. *Thank God for the wind.*

"Fire!" He had to repeat the order to make himself heard. *"Fire!"*

Undine's disengaged gunports were also awash, and her runout battery was pointing almost towards the sky as each captain jerked his lanyard.

Even above the roar of cannon fire and the wail of the wind Bolitho heard the chain-shot whimpering through the air and ripping into *Argus's* fully exposed topsails and braced yards. He heard, too, the immediate clatter of severed rigging, the louder explosions of bursting stays and shrouds as foremast and main-topmast swayed together like great trees before booming and splintering into the smoke.

Bolitho waved his sword above his head. "Hold her steady, Mr. Mudge! She'll be alongside directly!"

He ran to the gangway, and then stopped dead as the wind sucked the smoke downwind and away from the two drifting hulls. Dead and wounded lay everywhere, and as the marines ran to their places for boarding Bolitho saw Shellabeer mangled beneath a gun, and Pryke, the carpenter, pinned across a hatch coaming by a broken length of gangway, his blood linking with all the rest around him. And Fowlar, could that thing really be him?

But there was no more time to regret or to think. *Argus* was here, alongside, and as Soames led his men across the bows Bolitho shook his sword and yelled hoarsely, "Over you go, lads!"

The French seamen were struggling to free themselves from the great tangle of spars and rigging, the broken cordage lying in heaps like giant serpents.

But the steel was ready enough. Bolitho crossed swords with a petty officer and then slipped in some blood, the breath driven from his body as the Frenchman pitched headlong across him. He felt the man jerk and kick, saw the awful agony in his eyes as Carwithen pulled him away, a boarding axe locked into his collar bone.

On every hand men were fighting and yelling, the pikes and bayonets waving above the more desperate work of sword and cutlass.

Davy was heading for the quarterdeck ladder, shouting to the men at his back, when a rally of French seamen left him momentarily isolated and alone. Bolitho watched his contorted face above the thrusting shoulders, saw his mouth shaping unheard screams as they cut him down, their weapons not still even after he had dropped from sight.

Midshipman Armitage stood shaking on the gangway, his skin like chalk as he shouted, "Follow me!" Then he, too, was dead, pushed aside and trodden underfoot as the two opposing groups surged together again.

Bolitho saw it all as he fought his way aft towards the main quarterdeck ladder. Saw it, and recorded it in his mind. But without sequence, like a nightmare. As if he were a mere onlooker.

He reached the ladder and saw the French lieutenant facing him, the one named Maurin, who had an English wife. The rest seemed to fade into a swirling, embattled fog as the two swords reached out and circled each other.

Bolitho said harshly, "Strike, Maurin! You have done enough!"

The Frenchman shook his head. "It is not possible, *m'sieu!*"

Then he lunged forward, taking Bolitho's sword on the hilt, and deftly turning it towards the sea. Bolitho let himself fall back to the next step, seeing the desperation on Maurin's face, knowing, without understanding why, that this man alone stood between victory and senseless slaughter.

"Le Chaumareys is dead!" Bolitho tested the next step with his left foot. "Am I not right?" He had to shout at the top of his voice as more of *Undine's* men burst yelling on to the gun deck and attacked the French crew from behind. They must have climbed through the shattered stern, Bolitho realised dully. Again it was more of a reaction than anything. He added coldly, "So for God's sake *strike!*"

Maurin hesitated, the uncertainty plain on his face, and then made up his mind. He sidestepped and raised his hilt almost level with his eyes before lunging towards Bolitho's chest.

Bolitho watched him with something like despair. Maurin had been too long in the one ship, had forgotten the need for change. It was easy. Too sickeningly easy.

Bolitho took his weight on his foot, parried the blade as it darted towards him, and struck. The lieutenant's weight was more than enough, and Bolitho almost had the sword wrenched from his grip as Maurin fell gasping to the deck below.

A pigtailed seaman raised his boarding pike, but Bolitho shouted, "Touch him, and I'll kill you myself!"

He saw Herrick walking between the French seamen who were throwing their weapons on to the bloodied deck, the fight over. Their strength going at the sight of Maurin's last gesture.

He thrust the sword into its scabbard and walked heavily up the last few steps. He knew Allday was behind him, and Herrick took his place at his side as together they stood in silence looking at Le Chaumareys's body where it lay beside the abandoned wheel. He looked strangely peaceful, and amidst so much carnage and horror, almost unmarked. There was a dark stain below his shoulder, and a small trickle of blood from a corner of his mouth. Probably one of Bellairs's sharpshooters, Bolitho thought vaguely.

Bolitho said quietly, "Well, we did meet, Captain, just as you said we would."

Lieutenant Soames knelt to unfasten Le Chaumareys's sword, but Bolitho said, "Leave it. His was a bad cause, but he fought with honour." He turned away, suddenly sick of the watching dead, their pathetic stillness. "And cover him with his flag. His proper flag. He was no pirate!"

He saw Davy's body being carried to the gangway, and added, "A moment longer and he would have seen *Argus* taken. Enough prize-money even for his debts perhaps."

As they climbed across the trapped water between the drifting hulls Bolitho turned, startled, as some of the seamen gathered to cheer him. He looked at Herrick, but he shrugged and gave a sad smile.

"I know how you feel, sir, but they are glad to be alive. It is their way of thanking you."

Bolitho touched his arm. "Survival? I suppose it is a fair cause for battle." He forced a smile. "And for winning."

Herrick picked up his hat and handed it to him. "I'll set the people to work, sir. The pumps sound too busy for my liking."

Bolitho nodded and walked slowly towards the stern, his shoes catching at splinters and broken cordage. By the taffrail he paused and looked wearily along his command, at the broken planking and stained decks, the figures which were picking their way amidst the debris, more like survivors than victors.

Then he leaned back and loosened his neckcloth, and shook open his best dress coat which was torn and slashed in a dozen places.

Above his head the flag was flapping more easily, the sudden squall having passed on as quickly as it had arrived to save them from *Argus's* great guns. But for it . . .

He looked round, suddenly anxious, but saw Mudge in his place near the helm, cutting at a piece of cheese with a small knife which he had fished from one of his pockets. He looked very old in the dusty sunlight. Little Penn was squatting on a gun truck, having his wrist bandaged, and dabbing at his nose which had started to bleed when a charge had exploded prematurely nearby.

Bolitho watched them with something like love. Mudge and Penn. Age and innocence.

There was Keen, speaking with Soames, and looking very strained. But a man now.

Feet crunched on the debris, and he saw Noddall approaching him cautiously, a jug of wine clasped against his chest.

"I am afraid I can't yet find the glasses, sir." He kept his eyes fixed on Bolitho's face, and had probably had them shut as he had groped past some of the horror below.

Bolitho held the jug to his lips and said, "But this is some of my best wine."

Noddall dabbed his eyes and smiled nervously. "Aye, sir. All of it. The rest was destroyed by the battle."

Bolitho let the wine fill his mouth, savouring it. Needing it. They had come a long way since that shop in St. James's Street, he thought.

And in a few weeks they would be ready again. The missing faces would still be remembered, but without the pain which even now was getting stronger. Terror would emerge as bravado, and courage be recalled as duty. He smiled bitterly, remembering the words from so long ago. *In the King's name.*

He heard Penn say in his squeaky voice, "I was a bit frightened, Mr. Mudge." An awkward pause. "Just a *bit.*"

Old Mudge looked across the deck and held Bolitho's gaze. "Frightened, boy? Gawd, 'e'll never make a cap'n, will 'e, sir?"

Bolitho smiled, sharing the moment with Mudge alone. For he knew, better than most, that the truth of battle was not for children.

Then he looked along his command again, at the gleaming shoulder of the proud figurehead below the bowsprit.

Undine was the real victor, he thought, and he was suddenly grateful to have her to himself.

EPILOGUE

LIEUTENANT Thomas Herrick stepped into the stern cabin and tucked his hat beneath his arm.

"You sent for me, sir?"

Bolitho was standing by the open windows, his hands on a sill, watching the weed on the sea-bed and tiny, bright fish darting around the motionless rudder.

It was afternoon, and along the shoreline of Pendang Bay the trees and green fronds waved and shone in a dozen hues to a steady breeze. Good sailing weather, he thought absently, but not for *Undine*. Not just yet.

He turned and gestured to a chair. "Sit down, Thomas."

He saw Herrick's gaze resting on the opened despatches which had been brought aboard that day. A brig from Madras. Orders and news.

"Another Indiaman will be arriving shortly, Thomas. This despatch is from the Admiral Commanding the Inshore Squadron. He is sending fresh hands to replace some of those we lost in battle."

How easily said. *Lost in battle.* He glanced slowly around the cabin, knowing that Herrick was watching him, sharing his memories.

There was little to show of the mauling the ship had suffered under Le Chaumareys's guns. Fresh paint covered the repaired timbers, and the smell of tar and wood-shavings lingered throughout the hull. A month and two days since they had gone alongside *Argus*, but despite the back-breaking work, and the rewards of seeing the ship looking her old self again, the pictures of the fight hung in Bolitho's mind as if it were yesterday.

And how they had worked. Perhaps, like himself, the rest of the company had needed it, if only to hold the memories at bay a little longer.

Small moments stood out when you least expected them. Midshipman Penn crouching down as a gun recoiled inboard, wreathed in smoke, while its crew dashed forward again with sponge and rammer. A man had been hurled to the deck in a wave of flying splinters. Had lain there staring unwinkingly at the sky. Penn had reached out to touch him and had tried to jump away as the man had reached out to seize his wrist. He must have died at that very instant. Bolitho did not remember seeing the incident at the time, but it had lurked in wait within his mind. And Armitage leading his squad of boarders after Davy had fallen under those plunging blades. The clumsy, awkward midshipman, blind with terror, yet gathering his few reserves of strength only to find they were not enough.

And after the battle, the smells and the sounds, not least the surgeon fighting-drunk and being dragged bodily to his sickbay by three of his men.

When the wild cheering had given way to the realisation of victory, they had faced up to their own immediate situation. Wounded to be tended, the dead to be buried, and the work begun without delay.

Looking back, it was surprising they had reached Pendang Bay at all, Bolitho thought. Fore and main lower yards badly sprung, the mainmast itself so splintered and pitted that it was only quick work on stays and rigging which kept it upright, the tasks had seemed unending. More than a dozen holes below the waterline had kept the hands working at the pumps through every watch, as with the battered *Argus* in tow they had crawled painfully towards the land and safety. The captured frigate had already sailed under jury-rig for a yard in India where she would be quickly refitted and included in the Company's own private fleet.

Herrick asked, "Any further instructions, sir?"

Bolitho reached for a bottle of wine. "It is confirmed that Pendang Bay will be exchanged for another station now held by the Dutch East India Company." He looked up, seeing the astonishment in Herrick's eyes. "Now that we have established the settlement, the Dutch are more than willing to make the exchange, apparently."

He recalled with sudden clarity Rear Admiral Conway's face when the first despatch had been opened. Brought from Madras by Raymond himself.

He had said hoarsely, "So it was all for nothing?"

Raymond had looked away. "No, sir. The other settlement in the north is far more suitable to our requirements. Sir Montagu Strang has explained. You will see that your part in all this is highly thought of."

Later, when Raymond had left the room, Conway had said, "Highly thought of. But a *new* governor will be appointed."

Bolitho had replied, "I am sorry, sir. It is a bitter victory."

"Bitter?" Surprisingly, he had laughed. "This sort of work is more for shopkeepers than sailors, Bolitho. Remember that well."

He pushed a goblet across the table and realised that Herrick was still awaiting an answer.

"Once our replacements have been signed on, we will maintain a local patrol until ordered otherwise." He smiled gravely. "I am temporarily the senior officer in these waters. Not too surprising, since *Undine* is the only King's ship!"

Herrick grinned. "And well earned, sir. When I realised how you had put yourself inside the French captain's mind, I—"

Bolitho looked away. "If the wind had dropped, Thomas, you might think differently."

"Lady Luck, sir?" The grin was broader.

There was a tap at the door and Penn stepped into the cabin.

"Mr. Soames's respects, sir. The Indiaman has just weighed. He said you wished to be told, sir."

"Thank you."

Bolitho waited for the door to close, his heart suddenly heavy. Even Penn had not helped. Keen now stood above as acting lieutenant, and Soames had replaced Davy. The same story. One dies, another profits.

Herrick said quietly, "The Indiaman's sailing for Madras, sir. Our wounded will get better treatment there."

Bolitho picked up his hat. "We'll see her off."

The sun across the quarterdeck was harsh enough, but in the steady offshore wind felt less severe as with Herrick he stood by the nettings to watch the deep-hulled Indiaman spreading her topsails, her paintwork and company flag very bright against the land.

Bolitho looked along *Undine*'s deck and saw the hands pausing in their work to watch the big ship as she tilted to the pressure, her hull shining while she continued to tack clear of the anchorage. Thinking of home perhaps, where the Indiaman would eventually make her landfall. Or of old friends lying bandaged within her fat hull, and of the others who were not here to see anything at all.

Bolitho beckoned to Penn. "Your glass, if you please."

Only once had he been able to see Viola Raymond alone since *Undine*'s return. Because of Raymond, or because she understood better than he that it was pointless to add to the pain of parting, Bolitho was still not certain.

"A fine ship, sir." Herrick, too, had a glass. "To think my old father wished me to go to sea in an Indiaman. Things would have been very different, I suppose."

Bolitho tensed, seeing the pale green gown on the ornate poop, that same wide hat she had brought from Santa Cruz. He could hear her words to him, as if she had just spoken across the broad expanse of lively white-horses in the bay.

"If you come to London, please visit me. My husband has gained his promotion. What he wanted. What I thought I wanted, too." She had squeezed his hand. "I hope you got what you wanted from me?"

A gun boomed dully from the settlement, and another from the Indiaman's forecastle. Flags dipped in mutual respect.

Bolitho felt the ache returning. She was right. There must be no pain, only understanding. Peace, as after a great gale of wind. Something which they had seized, if only for a moment.

He thought of Raymond, going to a better appointment, while Conway returned to obscurity. It was impossible to fathom.

While he was much as before, except for that one moment. Or was he? By trying to mould him as she would have wished her husband, perhaps she had indeed changed him.

Penn called, "Signal, sir! From *Wessex* to *Undine*." He was straining his eye to a telescope to watch the flags breaking from the Indiaman's yards as she laboriously spelled out her message. *"Good luck go with you."*

"Acknowledge."

Bolitho kept his eye on the pale green figure. She was waving her hat slowly back and forth, her autumn hair blowing unrestricted to the wind.

Half to himself he said, "And with you, my love."

Some of the seamen were cheering and waving as the other vessel spread more canvas and heeled ponderously on a new tack.

Bolitho handed the telescope to a ship's boy and said, "Well, Mr. Herrick?"

Herrick watched him and then nodded. "Aye, sir. A glass of wine. I think we deserve it."

Bolitho held on to the mood, keeping his eyes away from the Indiaman as she stood purposefully towards the headland.

"At least we have *earned* it."

Allday watched them pass, seeing Bolitho's hand touch his side-pocket where he carried his watch. Just a brief gesture, but it told Allday a great deal. He walked to the nettings and stared after the departing Indiaman.

Sail away, my lady. You have left your mark, and for the better. But a closer embrace? He sighed. Neither of them would have weathered it.

Keen joined him by the bulwark.

"She makes a goodly sight, eh, Allday?"

Allday looked at him. "Aye, sir." *You don't know the half of it.* "But a bit too good for a poor sailorman, sir."

Keen walked away and began to pace the quarterdeck as he had watched Bolitho do a hundred times or more. He knew Allday was laughing at him, but did not care. He had been tested, and he had won through. That was more than he had dared to hope, and it was more than enough.

He paused by the skylight, hearing Bolitho's laugh and Herrick's quiet rejoinder.

And he had shared all of it with them.

When he looked again for the Indiaman she had slipped past the headland and gone from view.

He started to pace the deck once more. Acting-lieutenant Valentine Keen, of His Majesty's frigate *Undine,* was content.